# NO WAY OUT

# The works of Alan Jacobson

## NOVELS

*False Accusations*
*The Hunted*
*The 7ᵗʰ Victim**
*Crush**
*Velocity**
*Inmate 1577**
*Hard Target*
*No Way Out**

*\* Karen Vail novels*

## SHORT STORIES

*Fatal Twist*
*(featuring Karen Vail)*

*Double Take*

For up-to-date information on Alan Jacobson's current and future novels, please visit www.AlanJacobson.com.

# ALAN JACOBSON

A KAREN VAIL NOVEL

PREMIER
DIGITAL PUBLISHING

For Louis Brill, my junior high school English teacher. Mr. Brill had a long-lasting impact on my life—so much so that it might be said that my writing career would not have been realized had he not instilled in me a love of English and the beauty of the written word.

In what is undoubtedly a first for a dedication, I offer a peek at one of Mr. Brill's lessons, which dealt with the importance of using proper grammar—commas, in particular. Consider this sentence:

*Let's go eat, grandmother.*

Remove the comma and you are left with:

*Let's go eat grandmother.*

It's a simple illustration, but one that has stuck with me for decades.

Mr. Brill, this one's for you.

*Author's Note*

This is a work of fiction. The characters and organizations appearing in this novel, including the British Heritage Party and the British Shakespeare Academy, are products of the author's imagination. The events depicted are fictitious, and none of them really happened. Some literary license has been taken concerning geographical settings and standard police procedures, but these modifications are minor and, for the most part, will only be apparent to those familiar with the particular settings and procedures.

"Before you embark on a journey
of revenge, dig two graves."
- *Confucius*


"All warfare is based on deception."
- *Sun Tzu*


"Affairs are easier of entrance than of exit;
and it is but common prudence to see
our way out before we venture in."
- *Aesop*

# 1

"Could really do with a fag about now."

A number of responses flooded Karen Vail's thoughts—and not all of them politically correct. The one she chose was borderline, yet biting.

"I don't do fags," Vail said, knowing full well that the British man was talking about bumming a cigarette off her.

The homicide detective squinted, unsure of what to make of the feisty redhead—let alone her comment.

After a moment, he rocked back on his heels and said, "Your theory of finding signature within MO was quite intriguing."

FBI profiler Karen Vail, in Madrid as part of the Behavioral Analysis Unit's effort to provide instruction on criminal investigative analysis to the world's police force, held out her hand. "Karen Vail."

"Ingram Losner." The thin man paused, then said, "You did know I was talking about a cigarette, a smoke. Not a back tickler."

*Back tickler?* "I did," she said. "But that wasn't the first thing that crossed my mind. I don't know a whole lot of British expressions, but isn't that one outdated?"

"Old habits die hard. Kind of like smoking."

Vail looked across the tourist-filled plaza at a mime who was clad in thick green metallic paint, standing rock still and holding a broom. "I stopped smoking a while ago. Shitty habit." She faced Losner. "You do know what shitty is, right?"

"Of course."

"I'm just saying. You people say 'pissed' for drunk, 'fag' for cigarette, 'football' for soccer—personally, I think we Americans have improved the English language."

"Agent Vail," said a suited man with a thick Spanish accent.

Vail turned. "Oh, Detective—" She snapped her fingers. "Heredia."

"Very good, yes. I found your discussion of sexual homicide fascinating. It reminded me of a case I had four years—" His two-way radio chirped and he frowned. "Excuse me." He yanked it from his belt. "Estoy fuera de servicio." *I'm off-duty.* But a woman's staccato speech erupted from the speaker, and Heredia's expression hardened. He responded, "Sí, sí, estoy aquí." *Yes, yes, I'm here.*

Vail struggled to follow the exchange. Her conversational Spanish was poor and the brush-up audio course she listened to in the weeks before her departure required more time than she had to give.

Vail picked up a few words and missed several others, but she got this much:

*Two murder suspects. Your location. Gray and blue backpacks.*

Heredia's head moved left and right as he scanned the crowd in front of him. "There!" He brought the radio to his mouth. "Los veo." *I see them.*

Vail followed his gaze to two men a dozen feet away. They were carrying colored rucksacks like the ones the dispatcher had described.

"Policia," Heredia called out. "Necesito hablar contigo." *I need to talk with you.*

They turned to look, saw Heredia moving toward them, and took off.

Heredia followed, as did Vail. Losner's voice receded behind her as she charged into the throng: "You've got no jurisdiction—you're just a citizen!"

*No, I'm a cop. And those are fleeing murder suspects.*

Navigating through the dense horde of tourists and college students crowding the massive square, Vail saw the men running toward a side street. She did likewise, headed in their direction through the plaza's archway exit onto Calle del Siete de Julio.

"You see them?"

*Heredia.* Behind her, slightly to her left—and suddenly blocked by a heavyset woman with a stroller.

"Got a visual!" she said without taking her eyes off the fleeing men.

Whether or not this was her jurisdiction, Vail was an officer of the law down to her bones. True, she was unarmed, and in Spain her FBI creds were worth less than the brass alloy her badge was made from—but none of that mattered as she sprinted ahead, darting around, and into, passersby.

Something deep down—the inner voice she sometimes ignored—*Come on, Karen, admit it: you ignore me all the time!*—told her to back off, to remember what she was here for. No matter how she parsed it, she was not in Spain to engage murder suspects in a foot race through the streets of Madrid.

Yet here she was, pushing forward, hurtling toward…who knew what.

She followed the men as they turned left onto Calle Mayor, through the flow of tourists and city dwellers, although the crowd had thinned considerably as she and Heredia put distance between them and the plaza.

As she crossed Calle del Duque de Najera, one of the men peeled left down the side street.

"I got him," Heredia shouted.

Vail took the gray-backpacked man who continued straight. He slowed along Calle del Factor to dodge a passing taxi, its angry horn blaring.

On her left stood the imposing, brick Pallacio de Uceda. A soldier was stationed at one of the main entrances, a fully automatic machine gun slung over his shoulder. Asking him for assistance was out of the question; she had walked by the building two days ago and tried to chat him up about the best place to grab a taxi. He would not divert his attention to even talk with her, let alone join a harebrained chase.

Vail passed a Museo del Jamon restaurant on her left—with wrapped pig parts hanging in the window—and a cell phone store to her right.

The suspect dodged traffic and crossed the large avenue, Calle de Bailén. Slightly to the right and down the street was the massive complex of the Palacio Real de Madrid—the Royal Palace of Madrid.

But the guy toting the gray backpack was not headed toward the royal's home—too much security there.

He swung left toward a sizable gray and tan structure, sharply spiked wrought iron fencing rising behind what appeared to be a statue of Pope John Paul II. A dozen crosses sat atop spires of varying heights, the most prominent being the building's bell tower.

Vail's suspect turned left down the steeply sloped side street, then ran up some stone stairs and through the church's side door, the entrance to the Crypt of the Almudena Cathedral—a place one of the detectives had told her she "had to visit."

This didn't really qualify as a visit, but what the hell—she wasn't going to have time to see the place otherwise.

As she entered the cathedral, a short man with frizzled gray hair was on his feet, looking to his right, pointing beyond the entryway. He turned to Vail and yelled, "Él no pagó!"

"Yeah, and I'm not paying either, buddy," she said as she shouldered past him into the crypt. But the view immediately stopped her. "Holy shit—er, holy mother of God." *Please, God, don't strike me down. I meant no disrespect. But the view is kind of breathtaking.*

Charcoal-veined ivory marble tiles stretched a hundred yards down a long corridor lined with dozens of ornate columns and gold light fixtures. Strategic spotlights buried in the floor and accent lighting atop the columns lit the arching, atriumed ceiling, providing a dramatic aura in the dimly illuminated interior.

Vail couldn't decide if the place was exquisite or gaudy.

But one thing was clear: her suspect was nowhere in sight.

She moved forward cautiously, down the corridor, passing open rooms to her right—private crypts with carved mantles, religious figurines and some of the most complex stained glass windows Vail had ever seen. Angel-themed murals made of inlaid tile formed the backdrop for works of ancient porcelain pottery set on elaborate pedestals.

"Yo sé que estás aquí," Vail shouted. *I know you're here.* "Policía! ¡Salga!" *Police! Come out!*

*At least, I think that's what I said. Should've paid more attention to that audio course.*

Footsteps, twenty feet away, in the crypt off to her right.

Vail moved in the direction of the sound, reaching for her absent Glock. *Shit. What am I going to do, spit on him? Yell at him? Well, I'll definitely yell at him, but what's that gonna get me?*

As she passed the area where she had heard the noise, the clunk of something heavy striking the wall off to her left echoed in the corridor. She flinched and swung her head in that direction—but someone grabbed her from behind, locking the crook of his elbow into her larynx and yanking her backward. Vail pried at the man's wrist, attempting to leverage his arm off her windpipe, but the pressure against her neck only increased.

She slammed her heel into his foot— and he released his hold enough for her to turn her head to the side and squirm down, out from under his grip. But then he brought his left knee up and swung it around, slamming into her side and sending her sprawling deeper into the crypt.

She landed face down on the slick tile floor and was trying to get up when he grabbed the back of her shirt and flung her into the stone wall. Her shoulder absorbed most of the impact, and she bounced back enough to give her the momentum to stumble forward, toward the opening that led to the corridor.

But he fisted her blouse and yanked her back toward him, then cupped a hand across her mouth. She wind-milled her elbows, striking him sharply in the nose and cheek—yet his grip remained firm.

He clamped a hand over her eyes and tried to force her to the ground.

Vail reached out blindly and grabbed for something—anything—and felt two objects. She took one in each hand and heaved them behind her, above her head.

They struck her attacker in the face.

He froze on impact—and she drove the point of her elbow into his abdomen. As he released his grip, she spun around, put her head down and struck him in the stomach, driving him backward like a linebacker doing tackling drills.

He grabbed her hair and pulled—but momentum and adrenaline propelled her forward several steps until they both struck the wall. It knocked the wind out of him and he lost his hold on her. She fell to the floor, landing on her bottom.

Vail got on her feet, ready to strike if he came at her again. And that's when she realized that it was not the wall that had taken away his breath, but the wrought iron gate.

That, and the curved, razor-sharp pointed arrows atop the metal fencing.

As she advanced on him, it became clear that the murder suspect with the gray backpack was no longer a threat: the prongs had punctured the back of his skull, killing him instantly.

Footsteps. Running, echoing.

Shouting voices: "Policia! ¡Salga ahora!" Police! Come out now!

*Now there's a new one. Wish I'd thought of that.*

Two cops appeared with handguns, pointed not at their dead suspect, but at her.

Vail did what all people are supposed to do when armed law enforcement personnel yell at you: she lifted both hands above her head. The universal sign for "I am so screwed."

"FBI," she said, not knowing if they understood English. And there was no way she'd be able to translate Federal Bureau of Investigation into Spanish. But she tried anyway. "Bureau Federale de Investigación."

They looked at one another, hesitated—and then handcuffed her.

*Typical cops. Don't like fibbies.*

As they led her away, she realized she had a problem. Murder suspect or not, she had killed a man in a foreign country. She was, as a buddy of hers liked to say, "in the shit."

*Lucy, you got some 'splaining to do.*

VAIL FORCED A SMILE. She had been in the police interview room for thirty minutes, doing her best to explain her actions. But her piss-poor Spanish and their piss-poor English made for a lot of confusion and misunderstood hand gestures. Unfortunately, the one hand gesture Vail preferred to use would not have done her much good.

They finally summoned a translator.

"As I've been trying to tell you, I'm a Supervisory Special Agent for the FBI in the United States. I'm teaching a conference on behavioral analysis to your detectives." She stopped and waited for the man to finish turning her English into Spanish. Accurately, she hoped.

A few exchanges later, she wondered if the interpreter understood English either. As he and the police official discussed the score of the soccer game between Real Madrid and Barcelona—they couldn't have been talking about what she had just said because she had only uttered three sentences—Vail realized that her do-it-yourself attempt to save her ass was falling short.

"Find Detective Heredia. He'll tell you. There was a call over his radio about two murder suspects." She finished the story, and then the interpreter stopped and waited for her to continue. But she felt she'd already provided the police enough information for him to laugh, slap her on the back, apologize for putting her through the embarrassment of getting arrested—and then offer to take her out for tapas and beer.

He did none of that. Instead, he turned to face her and said, through the interpreter, "The Almudena Cathedral is the seat of the Madrid archdiocese. You disrespected our national treasure and destroyed valuable artifacts."

*Yikes, the archdiocese? For sure I'm gonna burn in hell.* "It's a really beautiful church." *Over the top gaudy, if you must know.* "I'm truly sorry. I should've let the murder suspect get away."

Some rapid-fire Spanish, and then the translation. "You have no jurisdiction here. Why did you initiate foot pursuit?"

*I'm sure my boss will be asking me that same question.*

"Instinct," she said with a shrug. "I'm a cop. No matter what country I'm in, I live to catch the bad guys."

The man frowned and shook his head.

*Really? Not even a thank-you?*

He walked to a phone, babbled something into the receiver, waited, then babbled some more. He finally returned and said, "Your FBI will be handling this."

*I can't wait.*

VAIL SAT IN THE STATION for another forty minutes, waiting for things to get sorted out. Because of the time difference, she was sure the delay was due to an inability to reach someone at the Bureau. She didn't even know the protocol for a situation like this. It probably involved the Madrid FBI Legat, or legal attaché, calling his contact in the States, who would then alert an assistant director in charge, who would then call her boss. If that scenario was correct, she was not looking forward to hearing her name tossed about in hushed curses—not only for what she had done but because she did it at an "inconvenient" hour.

Finally Vail was led into a large room where the detectives had their desks, computers, and files. She was put in a chair and handed a phone. A line button was pushed and she said, "This is Vail."

"Karen."

It was the voice of the Assistant Special Agent-in-Charge of the behavioral analysis units, Thomas Gifford.

"You can imagine my surprise when I got a call from Director Knox about some trouble one of my agents got herself into. And the first thing I thought was, 'Must be Karen.' Now why is that?"

"I'm sorry they got you out of bed for this, sir."

"I wasn't in bed."

Vail did a quick calculation—but before she could arrive at the answer, Gifford said, "I sent you to Madrid because I thought you'd do a good job representing the Bureau. But maybe that's my fault for having unreasonable expectations."

*Ow. Did I deserve that?* "You realize, sir, that none of this was my fault."

"I'll withhold judgment for the moment. But only because something's come up. I need you to go to London."

"London." She looked around for a hidden camera crew capturing her surprise. "What's in London?"

"There's been a bombing and we were asked to provide support and analysis. Threat assessment."

"What about my conference?"

"Postponed. If you wrap up your assignment in London quickly, you can go back to Madrid. But we're also discussing a way of finishing it on Skype. Not ideal, but right now the priority is helping New Scotland Yard with this case. And—I can't stress this enough, Karen—I want you to make like a good soldier and get along with others. Show respect to the other law enforcement personnel you come into contact with, especially the London Legat. Okay?"

"Okay."

"That's extremely important. I don't want anymore phone calls."

"No more phone calls. Got it."

"Karen, I'm serious."

"I am, too, sir. Phone calls are bad. I don't want any phone calls either."

"Karen—"

"No worries. Sarcasm's in check. No insubordination. I will be a good soldier."

"I'm not going to hold my breath."

"Probably smart, sir."

"Lenka worked with the travel office," Gifford said, ignoring her comment, "to get you a room. London's usually 80 percent occupied, and it's particularly busy now, so it wasn't easy. You're booked into The Horatio Nelson at Charing Cross. It's by Trafalgar Square, centrally located and very expensive. The British government is footing the bill. Please be courteous to the staff. Got it?"

"Courteous. Got it."

"That means no attitude. That's an order."

"Yes sir. Got your order. A side of courteous, hold the attitude. When do I leave?"

Gifford groaned. "This isn't going to work."

"Sir, have I ever let you down?"

Gifford chortled. "Plenty of times."

Vail furrowed her brow. *This is a new leaf. No argument. Go with it.* "Yeah, but here's the thing: all that stuff's behind me. I'm not gonna let you down. Clean slate."

Gifford was quiet, no doubt wondering if she was serious—but hoping that she was. He said, "I'm going to hold you to that. Because I don't have a choice and I've got someone from the Madrid Legat packing up your stuff as we speak. Head directly to Madrid-Barajas Airport. Your Lufthansa flight leaves in two hours."

# 2

Vail arrived at Heathrow—a city within a city—and hiked about four miles to the entrance of the Underground, London's subway system. Fine—it was only about three-quarters of a mile. It just felt like four.

Per Lenka's emailed instructions, Vail went to the ticket window and purchased a week's pass. The man handed her a blue card with "Oyster" lettered across it. She wasn't quite sure what an ocean mollusk had to do with a subway system, but she had other things to worry about—like where she was going.

She navigated the long, narrow tunnels to the tracks and arrived just as the train pulled into the station. As she lifted her suitcase up into the car, a female voice filtered through the speaker. In "The Queen's English" she announced, "This is a Piccadilly line train. Mind the gap."

Vail turned to the woman seated to her left. "What did she say? Mind the what?"

"The gap. There's a step up into the train and there's a space between the car and the platform. I think you Americans say 'watch your step.'"

Vail got off at Leicester Square station and "minded the gap" as she disembarked. Then she wheeled her suitcase back and forth, looking for the exit. There was none.

"Excuse me," she said to a suited man heading toward her. "How do I get out of here? I don't see any exit signs."

"Just look for the way out."

Vail drew her chin back. *Does this guy understand English? Silly question. Of course he does.* "That's what I said. I'm trying to get the hell out of here."

He pointed up and behind her.

Vail turned and scanned the ceiling. A black and yellow sign said "Way Out," with an arrow that pointed right. *You've gotta be kidding me.* "And I suppose outside there's a sign that says 'Way In.'"

The man tilted his head. "What else would it say?"

"I don't know. Maybe something simple like…'Entrance'? And Exit?"

He frowned and hurried off.

Vail carried her suitcase up the stairs and then boarded an exceptionally long escalator that featured dozens of small, rectangular advertisements evenly spaced along the tiled walls of the tube-shaped tunnel.

At the top, she wheeled up to the electronic turnstile and placed her Oyster card over the reader. After another flight of stairs, she exited onto a rainy street. *Lovely. No umbrella.*

Ten minutes later, she arrived at her hotel, which sat adjacent to the Charing Cross underground station on The Strand, a busy commercial street lined with retail shops. She walked through the curved glass of automatic doors and into the soapstone floored lobby. A strong floral scent curled her nostrils.

She stepped up to the semicircular registration desk and was greeted by a Frenchwoman sporting a smile and a name tag that read, Aimée. Her heavily accented speech was nearly unintelligible.

"Checking in. Karen Vail."

"Welcome to London," Aimée said, punching the keys on her terminal. "How was your journey from the airport?"

"Did my best to mind the gaps. They're very scary."

Aimée's smile faded. "Come again?"

"Who knows? Let's first see if I like your city."

Aimée stared at Vail a long moment, apparently confused. She recovered and fell back into her spiel. "We're a full service facility. Would you like to know about the area? See the sights?"

"I'm here for work. I won't have time for pleasure."

"Well, if there's anything you need, just ring us up." She handed her a key card and said, "Oh wait. Room 204." She hesitated, bit her lip, and looked back at her screen.

"Something wrong?"

"I will find you a different room. If you give me a moment." She started tapping her keys again.

"What's wrong with 204?"

Aimée's eyes tracked up and met Vail's. "I'm not supposed to tell the guests this, but you're a woman, and, um…" She glanced left and right, leaned forward, and said, "Jack the Ripper supposedly stayed there, in 1888. I don't think you'd find it to your liking."

*Jack the Ripper. How perfect is that?* Vail grinned. "The room's fine. I'll take it."

AFTER SETTING HER SUITCASE on the bed, Vail called her significant other, Robby Hernandez, and her son, Jonathan. She told them both she was in London, prompting Jonathan to ask her to buy him a sweatshirt—and a shot glass.

"A what? You're fifteen years old."

"It's not for drinking, mom. My friend collects them and they're cool."

"Let me think about that one."

"God, ma, sometimes you're such a—such a—"

"Mother? Guilty as charged. I'm not saying no, I'm just saying I have to think about it." *Then I'll say no.* "Okay?"

"Whatever."

"I'll talk to you soon. I love you, sweetie."

"Love you, too."

After hanging up, Vail took a cab to the American embassy in Mayfair. The massive building occupied an entire city block, fronting the adjacent heavily wooded and grassy Grosvenor Square. Statues of Ronald Reagan and Dwight Eisenhower stood heroically at either end of the park's planters.

Multiple Delta security barriers rose from the ground along a semicircular foot path that brought visitors to two sizable bronzed glass guard booths that sat astride the embassy's front steps.

An American flag ruffled in the breeze, just above a massive eagle that extended from the center of the roof. Despite the ugly uniformity of the building's dated and uninspired design amid a city of classic, centuries-old architecture blended with contemporary glass marvels, Vail felt a sense of pride well up inside her chest as she paused to watch the stars and stripes ripple above. The founders were not only visionaries relative to the new government they were forming, but they selected a flag design that was inspiring—and timeless.

Vail had heard that the embassy was moving to an ultramodern facility and that the existing complex had been sold to a Qatari developer. She had little doubt the London demolition crew would enjoy ridding the city of this eyesore.

Vail stepped up to the guard booth. Ten feet away, behind tall wrought iron fencing, men toting large machine guns paced the grounds. The one closest looked her over—at a fit five-seven with a mane of curly red hair, it was something she was accustomed to—but his was not the lusty gaze men often gave her. His expression was stony. All business.

He evidently decided she was not an immediate threat, since he turned his attention to an approaching tourist snapping photos of the embassy.

Vail entered the booth and placed her creds on the security scanner, then walked through the magnetron while one of the British guards called the Legat's office to confirm her appointment.

Nothing was taken for granted. Such was the state of the world these days.

MOMENTS LATER, VAIL EMERGED from the elevator. The administrative assistant, whose name plaque read Annette Winston, glanced up. "Agent Vail. Welcome. The legal attaché will see you in a moment."

Jesus Montero, dressed in a finely tailored dark blue suit, white shirt, and bright red tie, sat down behind his large desk. He opened a folder and turned a page.

He did not invite Vail to sit, and since she intended to keep her promise to Gifford to be a good soldier, she waited for Montero to offer her a seat.

"So how was your time in Spain?" he asked, turning another page in the file.

*Crap. Don't ask me about Spain.* "Fine," Vail said. "Beautiful city. My first time there. Lots of churches and antiquities." *Fewer antiquities, unfortunately, after I left.*

Montero skimmed a file note as he spoke. "And ASAC Gifford sent you over here? Is that right?"

"Yes sir. He said it was important. I haven't been briefed yet. Some kind of threat assessment."

"Exactly," Montero said, scrawling his loopy signature across a document. "Bombing at an art gallery. High profile location. Lots of media. The nature of the target makes it a big deal to the British government. You're going to have your hands full."

*And here I was, hoping to see the town, get in some shopping at Harrods. Damn.*

For the first time, he looked up from his paperwork. His eyes were cold and dark, penetrating. Serial killer-like.

"What?"

*Did I say that out loud?* "Nothing. I didn't say anything."

Montero let his pen drop and leaned back in his chair. "You didn't have to. Your face said it all."

*My face? Shit, it's harder to master this good soldier thing than I thought.*

"I'm going to be honest with you, Agent Vail."

"Honesty is always best, sir." *Bullshit. Sometimes that white lie is worth something. Jesus, Karen. Stop it. He can read the sarcasm on your face.*

"It's your record," Montero said. "It concerns me. A great deal."

Vail narrowed her eyes. "I think I've got an exemplary record."

"Yes, I've no doubt you'd think that. I've had agents like you before under my command. Problems, every one of them. Their value to the Bureau never surpassed the shit they stirred up."

Vail narrowed her left eye. She felt blood rushing to her face. *Oh crap. Keep your cool, Karen. You're a good soldier. You're a good soldier.* She put her hand to her mouth and forced a few deep coughs to mask the flushed skin.

"You've had some problems with ASAC Gifford. And a domestic violence complaint—"

"And a lot of very important arrests. Are those in your file, too?"

"Yes," he said with a dismissive wave of a hand. "Somewhere."

*Smile. Lighten the mood.* "The reports of my insubordination have been greatly exaggerated." *Is quoting Mark Twain over the top?*

Montero squinted. "Are you trying to be funny?"

She straightened her shoulders. "No sir."

The door opened and in walked Annette Winston. She marched over to Montero and handed him a message slip.

He glanced at it, then his eyes narrowed and he shifted forward in his chair. "Thank-you, Annette." The woman turned and headed out.

Montero looked at Vail. "You've gotta be kidding."

Vail swiveled to look behind her. "You talking to me, sir?"

"There's no one else in the room," Montero said. "And no one else here who needed her ass bailed out of trouble by the Legat in Madrid."

"Oh," Vail said, swatting the air with a hand. "That. It was nothing, really."

"Let's get something clear, Agent Vail. You're here until I say you can't be here anymore. In this country, I *am* the FBI. I am the director here. There is no higher authority. Kind of like God. Get it?"

"Yes sir. After all, your name is Jesus. I get it."

He studied her face a long moment, then asked, "Do you? Do you really?"

"I think so. God is pretty absolute."

Montero rose from his chair. He walked up to Vail, very close—too close—invading her space—and looked down at her.

"I think you should take a step back, sir. With all due respect, of course. The last man who tried to intimidate me by getting in my face ended up—well, it didn't end well for him. But you probably saw that in my file."

Montero ground his molars and took a long moment to respond. But he did not move. Finally he said, "Don't bother unpacking your bags, Agent Vail. You won't be staying in London. Wait outside with Annette."

VAIL ENTERED THE ANTEROOM and took a seat. Annette was on the phone.

"Yes sir. Please hold." She glanced at Vail with a concerned expression on her face, then pressed a button and dialed a long string of numbers. Moments later, she said, "This is Annette Winston at the London Legat office. Mr. Montero would like to speak with Director Knox…Yes, I'll hold."

*Oh shit, Karen. The director? Not my biggest fan. But what was I supposed to do?*

Five minutes later, Montero's door swung open. "Agent Vail. Come in."

Vail pulled herself out of the chair and made her way into Montero's office.

"Look, sir," she said, trying to strike a conciliatory tone. "I'm sorr—"

"You will complete your assignment in England," Montero said. "You will report everything to me, no matter how inconsequential."

Montero kept his eyes on the desk. Unlike before, his penetrating gaze never once made contact with Vail's face.

"Okay," she said, trying to hide the shock. "Can I have a handgun to carry while in-country?"

"No." He sat down and shuffled some papers. "England's very different from the States. There's no tolerance for guns here. Even the police officers—even the detectives—don't carry." He shifted a stack of files—and had still not looked at her. "We're done here. You can leave."

Vail rose from her chair and turned to leave, but Montero stopped her.

"Stay out of trouble, Agent Vail. I don't want to have to clean up any of your messes."

*Yeah. I got that speech already. No phone calls.*

Vail left the room without responding, still confused about what had happened. As she exited the building, she realized none of that mattered. The faster she could complete her threat assessment, the sooner she could head home.

# 3

Hector DeSantos sat in CIA Director Earl Tasset's office beside the man's FBI counterpart, Director Douglas Knox, and DeSantos's own boss, Secretary of Defense Richard McNamara.

All that authority in one room had DeSantos feeling uncomfortable and overmatched—a new experience for him. DeSantos had gone up against far more intimidating men during his career as a black operative. And if there was one skill he had mastered, it was disguising his weaknesses by projecting the opposite.

McNamara had seen the rigors of the battlefield—and had the physical scars to prove it. But his outwardly casual demeanor belied an inner strength that some, including those who knew him well, feared.

DeSantos did not know McNamara well; in fact, he did his best to steer clear of the man. The Secretary of Defense—SecDef in military parlance—knew of DeSantos and the Operational Support Intelligence Group's exploits: "A useful tool if there ever was one," he called it when taking his new post. But useful or not, OPSIG was a device he preferred to keep locked away in the basement—the subterranean bowels of the Pentagon. That was fine by DeSantos, since he already had two bosses, Deputy Secretary Wesley Choate, the man DeSantos reported to officially, and Douglas Knox, the man DeSantos reported to unofficially.

Perhaps the friction between McNamara and Knox had to do with Knox's disproportionate, and unprecedented, amount of say over the men in OPSIG. Knox, its founder and chief architect, and currently the FBI director, possessed a résumé like that of a summa cum laude intelligence master. In essence, he was a puppeteer whose positions of power enabled him to build a moat of impenetrability, a force field that could repel adversity, a man who pulled strings behind the scenes to make things happen. More than that, though, Knox enjoyed the loyalty of allies and elicited fear from adversaries; and in the process, he had developed a cache of dirt on the Washington elite.

Perhaps related and perhaps not, discord existed between McNamara and Knox going back two decades. DeSantos never asked Knox about it because it was something he did not need to know—and those would be Knox's precise words should DeSantos venture onto the topic.

Tasset, with his wavy, uncharacteristic collar-length hair and professorial metal-rimmed glasses, pressed a button and a small green LED lit up on the conference room table. "We can talk securely." He turned to Knox and sat back in his seat. "You said this involved Anthony Scarponi."

"Hector would like some time with him," Knox said. As Tasset raised a hand to object, Knox continued: "Secretary McNamara and I have briefed Hector on the dangers and we've consulted the doctors. They all feel Scarponi is past the point of relapse."

Tasset frowned and leaned forward, placing his forearms on the tabletop. "You've already spoken with the doctors? Why am I only hearing this now?"

"We didn't see any harm," McNamara said.

Tasset ground his jaw. "After all we've been through with Scarponi, after all the damage he's caused and all the money we've dumped into his rehab, I can't imagine this is important enough to jeopardize—"

"The doctors cleared it," DeSantos said. "Sir."

Tasset's gaze shifted to DeSantos. His long stare was meant to antagonize, unnerve. Though Tasset was an outwardly passive man, DeSantos knew he had an explosive temper and defended his territory ferociously. Like a guard dog.

But when it came to Anthony Scarponi, it took a lot more than a Washington power broker to deter Hector DeSantos.

Scarponi had been a key CIA operative working covertly in the Pacific Rim when his cover was compromised in the Ames spy scandal, which made headlines around the world. The fallout included Scarponi's capture by the Chinese, who proceeded to run unsanctioned medical experiments on him. But not Mengele-type atrocities; these dealt with mind control. China had pioneered the field of *xi nao*, or "washing the brain," in the 1950s, though the concept of exerting influence over another individual's actions extended back to the thirteenth century.

The Chinese succeeded in turning Scarponi into a skilled assassin who operated around the world—and conveniently bore the fingerprint of the United States. The US government, unaware that their former operative had been turned, received its first indication of a problem after Scarponi's initial hit—a Taiwanese official negotiating an arms deal with America.

After Scarponi's only assignment on domestic soil—the murder of Deputy White House Counsel Vincent Foster, officially ruled a suicide—the FBI apprehended him and the US Attorney delivered a conviction. But new evidence emerged after Scarponi had served several years in prison, and he was released pending a new trial. His attempt to exact revenge against the prosecution's key witness resulted in an intensive effort to recapture him. But during the op, DeSantos's partner, Brian Archer, was killed by Scarponi and his accomplices.

Rather than being returned to his jail cell, however, Scarponi landed in a secure facility at a Department of Defense medical facility overseen by doctors, researchers, and scientists working covertly with the CIA. There, while being studied to determine what techniques and psychoactive drugs had been used on him, and how they could be reverse engineered, he received specialized rehabilitative deprogramming therapy.

Tasset rose from his chair and leaned both hands on the table. He looked down for a moment, then said, "My better judgment tells me we should wait. If there's no rush—"

"But there is." DeSantos inched forward in his seat. "I have reason to believe that one of Scarponi's former accomplices is planning a hit on a target of interest to us."

"Who? And what?"

DeSantos and Knox shared a look.

"That's unimportant," Knox said.

"Bullshit. You want my permission on this but you won't provide full disclosure? That's not how this—"

"We don't need your permission," Knox said. He glanced at McNamara, whose impassive facial expression provided Knox all the support he needed—which was not much. "I'm sorry if I didn't make that clear. This is a domestic issue. And that's my purview. So this is—" Knox shrugged a shoulder—"a courtesy visit."

Tasset's skin tone flushed crimson.

Knox held up a hand in contrition. "Earl. Let's be frank, okay?" Tasset took his seat and motioned him to proceed. "This is important and we wouldn't be here if I thought it was unreasonable. I would've just gone ahead and let Hector meet with Scarponi and informed you after the fact."

"You son of—"

"But you know that I believe inclusion and openness is preferable. Because that's what I'd expect in return if the situation were reversed."

Tasset worked his jaw muscles, but finally, through clenched teeth, said, "Fair enough."

"We didn't go about this recklessly. And you have my word that we'll handle the meeting with the utmost care to prevent a setback in Scarponi's retraining."

"I think we owe this to Mr. DeSantos," McNamara said, drawing attention away from Knox.

Tasset swung his head toward DeSantos. "I don't care who your father is, Hector. This is an ill-advised—"

"This has nothing to do with my father, and you know it."

"Dick," Tasset said pointedly, "you've been very quiet. But I know you. You've got an opinion on this. And it's rarely in sync with Douglas's view of the world."

McNamara narrowed his left eye. "This will be an important test to see if Scarponi is truly as far along in his recovery as the doctors have led us to believe. If he can't handle this, he has no business going back into the field. All issues aside, that's reason enough to support us in this."

Tasset chewed on that a long moment, then threw up his hands. "As you said, you people don't need my permission. Do what you want. But no, I'm not sanctioning it. Something goes wrong, you two are going to answer for it. Not me. Are we clear?"

Knox and McNamara rose. DeSantos followed.

"Thanks for your time, Earl." Knox forced a smile. "Always a pleasure."

Rather than offering his hand in peace, Knox turned to leave—with McNamara at his side and DeSantos following close behind.

# 4

*United States Department of Defense*
*Defense Advanced Research Projects Agency*
*CARD: Covert Arms Research Division*
*Memogen Study Facility*
*Undisclosed location*

Hector DeSantos, accompanied by Douglas Knox and Richard McNamara, cleared security procedures that rivaled those of the NSA. After stowing their weapons in a locker in the Sally Port, they were escorted to the basement by four Military Police officers and Dr. Saakaar Poola, CARD's assistant director of research.

Stainless steel lined the walls, with closed-circuit cameras mounted every fifty feet, blanketing all corners and angles.

"Mr. Scarponi has been a model patient," Poola said as they walked. "He's extremely motivated and has done everything we've asked. His retraining and rehabilitation programs are progressing precisely as expected and he's hitting the milestones I and my staff have set for him. In short, we expect a full recovery."

DeSantos fought the urge to snort disapproval.

They turned a corner and entered a room that featured a large window inset in the Navajo white cinder block wall. Inside sat Anthony Scarponi, sitting at a table and staring at a Nook eReader.

DeSantos felt bile rise into his throat. His abdominal muscles contracted. And his mind was seized by a single thought: *I want to kill the bastard.* Instead, he stayed within himself and asked, "Are you implying, Doctor, that you feel Scarponi can go back out into the field?" DeSantos made no attempt to hide his doubt.

"Not for me to say, Mr. DeSantos. My job is to make recommendations based on the patient's clinical progress, analysis of his applied test results, and studies of his rigorous psychological testing."

"You sound like the Mikhail Baryshnikov of the research community, Doc."

Poola tilted his head in confusion.

DeSantos turned away and looked through the glass. "You danced around that question with remarkable skill."

Knox cleared his throat. "Hector. Please."

DeSantos held up a hand, as if to center himself. Now was not the time to antagonize. "My apologies. Sorry for putting you on the spot."

McNamara, remaining in the background and observing—some might say looking for weakness and waiting to pounce—spoke up. "You sure you're up for this, Hector? I'd rather do this another time if you're going to have a problem with—"

"No problem, Mr. Secretary. I'm good." He was incensed and filled with murderous rage, but he was good.

McNamara motioned to Poola. "Doctor, a word, please."

Poola and McNamara moved into the corridor.

DeSantos felt Knox's glare on his neck. "What. Sir."

"You know what. I don't want any drama. I made this sit-down possible. It can't come back on me."

DeSantos did not look at Knox. "I hear you, sir."

"Do you? In all the years I've known you, I've seen you like this only once before, and you ended up doing something really stupid."

"Thanks for the vote of confidence." He waited a beat, realizing he needed to lighten the moment before he lost his lone supporter. He said with a slight smile, "And thanks for the reminder."

"What I really want you to remember is why you're here. Make the most of your visit because you won't get another one. And if Scarponi is released, and if he does return to the field, you're going to have to stay a mile away from him. McNamara is not going to be understanding. And I don't want to have to step in to clean up your mess. Not on something like this."

"Understood."

"Keep your head, get your answers, get out of there."

McNamara and Poola reentered the room.

DeSantos stepped over to the adjacent door. "I'm ready."

"You've got ten minutes," McNamara said.

DeSantos put his hand on the knob and paused for a second as he slipped a tiny sliver of metal into the lock. He took a deep breath, cleared his mind to get into operations mode—and wiped all emotion from his face. Focused on mission success.

He pushed through the door and grinned. "Anthony, I'm Hector. Department of Defense."

Scarponi rose from the chair and set his Nook on the table. He shook DeSantos's hand with confidence. "Good to meet you."

*We came close to meeting once before, asshole. On a street in Fredericksburg. When you and your buddies killed my partner.*

DeSantos motioned him to return to his seat. "How's your... therapy going?"

"Far as I can tell, real well. The doctors are very happy."

DeSantos pursed his lips and nodded. "I'd like to talk to you about your time in China."

Scarponi leaned back in his chair. "I'd like to help you out, Hector, but I've been through this with the doctors. I'm like a blank sheet of paper. I don't remember anything from those years. It's like it's been erased."

"Erased," DeSantos repeated.

"Best way I can describe it. I can't remember a thing."

DeSantos leaned two hands on the back of the metal chair in front of him. "When does your memory begin? What's the farthest back you can go?"

Scarponi looked up at the ceiling. "I really don't remember much before my first few days here. At some point I was in the hospital and doctors and nurses kept coming and going from the room. It seems like a dream, but apparently that's what happened. As for childhood memories—or anything else, really, before those first days in the hospital—I've got nothing. They even had to tell me my name."

His better sense told him that Scarponi was bullshitting him—but he had no proof and the man's body language was flawless; he gave nothing away. In this setting, DeSantos was powerless to force answers from him.

He wished he had Scarponi hooked up to a polygraph. Then again, a man like this—an international assassin, one of the most efficient and revered surgically accurate killers the world has known—would reveal nothing of use in a "psychophysiological detection of deception" examination. Despite all the sensors recording blood pressure, pulse, respiration, and skin conductivity, Scarponi would have long ago mastered incontrovertible control over his body's physiological responses.

"So if I asked you about the guys you used to work with—"

"I wouldn't know who you're talking about."

DeSantos had considered the possibility that Scarponi would refuse to provide the names of his former colleagues, let alone their tendencies, and where they had an inclination to pitch their tents. But he had not figured on Scarponi taking a passive-aggressive approach. It was a brilliant strategy because DeSantos could do nothing with it. That's assuming, of course, he truly did not retain his prior memories.

DeSantos was willing to bet that it was an act. But was he willing to stake his career on it?

He took a seat opposite Scarponi and locked his gaze on the man. He had been evaluating his body language, the movement of his eyes, the visible—as yet nonexistent—moisture content of his skin. So far, unsurprisingly, his adversary had given away nothing.

"I read the reports of your escape from federal custody," DeSantos said. "When you cut out the tracking transmitter. That was real good, by the way—very cool. There aren't a lot of guys with the balls to do that. Not sure I could've done it."

Scarponi shrugged. "A tracking transmitter?" He lifted his brow in genuine amazement. "Don't remember. But that does sound pretty impressive."

DeSantos smiled out of one side of his mouth. "It was. Still," he said, leaning forward, "the thing that really caught my attention was when you had Lauren Chambers in that cabin. I mean, you had her tied up. How'd she get out?"

"Like I said. Can't help you. But I'm surprised it's not in the report."

"Oh," DeSantos said with a hearty laugh, "it is. I just wanted to hear it from you. Because I don't believe what's written there." He stared at Scarponi, watching for facial tics. And waited.

Finally, Scarponi spread his hands in innocence. "I don't know what you want me to say."

"Well, I mean, you're a big, strong, tough guy. You killed people for a living. A lot of people. Some you shot—not so hard, really—others you poisoned. But then there are the harder ones, the up-close-and-personal hits: you stuck a knife in their stomach, twisted it, and sliced open their insides. That's impressive."

DeSantos stopped, observed. No reaction.

"And then there were the ones you strangled with your bare hands. Truly exceptional. It's what made you so good at what you did."

Scarponi shrugged. "I'm told that the drugs the Chinese used on me were very powerful. The training they gave me, the psychological techniques they taught me, perfected through decades of research and experimentation."

"Yeah—I don't doubt that for a minute. But here's the thing." DeSantos leaned in to Scarponi's face and said, "This woman, only about five-four, a hundred ten pounds, she gets the upper hand and beats you silly. Pounds your face to a pulp." He stopped and watched. And got what he wanted. A narrowing of the right eye, a tightening of his jaw muscle. *The face is a wonderful thing—unless you're being interrogated—in which case it's like a junkie who needs a fix.*

"Big, tough man beat up by a woman. See, that's what the report says about how she got away. She beat you and left you in that cabin."

"No, that's not—" Scarponi stopped, blinked. "I doubt that's the way it went down." He chuckled. "I mean, really. Look at me. Do you think that's even possible?"

"I think a lot of things are possible, Hung Jin," DeSantos said, using the name Scarponi had adopted when he was working for the Chinese.

"Who is—who's Hung Jin?"

DeSantos grinned, broadly. "That's good." He rose, paced a bit, passed in front of the door, leaned against it—and locked it discreetly. "*You're* good. But I've had enough of your bullshit. You're going to tell me what I want to know—the names of your accomplices, the ones you worked with on US soil."

Scarponi looked over at the observation window and spread his hands. "I don't know what this man is talking about," he said to the glass.

DeSantos stepped forward and jabbed Scarponi so fast and hard in the face that the man's chair tipped backward and he went sprawling onto the floor.

DeSantos was on him immediately.

He grabbed Scarponi by the collar and slugged him again, his skull slamming against the concrete. Scarponi's eyes rotated back into his head, then settled back in their center, jittering slightly as they fought to focus on DeSantos.

"Names. I want names! Now, or I swear to God, I'm going to kill you." He grabbed Scarponi's neck and dug both thumbs into his trachea.

Scarponi lifted his chest off the ground, throwing DeSantos off balance—and then rolled and spun out from under his weight. Scarponi scrabbled to his feet, but DeSantos was a half second faster, and he landed a vicious kick to Scarponi's chin, snapping his neck back.

He lowered his head and slammed his shoulder into Scarponi's chest, driving him back against the wall. He struck it forcefully, and the impact emptied the air from the man's lungs.

DeSantos pulled flexcuffs from his back pocket and tightened them around Scarponi's wrists. He fed another around the metal leg of the table, which was bolted to the floor. Pulled it tight.

DeSantos threw his forearm against Scarponi's neck and put his weight behind it. "Names!"

Scarponi struggled, trying to swing his head side to side to dislodge DeSantos's grip.

Somewhere off behind them:

*Banging against the door.*

*Blaring alarms.*
*Flashing red lights.*

DeSantos knew he didn't have much time before the MPs stormed the room. With his other hand, he grabbed Scarponi's testicles and squeezed as hard as he could. Scarponi stiffened in pain. DeSantos pushed his forearm harder into his windpipe.

Tears streamed from his eyes, but Scarponi refused to talk.

"They've treated you like royalty, anything and everything you wanted. Coddled you, nurtured you like some poor little sick puppy. Well, see, here's the thing, *Tony.* I'm like you, a killer. And I'm here for information. If you don't give me what I want, I'm gonna do what you and your thugs did to my partner. So you can keep your mouth shut, let me take my revenge and settle the score. Or you can give me the names I want."

Scarponi's face shaded deep red, his eyes bulged, and he continued to struggle, moving his neck, attempting to suck air into his chest.

"What's it going to be?"

Still no indication he intended to talk.

*Banging.*
*Yelling.*
*The whine of a drill on metal.*

"I know what you're thinking—they're gonna break in and pull him off me. And they're definitely trying. But are they gonna get in before I kill you? Ask yourself—are they gonna drill out that lock in the next ten seconds? 'Cause that's all you've got left. You ready to die?"

Scarponi locked gazes with DeSantos, who leaned harder on his neck.

"Give me the names and you'll live another day. Your choice."

Scarponi opened his mouth and his lips tried to form words. DeSantos released a bit of pressure on his neck.

"Vince Richter. Mike Hagel." He coughed. "Can't breathe—"

DeSantos loosened the pressure—slightly—and said, "Who else?"

"Kyle…Walker."

"There's more!" DeSantos squeezed harder. "I want all of 'em!"

Scarponi's face reddened, his eyes intense pinpoints of anger.

"Hussein Rudenko. Where can I find him?"

Scarponi's eyes widened—recognition—and he parted his lips, as if to answer. But he spit on DeSantos's cheek instead. There wasn't much force behind it, but the message was clear.

DeSantos slammed his forehead into Scarponi's nose, breaking it and raising a corresponding lump on DeSantos's brow.

"Rudenko! Goddamn it, where is he?"

Blood running out of both nostrils, struggling to breathe with DeSantos's forearm pressing into his trachea, Scarponi laughed defiantly, telling DeSantos that his time had run out.

And that he was not going to get what he came for.

The door to the room blasted open and four MPs poured in. Two grabbed DeSantos, wrestled him to the ground, and cuffed him.

Knox and McNamara crowded into the small room as the remaining MPs took control of Scarponi.

"Lock him up," Knox said. "Scarponi, I want him in full restraints. He and I are gonna have a little chat." He gave DeSantos an angry scowl and then walked out of the room.

DOUGLAS KNOX WALKED into the holding cell where DeSantos was seated. Twenty minutes had passed, yet DeSantos's pulse was still galloping at an unhealthy pace. He was perspiring and on the verge of hyperventilating.

DeSantos opened his mouth to speak, but in that moment Richard McNamara pushed into the room, shoving Knox aside. Dr. Poola was barely visible in the entryway.

DeSantos struggled to read Knox's face. He was not pleased, that much was evident—but had DeSantos gone too far? Was Knox going to dismiss him?

His eyes shifted to McNamara, whose expression reeked of disgust.

"What the hell was that in there?" McNamara asked. "You're one of my best operatives, but I've got good reason to send your insubordinate ass packing. You were under direct orders to keep yourself under control. The director and I put our reputations on the line for you. Why, I'm not really sure, given how you just fucked us over."

They were all looking at DeSantos, who sat back, incredulous. "Did I miss something? With all due respect, sir—sirs—did you see what happened in that room?" No one answered. "Dr. Poola—you saw it, didn't you? Your patient's been gaming you. He's not *progressing* with your retraining. He's playing you. Hell, he's the same person you brought in here—"

"Hector," Knox said. "Don't deflect attention off yourself. What you did—"

"Probably saved a lot of lives. *Sir.* Because the good doc here was convinced his patient was safe to release into the field with a handgun and a US passport."

"You've bought yourself some time off," McNamara said. "You need to cool down. *I* need some time to cool down." He held out an open palm. "Your creds and clearance."

DeSantos made no move to his pocket. "For how long?"

The two men stared at one another. McNamara did not provide an answer—or even a facial twitch.

Finally DeSantos turned to Knox—who DeSantos felt would always have his back. The man frowned, then looked away.

DeSantos stood up, pulled out his credentials case, and handed it to McNamara.

"Leave your gun in the locker. There's a driver out front who'll take you to your car. Someone will be in touch."

DeSantos made eye contact with each of the men, trying one last time to ascertain if they did, in fact, see the important role he had played in exposing Scarponi. None of them reacted.

DeSantos walked out of the room, where he was joined by two MPs who escorted him off the complex.

As the bright sun struck his eyes, he wondered if he would ever step through those doors again.

# 5

*Present Day*
*The Horatio Nelson at*
*Charing Cross Hotel*
*London*

Vail had been in her hotel room ten minutes when she heard a knock at the door. *Nice to be welcomed, but no one knows I'm here.* She reached for her Glock—and found nothing: no holster, no gun. *This is going to take some getting used to.*

She stepped up to the door to peer out the peephole, but there was none. *No wonder Jack the Ripper liked staying at this hotel.*

"Who is it?"

"I'm looking for Karen Vail."

*So are a bunch of serial killers back in the States.* "And who exactly is looking for her?"

"Clive Reid. I'm with the Met—New Scotland Yard. I was sent to escort Agent Vail to the crime scene."

Vail pulled open the door—and found a man a few inches taller than she, late thirties, dressed in a dark gray suit.

"Madam. Am I to assume you're Karen Vail?"

"What was your first clue?"

"First one would have to be the hotel registry. Second would be the description the guv'nor gave me. Pretty redhead."

"Pretty. Really. Were those his words?"

Reid grinned. "Yes, Madam, they were."

"Okay, let's get one thing clear. I don't go by 'madam.' Sounds like a grandmother wrapped in a shawl."

"Very well, Madam. I—I mean...what is it I should call you?"

Vail flashed on a number of different terms the guys in her unit used, but didn't want to poison the water she'd be drinking from. "Karen would be fine. Vail works too. Just don't call me Karen Vail every time."

Reid squinted. "Right."

"I hope you have a sense of humor, Reid."

"I have a *sense* of it, yes."

Vail nodded. "Very good." She glanced around her room. "I'm ready to go. Your car or mine?"

"Oh—I didn't...I didn't realize you had a car."

"I don't. So I guess that answers that question." Vail grabbed her purse and walked out, past a perturbed Reid.

AS REID NAVIGATED THE CLOGGED streets of London, Vail noticed a photo of a teenager that was taped to the dashboard.

She gestured to it and said, "Is this guy wanted?"

"Wanted?" Reid snickered. "No, no. That's my son."

"Yeah, I didn't want my son, either. He was an accident."

Reid hesitated, then got the joke and gave a belated, pity-laden chuckle.

"No photo of the wife," Vail said. "Divorced?"

"Passed on."

*Oops.* "Sorry."

"Don't be. We didn't much fancy each other. Well, we did for about ten years, and then she stepped out on me. It's complicated."

"Sounds pretty straightforward to me."

"My son is really my nephew."

Vail nodded slowly. "Okay, I see what you mean. Didn't see that one coming."

"His parents were killed a year apart when he was a kid. My brother's helicopter was shot down in Afghanistan about ten years ago. My sister-in-law died in childbirth with their second son a few months later." He shook his head. "Tragic, really."

"More like devastating."

"Devastating, quite." Reid twisted his lips, then said, "Anyway, that brought things to a head with my wife. She didn't like the late nights when I was trying to make detective. So she had a fling with a bloke from Brighton. I chose the right profession, I guess, because I knew something was up. Around the same time, my brother and sister-in-law passed. I wanted to adopt my nephew and she said no. I didn't even have time for *her*, so if we adopted a kid it'd be her burden. That's how she phrased it. Her 'burden.' I did it anyway and she left me for the arsehole from Brighton."

"Is that why you offed her? For cheating on you?"

"Offed?"

"Yeah, you know, killed her."

Reid took his eyes off the road, apparently to see if Vail was serious. Satisfied that she was not, but still not quite sure, he chuckled nervously.

"Just kidding," she said with a dismissive wave of a hand. "It was me, I'd have cut my husband's balls off. Kind of hard to do with a woman, though."

Reid laughed again, this time more genuinely. "Are we talking off the record here?"

Vail twisted her head in both directions. "There *is* no record here."

"Fine. Then I poisoned her. Much cleaner, harder to trace than gunshots or knife wounds." Reid looked at her, hard.

Vail turned to him, examined his face, and then they both burst out laughing.

"I had you there. For a minute—"

"No, you didn't. Give me a break."

"No, I did. I insist."

Vail smirked. "Fine, you did. For a couple of *seconds*."

"I knew it. I saw it on your face." He grinned at her again, then asked, "So how old's your son?"

"Jonathan's fifteen."

"Brant's sixteen. Birthday's today, actually."

"Today. Too bad you didn't get the day off."

"I did. Until the guv'nor called and said I had to take you round, so, well, that's that. But I don't want you to feel bad. I mean, can't be too upset about spending the day with a pretty woman."

*"Pretty" again. I could get used to this.* "I'm a big girl, Reid. I can look after myself. I'll rent a car. You go spend the rest of the day with your son."

"Ever driven on the right side of the road?"

Vail looked out at the street. "Don't you have it backward? You're driving on the left."

"It may be the left, but it's the *right* side. You Americans drive on the wrong side."

*Oh. He's trying to be funny.* "Got it. Not bad."

"Can't take credit for it. It's an old one in these parts. I got it from a coach driver."

"No," Vail said, "I've never driven on the left side of the road. How hard can it be?"

"Judging from some family members who've visited from the US, quite. It's harder than you think. No worries, though. I've got the assignment."

*So now I'm an "assignment." Liked it better when I was the pretty redhead.* "Can you tell your…guv'nor I don't need a babysitter?"

"Let's get this squared away and we can re-evaluate the situation at that time. What do you say to that?"

"Just thinking of your son."

Reid made a number of turns, navigating among the dozens of black taxis and those blanketed from bumper to bumper with corporate advertising graphics.

"He'll be fine. Not the first birthday he spent alone. Besides, he's going out with some friends for fish and chips after school. He won't be missing his old man, I can tell you that."

Reid pulled down a swanky street lined with expensive-looking shops.

"Whoa," Vail said. "Where are we?"

"Someplace the likes of you and me visit but don't have any business shopping at. Bond Street. Heard of it?"

Vail snapped her fingers. "Where that guy James lives. Bond. James Bond."

"More like where Daniel Craig *shops*. And lots of other celebrities. Just last week I ran into Robert Downey Jr. and his wife in that shoe store on the corner. Bond Street's famous for its luxury shopping, exclusive brands, designer fashion, one of a kind jewelry pieces, fine art, and...rare manuscripts. I reckon it's probably one of the most expensive strips of real estate in the world."

Just ahead, a police cruiser was parked at the curb, yellow crime scene tape stretched across and around the sidewalk. A news truck with its corkscrew antenna rose from the van's center, and a suited reporter and his cameraman stood off to the side, framing their shot.

Reid pulled over to the curb behind the police car and set the brake. "C'mon now. This is it."

Vail got out and looked up, where blown out windows and charred studs were visible on the second floor. She was about to duck beneath the police boundary when she was met by a reporter.

"Anything more you can tell us?" the man said, shoving his mike in her face.

Vail, straight-faced, said, "Yes. I can tell you that you're standing on my foot and that it hurts."

The reporter jumped back and Vail fell in behind Reid, who was entering the office building through the modern storefront.

Reid acknowledged the bobby who was stationed at the entrance maintaining the integrity of the scene. He and Vail signed the logbook and continued up the staircase.

"Have you worked many bombings?"

"You probably heard about an assassination attempt on our president-elect?"

Reid laughed. "Heard about it? It was all over the bloody news, even here."

"I worked that case. Among others. So yeah, no worries, I can handle this threat assessment." Out of the corner of her eye, Vail caught the names of the businesses listed on the directory placards as they ascended the steps. "Turner Gallery. That the place?"

"That's the place."

"An art gallery?"

"The owner's an art, antique, and rare manuscript dealer. Half his gallery was destroyed by a potent firebomb. Fairly well-defined in its ignition source, which makes me think the target was the item or items contained in the safe."

Vail stopped at the top of the second flight. "What explosive was used?"

"Flash powder, set to go on a timer."

*Aluminized perchlorate. Whoa.* "Where was the evidence taken?"

"Military lab, a couple hours away. Why?"

"With flash powder, we should be able to determine the supply source of the explosive material. We'd want to know if it's commercial, if it's factory-made, if it's been obtained through legitimate means, if it's been stolen, if it's military ordnance or if it's been improvised. It'd tell us about who we're dealing with, what his skill-sets are, and what limitations he has on his ability to come up with the materials he needs to make a bomb."

"I imagine all that's being looked at. Our lab's very thorough. You know a lot about this stuff."

"Picked it up from one of my mentors. He's an ATF profiler—Alcohol, Tobacco, and Firearms—our agency that handles arsons and bombings, that kind of thing. There's not a whole lot of research on bombers, so I've made it a point of picking his brain."

"Obviously," Reid said, "you've picked him clean on the subject of flash powder."

Vail chuckled. "Not really. But I do know a few things. Combined with what your experts know, it should help figure out how serious this offender is, and how likely it is that he'll strike again. First thing—flash powder's aluminized perchlorate. Almost always an improvised mixture and very dangerous to work with. It's sensitive to pressure, heat, shock, and static— it's basically one of the most dangerous explosives you can get. Dangerous for the offender, as well."

Reid tilted his head back. "You're talking like it's a lone bomber, an individual. I wouldn't make that assumption. We don't have lone bombers in the UK. It's very, very unusual. Our bombers tend to be organized groups. And they tend to know what they're doing."

"I was speaking generally, but let's test your theory. I take it there was an arming switch."

Reid squinted. "Yes. How—"

"Groups use arming switches as a personal safety measure to keep the device from exploding on them while they're setting it. These guys want to stick around to further their cause. So they take precautions. Like an arming switch."

Reid removed the crime scene tape that was strung across the entryway.

"Another thing to keep in mind," Vail said, "is that if we're dealing with a situation where access is an issue—like if the flash powder's military in origin—then that might make your job a hell of a lot easier because it should help narrow your search."

"Because only a limited number of people have access to that stuff."

"Theoretically," Vail said. "Yeah."

Reid jiggled the key a bit as he unlocked the door. He turned back to her and said, "There was also a separate fire ignited across the room, where other artwork and manuscripts were on display."

"Casualties?"

"None." He pushed the door open and led the way inside. "There are three rooms to this place. Two were untouched, and one—this one—was destroyed."

A pungent chemical smell hung in the air, despite the fresh air leaking through the damaged wall at the far end of the gallery, which had been demolished by the blast. A clear plastic tarp covered the opening, flapping gently in the wind. The interior—and everything inside—was singed beyond recognition.

"Looks like whatever they were going for was in this room." She ran an index finger through the black soot that had accumulated on the counter. "This was one hot fire."

"Extremely. According to the Fire Brigade, these people knew what they were doing."

*I'm starting to get that impression.*

"What's Islamic terrorist activity like in the UK these days?"

"We've got our share of problems, but we do a decent enough job of staying on top of it. Sleeper cells, yeah. Threats on a regular basis, yeah. Affiliates, we've got those too. But al-Qaeda specifically, they've claimed for three years to be planning a 'spectacular attack' in Britain. Hasn't happened. And we haven't had another 7/7, so that's all we can hope for. Why? You think they, or some group like them, is involved?"

"Don't know enough yet."

"Let's see if we can remedy that. I've asked the owner to join us here in case you had any questions. He should arrive momentarily."

"I assume you haven't released details to the media."

"Almost nothing. Hasn't stopped them, though. They're good at speculating, filling in the blanks with talking heads."

Vail strolled around the flat, assessing the layout and orienting herself: what was located where, what areas were most damaged, and taking in the view of Bond Street from the destroyed windows.

The sound of crunching footsteps snagged Vail's attention. Reid unlocked the door leading to the undamaged room and pulled it open, revealing a lithe man in a cream-colored suit with graying temples and a tan complexion.

"Idris Turner," Reid said, "this is Karen Vail, from the FBI. She's here to help us assess what's happened and determine whether or not substantial threat exists for further bombings."

Turner glanced around his damaged gallery. "I don't have to tell you that this is very upsetting. They almost succeeded in destroying my life's work—and something extremely important to England's heritage."

Vail stole a skeptical look at Reid, then said, "Forgive me for being so direct, but that sounds a bit over the top. What are we talking about here?"

Turner pulled over three metal stools and brushed off the ashes with a handkerchief that he pulled from his breast pocket with a flourish. He slid a seat over to Vail and he and Reid took the others. "A few weeks ago, I purchased a very rare manuscript: an early draft of Shakespeare's *A Midsummer Night's Dream* that I believe dates back about 420 years. It was the find of a lifetime. All of us in the rare manuscript business fantasize of finding something of Shakespeare's, something written in his own hand. Nothing exists with his original writing. But all hope had been given up long ago because of the fire in 1666 that destroyed just about all of London, and so much of our history with it."

"There're no handwriting samples?" Vail asked. "Anywhere? No signatures, on a land deed, a bank check, a signed first edition of *Romeo and Juliet*?"

Reid chuckled.

"There are six signatures," Turner said, not joining in the joke, "and they're all different. Some could've been made by law clerks. But this—this manuscript—is written by hand. Entirely by hand. Goose quill and ink. That's the way they did it back then."

"No offense, Mr. Turner," Vail said, "but I'm an FBI agent, not an archeologist."

"Please, call me Idris. But you don't understand my point. I believe that manuscript is the reason for this bombing."

"Why? Who'd care that you found a manuscript written in Shakespeare's hand? Wouldn't that be a great thing?"

"It depends. Most people would be intrigued. But some may not be. Just the opposite, in fact. I believe that whoever is behind this did it to destroy the manuscript."

"The offender bombed a building in the heart of London's most posh luxury shopping area, to destroy an old manuscript?" Vail chortled. "I know you British are a bit buttoned down, but that seems extreme."

"I'm not doing this justice. It would be better if you could talk with John Hudson."

Vail looked to Reid for an explanation.

"Hudson is a Shakespearean scholar." Reid consulted his watch. "He was here in London but he's now back in New York. Middle of the night—I'm sure he's in bed. But his associate with the Dark Lady Players is still in town."

"Dark Lady Players?" Vail asked.

"An interpretive/experimental theater group of Shakespeare players out of New York. They just finished a week of performances here in London at the Donmar Warehouse."

"Can you get his associate on the phone?"

"I can do one better. Let's see if he can grab a coffee. My sense is that this is best handled in person."

VAIL AND REID FOLLOWED TURNER to a Costa coffee shop in Piccadilly Circus. It was not too different from a Starbucks in the States; in fact, they had passed a Starbucks along the way.

Costa's walls featured earth red and brown tones along with contemporary furniture and lighting fixtures. The café was larger than it looked from the outside; it extended far back in a long, rectangular shape, with signs directing patrons to extra seating downstairs.

They took a seat at a table in the middle third of the restaurant while Reid waited in line to get their drinks. A moment later, a man with dark hair and ripped jeans approached them.

"This is Simon Wilkinson," Turner said. "Simon, FBI Agent Karen Vail."

"Thanks for meeting me," Vail said. "I'm a little out of my element and I'm hoping you can shed some light on this whole Shakespeare obsession."

"Yes, well. As you can probably tell from the way I talk I'm at heart a native Brit. I've lived in New York the past fifteen years working with John, so I guess I can give you a good view of what you're looking at from the British point of view. 'Obsession' is a bit strong, but really, not far from the truth."

"You know about the bombing then."

Wilkinson laughed. "Everyone in England knows about the bombing. The discovery of this manuscript has gripped the country. When the media broke the story, it caused quite the stir. On a smaller scale, it's like the Olympics all over again. That's all that's been on the television. Blogs haven't stopped talking about it. Idris and Gavin have been under siege."

"Who's Gavin?"

"My curator and resident rare art expert," Turner said. "Gavin Paxton. He does some restoration, too. He's very good."

Reid came over with a tray of squat, oversized mugs. "I took the liberty of getting you a coffee. White, that okay?"

Wilkinson took it off the tray. "You remembered. Perfect."

"White?" Vail asked.

"White," Reid said. "With milk."

"Is it me, or do you Brits have weird ways of looking at things?"

"It's you."

Vail grinned. "Probably right. So. What is it about Shakespeare that enraptures British society—and why is this rare manuscript so important that someone'd be willing to kill over it?"

"Two very good questions," Wilkinson said.

*Two. Wow. In one breath.*

Wilkinson turned to Turner. "How much have you told her? The authorship?"

"Haven't gotten to that yet."

"Why don't we start with your first question." Wilkinson sucked on his bottom lip a moment. "In a sense, Shakespeare is synonymous with England. He's so deeply steeped in our society and culture that you can't separate one from the other. Kind of like the monarchy and the Beatles. A few months ago a think tank did a study of which symbols give Britons a sense of pride. Shakespeare scored 75 percent. The monarchy only got 68 percent."

Vail lifted her brow. "What about John, Paul, George, and Ringo?"

"The 'Fab Four,'" Wilkinson said, "scored 51 percent. If that doesn't say it all, I don't know what does. Shakespeare's ingrained in our identity, a tremendous source of national pride, our greatest cultural export.

"Not to mention Shakespeare's arguably the finest writer of all time. Certainly the greatest dramatist in history. His contribution to literature is unparalleled—he introduced nearly three thousand words into the English language. And when you look at the themes, the story construction in his plays—so much of what we take for granted in storytelling nowadays has its roots in Shakespeare's writings. Some academics and social psychologists even feel that our understanding of human relationships and emotions comes from his works. The plays and sonnets are an integral part of school curricula, studied by half the world's children."

"Okay," Vail said, "I get why he's an important figure in English literature. But—"

"Then there's the financial angle," Turner said.

"Okay, now we're talking." *As in, now we're talking* motive. "But what kind of financial angle can there still be for old plays? Other than selling books and Cliffs Notes to college students."

Wilkinson chuckled. "Surely, you can't be serious."

"Ironically, this is one of those rare occasions when I am."

"John—John Hudson—did an estimate and found that Shakespeare is a multibillion dollar enterprise worldwide. Not to mention that an entire city in England is built around the Bard: Stratford-Upon-Avon."

Vail grabbed a box of chocolate covered espresso beans from the table and peeled open the tab. "Stratford—his birthplace, right?"

"Right. Over three million tourists a year. The house where Shakespeare was born and raised is the main attraction, but everything else, from hotels to restaurants to shopping malls and theaters, all revolve around William Shakespeare and his universally recognizable portrait that's become a marketing logo."

"And don't forget the World Shakespeare Festival," Turner said.

"I saw the signs," Vail said. "What's the deal with that?"

"It's why you probably had a tough time getting a hotel. Think of it as a cultural Olympics. Millions of people from all over the world are in London to celebrate the Bard. Sponsorships, live performances, concessions, events, exhibitions, lectures. Tens of millions of pounds to be made by lots of businesses and vendors."

Vail popped an espresso bean in her mouth and crunched. The taste of chocolate and coffee spread across her tongue and was instantly pleasing. "You think there's something to the timing of your bombing and the festival?"

"I'd be a fool to think it's a coincidence," Turner said.

"Okay," Vail said, "so I get the fact that William Shakespeare is big business, and that he means a lot to your national pride. But what's your *Midsummer Night's Dream* manuscript got to do with this?"

"That'd be the authorship dispute," Wilkinson said.

"Dispute?" Vail asked. "Disputes are always good for murder."

Wilkinson brought his mug to his mouth and blew on the drink. "Are you aware that there's disagreement over who wrote the Shakespearean plays?"

Vail looked at him out of the corner of her eyes. "This isn't a trick question, is it? Like what color was Washington's white horse?"

Reid laughed. "That wasn't a trick question."

"Wait," Vail said. "That movie. Is that what you're talking about? I never saw it, but the trailer looked interesting. Something like Shakespeare didn't write Shakespeare, right? But really. Seems absurd, no?"

Wilkinson set down his cup and paused a moment. "Let's talk fact, not the fiction of a Hollywood producer's dream. There are a lot of theories that a different man was the author of the plays. And there are dozens of names on the list, many with proponents who can make a case. But there's really only a handful that are serious contenders. The people championing these theories are academics, Shakespearean scholars, not some whacked out bloggers who're trying to make a name for themselves."

"Okay, so this topic is taken seriously."

"Extremely seriously. From an academic point of view, the most commonly advanced theories involve Edward de Vere, the Earl of Oxford; Francis Bacon; and Christopher Marlowe. Each one of these men, as well as a few dozen more, have treatises written about why they are the true authors of Shakespeare's works."

"But nothing's ever been proven," Vail said.

"No. But keep in mind we're talking about a very long time ago, and a lot of potential evidence could've been destroyed."

"I'm no English major, but big deal. These plays are over four hundred years old. Is it just me, or does someone really care about whether some guy named William Shakespeare wrote them or if Francis Bacon wrote them and used a pseudonym?"

"Oh yes, very much so. It's an important matter that's been debated for over 250 years."

Vail spread her hands. "I don't see why. I mean, the financial machine that generates all the money's gonna be around whether Will wrote 'em, or Francis. Right?"

Wilkinson sat forward in his seat. "You have to understand that entire industries have been built around the concept that the man from Stratford named William Shakespeare wrote the Shakespearean plays. Theaters and academia worldwide are threatened by challenges to that belief, and will do anything possible not to have to face the prospect of their careers being in ruins.

"Just here in England," Wilkinson continued, "the Stratford-Upon-Avon tourism trade is based on that 'truth,' and now you have the World Shakespeare Festival bringing millions into London's economy. It'd be devastating if it came out that Shakespeare was built around a lie.

"And then you have the British Shakespeare Academy—which cleared £900 million in profit last year. The principles expressed in the plays are overseen, protected, and cultivated globally by that group—with a very firm hand. More so than even the Royal Shakespeare Company. But it's not just about the plays. It's about the times the plays were written in, about the monarchy, and just as importantly, the church. One can't be separated from the other, because they'd lose their context."

"This is more than merely someone trying to destroy, or even steal, a rare manuscript," Reid said.

Wilkinson nodded animatedly. "Yes, yes. There are also many aspects to 'William Shakespeare,' beyond his writings: his name's synonymous with Elizabethan English—a close cousin to today's English. He's synonymous with England, with our society. To think otherwise is like trying to rewrite the past...pulling the rug out from under a country's history and, well, its very identity."

"Google 'William Shakespeare,'" Turner said, "and you'll get 100 million results. And among those, you'll get scholars claiming that Shakespeare was Italian. Or Brazilian. Everyone wants a piece of him."

"Still," Vail said, "what matters is the plays, right? They were exceptional stories with themes that are still emulated today. But—and I keep coming back to this—what does it really matter who wrote them? I mean, William Shakespeare was just a name printed on the plays."

"First of all," Wilkinson said, "let's look at this as a UK issue, in the context of the past as well as the present. William Shakespeare was a Catholic Caucasian whose very identity fit—and fits—the identity of the male-centric British society."

Vail chuckled. "You've got one of those too, huh?"

"I think you need to tell her John Hudson's theory on authorship," Turner said.

Wilkinson inched his chair closer to the table and lowered his voice. "What if it's not just that Shakespeare wasn't written by William Shakespeare? What if it was a *woman* who wrote the plays?"

# 6

"A woman," Vail said. "I'd think that'd be pretty awesome."

"*You* might," Wilkinson said, "but the rest of the world might not. And what if she was a woman of color?"

"Even better."

"If that's not enough, what if that woman of color was not a Catholic but...a Jew?"

"Is that supposed to scare me?"

Wilkinson frowned. "You don't understand. English society in the Elizabethan era was extremely anti-Semitic: Jews were expelled in 1290 and weren't allowed to return for almost four *centuries*. So there were hardly any Jews there, and hardly any people of color, in England in the sixteenth century. Jews were presented on the Elizabethan stage in a very negative light, in hideous caricature with hooked noses and bright red wigs.

"Point being, England was no place for a black, Jewish woman to write plays that would be performed in public—certainly not ones with concealed religious allegories that were highly critical of the church."

"So," Vail said, "William Shakespeare, white bread legend of national and international stature, wasn't a white church-going Catholic but a black Jewish *woman*." *Okay, I can see that not sitting well with some.* "But that was over four hundred years ago, and my job is to assess the threat as it stands now."

"Fine. Fast-forward to the present. There's considerable unrest among a rising minority base in this country. British society is under pressure from an Arab Islamic population that's growing rapidly. And there's a substantial population of disadvantaged minorities that are aligned against the white establishment, an establishment that supports the Shakespeare fiction through high-browed elitist organizations like the government-backed British Shakespeare Academy.

"Given everything the government's dealing with, keeping the peace, if proof emerged that Shakespeare was actually a minority woman it'd almost be too much for the country to bear." Wilkinson shook his head. "I'm not doing this justice. John Hudson, the man who's been championing this theory, would do a better job of—"

"You're doing fine. Keep going."

Wilkinson leaned back. "If you're to truly understand the motive behind this bombing, you need to see the whole picture."

"What's John Hudson's role?"

"John's a Shakespearean scholar and a graduate of the Shakespeare Institute at the University of Birmingham. A brilliant bloke, really. But he's not exactly beloved in traditional Shakespearean circles. Actually, anyone who raises the theory that Shakespeare didn't write Shakespeare is looked upon as so much rubbish. But John's presented an extremely compelling case. And with the discovery of this *Dream* manuscript, Idris's got something none of the other anti-Stratfordians have ever produced: proof of authorship."

"Anti-Stratfordians?"

"Scholars who challenge the notion that William Shakespeare wrote the Shakespearean plays."

"This manuscript," Vail said. "I'm beginning to see why I now find myself sitting in a café in London discussing Shakespeare." *Gotta admit, that's something I never thought would happen.* "Why's it so important? How does it provide 'proof of authorship'?"

"Are you familiar with *A Midsummer Night's Dream?*"

Vail frowned. "I was no English major, but I'm familiar with the plays—and I've seen a number of them performed."

"This manuscript is an early draft of *Dream*, so parts of the story are a bit different, but even more significant, it's handwritten. There aren't any known examples of Shakespeare's handwriting, but we do have samples of writing from Amelia Bassano Lanier—she's the black Jewish woman I mentioned a few minutes ago. Anyway, in the margins of the *Dream* manuscript are notes, some of which outline edits that would ultimately end up in the final *Dream* play that was performed at The Globe and later published in the First Folio."

Vail took a sip of coffee. "Very compelling. Great. So, case closed?"

"John's 'case' was solid *before* this manuscript surfaced. His proof is based on a scholarly analysis of Amelia's work, her background and upbringing, and the content and writing style of the plays themselves. He doesn't need the manuscript. That said, it *is* the final piece to the puzzle, so to speak, and should help throw water on the critics' fire. But if you look at the dispute, it largely starts with the fact that William Shakespeare was not a well-educated lad. And he didn't have the training to write such eloquent prose."

"So there really was a William Shakespeare."

Wilkinson chuckled. "Well...truth be told, there was a Gulielmus Shakspere born in 1564. 'William Shakespeare' doesn't appear until 1594, as an actor in the Lord Chamberlain's Men theater company that subsequently performed a number of the Shakespearean plays. But the name actually appears before that, because Amelia used it as a pseudonym to write under."

"Why use a pseudonym?" Reid asked. "What'd she have to hide?"

"Plenty. But let's start with two early works she wrote around 1592—*Venus* and *Adonis* and *The Rape of Lucrece*—long pornographic poems. The pseudonym she wrote these under was Will Shakespeare—spelled exactly like we spell 'Shakespeare.' Except that in Elizabethan slang, 'Will Shakespeare' means 'prick masturbator.' Pornographic poems written by a prick masturbator." He smiled. "It was done tongue-in-cheek."

"Sounds like she had a keen sense of humor," Vail said. "A woman after my own heart."

"Yes, well," Wilkinson continued, "two years later, after Amelia started writing the plays, she came across an actor named Gulielmus Shakspere and persuaded him to change his name to her pseudonym, William Shakespeare."

"Why would she do that? And why would Gulielmus agree to name himself a 'prick masturbator'?"

"Second question first. He agreed to change his name because she paid him to act as a front man for her writings. Actors of that time weren't like George Clooney or Angelina Jolie. They were like beggars or harlots. Paid very, very little. So when Amelia offered to pay him for merely changing his name and using it on her plays, his decision wasn't difficult. As to why she used a pseudonym, that's a much more compelling question. Let's go back to the plays for the answer. Actually, let me start with a contemporary analogy. Remember *Star Trek*?"

"Whoa," Vail said, "How'd we go from sixteenth-century Shakespeare to twentieth-century *Star Trek*?"

"When *Star Trek*'s creator, Gene Roddenberry, pitched a sociopolitical commentary drama to NBC in the early 1960s, they flatly rejected him because they didn't have the stomach to deal with controversial issues like the Vietnam War and the concept of the US interfering in another country's culture. So Roddenberry set the show in Twenty-third Century outer space, changed the Americans and Vietnamese to alien races, and bang—suddenly the network loved the concept. The disguise worked: the network never got wise to his veiled attempt to tackle these difficult sociopolitical issues that the country was dealing with at the time."

Vail tossed a couple of chocolate espresso beans into her mouth. "And how does this relate to Shakespeare?"

"John believes that Amelia Bassano Lanier did the same thing. Amelia was the first woman in England to publish a book of original poetry, so she had some standing as a writer. But the Shakespeare plays are filled with religious allegories, *powerful* religious allegories that were anti-Christian and anti-church. In fact, many of the plays' allegories dealt with the church as an apparatus for control. If the deeply couched allegories were discovered, Amelia and her family would've been executed. But packaged in cleverly disguised stories—and written under a pseudonym—they were safe from retribution."

Vail chewed on this a moment, but Reid spoke first. "What was Gulielmus, a dim-witted bloke? He agreed to take on a name that meant 'prick masturbator,' and if the Queen saw through the religious allegories in 'his' plays, he'd have been killed."

"Exactly," Wilkinson said. "Gulielmus wasn't well-educated, remember? He didn't recognize the allegories, and he didn't realize the risk he was taking on. He took the money, so maybe he was the smart one after all. The world thinks he was a literary genius who created legendary works of art."

"Good point," Vail said.

"What about Amelia's education?" Reid asked. "Is there reason to believe she had any more knowledge to write these plays than Gulielmus did?"

"Amelia's family was made up of Venetian-Moroccan Jews who came to London from Venice. They were all musicians and played Elizabethan stage music for plays that were performed at the English Court.

"Now, it's reasonable for a Jew from Venice to know both Italian and Hebrew, and a woman from a professional musician's family to have a knowledge of music. But Gulielmus didn't know Italian or Hebrew, and yet these languages are utilized in a lot of the plays as clever, complex puns.

"We know that Gulielmus didn't have a musical background of any kind, yet there are, again, sophisticated musical references throughout the plays. They also contain mentions of hundreds of literary works. Gulielmus would not have been exposed to many, if not any, of these, coming from his modest Stratford upbringing in Warwickshire. He just didn't have the social context to write the works that are attributed to him. But Amelia did."

"At Scotland Yard," Reid said, "I do believe we call that circumstantial evidence."

"Then here's something a little more direct for you. Amelia left some clues for us. Years after writing *Othello*, she added 163 lines in 1623, when the plays were officially published in what's known as the First Folio. These lines contain specific references to herself. First, the section that she added expands the part of Amelia, one of the characters in Othello. Second, it includes the 'Willough Song,' which repeats the name Willough, Willough, Willough—dying like a swan to music."

"What's the significance of 'Willough'?" Vail asked.

"Amelia's father died when she was seven, and her mother was very ill. Amelia was adopted by Susan Bertie, the dowager Countess of Kent, and lived with her, her brother the Lord Willoughby, and her mother Katherine

Willoughby the Duchess of Suffolk. When Amelia was thirteen or so, she became the teenage mistress of Henry Carey, Lord Hunsdon, the Lord Chamberlain. He was the most important man in London's theatrical life, and would become the patron of the Lord Chamberlain's Men. Remember, I told you a few minutes ago that it was in 1594 that Gulielmus changed his name to William Shakespeare and appeared as an actor in the Lord Chamberlain's Men theater company."

"The theater company run by Amelia's lover," Reid said.

"Exactly." Wilkinson warmed his hands around the large white mug. "One other thing to keep in mind: Amelia gave birth to Lord Hunsdon's illegitimate son, Henry."

Vail took a sip of her coffee. "Go on."

"During his research, John identified a pattern of what he terms 'the swan signatures' that's prevalent across all the Shakespeare plays in which the image of a swan dying to music appears. It's actually a Renaissance image for a great poet. There are two other plays in which it's mentioned, *King John*—where it's referring to *Henry*, who is John's son, and in *The Merchant of Venice*, wherein the person the song's referring to is Bassanio, who's 'going to die like a swan in Portia's tears.'

"Now—one other thing you should know: Amelia's maternal cousin was Robert Johnson, who wrote music for the playwrights as well as for five Shakespearean romances—including *The Tempest*, *Cymbeline*, and *The Winter's Tale*.

"So let's put this all together and look at what we have here in *Othello*: there's a character named Amelia who sings the Willough song—wherein a swan dies to music. Willough is the name of the family that brought her up after her father died.

"Then in Shakespeare's play *King John*, the same imagery of a swan dying to music is used, this time with the song referring to Henry, which is the name of both her son and her lover. In the play, Henry is John's son. *Johnson.* Johnson is her mother's maiden name and her cousin's name. Her cousin wrote music for a number of the Shakespearean plays. So do you see what she's done?"

Vail put down her mug. "Amelia buried her family names in Othello so that no one except her family would get the inside joke."

"Right. The great poet, Amelia Willoughby Johnson Bassano. You can run a probability analysis on it. It's no coincidence."

"And," Turner said, "Gulielmus—or William at this point—wasn't alive in 1623 to write those 163 lines that were added to Othello. Amelia was. And—before you ask—according to my independent expert, although it's nearly impossible to *date* a writing sample that's so small, these lines were written in the same stylistic 'hand' as the rest of the play, and consistent with the style of many of the other Shakespearean plays."

"Another thing to keep in mind," Wilkinson said, "is that the Shakespearean plays are the most musical plays in the world. They contain nearly two thousand music references. *Taming of the Shrew* contains 110 music references alone—that's about one every minute. *Twelfth Night* has ninety-one.

"Remember, Amelia was brought up in a musical family. It's only natural she would have a proclivity for writing stories that so elaborately incorporated music into their storylines. By comparison, the other playwrights of her time—Marlowe, or Lodge, or Green—used on average only about eighteen music references in their plays. Gulielmus had no known musical knowledge, let alone any as complex as the writer of the Shakespearean plays clearly demonstrates.

"And you can't overlook the influence that the accomplished Lord Hunsdon had on a bright, impressionable young woman. Hunsdon was Henry VIII's illegitimate son, so he was both a half brother and cousin to Queen Elizabeth. John believes that Hunsdon's knowledge as a judge, lawyer, general, falconer, and diplomatic envoy to Scotland and France exposed Amelia to the types of experiences and skills needed to write such complex literature. And we see all of these influences in her works."

"From what I remember of my history classes," Reid said, "that was highly unusual in those times. For an English woman to be so accomplished."

"Absolutely. There were very *few* women in England who were educated. We're talking maybe several dozen in the entire *country*. But Amelia was the polar opposite, as was Anne Locke, who lived next door to the Bassanos when Amelia was growing up. Locke became one of the most highly educated women in England. She invented the sonnet sequence—a group of sonnets thematically linked to create a longer work. And again, we can see the effect which that kind of influence would have on Amelia in shaping her writing style. Remember I told you that Amelia was the first woman in England to have a book of original poetry published?

"It was titled *Salve Deus*—and it contains a comical crucifixion parody, something no good Christian would write. But the same type of crucifixion parody also appears in *A Midsummer Night's Dream*. Again, this is not something a Christian would write—yet more evidence why Amelia, a Jew, wrote that play—and all the other Shakespearean plays."

"And that," Vail said, turning to Turner, "brings us full circle, back to the *Midsummer Night's Dream* manuscript you've found."

Reid, having drained his coffee mug, set it down on the table. "Indeed it does."

Vail leaned back in her chair. "Sounds like John Hudson has done some groundbreaking work here."

"You haven't heard all of it, I'm afraid," Wilkinson said. "John's writing a couple of books on it, assuming he isn't prevented from getting them published."

"So saying you had proof that William Shakespeare did not write the plays is like saying you've got proof that Jesus was a mere mortal. In my business, that translates into lots of reasons for someone to want that manuscript destroyed."

"Likewise," Turner said, "there are lots of people in this multibillion dollar industry who'd lose a great deal of money if 'Shakespeare' was a fraud perpetrated by organizations supported by the government for financial gain."

"Not to mention the loss of national prestige," Reid said.

Vail tossed a handful of espresso beans into her mouth. As she crunched them, she said, "You'd run yourselves ragged trying to assess all the angles of who'd want to destroy this manuscript. The list of suspects would be too numerous. You have to find a way to narrow it down."

"What's your role in all this?" Wilkinson asked.

"I'm helping Scotland Yard draw up a threat assessment. More than that, I don't know. I haven't even been fully briefed yet." She looked to Reid, who shrugged.

"Don't ask me. I was just handed this assignment."

*I'm an "assignment" again? "Pretty redhead," remember?*

Reid's cell phone rang. He glanced at the display, then answered it. "Yes, guv'nor." He listened a moment, then said, "Yes sir. Got it. I will."

He dropped the phone from his face and turned to Vail. "Looks like we should suspend show-and-tell for a bit. We've got one answer to your question. A group just claimed responsibility for the bombing."

# 7

R eid pulled the car to a stop in the parking lot of the Kennington Road Police Station.

"Where are we?" Vail asked, craning her head around.

"South London. That big, winding river you probably saw from the plane? That's the Thames. Pretty spectacular, anyway. If you've got time, you should take one of the sightseeing boats all the way to Canary Wharf. The architecture is stunning. You can't get into any of the buildings, but you can gawk from the outside."

"Why can't I go inside?"

"Financial district. Security's tighter than a virgin's—oh, sorry. Tighter than a rusted nut."

"Where's your mind, Reid? Virgins and rusted nuts?"

"Did I say rusted? I meant roasted. The street vendors sell tasty roasted nuts right across from Big Ben."

Vail tilted her head. "Virgins, rusted nuts, and *Big Ben*. I think I misjudged you."

"Anyway," Reid said, looking a bit flustered, "London's not divided into a north-south-east-west grid like some cities. It's arranged in boroughs."

Vail pushed open her car door. "Doesn't look like a great area."

Reid joined her around front. "It's no Bond Street or Chelsea, that's for sure. It's an immigrant area, fairly poor. Not a place for a woman to be alone at night."

They walked up the steps to the entrance, where salt-and-pepper granite tile and white marble facing seemed out of place in the neighborhood. The glass doors slid apart and they walked up to the front desk.

"We're here for DCI Grouze," Reid said to the desk clerk, who moved to her left and lifted a phone.

"So this station has jurisdiction over the bombing?" Vail asked.

"Not exactly. Policing is very different here in the UK from what you're used to back in America."

"Yeah, been meaning to ask you—How do you cops do it? Not carry a gun? Mine's like a third hand."

"Simple. We don't need 'em. We don't have a gun problem like you do in the US."

"So let me get this straight. A perp's just robbed a bank and you're in foot pursuit. What do you do, yell? Stop—or I'll yell 'stop' again?"

The clerk behind the desk gave Vail a full-mouthed frown.

"We have ways of dealing with those types of situations. We surround the perp and use manpower over gunpowder."

Vail grinned. "Cute. But what if he draws down on you?"

"There aren't many handguns in the UK. Knife-related violence is a much greater threat. But if we do have reason to believe the perpetrators are armed, we call in SCO19—better known as CO19—our elite gun squad. It's similar to the group you've got—you know, the thing you do with flies." He wiggled his fingers.

"SWAT."

Reid winked at her. "Yeah, that's it."

"Seriously—your offenders don't carry guns?"

"Well," Reid said with a tilt of his head, "I didn't exactly say that. There was a case we had a couple years back. Some gang banger had a gun stored away in a vault. He'd have his crew bring it to him, he'd do his job, and then they'd ferry the gun back to their home base and put it back in the vault."

Vail stood there staring at Reid. "You're bullshitting me, aren't you?"

"I'm not." Reid checked his watch. "Just because we speak English doesn't mean our societies are the same, or even similar."

*Yeah, I got that.*

The clerk handed Vail a visitor's badge and they proceeded up the concrete stairs to the fourth floor. Reid pulled open the metal door and motioned Vail through. A sign indicated she was entering the area that housed the Lambeth Murder Investigation Team.

The long rectangular room accommodated a dozen or so detectives sitting at stout wood desks, a computer at each station. Along the left side, an expansive white board showed assignments hand-lettered in colored marker against a light mint-colored wall. A monstrous, industrial-sized HP LaserJet stood beside well-worn metal cabinets and filing drawers perched atop flooring made of blue commercial carpet squares.

"There he is."

A voice from behind; Vail and Reid turned. Ingram Losner was standing there, hands on his hips.

"You're back," Reid said.

"From Madrid? Yeah, the conference got cut short. The FBI profiler they brought in ended up getting arrested. Boom. Conference over."

"I heard about that," Vail said. "Can't take those profilers anywhere. Never know what trouble they're going to get into. Degenerates, every one of 'em."

Reid looked at Vail, then at Losner, then back at Vail. "Wait, you were the one teaching the conference? And you got arrested?"

Vail hiked her brow. "Guilty as charged. Of course, that's not what I told the judge."

"Judge—"

"Kidding. But it all turned out okay. Calls were made, strings were pulled, and, well, here I am, at your service."

"Let's hope you don't get nicked in the UK."

"I promise to leave your country in better shape than I did Spain. I'm looking forward to getting back home, so I'll be outta here faster than you can read one of Churchill's addresses. Besides, I promised the legal attaché I'd be on my best behavior."

Reid made a twisted face. "I think I've gotten to know you well enough by now to ask if your best behavior will do the trick."

Vail fought back a grin. "You keep impressing me, Reid.

A woman approached from behind them. "The guv'nor is ready to see you now."

"This way," Reid said. He led them down a long corridor and turned right into a small room that was deeper than it was wide.

The lanky man seated behind the sizable desk closed the file he was reading and set it beside his nameplate, which read, "Lance Grouze, Detective Chief Inspector."

Vail leaned forward and extended a hand.

"Oh, right." Grouze looked at it a long second, then took it and shook— but did not make eye contact. "Have a seat."

Vail and Reid took the chairs in front of the desk and Losner sat off to the side, behind them.

"So we got a phone call," Grouze said as he removed his reading glasses. He tossed them onto the file in front of him and looked at Vail for the first time.

He seemed to frown. *Gotta be my imagination. I haven't even opened my mouth yet.*

"The call was different from the first one. A computerized male voice. He said more attacks are coming."

"Wait," Vail said. "There was a call? Claiming responsibility?"

"Ten minutes after the bombing," Grouze said.

*That would've been nice to know.* Vail turned to Reid and gave him a less than pleasant look.

"The caller," Grouze said, "railed against 'the powers'—he looked at a pad on his desk—"'the powers that seek to destroy the English legend of William Shakespeare, to muddy the British people's reputation, to demoralize the country's pride.'"

"Can I listen to the recording?"

"There wasn't any," Reid said. "It didn't come in on a recorded line. The inspector who answered the phone jotted down notes. It's not word for word."

*Great.* "And the new call?"

"Not recorded either," Grouze said. "They identified themselves as the Army of English Anarchists."

After a moment of quiet, Vail shrugged. "If that's supposed to mean something, the reference is lost on me."

"I would think your superiors would do a better job of preparing you."

Vail squinted. "Then you would think wrong. I pretty much just got here. You want my assistance, it might be helpful to provide some background."

"They're an offshoot of the British Heritage Party—the BHP. For now, let's just say that the BHP is a party in our government opposed to combining England with the European Union to make a US-type country. Their position has gotten more traction after the Greek financial crisis. But worse than that, the BHP has spawned a number of minority fringe movements that want to prevent Turkey from joining the EU, groups that've been covertly spearheaded by the BHP. They're basically neo-Nazis who fear immigrants. They complain that Slavs and Croats have been taking their jobs and living off the state."

"Living off the state, how?"

"Britain offers free health care and other very generous entitlement programs."

"And what's the problem with Turkey?"

"Turkey," Losner said, "has the death penalty, which no EU country has. And Turkey would be the first Islamic country in the EU, which has stirred a range of feelings. And paranoia, as you might imagine."

"But the BHP is legitimately part of the Parliament?" Vail asked.

"They are," Reid said. "Because a lot of what they stand for strikes a chord with the common man."

Grouze leaned back in his chair and swung it half around, facing the window. "There's also the Euro Zone and Schengen Agreement. The Euro Zone allows member countries to have a single currency—the euro—and Schengen allows freedom of movement from one country to another. No passports needed among the twenty-six member countries. No border control, no customs. The UK's chosen not to be part of Schengen—or the Euro Zone. There's pressure from both political and industrial economic groups for the UK to join the Euro Zone, to have one currency and no barriers to business."

"Sounds like they want what the US has."

"Quite. They want to move toward a US model, a 'United States of Europe.' But some Brits don't want to give up their sovereignty. They feel they'd be getting the short end of the stick because England is, well, England. The British culture is rich, its economy healthier and more prosperous than most of its EU cousins."

"They feel they're superior to the rest of the EU."

"I didn't say that."

Vail smirked. "You kind of did. Not in so many words, but—"

Grouze swung his chair around. "We've only been invaded once in a thousand years, Agent Vail. And it failed. And yes, we're afraid of diluting our heritage, of becoming one big melting pot of nothingness. We'd lose centuries of culture with the swipe of a pen."

"It's not my place to comment on that." *Except that you switched to "we" from "they." Interesting.* "But if you don't mind me saying, you sound a bit like that first caller, who seemed to be talking about the discovery of the Shakespearean manuscript of *A Midsummer Night's Dream*. And since that manuscript is a flashpoint for the media—and apparently all of British society—it would appear that there's a relationship there."

"Maybe," Grouze said. "But to me the question seems to be, Is the second caller—The Army of English Anarchists—the same as the first? My sense says no, but unfortunately, we've got no way of knowing."

"Tell me about these Anarchists," Vail said. "You said they were an offshoot of the British National Party?"

"No, no. The British National Party's a different organization. They're not part of Parliament. This is the British *Heritage* Party. The BHP."

"So these Anarchists are a splinter group of the BHP?"

"Exactly. To try to achieve their objectives from within the legitimate political system, the BHP has attempted to go more mainstream by removing some of the more odious parts of their agenda. That's given power to the extreme factions within the group, who think the party's gone 'soft,' selling out to the establishment. They've formed a number of spin-offs, extremists in the strictest sense. We've had problems with these groups before. Good news is that, despite their name, we've never seen violence from the Anarchists. They surface from time to time, but the bad news is that we don't know who they are—beyond a name."

"They may be trying to bring more attention to themselves with a high profile bombing," Reid said.

"Possibly." Vail thought a moment and then asked, "What're their demands?"

Grouze shrugged. "They haven't made any. They've just stated that there'll be more attacks and that they'll be in touch with their demands when we've felt enough pain."

*Lovely.* "That tells me that they feel like they're in total control, that they don't feel we're capable of figuring out who they are, or that we can catch them."

Grouze laughed. "You got that from two sentences? Give me a break."

*Here we go again. C'mon, Karen. Win him over with your charm. And when I find that charm, I bet it'd be very useful.* She held out her hands and splayed her fingers. "Hey, you brought me here for my skills in developing a threat assessment. You don't want my help, just call my boss and I'll be on the next flight out."

Grouze's jaw muscles flexed.

"Before we get too far down this road," Reid said, "how 'bout we take a break and let the air clear?"

"Fine," Grouze said, rising from his chair. "That's why I keep you around, Reid. Go grab some coffee. And be careful Vail doesn't profile you down the wrong road. We all know how that story turns out."

Reid and Losner, likely sensing that they needed to head off a conflict, rose from their chairs and ushered Vail out of the room.

Outside, Vail shook her arms free of their gentle grasp. "What the hell was that in there? What's his problem?"

"Oh," Reid said, "you picked up on that."

Vail gave him a look.

"Yes, of course you did."

"I'm gonna go grab us some coffees," Losner said.

As he walked off—rather quickly—Vail turned to Reid. "So what the hell?"

Reid lowered his voice and said, conspiratorially, "He can be a bit of an arsehole at times."

"Then we've got something in common." Vail turned and started back down the corridor where they had come from a moment ago.

"Where are you going?"

"To stir up a hornet's nest."

Reid started after her. "You're not going back in there."

"Everything tells me I shouldn't. But yeah, I am."

"Karen, don't do this—"

She pushed through the door to see a surprised—and annoyed—Lance Grouze. "So what's your problem?" she asked.

"You realize you just barged into my office?"

"Answer my question." *Take a breath, Karen. And take it down a notch.* "Please."

Grouze buried his gaze among the papers on his desk and then lifted a folder. "I don't have a problem. If you'll excuse me, I've got work to do. Real policework."

"I read people for a living, Grouze. You avoided looking at me when I walked into your office, and then you treated me like I'm carrying the Black Plague."

Grouze picked up a pen and jotted a note on the outside of the folder. "I don't know what you're talking about. And I really do have work to do. Please close the door on your way out."

"I usually know when I've pissed someone off." *And I've tried hard not to, because, well, I promised both my bosses I wouldn't cause problems.* "Did I do something wrong?"

Grouze tossed the pen onto the desk. "Fine. You want to know what's bothering me, I'll tell you. We don't need you here. We're perfectly capable of handling a bombing and threat assessment without your help."

"'Your' meaning me? Or a woman? Or an American?"

Grouze removed his glasses and threw them onto the file, beside his pen. "Well, you are perceptive, I'll give you that."

"And you're unbelievably direct. For a Brit."

"It's not a virtue. It tends to get me into trouble."

Vail couldn't help but smile. "Yeah? Me, too."

Grouze's lips reluctantly thinned into a grin.

"If it's worth anything, I didn't want to come here. But I wasn't given a choice."

"Neither was I."

"So maybe we should agree to work together. Doesn't mean we have to like each other."

Grouze considered that a moment, then lifted his glasses and slid them back on his nose. "I never said I didn't like you, Agent Vail." His eyes flicked up toward hers and remained there a long second before he turned back to his paperwork.

Vail took the hint and, having reached some kind of détente, figured it was best to leave with a small win. When she walked out into the corridor, Reid was standing there.

"I'm afraid to ask how that went."

Vail chewed her bottom lip. "Actually, I think we came to an understanding."

"Really." Reid hiked his brow and turned to the door, as if having a hard time fathoming the concept of Vail and Grouze reaching any kind of an accord, let alone an understanding.

She started down the hall, Reid following.

"So all's good?"

Vail chuckled. "I didn't exactly say that. I'm not sure if he didn't like having to ask a woman, or an American, or an American woman, for that matter, for assistance."

"Now that does sound like my boss. But I think I know what the problem is."

"Oh?"

"Here you go," Losner said, holding a cardboard carrier with three cups of coffee. His gaze flowed across their faces and he tilted his head. "You're both too calm. What happened?"

"Your boss and I came to an understanding."

Losner snickered. "Good one."

Grouze's voice boomed down the corridor. "Reid—where the bloody hell are you?"

Reid took a step forward and peered down the hall. Grouze's head was barely visible around the edge of the doorframe. "Here, sir."

"We just got another call from our English Anarchists. They've given us twelve hours. Then there'll be another bombing. And this time someone might get hurt. Their words, not mine."

Vail came up beside Reid. "I can help. That's what I'm here for, right?"

Grouze ignored Vail and spoke to Reid. "Get everyone together in five in the murder room. And notify SO15 and MI5 that we've got a viable threat."

# 8

Vail followed Reid as he moved about the floor, informing the inspectors of the meeting.

"What's SO15?"

Reid consulted his watch, then glanced around the room. "Counter Terrorism Command, part of the UK's Police Special Operations unit. Wouldn't be surprised if they took the lead in this investigation."

"What does that mean for us?"

"Not much. We still do what we do. But we'd be reporting to them. Them and MI5, who'll be supporting us, taking on a domestic intelligence role."

"Don't take this the wrong way, but it sounds like you're locked and loaded. You still need me?"

"A couple of minutes," Reid said to a colleague, then gave a thumbs-up to Grouze, who was talking to an inspector down the hall. "Honestly, Karen, only a fool would send you away right now. We Brits may've screwed things up a few hundred years ago with you Americans, but we're not daft. That said," Reid went on with a chuckle, "I hope you brought your A game. Looks like we're going to need it."

*I didn't bring a whole lot with me to England, but my A game is one thing I always pack.*

Vail's phone vibrated. She stole a look: Jesus Montero, her Legat. She hit "ignore." "You said you know what Grouze's problem is with me."

"I thought you squared things away."

"A truce. I didn't want to push it."

"Ah, right. Well, it's not you. It's profiling he has the problem with. He doesn't believe it's scientific. He can't justify making an arrest on the say so of someone who tells you the offender will be five foot six, lives with his mum, watches football on the telly Saturday afternoons, and likes milk chocolate. He can't get that evidence in front of a court. That's just not enough to make the case."

"That's not a fair appraisal—"

"This is the guv'nor's position, not necessarily mine. Problem is, he's got a history with an offender profile that blew up in his face. He had a profile done up by a criminal psychologist and it led to the arrest and conviction of Colin Stagg for the Rachel Nickell murder back in '93. Problem is, the profiler took over the investigation and led us down the wrong road. Stagg was innocent, he sued, got lots of money. It was a big embarrassment on a high profile case."

"I'm beginning to get the picture."

"Years after, the guv'nor did a dissertation on offender profiling and he concluded that a lot of it was based on gut instinct and guesswork. At the best, it provided circumstantial information. Not enough in our courts, which tend to be very adversarial. You really need a strong case."

"Why didn't he just tell me all this?"

Reid tilted his head, indicating she should look behind her. She did and saw Grouze approaching. Not only that, but every seat in the long rectangular room was filled with inspectors. They had pushed their files aside and sat at their desks facing Grouze, Losner, Reid, and Vail, who stood with their backs to the windowed office of the detective inspector, who ran the Murder Investigation Team.

Grouze addressed the squad, pressing the need for a swift resolution because of the threat of further attacks, and going over the details of the bombing. He highlighted the three phone calls laying claim to it, and their potential lead involving the Army of English Anarchists. Everyone was familiar with BHP politics, so there were few questions. Vail stood in the background, her bottom against one of the wood desks, observing.

That is, until Grouze turned to her. "I'd like to introduce Karen Vail, a profiler with the FBI. Now," he said, holding up a hand, "I know I've not been a positive sort on profilers over the years, and been known to throw a wobbly over profiling in general—and I don't want to hear any bollocks from any of you—but she's here, and the Anarchists have got us by the short and curlies, so we should listen to what Agent Vail has to say. We don't have to follow any of it, but we should listen." He turned to Vail.

*Now there's an intro for the ages.* She pushed away from the desk. "Well, I don't ever want to be accused of making your boss throw a wobbly." *Whatever that means. A bad Frisbee toss?* She scanned the faces in her audience. No reaction—so far, so good. "So let me just give you a very brief background on bombers. My goal is to help you narrow down the suspect pool, so you can identify the *type* of person we're looking for. That's a good place to start, since we don't know who these English Anarchists are. And we've got no way of verifying if these guys are really behind it just because they say they are, or even if they're the same group or individual who made the first claim.

"The FBI's Behavioral Analysis Unit has studied bombers for years. We've charted the commonalities in their crimes, we've looked at their demographic and behavioral characteristics and the things that motivate them, and we've studied the techniques these people use to deploy their devices and the techniques they use to keep themselves off the grid. Based on all this, we've developed investigative approaches that could help police agencies identify the type of person who's most likely to commit this kind of crime.

"Now, time's ticking. So before your boss gets his short and curlies balled in a fist, let's talk about how this helps you catch these people. First, let's look at the different kinds of bombers there are, which'll lead us to motive. And if we can figure out their motive, we'll know what their purpose really is. Sometimes what they say they want when they call in a threat isn't really what they're after. And we have to know that, or we'll be chasing wild geese."

"Wild geese?" one of the inspectors asked.

"I'll get to that later. Moving on...A researcher named MacDonald categorized the different types of offenders: the compulsive bomber, the psychotic bomber, the sociopathic bomber, the Mafia bomber, and the military bomber."

"Isn't that a little too neat?" Reid asked.

"These are just general categories," Vail said. "And yeah, you're right. The assholes don't read the research, so our attempts to fit them into cubbyholes screams 'error.' So we should look at these as *guidelines*. An offender is often a blend of one or more of these types. The point is to understand the concepts of why these people do what they do, to help us look for the right person and to cut through the crap, so we can zero in on what's really going on.

"First. The compulsive type has been around explosives all his life and may even work in an industry that gives him the opportunity to blow shit up. So, he'd be a soldier, a stunt man, a demolition expert in a mining company or a construction company. That type of thing. Their motive is power and excitement. Sometimes that excitement takes on a sexual nature.

"Next one. Psychotic. As you might think, he's driven by paranoia, schizophrenic tendencies, or even sadism. He can be just about anyone, but certainly a check of mental health databases may be helpful. Then again, that's a large number, so it'd have to be combined with some other filter we devise so we can narrow down that list.

"The sociopathic bomber doesn't feel remorse, guilt, and so on—they have no emotions in general, and that certainly applies to killing people. According to MacDonald, his goal would be profit, revenge, power, hatred of something or someone who's pissed him off. He also may bomb to conceal another crime—a diversion."

"But those categories," Losner said, "don't include political motives. And with Northern Ireland, we've certainly had our share of that."

"You're absolutely right." Vail turned away from Losner and addressed the room. "Other motives we've observed include vandalism, protest, crime concealment, experimentation, fraud, burglary, and ideological—which obviously includes all things political, terrorism, religious, and so on. And remember, there are times when we get an overlap of one or more of these." Vail sat down on the edge of the desk. "There's a lot more detail to each of these categories, but for our purposes, I'm going to try to narrow it down a bit so we're not here for the next three days while more bombs go off in the city.

"If we believe that the Anarchists are behind this attempt, then we're dealing with a 'group cause' motive, something that Robert Ressler, one of my profiling unit co-founders, studied. I think we should focus on this—but we should also keep in mind that they could be using the bombing as a front for something else. Here's an example: in the late eighties, a federal judge was killed by a mail bomb. Two days later, another bomb killed an attorney in the same town.

"A third one targeted another federal judge and a fourth the National Association for the Advancement of Colored People. It appeared that the judges, attorney, and organization were targeted because they were known for their work in civil rights. But the investigation turned up a series of connections between the accused bomber and his first two victims. The offender had a pattern of experimentation with bombs.

"In the early seventies, one of the bombs he built accidentally injured his wife. He was found guilty and did prison time. That conviction and his failed appeals gave him a deep resentment of the court system, and the federal judge in particular—the same judge he killed in his first bombing attack. The third and fourth bombs were meant to lead the FBI down the wrong path—red herrings—by making us think the crimes were racially motivated.

"So if we look at that case, we see a combination of motives and offender types: experimentation, sociopathic, revenge, concealment—with a deliberate attempt to make us think his motivation was ideological.

"Point is, the Anarchists may've had nothing to do with this bombing, and they're being opportunistic, taking credit for something they didn't do. Just to raise their profile. And if that's the case, they'd know that until we have proof of their involvement, we can't prosecute them just for saying they did it. No evidence, no conviction. I'm sure that's as true in the UK as it is in the US."

"So we've got to get some evidence," Losner said.

*That'd help, yeah.* "The type of person we're looking for is not your typical killer. He's a male, often married with children, who has a good relationship with his loved ones. He's probably not the product of a broken home, and he wasn't abused. He is intelligent and well-educated. Chances are good that religion played a role in his upbringing, with a majority being Protestant. Catholics are a close second. Perhaps most importantly, there's a very strong likelihood that he has an extensive criminal history.

"I should qualify all this by reminding you that this is a guide, looking at percentages and likelihoods. If your Anarchists fall into the 20 or 30 percent that don't follow this profile, we'll be off."

"Sterling," Grouze mumbled.

"And—" she looked over at Grouze—"just a guess here, but that's probably why your boss is a bad Frisbee player."

Reid made a face that could only be interpreted as, "Huh?" The other inspectors shared a similar, puzzled look.

Vail brushed it aside, spent another few minutes hashing out the profile, and then sensed it was time to turn the inspectors back to Grouze.

When the meeting was over, Grouze left the room in a hurry, possibly to avoid getting into it again with Vail.

"We don't have a lot of time," Losner said. "In less than a day, there'll be another bomb."

Reid pushed through a set of doors into the stairwell. "Ingram. Why don't you set up a meet for us with Leon McAllister. We'll follow up with Idris Turner."

"Who's Leon McAllister?" Vail asked as they descended the steps.

"The leader of the BHP." As they reached the second landing, Reid said, "Oh—what was that about the guv'nor being a bad Frisbee player?"

Vail shrugged. "He said he's been known to throw a wobbly."

Reid snorted. "It means to throw a tantrum, have a fit."

Vail stepped outside, into the rain. "Why can't you Brits just speak English?"

# 9

Vail and Reid arrived on New Bond Street to find a line of news vans and satellite-outfitted trucks against the curb, coiffed reporters primping behind their mikes, and cameramen setting up their shots. Vail and Reid "no commented" their way to the building's entrance and ascended the stairs to Turner's Antiquities, Contemporary Art & Rare Manuscripts—or what was left of it.

After signing in with the duty officer, they stepped into the soot-covered gallery. Vail gave a sweeping look around and saw a beefy man crouched over a hunk of metal in the far corner. His build, close-cropped hair, and thick neck gave him the look of a boxer. He uncoiled himself and his eyes searched their faces.

"Clive Reid, DCI on the ICS out of Kennington."

"Ethan Carter, MI5, for JTAC. Thames House."

"Karen Vail, FBI, for the DOJ. Quantico." She chuckled. "These acronyms make me feel right at home."

Carter twisted his lips into a frown. "ICS is the International Counter Terrorism branch. JTAC is Joint Terrorism Analysis Centre. What does DOJ stand for, Department of *Jackasses?*"

Vail nodded slowly. "Actually, sometimes, yes."

Carter didn't seem to know what to do with that, so he merely extended a hand to Vail, and they shook.

*Hey, maybe I can master this art of being a good soldier. It's not so hard.*

"I was told to expect you. We really don't need your—"

"I've heard it and I get it. But I'm here, and I don't really want to be here, so I think that makes us even. Now, how about we wrap this thing up so I can be on my way?"

A knock behind them grabbed their attention. Reid stuck a key in the lock and pulled open the charred door.

"Can I come in?" It was Idris Turner, a jeweler's monocle strapped to his forehead.

Reid moved aside. "Of course."

"A might ridiculous that I have to ask permission to step into my own gallery."

"Until we release the scene, that's the way it's gotta be, mate," Carter said.

Turner grumbled and pulled the magnifying lens from his face. "Not like there's anything left to care about."

"Which reminds me," Vail said. "What happened to the manuscript? The safe didn't look so good. A fire that hot doesn't leave much behind."

Turner hesitated a moment. "It wasn't here at the time of the explosion. I moved it a few days ago."

Vail's eyes widened. "Did anyone know that?"

His gaze shifted from Reid to Carter, and then back to Vail. "I don't tell anyone where I keep my most valuable pieces. I never open the safe in front of anyone. In fact, I never open it during regular business hours. If a buyer's interested, I arrange a meet. And even then, I will have added security, and I give myself a buffer to get the piece here safely. You can call it being paranoid, if you want. I call it being smart."

She crooked her neck and peered into the adjacent room. "What's the layout of the rest of this place?"

"Come, I'll take you around."

Vail followed Turner into the other portion of the gallery, which was meticulously designed with contemporary displays, earthy, rich colors, and tight halogen spots suspended from wires. When they were alone, Turner leaned closer to Vail and whispered, "I have a flat that's not leased under my name. That's where the manuscript is."

"And no one knew this?"

"No."

In a back workspace, off to the side, Vail spotted someone bent over a table, a large, lighted magnifying glass a few inches from his face.

"Who's that?"

Turner followed her gaze to a man with thinning hair and a middle-aged paunch. "That's Gavin Paxton. I mentioned him at the café—"

"Your curator and art restorer."

"Good memory. Yes."

Vail turned her attention back to Turner. "If no one else knew the manuscript was stored elsewhere, is there a reason they would believe it'd be in that other room? I mean, the attack was very specific to the contents in that safe, and in that portion of the gallery."

Turner cocked his head, thought a second, then said, "Mr. Carter told me that the safe was the source of the explosion, and that because of where the explosive was placed, they likely wanted to destroy what was in it. It's the only safe I have in the gallery, and I don't publicize the fact that I keep certain antiquities offsite."

"Who had access to the safe?"

"Only me and Gavin."

"And I assume that anyone who knew that you had the manuscript—which was the entire country, based on the frenzy and extensive media coverage—would conclude that you'd store it in the safe."

Turner shrugged. "Logical assumption."

"So where exactly is this secret flat?"

Turner hesitated. His gaze moved around the walls above, behind, and to the side of Vail.

"Look, Mr. Turner. I'm here to help. I know you don't know me, and you don't know the FBI. But I've got no ax to grind here. And I recognize the importance of the find. Personally, I think it'd be pretty cool if a woman wrote Shakespeare." She paused, then added, "It's my job to help catch the people behind the bombing."

Turner thought a moment longer, then said, "It's nearby, on Moulton Street. Follow me." He led her through a metal fire door into the stairwell. But as soon as he broke the seal, an alarm began blaring. Turner stuck his head back in and yelled, "Gavin, can you please take care of that?"

As they descended the steps, the noise stopped.

"You're sure no one knows you've got this other place?"

"Oh, yes, Agent Vail. I've been very careful."

"What if someone follows you—"

"I never take a direct route, and I always check to make sure I'm not followed. I took a course in surveillance, so I know how it's done."

*Oh, he took a course. Great. He's an expert.*

He started walking down the stairs, and Vail followed. He pushed through the door and dodged the reporters who swarmed around them.

"Any leads on the case?" one shouted.

"Did the manuscript burn in the fire?" asked another.

Vail turned left and cleared the way, no commenting until they were free of the throng.

After crossing Bruton Street, Turner's gaze covered the area, his head swinging both ways as he seemed to take note of everyone who was in the vicinity. He stopped and faced a man who was behind them.

Vail recognized him as one of the reporters.

"Can't I have some peace?" Turner yelled at the journalist.

"Go back to the gallery," Vail said. "If you're good, maybe I'll have something for you when we get back."

Vail turned and started walking.

"You will?"

"We'll see. I didn't say it'd be anything he didn't already know. Now— you were telling me about your 'secret place.'"

Turner glanced around again before speaking. "The entrance is underground. I had it specially built and there are no plans, no permits on file with the city. And like the gallery, I've got state of the art security cameras."

"Security cameras—so you've got footage from the night of the bombing."

"Mr. Carter has it—MI5 was analyzing it in their communications lab."

"I need to see it. And the video from your secret hideaway."

"I've already looked at it. No one except me is on that recording. I checked all the way up to two weeks before. There's nothing. Just me."

"You were able to go through two weeks in just a couple of days?"

"It's digital. I can search for any movement that set off the sensors in a matter of seconds."

Vail stopped walking in front of Louis Vuitton, just before crossing Clifford Street. The limestone storefront featured twenty foot tall windows with overlying decorative mirrored circles that also lined the interior walls. She pulled her attention back to Turner. "Do the ones from the gallery use the same technology?"

"Same system, yes."

"What if their movement didn't trigger the sensors? Could someone who knew what they were doing defeat the sensor?"

Turner shifted his weight as he thought.

"Could they?"

"I—I don't know. I've never thought of that."

"Based on what I know of these things, I'm guessing the answer's yes. But we'll have to ask Carter what MI5's doing with the recordings."

"'Enhancing' them is what he said."

"I want a look—an analog look, not a digital one." Vail glanced at the high end merchants, as far as her eyes could see down Bond Street. Many competed with Vuitton for elaborately designed, sparkly storefronts. "Where'd you get this manuscript? Seems like it'd be the find of the century."

Turner took a small, but noticeable, step backward. "Why's that important?"

"Maybe whoever sold it to you didn't realize what he had, and after you went public with it, the country went nuts, and he had seller's remorse."

"First of all, I didn't go public with it. Something like this...I'd never announce it publicly. It'd bring out all the nuts and I'd be placing myself in danger—and it'd be a media circus. Exactly what happened is why I would keep it under wraps."

"So who leaked it? Who else knew of it?"

"Just Gavin. And he's been very bothered by all the media scrutiny. He hates the spotlight. He'd be the last person to tell. Me, I never paid much attention to TV and the paparazzi. Now I've got people following me. Trying to see where I go, who I'm meeting with. I don't know if you noticed the black car that followed us when we went to the café."

"Black car." *Uh oh. Is this guy a nutcase?* "No, other than all the black taxis, I didn't happen to notice anything unusual. But tell me more about Gavin."

Turner shoved his hands in his pockets. "I'm out of town a lot, Ms. Vail, scouring the world for art and rare artifacts. Gavin's been a godsend, day after day, always here. Very dependable and trustworthy. I've never had an issue with missing money, embezzled funds, none of that. As you would imagine, that's very important to me." He chuckled. "If you're thinking Gavin had anything whatsoever to do with this, you're wasting your time."

"Fair enough. I just want to make sure I don't overlook something."

"Mr. Reid already checked Gavin out. You can ask him, he's been very thorough."

"Then let's get back to the source of the leak."

Turner shook his head. "It's been very upsetting. Two days ago, the tabloids were hounding me as if I were some sort of criminal." He spread his arms. "And now, it's like I'm the bad guy for buying this manuscript. Some kind of smear campaign."

"So where'd you get it? We have to eliminate the seller as a suspect."

"I don't think so."

Vail folded her arms across her chest. "I'll be the judge of that."

Turner looked away.

"Did you steal it?"

Turner swung his gaze back to Vail. "No! How could you suggest such a thing?"

"I read people. Your body language tells me something's not Kosher."

Turner sighed, then started walking again. "You've heard of the Curtain Theatre?"

"Haven't had the pleasure."

"What about the Globe?"

Vail checked traffic before crossing the side street. "The theater where Shakespeare's plays were performed."

"Right. The Curtain Theatre came before the Globe. It was the main theater for Shakespeare's plays from 1597-1599."

"Okay," Vail said. "Thanks for the history lesson, but I don't see—"

"It was recently discovered, totally by accident. The government excavated a good part of it. Including the theater itself, the manuscript was by far the most significant find."

"What's the saying? Something smells rotten in Denmark?"

Turner chuckled. "You're quoting Shakespeare?"

"Seemed appropriate. This doesn't add up—why would the British government sell you one of its most prized artifacts?"

"I could argue that they don't want to acknowledge it, that it's something they'd want to stay buried."

"You could argue that, but that also makes no sense. They found it. If they didn't want it known—and I'd hope the UK government would embrace its history, no matter where it led—they could've destroyed it or locked it away in a secret vault somewhere, never to be found."

Turner stopped walking and took a long look around the street. He ground his molars, then stepped closer to Vail. "I bought it off one of the archeologists working the site for a tidy sum. He said no one else knows that he found it. He was in a secluded area and had a sense it was important because of the handwriting in the margins. But he didn't realize how important it was. He set it in his lunch box and after work he showed up in my gallery." Turner looked down at the ground. "I'm only telling you in case it's relevant to the case. I'd appreciate you keeping it to yourself."

Vail tilted her head, making no effort to hide her displeasure.

"Look, Agent Vail. The bloke approached *me*—I did nothing wrong."

"If that's true, why don't you want anyone to know?"

"It's in everyone's best interest if this information remains between us."

"Do you have any rivals? Would any of your fellow rare manuscript dealers be insanely jealous of your 'find'?"

"It's not like that. That said, I can't remember the last time something of this magnitude has been made available."

"So you don't know of anyone in your circle who'd have a problem with missing out on the opportunity of having something so valuable *made available* to them?"

Turner held her gaze as he said, "No. If there was, I would've told Mr. Reid and Mr. Carter the second they stepped into my gallery."

"And you say you don't know who leaked it to the press?"

"Again. If I did, I'd tell you. Having the media on my arse is obviously the last thing I'd want. They ask questions, lots of questions. I've been able to avoid talking to them because of the police investigation, but I don't know how long I can keep that up."

"And other than the people we discussed—the ones who'd want the manuscript discredited—are there others who'd benefit from seeing it go away? I'm looking for motive here."

"Other than what we talked about over coffee, no."

"Does the Army of English Anarchists mean anything to you?

Turner's eyes rotated up and about. "I've heard of them. But no, they don't mean anything to me. Why, you think they're involved?"

"So you haven't heard anything from them. Haven't had any contact with them."

"Nothing," he said firmly—with a bit too much volume. He held up a hand and tucked his chin as he composed himself. "Look, Agent Vail. I don't want any trouble. Are you—are you going to tell anyone about where I got the manuscript?"

Vail looked at him a long moment, then said, "I only need the info for the threat assessment. I'm no expert on British law regarding archeological or historical preservation, but I have a feeling that what you did is not above board. I think you already know that. As would Inspector Reid. That said, if you did the right thing by selling it to a reputable party, Reid and I would have nothing to discuss."

"Of course," he said, nodding. "Of course."

"I'm thinking you should start by contacting the leading British museums and see if they're interested." She winked at him and gave him a hard, long look.

Turner frowned. "First of all, they're going to want to know where I got it. Not to mention who knows what they'd do with it once they had it in their possession—"

"Given the timing of the Curtain excavation and the discovery of the manuscript in your gallery, a museum curator would be able to put the pieces together. You could simply say a man approached you—which is true. Any museum worth a shit would salivate over a find like this. And my sense is that they'd want to display it and boast that they've got one of the most significant pieces of literature in world history—and let the historians fight over its relevance to British society and culture."

Turner looked away.

"Call them before close of business."

Turner's shoulders slumped. "They've already rung me up."

"Then I suggest you call them back and make the offer. A very reasonable offer." Vail's BlackBerry vibrated. She fished it out and answered. "I'm a few blocks from the gallery, down New Bond, in front of—Okay. I'll be here." She shoved the handset back in her pocket and said, "I have to go. Make the call, Mr. Turner. Or I will most definitely have something for that journalist hanging around outside the gallery."

Turner sighed in resignation, then turned and headed back the way they had come.

# 10

"Merlin Hughes is the guy we'll be meeting with," Reid said. "He's the legislative aide to Leon McAllister."

Carter was seated in front of Vail, who was sweating the tight quarters. She opened the car window, despite the drizzle coming down, and the cool, damp air helped her breathe. "What can you tell me about the British Heritage Party?"

"Essentially," Carter said, "the past twenty or so years they've tried to go 'mainstream' and become 'respectable' to reel in a broader spectrum of the British public. They prey on the disaffected, exploiting the economic situation and particularly the 'threats' to employment."

"What threats?" Vail asked.

"Immigrants taking 'our' jobs," Reid said. "Remember what Grouze said about Croats and Slavs? Immigration rates over the past fifteen years or so from the poorer parts of southern and eastern Europe have gone through the roof."

"Because of their history," Carter said, "the Security Service used to keep a close eye on them."

*Maybe it's time to start again.* The rain picked up and Vail's sleeve got wet. She rolled up the window a few inches.

"Leon McAllister," Reid said, "is an elected Member of Parliament for an area of the UK that's got a high concentration of immigrants. McAllister's a sharp bloke, Oxford educated."

Vail nodded. "We see that a lot in the US too, with our extreme right-wing groups. The leadership's bright, the followers not so much."

"They're essentially a 'Britain for the British' party. They cater to white, lower-middle-class voters who are feeling increasingly marginalized—but are turned off by radicalism. So the party dialed back on the extremism to capture their votes. Even so, BHP policies still tend to be isolationist and xenophobic, and they're still trying to extend their base using fear by exploiting deeply held and often buried prejudices."

Reid pulled up to the curb across the street from the Nags Head Pub in South London.

Vail peered over the top of the partially open window and gazed up and down the street. "Where the hell are we?"

"Our meet with Merlin Hughes," Carter said with a wink.

"All I see are bars and...more bars."

"Right observant you are, Agent Vail."

"I figured we'd meet him at Parliament or something. Don't they have offices?"

"I thought this might be more conducive to an open chat. And on neutral territory, to boot."

Vail rolled up the window. "What's this Hughes guy like?"

"A party operative," Carter said. "A disaffected Conservative, not as well educated as McAllister, but no pushover. Former worker bee for the Royal Mail, the postal service."

"Shall we?" Reid asked, propping open his door.

Vail followed, dodging the driving rain and stepping in a puddle. "Carter, Turner said that MI5 had his surveillance footage at the lab."

"They're being reviewed and enhanced."

"I'd like to see them."

Carter glanced at her, a dubious look. "We do a thorough job, Agent Vail."

"Of course. Can you arrange to get me a copy?"

With a frown, Carter said, "I'll see what I can do."

Reid reached forward and grabbed the handle of the pub's front door. "Word of advice. Probably best if you didn't meddle in those affairs."

*Meddle?* "Excuse me. Reviewing those recordings is a basic part of any investigation. Do you have a problem with me seeing them?"

"Not at all," Reid said. "Just trying to head off a problem with my boss."

"I can handle your boss."

Carter chuckled. "No doubt."

They pushed through the door and the low rumble of male conversation sat like fog over an old London street. In the dimly lit room, Carter wove his way past the tables to a rickety staircase that led downstairs. A large placard above the entry read, "No smoking. No exceptions."

The steps were shallow, and Vail grabbed the handrail to make sure she didn't take a header. The stairwell's red and white wallpaper was peeling at the corners and rolling inward along its seams, as if it had fought years of dampness and lost.

They turned left at the landing, past a sign that posted the gastropub's "recommended dishes": lamb shoulder, braised ham hock and mash, smoked rabbit, and bread and butter pudding. She clamped a protective hand over her stomach. *I think my appetite just went on vacation.*

"What's a gastropub?"

"Latest craze," Reid said. "A restaurant within a pub."

*Food in a bar? Now there's a new concept.*

The moldiness of the damp room flared Vail's nostrils. A patron occupied a table to her right, but in the back, against the wall, another man sat with his elbows leaning on the table, a Lambert & Butler cigarette burning in an ash tray by his left forearm.

*So much for the "no smoking, no exceptions" rule.*

By the man's right elbow sat a glass inscribed "Aspall Est 1728," filled with amber liquid topped by a half inch of white foam.

Reid and Carter greeted their contact, then parted and revealed Vail. The man's face brightened when she stepped forward.

His eyes traced her body from feet to face, lingering a tad longer on her chest. "They don't make cops like they used to, eh? Who's the dishy one?"

"She's visitin' from the States," Reid said as they took seats around the small circular table.

"So what can I do for the 'Yard today?" Hughes asked. "Always happy to help."

Vail had to resist rolling her eyes. *One of those.*

"Must be serious if we've got this many coppers coming to have a beer with me." He turned to Vail. "But you're not a copper, are you?"

"FBI."

Hughes tilted his head, then slowly found Reid's face. "This is about the bombing. Your partner didn't tell me—"

"Didn't think it mattered. I mean, since you're always happy to help. Doesn't matter what we talk about, eh, mate?"

Hughes tightened his jaw and nodded slightly. "Not much I can tell you."

"We have reason to believe that the Army of English Anarchists is involved," Reid said.

A waitress walked up to the table, apparently oblivious to the nature of the conversation. "Can I get you anything?"

Being good law enforcement officers, the men demurred.

Vail was not so constrained. "I'll have what Mr. Hughes is having." It wasn't so much that she liked beer, and with one exception in Napa awhile back, she did not drink on the job. But she wanted a way to connect with Hughes, and she'd given up smoking and did not want to tempt the pull of nicotine.

"From what little I know," Vail said, "there's some alignment of the Anarchists' philosophy and yours. Yours being the BHP."

Hughes leaned back and chewed on that a bit. "The British Heritage Party does not condone the bombing. And we don't control these splinter groups. Nor can we. Just because someone came from the BHP doesn't mean we endorse or even support their beliefs or that their beliefs mirror ours."

"All due respect," Carter said, "your group is intolerant of others. It's not surprising that these Anarchist nut jobs have a tie to the BHP."

Hughes studied Carter's face a moment. "Why don't we agree to say that it's no secret that their leadership were once BHP members."

*Well, it's news to me.*

"But that doesn't mean we had anything to do with the bombing."

"We're not accusing you of anything," Reid said. "We just thought you might have some insight into the Anarchists. Let's start with who they are."

Hughes chuckled. He reached out and took a pull of his beer, then licked his lips and set it back down. "I don't rightly know."

"With all due respect," Carter said, "you just stated that their leadership came from BHP."

"Rumors." Hughes locked gazes with Carter. "We've all heard them."

The waitress brought Vail's beer and set it in front of her.

Reid scooted his chair closer to the table. "You've had a number of people leave the Party the past few years. People who were frustrated with your shift in philosophy."

"Sometimes you have to change your spots to blend in better in the wild," Hughes said. "The party felt this was the best way to grow."

"But you don't agree," Vail said.

He thought a moment, studying the table in front of him. "I think you stand by your principles. Plenty a people agree with us. But to those who don't like what we stand for, I say, fuck 'em."

Vail lifted her glass and held it out to Hughes. He squinted, then raised his own and tipped it against Vail's. "I happen to agree with you, Mr. Hughes. We've got problems like that back in America. 'Course, I can't say that shit when I'm in the States, because the Bureau has to be politically correct, but our country's being overrun by Hispanics and Asians. The Hispanics take our blue collar jobs and the Asians take the high paying jobs in banking and engineering." *Jeez, am I laying it on too thick?*

Hughes studied her face a bit, then said, "People from poor countries come over here to live off the government, sucking our benefits dry. And British taxpayers pay the tab. It's not right. We're tryin' to change all that—from within. No bombs." He drove his index finger into the distressed wood table. "Legislation, that's what we're doing. Getting support for issues that appeal to the common man." He turned to Reid and Carter. "That's why we don't know anything about that bombing."

"But this bombing," Vail said. "Does it sound like a tactic the Anarchists would take?"

Hughes laughed. "If I did think that, why would I tell you people?"

"Because you're always happy to help Scotland Yard," Reid said with a straight face.

Hughes grumbled, then grabbed his mug and threw back a swig of beer. He let the glass slam down a bit harder than necessary. His eyes flicked over to the table where the other patron sat, then back to Reid. "There were a few blokes who got upset years ago when Mr. McAllister started advocating change. They thought the party'd gone soft, that we were selling out to the mainstream, gettin' in bed with the establishment—the people we've opposed for decades."

"So they split off from the party," Carter said.

Hughes took a pull from his Lambert. "We weren't radical enough for them anymore."

*Or, apparently, for you.* "Sounds like you envy their position."

Hughes sucked another mouthful from his cigarette. He locked eyes with Vail and leaned back in his chair. "Sometimes you have to make certain...compromises in life. But I'm not complainin'. I like my job. And I like working with Mr. McAllister." His gaze again wandered over to the man at the other table. "Besides, being a radical is better suited to young bucks. I'm too old for that shit."

Vail turned and glanced over her shoulder. The customer seated there wore a serious expression, his attention clearly focused on their table. Vail grasped her beer and rose from her chair.

"Where you going?" Reid asked.

She walked over to the other man's table and took a seat. "Karen Vail. Good to meet you."

Her new friend did not move, his vacant stare remaining on the formerly empty chair.

"Are you the leader of the Army of English Anarchists, or just a sympathizer?"

His eyes rose and met Vail's. "I'm in charge."

Vail nodded slowly. "Do you have a name?"

"I do."

Vail waited, but he didn't volunteer it. "You look like a Billy to me. So, Billy—"

"Nigel. Name's Nigel. And I know why you're here. No need to be troubling my friend over there. He ain't got nothin' to do with anythin'. BHP's a bunch of pussies. Talk a lot, no action."

"How about you, then?"

Nigel played with his empty glass. "I don't have any comment on that."

"I'm not a newspaper reporter. I'm a cop. In case you don't know, if you wanna keep your ass out of jail, you answer us when we ask questions. Unless you've got something to hide."

Nigel kept his chin down but raised his eyes to meet Vail's. After considering her point, he said, "Arrest me then if you think I did the deed. If not, I guess this conversation's over." He gestured at the waitress, who knew the signal and nodded back. "But you don't have anything on us. You can't. Because there ain't nothin' to have, is there?"

Vail looked over at her colleagues. They had all turned their seats and were watching; they were either impressed that she picked up on Nigel being with the Anarchists, or they were keeping their distance to allow her room to operate.

"You took responsibility," she said. "Just being opportunistic, or did you set that bomb?"

Nigel squirmed a bit. The waitress brought another beer and set it down. But as Nigel reached for it, Vail grabbed his forearm.

"It's not nice to ignore a lady," she said firmly. "I asked you a question."

His face was taut, angry. "You ain't no lady. You're a copper. And get your fuckin' hand off my arm."

Vail released it but held his gaze.

He took a swig of beer, then set the glass down. "That guy thinks he can destroy Britain's history, the essence of what makes it great, by claiming some nigger Jew bitch wrote Shakespeare. And then the media keeps repeating the lie, making it seem like the truth." Nigel frowned, as if his beer was suddenly bitter. "He needed to be shut up."

*Now we're getting somewhere.*

"How'd you do it?" Vail said nonchalantly. "The bomb."

"Didn't say we did."

"But you called in, claimed responsibility."

Nigel ground his jaw.

Vail drank from her glass, swallowed, and watched Nigel's expression. She knew very few details of the bombing were made public—standard procedure for any metropolitan law enforcement agency, especially one of

Scotland Yard's renown. "Let's back up a minute. If—hypothetically—you were to do the deed, how would you do it?"

"I'd plant the bomb using an undercover guy, who'd leave a package near where the manuscript is being stored. I'd make sure the arsehole was in his gallery, then I'd detonate with a remote."

"Semtex? Ammonium nitrate? Pipe bomb? M112 demolition block?"

Nigel studied her face but did not answer.

He may not have replied, but Vail had her answer. She finished her beer and set the glass down firmly on the table. "Thank-you, Nigel." She extended a hand and the man slowly took it, head tilted and mouth open in surprise. She grinned. "I appreciate your time."

BACK OUTSIDE THE BAR, standing in the drizzle, Vail turned to face her colleagues. "We've got our work cut out for us, gentlemen. Because if Nigel is truly the head of the Anarchists, they did not set the bomb."

# 11

"Hang on," Carter said, skirting a large puddle as they headed back to the car. "That's it? You have a five minute chat with the guy over a beer and you decide he's not our man?"

"I have to agree, Karen," Reid said. "Bit of a rush to judgment. They claimed responsibility. Their ideology fits."

"Opportunists," she said, stepping off the curb.

"Wait a minute." Reid moved in front of her. "I don't see—"

"You're skeptical because he was willing to put himself out there," Carter said, "putting a face and name to his organization. But it could be he's confident they covered their tracks and knows we won't find any proof linking him to the crime."

"No."

"No?"

"They're piggybacking on this," Vail said. "They didn't plant it."

Carter squinted. "How the fuck do you know that?"

"He said he'd use a remote detonator. Our offender used a timer."

Carter turned up the collar of his trench coat. "He told you he used a remote detonator? I thought you said they didn't plant the bomb."

"We were talking hypothetically," she said. "But I was reading his body language."

"Body language?" Carter snorted. "That's what you're basing this on? Gobshite."

"Carty," Reid said, holding out a hand, as if cautioning him against challenging Vail's opinion. "Karen's got a different way of looking at things."

"When I asked him what type of explosive he'd use," Vail said, "he didn't answer. He couldn't—because you didn't release that to the press. Am I right?"

"Yeah, but—"

"So that means that if they didn't do it, he'd have to guess. And if he guessed wrong, he'd be exposed as a bullshitter. His only reasonable move was to not answer me."

Reid stepped aside and they fell in behind Vail as she led the way to the car.

"I've still arranged for your buddy Nigel to be followed," Carter said, nodding at an undercover copper in a sedan a block away. "I was gonna have him tail Hughes, but we need some intel on the Anarchists. Just in case you're wrong."

"I'm not."

As Reid inserted his key, he said, "What'd you think of Hughes?"

Vail pulled open her door. "I assume you're asking relative to the bombing, not my personal opinion of the guy."

Reid twisted his lips.

She stood there, peering over the car at him. "I don't know. He may know who did it, but I doubt he or the BHP was involved. I think your assessment of the man's right. He'd like to be doing the more radical stuff—he's an action guy—but he's also loyal to Leon McAllister. So he's learned to temper his anger and toe the party line, no matter how tempted he is to pull the trigger, or how frustrated he got with McAllister's decision to take the group in a different, more mainstream direction." She got in and closed the door, and the others followed.

"Not sure I buy it," Carter said. "I'm not ready to give up on the Anarchists—or Nigel. Security Service is putting together a backgrounder on him right now. Until we've checked him out, he's still on my list."

Vail clicked her seatbelt closed. "I'm just here to advise. It's your show." *Robby'd be proud of me—I'm really getting the hang of this good soldier routine.* She looked out the window as Reid pulled away from the curb.

*Yeah, right.*

# 12

R eid dropped Carter at Thames House, MI5's headquarters, then continued on toward Turner's gallery.

"How long till that other bomb goes off?"

Vail consulted her watch. "I'm not sure we can still consider it a credible threat. But if it's an opportunistic strike—the most likely reason, if it does happen—we're looking at a little over two hours."

"If we're lucky, it's all just a bunch of bollocks. A hoax."

"I'm curious," Vail said. "How long have you known Carter?"

"Carter?" Reid asked. "Just met 'im."

*Bullshit.*

"Why?"

"I got the impression you two had known each other." *First clue'd be when you called him Carty.*

Without looking at her, he said, "Nope."

Vail's phone vibrated. She consulted the display and said, "Hmm. Speak of the devil. Your mate's arranged for me to see Turner's surveillance tapes."

"He's not my mate."

"Okay."

"He's not," Reid said, brow knitted firmly. "But you don't really want to waste valuable time watching security footage the service has already been through, do you?"

"I do. He said we can access the digital file from Scotland Yard. Know how to get there?"

Reid, making no effort to hide his frown, hung a left at the next intersection. "Should've stayed home and spent the day with Brant," he mumbled.

THEY WALKED UP TO THE main entrance, which sat inside a secured perimeter. To their left, a small, blue sign rotated slowly atop a white pole, its text reading either New Scotland Yard or Metropolitan Police depending on which side faced outward. The immediate vicinity was hardscape, a one-lane rain-slick road fronting the entrance.

They stepped into a glass-enclosed turnstile one at a time. After they entered the tube, the convex door swung shut behind them and the one in front opened a second later. For Vail, it was a second too long, a sense of claustrophobic anxiety building in her chest. She took a breath and stepped into the administrative area, where a contemporary semicircular wood desk dominated the space. Museum-worthy displays peppered the bright room commemorating milestone achievements in London policing.

After the officer at the front desk issued Vail a visitor's pass, Reid led her to an identical set of curved security pods.

*Great. Another glass coffin.* She steeled herself and made it through, then followed Reid to the right into a waiting elevator. They took it up to the cafeteria level, which was well-lit and cheerful, filled with modern white plastic-and-metal tables and chairs.

Rows of computers sat atop a midnight blue counter that ran along the periphery of the sectioned-off work area of the cavernous room.

They walked along the Pergo flooring and took seats in front of one of the monitors. The screen read, "Standard Workstation," with a Windows XP login. "Good to see you stay up to date on technology. XP is, what? A dozen years old?"

Ignoring her, Reid logged in and navigated to the correct folder on the server where the security footage was located. "Here you go. Fancy some coffee?"

"That'd be great, thanks. White."

Reid set off down the open hallway to the end of the room, where the vending counter was located. Vail inched the chair closer and oriented herself as to what she was looking at: a screen with an irregular line that

resembled an electrocardiogram. There were lengths along the time line
where the pattern was flat, with peaks at various points. She had seen
digital surveillance systems like this before: you clicked your mouse on
the areas where the line became elevated, which were moments when the
motion sensors had been triggered.

After having watched several segments that showed Gavin Paxton
moving about the gallery and then leaving for the evening, Reid joined her
with two steaming coffees in his hands.

"Anything?"

Vail leaned forward to get a better look at the screen. "What time does
Paxton normally leave the gallery?"

"Turner leaves at six, Paxton locks up at seven. Why?"

"Just saw Paxton leave, so I wanted some reference." She clicked on
the next peak and the video started again, with Paxton moving through
the gallery door.

"Time code's visible if you hit F4—it activates the onscreen display."

Vail did as instructed, and the milliseconds started cascading across
the bottom portion of the screen. "What the hell's he doing back at the
gallery at 11:30 at night?"

"He's got a key and permission to meet with clients anytime, even
after hours."

Vail paused the video. "Don't you think that's strange?"

Reid shrugged. "I asked Turner about it. Didn't seem fazed by it. Said
he gave Paxton the go-ahead. He's supposedly made a lot of after-hour
sales."

"Why can't he do the same business during regular hours?"

"Turner said he's got a very affluent clientele—not that all the people
who shop on Bond aren't affluent. But these are supposedly *very* well-off."

"The one percent," Vail said.

"The one percent are comfortable," Reid said. "These would be the point
one percent—maybe even the point-oh-one percent." Reid shrugged.
"You'd have to ask Turner."

"Or Paxton." She started the recording again and watched as two men
entered the gallery. "Who are these guys? I saw them come in before.
Paxton showed them a few things, but they left without buying anything."

"They made a purchase the second time they came in. A bronze statuette. Then they left. Paxton left a few minutes after them, and about an hour later, the bomb went off." He gestured toward the screen. "You'll see."

Vail observed the events play out as Reid described. When she clicked on a particularly pronounced spike in the line, a bright flash of light filled the screen, followed by dense smoke, and then a few seconds of voracious fire. "And that's all she wrote. Pretty intense."

"See?" Reid said, checking his watch. "Nothing there. I've been through it, MI5's been through it, probably even SO15. Waste of time."

"Uh huh." Vail clicked on the rewind icon and scrolled back to the activity prior to the explosion, when Paxton met with his two customers. She played it through in full motion, then rewound and replayed it. And again.

"What are you doing?"

"My job."

The images played out before her: Paxton welcoming the men, shaking their hands, and then chatting for three minutes and ten seconds. One appeared to pull out his wallet and extract a number of bills. He gave them to Paxton, who gingerly lifted a statuette from a lighted display stand and then disappeared off-camera. He returned a moment later with a medium-sized box. The men shook hands and they left. Paxton turned off the lights and exited the gallery ten minutes after his customers.

"Well?" Reid asked. "Do you see anything? 'Cause I sure don't." Vail didn't reply, so Reid continued. "I've watched the footage for the seven days prior to the explosion, including the day it went off. I never saw anyone setting it."

"Did you notice there's a section missing from the recording?"

Reid leaned closer to the screen. "What?"

"The seconds fly by too quickly, so don't look at those. But watch the minutes." She rewound it and then pressed "play." The digital numbers jumped, skipping numerals. "Twenty minutes are missing, starting fifteen minutes after Paxton and his friends left."

Reid continued to stare at the screen. "I'll have to ask the lab, see if they noticed that."

"Certainly raises a lot of questions." She clicked back to the moment when Paxton entertained his two guests. "These two guys are standing near the safe, where the bomb was placed. Right?"

"Yeah, but they don't look like they plant it. I mean, the safe has to be open for them to put the bomb inside."

"That's the point, isn't it? Remember I talked about access being one of the keys? So the question is, Who has access to the interior of the safe?"

"How the hell am I supposed to know?"

"As a skilled inspector, you might have just asked. Like I did."

Reid leaned back in his seat. "Bugger. I should've asked. So who had access?"

"Turner, obviously. And Paxton, because there are times when he's in the gallery when Turner isn't. That's it." She pressed "play" again and watched, this time in slow motion. Vail paused the recording, then sat back and appraised the screen. "What do you see?"

"Two guys standing in the gallery, in front of the safe, their backs to the camera."

"Exactly. And the day before, what did you see?"

"Pretty much the same thing."

Vail nodded. "Yeah, pretty much the same thing. Two guys, they come into this gallery, and they stand in the same spot." She indicated the frozen image. "We can't see their faces, not even a profile or one-quarter view. They could be anyone, really." Vail leaned closer, thought a moment. "They're kind of crowding the camera. On purpose?"

Reid moved forward and seemed to consider her comment.

She harumphed. "We can't see the front of the safe, can we? That guy on the left, he's positioned himself well, blocking a good part of the camera's angle into the safe."

"Or he just shifted his weight and happened to block the view."

"Or that," Vail said, continuing to look at the screen. "Then there's those missing twenty minutes. But for now, let's deal with what we have in front of us. First, they show an awareness of the cameras. Second—"

"How can you say that? Because they *happen* to be standing in a spot that *happens* to be obstructing our view?"

"Second," Vail continued, "not only do they know that there are cameras, but they know where the cameras are located. Third, the fact that they've positioned themselves to block the safe indicates that they have something to hide."

"Whoa." Reid rolled his chair away from the screen and rotated it to face Vail. "You're so far from the facts, I don't even think that theory warrants a response."

*Maybe. But something doesn't feel right about this.* "If the other guy opened the safe, we wouldn't be able to see. So what if…What if Paxton opened it and they inserted the bomb?"

"You can't be serious."

"Paxton was standing right there. And if he did nothing to stop them, he knows about it—which means he's in on it." Reid started to protest, but Vail silenced him by raising her hand. "At the very least, Paxton knows these guys. And even if he didn't plant it himself, if they're involved, he could be, too—or he'll know where to find them."

"Think about this a second, Karen. We have zero evidence. If Paxton's involved and we go off half-cocked, we could put the frights into 'im. He'd disappear somewhere in Europe and we'd never find 'im."

"Then we can't let that happen."

Reid folded his arms across his chest. "This is a bunch of bollocks."

"Always wondered. What the hell does that mean?"

Reid tilted his head. "You're seriously asking me that—now?" He saw that she was waiting for an answer. "Literally, it means testicles. But we use it to mean 'nonsense.'"

"Testicles, eh?" Vail pondered that as she clicked the mouse to an earlier spot in the recording. After watching for a few seconds, she said, "If you were buying a piece of art like that statuette, wouldn't you bend down, look at it from different angles? Get closer, move back to, I don't know…examine it, appraise it? They look like they're just going through the motions of making a purchase."

"Maybe they've seen it before, liked it, but couldn't decide if they wanted to spend the money. I'm sure it costs a pretty pence."

"You watched all the footage. Did they ever look it over? I mean really look at it. Especially if it's expensive, I'd expect them to pay *some* attention to it." Vail waited a beat, then reached again for the mouse. "Because if you're not sure, I can rewind—"

"No," Reid said, "they never did." He ground his molars. "What you're seeing is the most interest they ever showed in it."

"Don't take it personally. Sometimes it takes a different set of eyes to catch a nuance like that."

"If there *is* a nuance. They could've been in a month ago and seen it, looked at it from every angle and examined it with a bloody magnifying lens." Reid waved a hand. "It's just a theory, and not a good one at that."

"That's the thing," Vail said as she clicked stop. "A theory is more than we had an hour ago." She noticed that Reid was still staring at the blank screen. "This is good. Why do you look like I just screwed up your day? Cheer up, mate."

Reid grabbed his sport coat. "Don't talk like a Brit, Karen. Doesn't suit you."

A smile flitted across Vail's lips. "Let's skedaddle, shall we? Time's a-wasting and the game is afoot."

Reid rolled his eyes. "You're serious about questioning him?"

"Yes, yes. Now hurry along. We need to inquire as to these odd goings on. I smell a rat."

"You're just going to confront him, straight up?"

"I go nose to nose with serial killers. A bomber?" She snorted. "Piece of cake. Besides, you may as well find out now: I've got a set of steel bollocks."

They headed over to the elevator bank. "You're not going to carry on this way for the rest of your stay, are you?"

"It *is* kind of fun. But no. I prefer my bastardized American English."

Reid lifted an eyebrow. "That makes one of us."

# 13

After stopping to use the restroom on the way out of Scotland Yard, Reid retrieved their car and drove to the Turner Gallery. He dropped Vail off in front and went to find a place to park—not an easy task in this area, particularly with media trucks taking up valuable spots. While the Met's vehicles did get exemptions from parking regulations for "police purposes," there still had to be curb space.

As Vail turned to face the reporters, her phone vibrated. It was Montero again. She hit "ignore" and dodged the journalists en route to the cordoned off entrance to the building when she heard her name called out from somewhere beyond the crowd.

She turned to see Hector DeSantos giving one of the heavy-set cameramen a hearty shove to the side.

"What are you doing here?" he asked as he approached.

"Talk about a loaded question." Vail ushered him under the crime scene tape and over to the side, so they could talk out of earshot of the press. "What happened to your cool glasses?"

"Contacts. You like the new me?"

Vail appraised him. "I'm not sure it's an improvement."

He shrugged. "My wife likes it."

"So what about you? What're you doing here?"

"Now *there's* a loaded question," he said with a laugh. "Let's just say I got myself into some hot water, so I was exiled to England for some stupid 'secret' diplomatic mission."

"You?" Vail asked, making a show of looking him up and down. "A diplomat?"

"I know, right? The only other person more unfit for diplomacy would be, well, you."

Vail opened her mouth in mock surprise. "I'd kick you in the bollocks for that comment if it weren't true."

"Bollocks?"

"Testicles."

"Yeah, I don't think you're using it right. It means nonsense. Bullshit."

"I'll have to remember that. So what's your *secret* diplomatic mission?"

DeSantos hesitated, looking past her at the nearby reporters. "Here's the thing. If I told you—"

"You'd have to kill me?"

DeSantos squinted. "No, Karen. If I told you, it wouldn't be a secret."

Vail eyed him. "Boy, you really are taking the diplomat role seriously."

"I want my job back, so I took the assignment—my first one in four months. So I've gotta play the good soldier. Not as much fun as being blunt. Saying what's on my mind, doing whatever I need to do. Having full autonomy to accomplish my mission."

"I guess it's fitting we're in England talking about having a license to kill."

DeSantos frowned. "I'm serious, Karen. Walking on eggshells and dancing around issues isn't my way. I suck at it. I need this thing to go smoothly so I can get back to doing what I'm good at." He nodded at her. "You really here on business? Or you here with Robby?"

Vail sighed. "Business. Definitely not pleasure."

"Didn't realize the Behavioral Analysis Unit did stuff internationally."

"Not to state the obvious, but violent crime isn't limited to the US. We consult all over the world, teach seminars on criminal investigative analysis, train foreign police forces on how to recognize when they're dealing with a serial offender—same thing we do in the US."

"So you're here teaching?"

"No, I was in Spain teaching. My boss sent me here to do a threat assessment on the bombing."

DeSantos craned his neck upward to the bombed out windows of the second story. "The crime scene?"

"See, you're smarter than you let on."

DeSantos smirked. "Since you think I'm so smart, let me look around, give you some feedback. No charge."

"Not up to me—this is Scotland Yard's case, or MI5's—not exactly clear on that."

"So? I'm here. I doubt they'd mind."

"Really? The Brits are—"

"Aw, c'mon," he said. "Where's the harm?"

Before she could object, he was two strides ahead of her and pushing through the entrance.

"I really should check, make sure—"

"Karen," he said as he legged his way up the stairs, "you worry too much."

Moments later, DeSantos was introducing himself to Carter and Reid. Turner and Paxton were standing in the doorway, pointing at a scorched item on the floor.

"Hector Cruz," DeSantos said, extending a hand and greeting both men. "I'm a friend of Karen's back in the States."

*Cruz? What the hell? Is that his diplomatic cover?*

"I've had some experience investigating bombings, years ago, in a former life." He laughed. Reid and Carter did not.

"I think we've got this covered," Carter said. "Thanks anyway."

DeSantos headed for the safe. "Looks like a very powerful explosive. Flash powder or—nope, definitely flash powder." He straightened up. "Aluminum perchlorate?"

Reid, Carter, and Vail shared a look.

"How do you know that?" Carter asked.

DeSantos shrugged. "It's pretty obvious. I don't—I don't mean to step on your investigation. But—wait a minute. Is that—?" He took a few steps forward, bent over, and peered through the open doorway to the area of the gallery that remained intact. "I think it is." He turned and said, "May I?"

Reid tilted his head. "May you what?"

"Mind if I go into the other room?"

"Fine with me, but I don't own the place." All heads turned to Turner, who nodded. With three cops around, even if he didn't know who DeSantos was, Turner had to be certain the guy wouldn't attempt a theft.

Paxton joined DeSantos in front of a small oil painting. The gold leaf frame was nearly as large as the artwork, and a pin spot shone brightly at an angle, illuminating brilliant colors and confident, tiny brush strokes.

"Allow me to help you, sir," Paxton said. "This is a—"

"Fregosi, isn't it?"

Paxton's brow rose. "Very good, sir. You are familiar with his work."

"My wife is. She goes nuts for some of this stuff. I guess some of it's rubbed off on me."

"This is a truly impressive piece. It was done in his early years, a rare work that until a few years ago wasn't even known to exist. As you may recall, he was primarily a sculptor in bronze and wood."

"He did some marble sculptures, too, I believe."

Paxton grinned. "He did! I'm impressed. But Fregosi also created a few dozen tempera paintings. We think he was underrated."

"Is this the original varnish?" DeSantos asked.

"Unfortunately, no," Turner said. "Because of how it was stored, we had to do some restoration. But it turned out famously, I think you'll agree."

Vail, observing from the doorway, stepped into the room. "Hector, what are you d—"

"Trish has an affinity for Renaissance artists. Our fifteenth anniversary is coming up in a month, but I haven't had time to shop for a gift." He turned to Paxton and extended his hand. "Hector Cruz. You are?"

"Gavin Paxton. Curator."

"Idris Turner. Proprietor."

After shaking Turner's hand, he said, "What are you asking for this piece?"

"Three hundred fifty thousand," Paxton said. "Pounds, of course."

DeSantos nodded slowly and looked again at the painting. He tilted his head, moved slightly to his right, and took a different perspective. "I like it. The price is a bit out of my range. But let me see what I can work out."

"Of course," Paxton said.

DeSantos turned to Vail. "Fregosi was a peasant, an understudy of the renowned Renaissance artist Pietro Lorenzetti—"

"Hector, you probably forgot I was an art history major. I know all about Arnolfo Fregosi."

DeSantos laughed. "That was so long ago, I wasn't sure you'd remember."

*'That was so long ago'? What the hell's that supposed to mean? And what the hell is he doing?*

"Anyway, sorry to interrupt your investigation. I saw the painting and—Just give me a few more minutes and I'll come back out there and give you my thoughts on the explosive. I really do think I can help you out."

Something in DeSantos's look—which no one could see at the angle she had—told her to do as he suggested.

"Come find me when you're done."

"Will do," DeSantos said, and then turned back to Paxton and Turner.

STANDING IN FRONT OF THE SAFE, Reid said, "How well do you know this geezer?"

Vail chuckled. "Let's just say we've been through a lot together on a couple of very tough cases."

"Did you know that he was in London?" Carter asked.

"He's here...as a consultant." *Add this up, Karen. He might be here as a diplomatic attaché, but I don't think they use aliases.*

"Nice guy," Reid said. "He seems to know his stuff."

Vail, lost in thought, refocused her attention; she didn't want to appear distracted and draw attention to DeSantos if his mission was sensitive. "On bombs or art?"

"Both," he said with a laugh.

"Speaking of bombs, how much time do we have left?"

Carter rotated a wrist to check his watch. "Forty-minutes."

With that, both their cell phones began vibrating.

"Effing shite," Reid said, moving toward the doorway.

"What's that mean?" Vail asked.

"I think you Americans say, 'Fucking shit.'"

Carter, reading his phone display, was now in step with Reid. "They set it off early. You coming, Karen?"

"Hector," Vail yelled, backing out of the gallery.

DeSantos appeared through the doorway. He did not look pleased.

"There's been another bombing. Wanna tag along?"

He cursed, excused himself from Paxton and Turner, and joined her on the staircase.

# 14

D ebris lay scattered across the entrance to the Embankment Underground station. A dense fog of fine dust hung over the narrow street, and shattered glass from the front doors to the adjacent Costa café littered the pavement. Body limbs protruded from among piles of jagged concrete chunks. Two emergency medical personnel performed triage, as a number of Metropolitan police constables hurriedly secured the crime scene. First responder vehicles were parked at right angles, blocking off the street.

Carter checked in with the crime scene manager and donned protective overalls before wading into the wreckage. Reid had a quick chat with the nearest detective inspector, then met up with Vail and DeSantos.

"Three confirmed dead so far," Reid said.

"Can we take a look around?" Vail asked.

"I'll have to clear it. Don't know how you do things across the pond, but we're real strict with fresh crime scenes here. One path in and out. Everything's very controlled."

"Get anything useful?" DeSantos asked.

"If by useful you mean a description of the bomber, we're not so lucky."

"So that's a 'no'?"

"Not exactly. Looks like they may have used Semtex."

"You sure?" Vail asked.

"When I say 'looks like they may have,' it means I'm not sure. It was a preliminary read based on a field kit swab."

DeSantos looked around at the scurrying workers. "Those swabs are usually pretty accurate. And these flashing police lights are starting to give me a headache. In case you care."

"Not particularly," he said.

Vail appraised Reid. "You're in a snippy mood."

"What, I should be all chuffed to find three dead people and another bombing investigation on my plate? This just went from potentially deadly vandalism to a bona fide act of terrorism."

"Chuffed?"

"Happy," DeSantos said.

*Can't these people speak English? Real English?*

Reid rubbed the back of his neck. "Looks like we've got ourselves a lovely situation here. We're totally knobbed. In case your expert profiling skills didn't pick up on that."

DeSantos cleared his throat. "He means we're fucked."

Vail nudged DeSantos aside. "You want to know what my expert profiling skills picked up on? This is not the work of the same bomber who hit the gallery."

"How can you be so sure?" Reid asked. "We haven't even processed the scene."

"Which reason would you like first? He used a different explosive, which means his ritual—without going into a long explanation, let's call it his subconscious way of doing things—is already very different from the first explosion. Since an offender's ritual doesn't change from bombing to bombing—nor does his signature—that tells me we're dealing with a different perp.

"At the gallery, the bomber made sure he didn't kill anyone—he detonated it in the middle of the night. Here, the offender set it off at a subway station, in broad daylight. We're lucky there weren't dozens killed. So everything tells me these are two different bombers and nothing tells me it's the same person or group. Got it?"

Reid looked away. "Got it." He rocked back on his heels, then turned slightly toward Vail. "It's been a day."

"I accept your apology." *If that was an apology. Sometimes I don't know what the hell they're saying.*

Carter joined them and Reid briefed him on Vail's theory.

Carter seemed to read their faces, which clearly indicated the residual effects of a disagreement. "There are two more dead inside the station," he said. "Device was placed on the side of one of the turnstiles. Could've been much worse."

"I guess that's something," Reid said.

Vail elbowed DeSantos. "You want to take a look in there?"

"No, I'm good."

"I thought you'd have some genius whiz-bang observations for us."

DeSantos puffed out his cheeks and shook his head. "Nope. No genius whiz-bang observations. I'm not feeling it."

Vail eyed him dubiously, then turned to Reid. "Are you guys hanging around?"

"For a bit. You need a ride?"

"Hector and I will take the tube."

"We will?" DeSantos asked.

"Yes, we will." She nodded good-bye to Reid and Carter. "Meet up with you later."

THEY HIKED SEVERAL BLOCKS along Northumberland Avenue toward the Charing Cross station, located adjacent to the entrance of her hotel. They walked in silence for a block, and then Vail stopped in front of a storefront for Garfunkel's restaurant, near Trafalgar Square.

"I'm hungry," she said as she pushed through the door.

"I'm not."

"Then you can watch me eat."

They were seated at a booth in the storefront window. She took a quick look at the menu and ordered an American Hot pizza and an iced tea. DeSantos asked for "loaded jackets" and "chilli" poppers.

"What's an American Hot pizza?" he asked.

Vail leaned back in her seat. "It said 'American.' Right now I find that comforting."

He laughed. "Fair enough."

"Okay, enough bullshit, Hector. I want to know why you're really here."

The smile faded from his face. "I knew that's where this was headed."

"Of course you did, because you're a semi-intelligent person."

"You didn't really mean that."

"You're right," Vail said an empathetic tilt of her head. "I didn't. That'd be giving you too much credit."

Hector turned away. "Fine. You're angry because I haven't been completely honest with you." After a moment's thought, he said, "I *am* on a mission. And I do have to be careful with what I disclose. That much is true."

"You're talking about me, Hector. We've trusted our lives to each other, more than once. Don't you think it's silly to keep things from me?"

"Not my decision. I also wasn't lying when I told you I got myself into some real deep shit."

"With Knox?"

DeSantos looked down at the table. "And others. Knox has my back, but...it's complicated." He met her eyes. "So you want to know why I showed up at the gallery."

"Good place to start."

DeSantos nodded slowly. "Gavin Paxton might be someone we're looking for."

"Who's 'we'?"

"Can't say."

"Give me a break." Vail stared him down but DeSantos did not yield. "Why are you looking for him?"

"Better if I answer that once I have confirmation that Paxton is the right guy."

"You're not giving me much information."

The waitress set the iced tea on the table and moved off.

"No offense, Karen. But that's the point."

"Are you really on a diplomatic mission?"

DeSantos laughed. "You really don't get this game, do you?"

"I didn't realize what we do is a game."

DeSantos grabbed the iced tea and took a drink.

"Hey, that's mine."

"I was thirsty. We'll get you another. And no, I realize this isn't a game. But you and me, we're sparring because you can't help yourself—you need to know. But I don't think you need to know; I think you just *want* to know—and as you know, that means I can't tell you."

Vail rolled her eyes. "I love it when you talk in circles to me."

"It *is* kind of like sex, isn't it? I tease you, you want more—"

"And if you have any hopes of staying in the relationship, you *give* me more."

DeSantos held up the tea in a toast. "Very good." He set down the glass and thought a moment. "Let me do this. If things work out the way I think they will, I'll read you in on what's going on. But until I know more, stay away from Paxton." He rose from the booth, pulled out a £20 note, and dropped it on the table. "Enjoy my jackets and poppers. And get yourself another tea. I'll be in touch."

# 15

As Vail headed to the Charing Cross Underground station, she couldn't put Gavin Paxton out of her thoughts, and the more she played back the security recording, the more she was convinced that the curator had a hand in the bombing. But what was his motive? What did he have to gain by seeing the manuscript destroyed?

Theoretically, it should be a positive for the gallery, and thus for him—the more money Turner made, the more secure his job would be. But she didn't know the finances of Turner's business. It was something Reid, Carter, and Losner needed to look into, if they had not already done so.

As she swiped her Oyster card in the stainless steel turnstile, she received a call from Losner about the visit he had set up with Merlin Hughes. He was on his way to join Reid and Carter at the crime scene.

"I hate it when things don't seem to be going anywhere and now we've got another mess to deal with. I hope these people don't keep setting off bombs about town, or we're gonna have a bloody hard time managing the media."

"Then I've got some good news for you, Ingram. We have a potential lead on the gallery bombing and if it helps you any, the Underground case is probably unrelated."

"How 'potential' is this lead?"

DeSantos's comment to stay away from Paxton echoed in her mind. "It's probably nothing."

"I've only known you a little while, Karen, but you blew me away with your presentations at the conference. I trust your judgment."

A man bumped her from behind—she was blocking passengers trying to reach the boarding areas.

She told him why she thought the cases were unrelated.

"And the gallery case?" he asked.

"What kind of backgrounder have you put together on Gavin Paxton?" *Just an innocent question.* Besides, she'd already told Reid about her suspicions—and DeSantos had no say over whether or not Reid or Losner decided to pursue Paxton.

"You think Paxton's involved?"

"Let's just say that I have some concerns."

"Clive was putting that together. Let me touch base with him. I'll ring you back."

"If you're at Kennington, I'll meet up with you in however long it takes to get there from Charing Cross.'

"Right then. See you shortly."

VAIL CLIMBED THE STAIRS and emerged in the Murder Investigation Team unit, where Grouze was arguing with one of his inspectors. He saw Vail and stopped in midsentence. He pushed away from the man and intercepted her before she could reach Losner's desk.

"What the hell is this bollocks about you having a lead on the gallery bombing?"

"I have a theory. You can ask Reid about it—"

"That's who I heard it from. See, this is the problem with your profiling analysis."

"We prefer behavioral analysis—or criminal investigative analysis."

"Oh, it's criminal all right. We finally agree on something."

"Watch the tapes for yourself. Reid was there. He can tell you what I saw."

"That's the problem. He thought you were seeing things. Imaginary things. Like they weren't doing something you thought they should be doing. But the absence of something can't be used to prove the existence of something."

*Here we go again. I've had this argument before. Problem is, there's no good answer.*

"I study human behavior. I know what I saw. Does that mean it's a slam dunk? I'd be the first to argue that it's not. But I do think it means we need to check it out."

"We can agree to disagree. The beauty, of course, is that what I say goes. So I'm putting this in Reid's hands. Thanks for your opinion." He turned and walked away.

Vail stood there—counting backward from ten—when Losner came up from behind her. "Let's take a walk, shall we?"

"I just got here."

"I need a change of scenery, stretch my legs." He led the way to the elevator, and then stopped. "Wait—you prefer apples and pears, right?"

Vail swiveled her head in both directions. "Did I miss something? Were we talking about fruit?"

Losner snickered. "It means stairs. It's kind of an outdated saying, but I still like it."

"You Brits," she said with a shake of her head. "You're right. I prefer apples and pears. I'm not too keen on elevators, especially small ones."

They exited the building and started down the street. "Ever been to the Imperial War Museum?"

"This is my first time in the UK. And I've been a bit busy since I got here."

"Let's head that way, talk through your theory on the way."

"But your boss said—"

Losner kept his gaze ahead. "Yes. I heard. But I also think he has some bias. You can't be arsed by those things."

"You think I'm on to something."

"I watched the recording. I'm not as convinced as you are, but I think there could be something there, yeah."

"I think your partner disagrees."

"No 'think' about it. He had some choice words. But this case has him on edge. Not sleeping, not a fun guy to be around, I say."

"Never would've guessed that. Until about an hour ago, he seemed very laid back."

"Wait till you really get to know him."

They walked briskly, hashing out Vail's theory. By the time they were done, Losner was more excited about Paxton as a suspect than she was.

"I'll poke around, see what there is in the system on him. We did a preliminary backgrounder on everyone involved and nothing came up."

"I don't think we've got enough for a search warrant."

"No solicitor would let us poke around his flat."

"Surveillance?"

"That'd take manpower—and Grouze's approval. Not to mention Clive would find out. But maybe we'll get lucky and turn up something that'll change their minds."

Losner led the way to the entrance of the Imperial War Museum. Two enormous rocket-shaped projectiles stood on the front lawn, pointed out toward the street.

"What the hell are those?"

"Fifteen inch naval guns, from 1912. They weigh something like a hundred tons."

"I can't believe how long they are—they must stretch fifty feet."

"A bit more, actually. The ultimate phallic symbol, eh? If you like that, there's lots more inside. Wanna take a look?"

Vail consulted her watch. "I'd better get back to my hotel. I've got a threat assessment to write up and reports due with the FBI's legal attaché. It's like having a watchdog." *A rabid watchdog.*

"We all have people we have to answer to."

Vail thought of DeSantos and his usual autonomy on missions. *Some of us more than others.*

# 16

Known by Londoners as the "Wobbly Bridge" because of a design defect that caused it to rock when pedestrians traversed it, the steel suspension Millennium Footbridge crossed the River Thames and sat between two noteworthy landmarks, St. Paul's Cathedral to its north and a reconstructed facsimile of Shakespeare's Globe Theatre to the south.

Workers hurried across the span as tourists gawked and shuffled along, stopping to aim their camera phones at the rising and falling metal cabling, which contributed to its sleek, futuristic angles. Below, the Thames flowed toward the Tower Bridge.

DeSantos rested on the steel handrail and casually checked his watch: his contact was four minutes late. Out of the corner of his eye, he saw a dark-suited man ambling toward him with a slight limp. DeSantos returned his gaze to the water, and a moment later his companion took a spot beside him.

After a moment of silence, the visitor pulled out his phone and brought it to his face. "I'm getting concerned."

DeSantos knew he was talking to him and that the phone was a ruse. "I can handle her. No problem."

"She's already a problem. If you can't rein her in, something will have to be done. And it might be better if you do it than if we do it. Am I making myself clear?"

DeSantos stood up straight. He was tempted to turn and make direct eye contact. But he knew better. "I said I can handle her. Stay out of it."

"I'm afraid this isn't America, Mr. Cruz, so you don't make the rules."

"I don't make the rules there, either."

"If you don't fix this, we will take appropriate action. This is a very serious matter. I don't have to tell you why you're here, do I?"

DeSantos clenched his jaw. He had a mission to carry out, and sometimes things had to happen that were both beyond his control and outside his comfort zone. It wasn't the first time in his career—and it wouldn't be the last.

He turned and walked away, leaving the man holding a dummy phone and staring out at the river. At least DeSantos was able to control one thing: the last word.

It meant nothing, of course—but it made him feel better.

# 17

The morning did not begin well. The hotel room phone rang at 4:30, rousing Vail from a dream of making love with Robby by the ocean. As she sat on the bed listening to the shrill ring, she realized how much she missed him.

She lifted the receiver while rubbing her eyes with two fingers of her right hand. "Yeah."

"It's Reid. We've got a body. I thought you could help us out."

"What kind of body?"

"A dead one. A very dead one. They think it could be a serial."

"I thought you didn't think much of my opinion."

"Don't take all this stuff personally. We have different opinions of how things work. It's not a crime to disagree with you, is it?"

"Of course not."

"And I do value your input. You know that. That's why I've defended you with Grouze. And—I wouldn't be asking for it now if I didn't think you knew what you were talking about."

"Fine. Give me a half hour to get ready."

"Make it fifteen. We've got a bit of a ride."

"Where is it?"

"Stonehenge."

"Stonehenge?"

"Do we have a bad connection, or are you suddenly mutt'n?"

*If I knew what mutt'n meant, I'd be able to answer that question.* "Fine." She fought back a yawn and said, "Pick me up out front at a quarter to five."

STONEHENGE SAT A GOOD distance southwest of London and carried a mystique that belied its outward appearance—a circular arrangement of large stones. Reid and Losner told Vail that it was one of mankind's most ancient structures at five thousand years old, with some of its pillars and cross-pieces weighing fifty tons.

"What's even more impressive," Losner said, "is that these weren't from native or even local rock. Whatever civilizations built Stonehenge, they mined the materials from 150 miles away and carted them here. No one's sure how they did that—the wheel hadn't been invented yet. But that's not even the most impressive feat."

Reid turned off the A303 and onto a secondary road. "Can't really see it in the darkness, but there's lush countryside all around us. We'll be there in a couple of minutes."

"The thing that baffles me," Losner continued, "is how they lifted fifty-ton boulders twenty-five feet off the ground and placed them atop the vertical columns to create cross-pieces."

"Dinosaurs? You know, like in the *Flintstones.*"

Losner chuckled. "Would have to be something like that. Makes as much sense as some of the explanations I've heard."

Reid gestured off to the left. "There she is."

The predawn darkness was yielding to a brightening sky, giving Vail a vague sense of the enormous circular structure. "It's fenced off, so we'll park in the tourist lot and walk through the underground tunnel."

They passed by the Hooker's green ticketing office pitching "English Heritage" passes and then came upon the café—which was closed. Its sign advertising baguettes and drinks elicited a hunger rumble in Vail's stomach.

They proceeded through a subterranean tunnel sporting forest-themed wallpaper and crossed beneath the roadway. It meandered left and right as it ascended back to ground level.

Upon exiting the underpass, they were greeted by a crime scene manager, who logged them in and gave them booties to wear. "Stick to the path, where it's marked. Walk there and only there."

Reid moved on without a word—he knew the drill. "I don't need a plastic policeman giving me orders."

"A what?" Vail asked.

"Ah, it's a bit derogatory," Losner said. "We try not to use it in public. Refers to community service people who sometimes handle crime scenes. They're not police but they get to boss us around in times like these."

As the sun continued its slow rise behind the dense cloud cover, Vail could make out the borders of the Stonehenge complex more clearly. It was an impressive sight—much more so than she had thought it would be, based on a description she had once heard from a friend.

"What's that nipple-looking thing at the top of the tallest column?" she asked as they walked closer.

"That," Losner said, "is part of the wonder of this thing. They carved holes in the bottoms of the horizontal blocks and corresponding pin-type projections in the tops of the columns. That way, when they laid the blocks horizontally across the columns, that mortise-and-tenon type joint served as a locking mechanism that prevented the blocks from sliding off. It's a concept used in wood-working—except these people were doing it thousands of years ago."

Vail looked at the construction as she followed Reid down the path. "Okay, I'm impressed."

An aura of diffuse light backlit the edges of the larger stones. Vail figured there were powerful halogen lamps arranged in the inner circle, illuminating an object of interest.

Losner led them another dozen yards and then stopped. They turned and saw the subject of the spotlights.

Losner shoved both hands in his pockets and said, "The thing that gets me is that we're so capable of building amazing things like this, and yet we can destroy other things like that." With his chin, he indicated the severed head that sat atop a stone pedestal in the middle of the circular periphery.

*And there we are.*

Vail moved toward the structure, following the red traffic cones that delineated the area where she was permitted to walk. As she approached, she saw three crime scene technicians documenting the scene, the camera flash stingingly bright against the foggy dawn.

"So we've got the head over there," she said, indicating a small round stone that sat toward the open end of the circle. "Where's the rest of the vic? Do we have an ID?"

Losner whistled over a technician and repeated Vail's questions.

"Torso's over there," the man said, flicking on a powerful tight-beamed tactical flashlight. "Right side, resting against that rock. Arms and legs are severed, hanging from the top of that column. You can only see them from inside the circle. It's pretty grotesque. Never seen anything like it, inspector."

Losner dry-heaved and put a fist to his mouth, stifling an urge to vomit.

"Oh, and there's something stuck in her bum and her fannt," the technician said. He turned to Vail and explained, "That's her rectum and, um, her vagina."

Vail nodded, taking it all in.

"And there are knife marks on the breasts, too."

"Do we know who she is?"

"Prints just came back as a prostitute who'd been picked up last year in a petty theft. Connie Waterford."

After getting permission to proceed, Vail led the way into the center of the structure. It was as the forensic technician had described. Vail looked it over silently for a few moments. What he hadn't described—and why it was important for her to be here—was the blood that was smeared across the rock face and the "666" markings carved into the victim's abdomen. And then there was the giant "Satan" spray-painted on the surface of the crosspiece above the body.

"Can I borrow that flashlight?"

The technician stepped forward and handed it to Vail. She raked the beam slowly across the interior of the circle, taking in details that the halogen lamps did not reach, moving in a grid pattern from the tops of the nearly three-story stones to the ground, and then left to right.

Reid did the same with his own flashlight.

Vail stepped forward to get a better view of a worn Bible that sat open on one of the ground-hugging horizontal boulders. "What page is that opened to?"

"Afraid that's not going to help us much," the technician said. "Wind was blowing pretty good when we got here, so the pages were turning. Impossible to say what passage the killer intended us to see."

In front of the body, dug into the grass, was a design of some sort. "Were you able to make that out?" Vail asked.

"We just finished a tracing before you got here. It's a pentagram."

*A pentagram, of course.*

Candles, long since blown out, sat on the flat surfaces of a number of foot-high rocks. A crude wooden cross was stabbed into the earth to the right of the torso, upside down.

Losner cleared his throat. "What do you think?"

Reid spoke first. "Looks satanic to me, some kind of ritual killing."

"There *are* theories that Stonehenge was a religious site," Losner said, "either a place for ancestor worship or a ceremonial church for burial. They've found a few hundred burial mounds in the area."

Reid moved his beam of light to the 666 carving. "I read one theory that said Stonehenge represented the ancient 'land of the dead.' A decapitated male body was excavated from inside the ring back in 1923, and a number of others were unearthed with traumatic deformities. Could be some bloody arsehole cult resurrecting the rituals they think were done here thousands of years ago."

"Is that what you think's going on here?" Vail asked.

Reid again focused his light on the numerals. "I'm not sure about all the stuff he did, like severing the arms, carving the body, sticking things in her orifices, but yeah. I do."

Vail bought her light back to the body. "So a ritual satanic killing, that's what you think. Ingram?"

Losner shrugged. "I—I don't know. Sure, it looks like that. A sexual homicide, like you talked about in class, a predator who dabbles in satanic rituals."

*Great. If that's what he got from my class, I was wasting my breath.*

"Okay." She turned to leave but hadn't gone three steps when Reid called after her.

"Where are you going?"

She pouted her lips and shrugged. "Seems like you've got it all figured out. No sense in me spoiling the party."

"Karen, hang on a minute. It was my idea to bring you out here. And don't think I didn't catch some choice comments from Grouze. So why on Earth would I want to send you away without you helping us? Come and look at things, draw up a profile."

Vail turned and walked up to Reid. "Look. I was asked to come to England to write a threat assessment on the bombing. There's something off about all that, but I can't figure out what it is just yet. I need to be spending my time on *that*—not this bullshit."

"Bull— What are you talking about? Some young woman was murdered."

Vail laughed. "That?" She glanced over at the humongous stone structure. "This is a marvel of engineering, something I'd probably find fascinating if I was here with my boyfriend on vacation. But he's not here and I'm not on vacation. Bottom line, this is a complete waste of my valuable time. I've got real cases back in the States, with real victims, that need my attention. So, honestly, I need to get back to Bond Street and make some headway on that so I can get home."

Losner shoved his hands in his pockets and coyly approached Vail. "Karen. What is it that you're not saying about this murder?"

Vail took a long, deep breath. "I've been doing this a long time. Maybe too long. But I look at this scene here and it's—it's like my bullshit meter goes off." By the expressions on their faces, she realized they weren't getting it. "It's like someone read a book on serial killers and tried to make this look like a real crime scene. But they didn't have a true understanding of why those sick bastards do what they do."

"Come again?" Reid said.

"It's an obvious staging. Someone constructed this crime scene to look the way he or she *thinks* a scene like this should look. The offender's done things to the body that make no sense from a behavioral perspective."

Reid again swung his flashlight toward the torso. "But how can you—"

"Look, you can try to poke apart my theories on bombers. And you might have some valid points. But this—" she gestured at the scene before her—"this is in my wheelhouse. And I've never seen an offender do stuff like this."

"There are always new things," Losner said. "I mean, you can't have seen it all."

Vail shook her head. "I'm not explaining this right. It isn't that I've never seen this stuff before. It's that I've seen *all* this stuff before."

Reid spread his arms at his sides. "So what's the problem?"

"It makes no sense. It's like some novelist tried to think up the most bizarre things a sexual offender could do, and thought he was being clever in dreaming up some sick plot. It may be well-written, but it's got no basis in fact. It's so far from reality it's laughable—bullshit to anyone who knows anything about the subject. This crime scene, gentlemen, is exactly that. Understand my point?"

"I get what you're saying," Losner said, "but that doesn't make any sense. Why would someone kill a woman and cut her up—to fake a crime scene?"

Vail stood there staring at the torso. *Yeah, that's a good question.* "I don't know."

"But the satanic stuff." Reid swung a look back at the center of the ring.

"There have been a few homicides that've been linked to actual satanic intent. But I've never seen or heard of a serial offender who has done that stuff as part of his *need-driven* behavior. Don't you see? These assholes don't do the stuff with the bodies because they're thinking about it, they're doing it because it's comforting to them. For some reason, they need to do it. It's hard-wired in their brains, exacerbated by their upbringing, their development. All the satanic stuff like we see here doesn't compute. It just doesn't happen that way."

"But is it possible?"

"Certainly not *all* these things in one scene. A couple of them—a bible, a pentagram, yeah. Okay, fine. But not all of them. I'll tell you where I've seen these types of things—at staged crime scenes. This is way over the top."

They fell silent while they considered what she'd said.

After a moment, Vail said, "What if this was about me?"

"I'm sure. It looks like they cobbled together all the serial killer ìventions they've read or heard about. Or, in the case of the satanic ff, seen in movies or on TV."

Reid said, "Grouze isn't gonna accept that, you know. He'll want us to rk this case up neat and proper. So that's what we're going to do."

Losner took a deep, conciliatory breath. "Let's have at it, then."

"When are we getting back to London?" Vail pulled her sleeve back l stole a look at her watch. "That's what I'm really here for, remember? ìink we're onto something with Paxton."

"I need to help the inspector who's gonna be running point on this," ìd said. "He's a bit green."

*If he wasn't before he saw the severed head, he is now.*

"We'll get back on the road as soon as possible," Losner said.

*Great. I'm stuck here while they yank their chains on a bogus case.* She stepped :k, away from the gaggle of crime scene personnel, and shoved her ìds into her pockets.

If Vail was right, and this was about her, who would do it? And why?

To keep her occupied? They probably thought she would go crazy ìng to figure out what kind of heinous offender was responsible for :h a gruesome crime scene. It would consume a great deal of her ìrgy, leaving less time to work the bombing case. Normally that would true. But that would also mean that they knew her personality. Or y did their homework.

*But why wouldn't they want me working the bombing?*

*To prevent me from finding something? Maybe I'm getting too close. Too close to ìt?*

But the prostitute. When killers choose a prostitute it's because she ìn't be missed, and that gives them time to get away, or for evidence to grade in the elements. But here, there was no need for that. They ìnted the victim discovered quickly; that was why they displayed the dy at one of England's most famous tourist sites.

Vail thought back to her interactions with DeSantos. Was he capable killing a woman and hacking her to pieces just to keep her occupied? e couldn't accept that. And how would that possibly tie in to his ìssion"? *Then again, I don't know what his mission is.*

Reid laughed. "No offense, Karen, but very few peop
even here, so—"

"Not true," Losner said. "Her arrival was all over the n
thing on it all night after she got here, and all day the nex
that they sent an FBI profiler here to work the bombing.
had it."

*Gee whiz. I'm world famous. Just like Ressler, Hazelwood, and Do*

"Blimey. That's bloody great."

Three vans with satellite dishes turned onto the frontag
toward the main entrance.

"Speak of the devil," Reid said as he watched the news t
the turn into the parking lot.

Losner buttoned his suit coat and palmed his hair into p
here? Why do it at Stonehenge? We're in the middle of now

"That may be the point," Vail said. "That, and the fac
well-monitored at night."

Losner nodded. "There are so many closed-circuit TV ca
London, they needed a place off the grid. But why do yo
about you?"

"Whoever did this doesn't know what I know about
Bottom line, these offenders do what they do for a reason
scene should look a certain way. What we see—the behav
leaves behind—come from his personality and life ex
whoever staged this doesn't know how a scene like this wo
more importantly, *should* look. They threw all sorts of c
together.

"But—and here's the point: they *did* know that you'd call
knew that I'd come. And they also knew that the press wou
deal out of it and blow it way out of proportion because
found at a famous tourist attraction, and satanic stuff lik
headlines. A religious execution at Stonehenge, whic
mysterious and has its own history of devil worship and d
She snorted. "They just didn't know I'd see through their bu
I'd do it so fast. And obviously they didn't know that the s
such conflicting behaviors."

The men again fell silent. Finally Losner said, "You sure ab

Vail found the forensic technician they had spoken with earlier. "You have a time of death on Miss Waterford?"

"We'll have to check on that back at the morgue. But liver temp indicates she was killed elsewhere and brought here."

"How do you get location from a liver temperature?"

"Simple, really. If I'm right, at the time she was killed, Stonehenge was still open and there were probably several dozen tourists gawking at the place."

"Right." *Maybe that means something, maybe not.* Vail stared off at the stone monstrosity before her. With the newly assertive sun fighting to break through the early morning clouds, she saw the arrangement of building-size rocks in a different light: an ambitious construction project taken on by an ancient people thousands of years ago. She had to laugh. As Losner had observed, as much as humankind had progressed in all these centuries, the nature of who we are has hardly changed. At our core, we are just animals with primal needs.

That was how she was going to solve the bombing case. Motive and opportunity. Good old-fashioned police work.

Vail crouched down and looked around at the lush countryside that surrounded her. She closed her eyes, took a deep breath, and cleared her mind. *If someone doesn't want me poking around, that means I'm close to figuring out something important. But what?*

# 18

It was three hours before Vail's ongoing plea to get back to London resonated with Losner. He agreed that their useful time at Stonehenge had drawn to a close and convinced Reid to hand the scene over to the junior inspector who would be working the case.

While waiting for them to wrap up their involvement, Vail sent a buddy of hers back in the States, Agent Aaron "Uzi" Uziel, an email asking him to do some digging on Clive Reid and Ethan Carter. She hadn't forgotten about the familiarity Reid had shown Carter—a man he claimed not to know. It could be that she was looking for things that didn't exist. But she was bored and it had bugged her, especially when coupled with the Stonehenge crime scene. She had learned a long time ago to keep a healthy dose of paranoia squirreled away in the back of her mind…just in case. It kept her sharp and—sometimes—helped keep her from being blindsided.

She wanted to ask Uzi about DeSantos, and if he had any information on his covert mission. But she knew better. If it was in fact a sensitive matter, DeSantos would not have told even his good friend about it.

By the time she, Reid, and Losner piled into the car for the drive back, the sun had burned through the cloud cover, casting shadows across the grass that carpeted the countryside in and around the stone landmark.

Flocks of sheep grazed on the rolling green hills in all directions, and for several moments, Vail enjoyed a sense of calm.

They arrived in London in time for a late lunch, so they stopped in for a box of assorted sushi at Abokado's, across the street from Scotland Yard. As she started to clear her plate, her BlackBerry buzzed. A text from Montero:

**report to me immediately**

Vail snorted. "I really don't like this guy."

"Who?" Reid asked.

"My Legat, my UK boss. More like the thorn in my side. I've been ignoring his messages for days."

"Never good to ignore superiors, Karen."

Vail laughed. "Wish someone would've told me that years ago."

On the way out, Reid paused to adjust his tie in the storefront, using it as a mirror. "I've got a meeting at the Yard. Strategy session over how we're going to spin this case. I don't have to tell you finding a mutilated body among a rash of satanic symbolism is a sensitive matter."

"Sure you don't want my input at the meeting?" She grinned.

Reid shared the laugh. "I'd like to avoid the firing squad, if you don't mind. I'm afraid associating with you is a bit poisonous these days. Guilt by association."

"Kind of like the Black Plague," Losner said.

Vail laughed. "That's hardly fair. I thought I was behaving."

Reid consulted his watch. "Ingram's gonna take you wherever you need to go. The embassy?"

"Paxton. I want to have a talk with Gavin Paxton."

Reid sighed. "Fine. Take her to see our friendly curator. But please, do me a favor. In the remotest of chances that he is involved in this—and I really only say this to stroke your ego—because there's no way in hell that he is—handle him with care. Be smart about it. We don't want him heading out of the UK on the next train. We good on that?"

"We're good."

AS THEY ASCENDED the stairs en route to the gallery, Vail's phone buzzed. She pulled it out but did not recognize the number.

"I'll meet you in there," Losner said.

She nodded okay as she brought the handset to her ear. "Vail."

"Karen, it's Hector. We need to meet. I've got some important info for you that I can't discuss over the phone. Do you know the Caffé Nero in Piccadilly Circus?"

"Do I know it? I've been in London a handful of days in my entire life. What do you think?"

"You're still angry with me."

"A bit."

"Fair enough. Pick up the tube at Bond Street station and get off at Piccadilly Circus. The café's a block away, on Piccadilly. Big blue sign, next to Cotswold Outdoor. I'm at a table against the wall. See you in about twenty."

As she headed back outside, she texted Losner that she had an errand to run. Five minutes after getting directions to the station, she was swiping her Oyster card and moving down the long corridor filled with large billboards advertising Hollywood films.

She was bumped from behind, and then she felt a sharp prick in her neck. Her vision instantly distorted into a myopic tunnel.

A second later, everything faded to black.

# 19

Her neck hurt. That was the first thought Vail had as her consciousness started to return—slowly at first, then in increasingly rapid increments as she began to regain her senses: vision, then smell, then hearing.

There was darkness all around her, save for a pin of light near the ceiling. A dank, damp, mildew-like odor tickled her nostrils. Off in the distance, footsteps.

*Where am I? What happened? I was going to meet Hector.*

She tried to shift her weight and realized that her limbs were encased in ringlets of iron. A broader band encircled her torso, and her arms were pinned against her sides, their movement restricted by the thin metal bars.

*Oh God, I'm in some kind of cage.*

Anxiety overcame her in that instant, sweat soaking her shirt, the need to move overwhelming. Something as mundane as stretching out her arms—a motion she did a thousand times a day—was now something she had to do—*needed* to do. She forced them away from her body, scraping her skin against the rough metal bars. *I can't, I have to get out.* She felt panic rising in her throat—

But she stopped herself. She willed her arms to relax, her breathing to slow. Claustrophobia was not her enemy; whoever did this to her, however, was—and she needed to regain her wits to think clearly, to figure out where she was, and why. She needed to conserve her energy and find a way out of this.

As clarity returned to her thoughts, she realized she was suspended above the ground. How far, she did not know…but her metal coffin was swaying, pivoting from an attachment above her head. She found the pin of light again and followed it, trying to locate the boundaries of her chamber. It appeared that she was in a dungeon of some sort, and— judging by the limestone growths on what appeared to be cement block walls, uneven mortar extruding its joints—it was one of considerable age.

The scratch of tiny feet below told her that she had company— rodents of some sort.

She moved her head and her lips touched the metal encircling her face. It tasted like iron—rusted iron.

The loud clomp of heavy shoes echoed; there was a hallway or tunnel of some sort off to her right. Three—no, four—men were coming.

*Let them come. I want answers!*

When they got closer, she yelled into the darkness, "Who are you?"

Silence, except for the continuing footsteps. Seconds later, they stopped. They were below her, meaning she was at least several feet off the ground.

Breathing.

Finally, one spoke:

"حماة ال مع نحن"

*Arabic?*

"We are with al-Humat," another translated. "You know who we are."

A statement, not a question.

Beyond the regular FBI terrorist briefings, Vail knew of al-Humat because of what one of them had done to her friend Uzi.

"Yeah. I know who you are. What do you want with me?"

Vail knew the question was pointless. Whatever the reason, it was a violent group known for doing bad things to those it considered enemies— basically anyone who did not share its beliefs. *Infidels.*

A captor lit a match. In the flickering light, Vail glimpsed her prison— a tall, narrow dungeon. Three other rusted metal devices hung from the ceiling, all of various sizes. One looked like it had once been used to stretch a body between two rolling pins utilizing a crank.

The match burned out and she was again lost in darkness. Suddenly she felt a jerk and her body was lowered toward the floor. It was disorienting, moving downward but not being able to see where she was going.

Her bare feet slapped the cold dirt.

A painfully bright halogen light was turned on, blinding her vision and blowing out her rods and cones.

More Arabic—but no translation this time. She realized they were using interrogation techniques well established in western law enforcement and military training: deprive your subject of her senses, disorient her, keep her guessing, speak in ways she could not understand, control her, provide personal information about her to give her a sense of invasion. In short, break her down, freak her out.

The light went off.

Thirty seconds later, the glimmer of another match revealed three men in black hoods. Fighting to see through her damaged visual field—which needed several more minutes to recover—she saw that one held a video camera, his comrade an AK-47 assault rifle.

More footsteps clomped down the adjacent hall as two of the kidnappers unlocked her from her iron prison. They pulled her out roughly and knocked her legs out from under her. The match again burned out.

Darkness.

*C'mon, Karen. Fight! Fight!*

She swung her arms and sliced through air, twisting her torso but striking nothing of significance.

A large, slick hand grabbed the back of her neck and forced her face down into what felt like a tree stump. She struck it hard and immediately tasted blood in her mouth.

The man holding the camcorder turned on the bright light again and settled the camera on his shoulder, aimed at Vail. The red "record" LED started blinking above the lens.

Another captor grabbed a fistful of her hair and yanked her head back. He shoved a sheet of paper into her hands.

"Read this."

She squinted at the document, trying to focus and use her peripheral vision to make out the words. It was a confession for America's transgressions—the typical treatise captives were forced to read prior to...decapitation.

"I'm not reading that," she said.

"Read it!" the man said, louder.

*Don't give in. Show strength. Don't let them win. They're just trying to scare you.*

She looked down again at the paper and scanned the bullshit babble—until she reached a paragraph that made her glance up at the masked man holding the document. The text mentioned Uzi—and that's when she realized she was in trouble. This wasn't some random kidnapping, it was done for a purpose. Retribution, for her role in a recent case involving Uzi and al-Humat's sleeper operative.

Her legs went weak and she had to lock her knees to remain erect. To maintain the appearance of resistance.

The footsteps again snatched her attention; as she looked up, the light went out.

Another match was lit. Her face was pushed against the stump again, and out of the corner of her eye she saw a new set of black boots appear at her feet.

Someone pulled her head back. She saw a hooded face with bloodshot eyes. And a long, curved, lethally sharp talwar in his hand.

"الكـــافر تطهــير يجــب ! الآن ذلـك تفعــل!"

She didn't know what he yelled, but the tone was forceful and primal. If she ever feared for her life without hope of escape, it was now.

*Jonathan, oh my God, my son—*

*Robby! Where are you when I need you—*

Her head was forced against the mildewed stump. A hand clamped against her skull, and then...

Blackness.

# 20

Hector DeSantos checked his watch one more time, then lifted his coffee cup and took a drink.

He dialed Vail, but it went straight to voice mail. Again. Something was not right.

In the States, he would have assets at his disposal to locate her based on her BlackBerry's GPS signal. Hell, he could call people who knew her and ask if they'd heard anything. Here he was running blind. Actually, he wasn't running anywhere. He was stuck waiting in the café in case she showed up, a scowl on her face complaining that she didn't have mobile service in the tube and the train had broken down and it was hot and—

Any number of scenarios could explain why she was late. But it was now approaching an hour past her expected arrival, and there weren't many things that could be responsible for detaining her that way without contact of some sort.

If she had been delayed, or if something had come up regarding her case, she would have texted him. His cell phone number was now in her call log.

But his attempts at contacting her went directly to voice mail. Her BlackBerry was likely turned off.

He had drained the third cappuccino when his Nokia rang. "Karen?"

He closed his eyes as soon as he heard the voice at the other end of the line. It was not Vail.

"Yes. This is Cruz." He listened a moment, then said, "Yeah. I got it…No, I know where it is…Fine."

He slammed the phone down, eliciting looks of dissatisfaction from the other patrons tapping on their laptops and iPads. He rose from his chair and began pacing, his heart rate fast and forceful.

Seconds later, the phone rang again, and he stared at it a long second before grabbing it up.

"Cruz."

He turned toward the window, his eyes scanning Piccadilly, looking for someone watching him.

"No, I heard you. I'm on my way."


DESANTOS MET THE MAN at the M&M's World Store in Leicester Square. It was not a typical low-key location for a meet between two covert agents. But that's what made it safe: no one would expect such a rendezvous to take place here.

The building that housed the store was a block square, an all-glass contemporary design with bright lights spewing purples, pinks, yellows, greens, blues—almost the entire rainbow was represented.

DeSantos walked in the entrance, at the curved corner of the building, and was greeted by two man-size M&M mock-ups. The interior did not disappoint. It consumed multiple levels, a red staircase spiraling to the lower levels, where he saw four large M&Ms striding in a crosswalk against a facsimile backdrop of what appeared to be the Beatles' *Abbey Road* cover.

Any other day, DeSantos would've at least smiled at the sight of the diorama. But right now he wanted answers.

He walked to the back room where M&M teddy bears were stacked on racks wearing clothing bearing the classic candy's colors. DeSantos picked up a red-shirted teddy bear—his signal for the contact to approach.

"Where is she?" DeSantos asked in a low, measured tone.

From the adjacent rack, the man said, "You should know that you are responsible."

DeSantos fought the urge to turn and get in the man's face. Wrap his fingers around his throat. "What's that supposed to mean? I told you I'd take care of her. You should've trusted me."

"You didn't, she was out of your control and was headed into very dangerous territory. Now, I'm afraid, there have been consequences that you will have to deal with."

"Where is she?"

"I am not responsible for the state she is in."

"Where is she?" DeSantos repeated, louder than he intended. But at this point he did not care.

The man gave him the location, and DeSantos left the store on the run, the red M&M bear flying from his hands, landing harmlessly on the floor.

# 21

eSantos arrived in Oxford ninety minutes later. His phone's GPS took him to the address he had been given, and despite the darkness that had settled over the town—which was always bleak, even on bright days—he recognized parts of it from a prior trip here years ago.

He knew the general area: one of England's most visited and historically important churches, the University Church of Saint Mary the Virgin, erected in the thirteenth century—and looking every bit its age. The exterior was in desperate need of retrofitting and refurbishment.

DeSantos drove down Catte Street and took it to the end, then parked his Peugeot—illegally—and took to the pavement with an old-fashioned incandescent Maglite that was woefully underpowered.

A few university students walked briskly past, probably en route to their dorm rooms, an evening party, or the library to study.

DeSantos started in Radcliffe Square and moved slowly around the several centuries-old circular Radcliffe Camera building, checking the crevices, alcoves, and doorways.

But there was nothing.

He returned to his car and then backed out of Catte Street, about to pull out his phone and ask what the hell was going on—when something caught his eye. He grabbed his flashlight and jumped out of the vehicle.

Beneath the archway of the Bridge of Sighs—an ornate covered connector ramp between two buildings—DeSantos saw three young men gathered in the darkness. Two items protruded from beneath the youths—women's black boots. He knew those shoes.

As he stepped onto the cobblestone gutter that paralleled the curb, he brought his Maglite up and splashed it across the backs of the men. They turned—and DeSantos's forearms tensed. These were not youths— certainly not the innocent type out for a night on the town. These were troublemakers: hooligans, in the local vernacular.

"Get that light the fuck out of my face," the older one said, a roughness to his skin and a squint in his eyes.

"What do you got there?" DeSantos asked.

"None of your business. Do yourself a favor and move on."

If he had his Desert Eagle, he would have pulled it by now. Its impressive mass would've been enough to give these shitheads a case of urinary release.

The hoodlums shifted position—as they prepared to do battle. In that moment DeSantos realized that he had been wrong. There were four of them, and they were larger, and not nearly as young as he had estimated at first glance.

Behind him, his car idled. The street was otherwise empty.

"Move away from her," he said.

The leader stepped forward. "Yeah? I think you need to do some arithmetic. There be four of us and only one 'a you."

DeSantos detected a Northern Ireland twang in his accent. These men were hardened veterans, likely brought up during the brutal and bloody conflict.

As if on cue, he flicked his right wrist and unfurled a long-bladed knife. Its bright chrome glinted in the yellow beam of DeSantos's Maglite. It looked clean and sharp.

"Is that supposed to scare me?" DeSantos asked, taking a step forward, followed by another. First rules of close quarter combat: take an attack mode—a fuck you stance. Show no fear. Control the situation. "I'm not gonna tell you again. Move away from her. Now."

"Or what?"

"Or I'll kill you." He said it with a cool casualness that lent credibility to his claim—no hyperbole; a statement of fact. He continued to advance on them; the thug's comrades shuffled position in response. "That woman means a lot to me. You're gonna have to go through me to get to her. And trust me. You don't want to have to go through me."

DeSantos had stepped within three feet of the man and had started moving laterally, his body squared up and his right hand extended, pointing at him.

The thug jabbed the knife toward DeSantos—who deflected it with a sweeping downward motion of his hand against the man's elbow, locking it and driving it backward, breaking it with a satisfying snap while simultaneously jabbing the edge of his right hand into his throat.

The man stiffened, and DeSantos yanked down on his attacker's left wrist, the pain from the fractured joint forcing the knife to drop from his hand. DeSantos snatched it up, swung it around, and sliced at the guy's abdomen, opening the flesh and releasing a line of bright red blood. He slammed the point of his elbow into the man's chest and he went down hard, back first, to the pavement.

DeSantos brought the knife up and prepared to take on the next banger. With two swift, continuous movements of his hands, he slit his adversary's bicep, then brought the blade down across his stomach and finished him with a quick stab into his groin. He dropped to the ground in writhing pain.

"C'mon," DeSantos yelled, facing the third criminal. "Let's go, asshole!"

The other two took a step back, eyes locked with DeSantos's.

"Last chance. Come at me or get the hell out of here. Three. Two. One—"

They brought their hands up and backed away, revealing his unconscious colleague, a rag stuffed in her mouth.

"Karen!"

He tossed the gag aside and moved the damp, matted hair off her face. He stroked her cheek gently, then checked her pulse: fast and thready.

He hoisted her over his shoulder and carried her to his car.

Goddamn it. He told them he would deal with her. Son of a bitch.

# 22

DeSantos stood in the treatment room next to the examination table where Vail was lying supine. He had burst into the quick care facility with her in his arms, telling the staff she had been attacked by street thugs.

"Do we need to do a rape kit?" the doctor asked.

"No, I got there in time. But it looks to me like she was given some kind of sedative."

After finishing her exam, the doctor slid her penlight back into her breast pocket. "Your friend's in shock and she's sustained some contusions to the face and head. But I'm not seeing evidence of a concussion. She's fortunate that you came along when you did. We'll infuse her with some fluids and let her rest for a bit. She should be well enough to leave in a couple of hours."

DESANTOS HELPED VAIL back to the car and fastened her seatbelt. She was more lucid now, and her disoriented questions of "What happened?" and "Where am I?" transformed into more forceful demands to know why she was taken and how DeSantos knew where to find her.

"Where are we?"

"Just outside Oxford, about an hour and a half from London."

"How'd I get here?"

When he didn't answer, she turned to him, intensity in her eyes. She was clearly feeling better. And that meant the questions were going to get tougher, more pointed. Anger would set in shortly after that.

VAIL RUBBED AT HER TEMPLE. The headache was subsiding, but bits of memories of being confined in a dark area flashed through her thoughts.

"I was in a dungeon," she said, staring at the dark road ahead. She hugged herself and shivered. "I was chained inside an iron cage."

"Sure it's not some kind of drug-induced dream?"

"No. Not a dream." She looked at her wrists and saw abrasions from the iron restraints. "Arabs. They were speaking Arabic." She turned to DeSantos. "What the hell? Does that make any sense to you?"

He blew some air through his lips. "Arabs. You sure you're not mixing this up with some other case you had?"

Another image. "Bright lights. They were wearing black masks."

"This is sounding more and more like a dream."

*That doesn't make any sense. None of this is making sense.* "It wasn't a dream."

DeSantos leaned forward to check an approaching road sign. "I don't know what to tell you, Karen. Someone grabbed you up. That's about all you know for sure. Everything else, well, sounds like a really intense nightmare."

"Nightmare for sure." She stared out at the dark roadway. The vivid, blue-tinged headlights of an approaching vehicle made her squint. *Lights.* "They were filming—there were movie lights. No, they were making a video. Of my death, my decapitation."

She realized DeSantos was looking at her strangely.

"I'm not making this up."

"Did I say you were?"

"That's what you're thinking."

"Look, Karen. I have no doubt something traumatic happened to you. But Arabs threatening to decapitate you? Taking revenge on you for Uzi's case?"

Vail looked down at her legs, pulled up her pant cuffs, and saw bloody scrapes all across her shins and knees. *Definitely not a dream.*

She turned to DeSantos. "Stop the car."

DeSantos checked his mirrors. "Why? What's wrong?"

"Stop the goddamn car, Hector. Now!"

"We're in the middle of the motorway."

"Pull over."

"Why? What's got into you?"

She reached over and unlocked her door and then grabbed the handle.

"Okay, hold on." He swung the car left onto the shoulder and stopped.

Vail popped open the door and walked around to the driver's side, where DeSantos was getting out. The Peugeot's headlights shone into the dew-heavy distance; the engine purred.

"You mind explaining what the—"

She grabbed hold of his collar. "Tell me what the fuck's going on! No more bullshit."

"What? Are you talking about our lunch the other day?"

"What the hell happened to me in that dungeon? Who was behind it, and why?"

"What makes you think—"

"All I said is that there were Arabs. You said they were taking revenge for Uzi's case. But I never mentioned that." She let go of his collar and slapped his face. "Goddamnit, Hector. I thought we could trust one another."

DeSantos's eyes narrowed, darkened. "I save your life and I get a slap in the face as thanks?"

Vail took a step back. "How do I know that you're not responsible for putting me in that situation to begin with?"

DeSantos tensed his jaw. "Hold on right there. How dare you? Do you really think I'd do anything to hurt you? *Anything*? Ever since I met you I've tried to keep you out of trouble, to watch your back, to make sure no one hurt you."

"Then what the hell is going on? You owe me an explanation—full disclosure."

DeSantos leaned his buttocks against the car door. Finally he said, "Why don't we get you a shower, grab some food somewhere, and talk this through."

"No. I want to know now. No more deceptions, no more half-truths."

He chewed on that a moment, then said, "Ever hear of Hussein Rudenko?"

Vail tilted her head. "Of course. Long and impressive résumé—if you're a criminal bent on wreaking havoc in the world. We're briefed on him once a year or so. I can't tell you what he's done, but I know he's number three."

"Number three?"

"FBI Ten Most Wanted list."

"Brief rundown? He's the world's most prolific weapons dealer and money launderer. He's sold deadly weapons systems to militias in the US, to the Taliban, the Northern Alliance, Hezbollah, and terrorists in Africa, the Congo, Sierra Leone. You get the point. But he made one mistake. He fucked with the wrong people: when he sold those surface-to-air missiles used against an Israeli passenger jet in 2002. Mossad's been looking for him ever since. Problem is, he's a tough guy to find. Interpol's been searching for him for two decades. But it's hard to find someone when no one knows what he looks like. And that's why I'm here."

"Here, as in England? I thought you were on a diplomatic mission."

"I never said that. I mean, really. Me? A diplomat?"

Vail looked at him.

"Okay, fine. That's my cover story. Repping the State Department and assisting the diplomatic attaché. That said, about three years ago, the CIA got intel that Rudenko was getting involved in planning and carrying out terror attacks. Some in The Agency felt he was trying to expand his business by stoking the embers, creating greater demand for his weapons. Others thought his sibling's death set him off.

"Whatever it was, Mossad stayed on Rudenko's trail. Two years ago they intercepted a shipment of chemical weapons that Hezbollah was transporting out of Syria, bankrolled by Iran and facilitated by Rudenko. But instead of confiscating it, they decided it'd be more valuable for them to see where it was going—because where it'd end up, there'd be a much larger cache. That was the Holy Grail. So to speak.

"They embedded electronic tracers and let the cargo go through. They were able to get actionable intel on the weapons depot in Libya, where it ended up. They weren't sure they'd be able to go in without being detected, so they watched it for movement. But they were bumping up against a deadline—they were worried the power source on the electronic beacons would run down. The tracers had been sending back signals for two years and the desert heat and dust are killers for electronics. And if they were stored in some kind of hardened bunker, that requires more power to get the signal out. Mossad couldn't risk losing track of the weapons.

"So they started prepping a mission to capture Gadhafi's chemical weapons stash when his government was overthrown. The cache wasn't being guarded, and munitions of all kinds were open to terror groups and weapons dealers. You name it—they had it. Bad shit when you're talking about it falling into the hands of bad shit*heads*.

"A huge red flag went up when the Israelis tracked a large shipment of weaponized ricin to the UK. London, specifically. They alerted MI5 immediately."

"And that's why you're here."

"That," DeSantos said, "is why I'm here."

"But why would MI5 need your help? They've got their own agents and informants. They can execute a black op as well as we can."

"They do have skilled operators. Or they did. Past tense. There was a cyber-attack during a mission six weeks ago and the identities of all of their operatives were potentially exposed. There hasn't been enough time to sort it out and figure out who's safe and who's not. Two have already been assassinated."

"How could something like that happen?"

"By exploiting the one and only weakness in the system. Someone figured out—or knew—which bank the Security Service and MI6 use to pay their operatives and they accessed its system. Hacked it, or got in through the normal portal, they don't know yet. It looks like the system was *not* hacked, which would suggest someone on the inside. A mole. But they don't know if that's really the case or if it's been made to appear that way.

"Point is, the identities of all their domestic and foreign agents are at risk. When Mossad sounded the alarm, the Brits had a huge problem. They couldn't send in some junior agent in training. And until they figured out who did it—mole or not—they couldn't risk using a compromised agent. He'd be killed—and the op would fail. Rudenko would take off, vanish into the wind. Again. And one of his compatriots would launch the attack. So they sent me here."

"Because no one here knows who you really are."

"Let's hope not. The MI5 director general had the idea of using an American black operative who was unknown in London, who had no known affiliation with the security service or with the CIA."

"And you fit their needs."

"Apparently. Director General Aden Buck called Knox, his counterpart, and my boss signed off on it."

"I thought you were in some kind of trouble."

"There was that, too. I was happy to get back out in the field, prove myself. They didn't need to ask twice. Actually," he said with a chuckle, "they didn't ask once."

"Why didn't you just tell me this when we first met?"

"Because then I'd have to kill you."

Vail smirked. "Now there's the Hector DeSantos I know and despise."

"Ow. That's not fair. Without people like me doing what we do, lots of innocent people would be blown up by terrorists, racially cleansed by despots, raped and dismembered by warlords. You don't want to know the entire list."

Vail stabbed at the dirt with her left shoe. "I know that. I just have a hard time with killing in cold blood. Circumvents due process." She held up a hand. "But I understand where you're coming from. And I appreciate your putting your life on the line. So what's this got to do with me? And why are you suddenly leveling with me? Or are you about to stick a knife between my ribs?"

"First of all, that's not how I'd kill you. Too painful. And despite what you think, I'm fond of you, Karen."

Vail tilted her head. "Thanks. I think. This conversation is not instilling a whole lot of comfort."

"You wanted the truth."

"Right. The truth. So what's this got to do with me and my time locked away in a dungeon?"

"We believe that Gavin Paxton is Hussein Rudenko."

Her mouth dropped open. "Holy shit."

"Yeah."

"When did they zero in on Paxton?"

"In retrospect, it looks like he started using Turner Gallery as a ruse, a front, for his weapons deals about a year ago, when Turner's former curator 'died' in a car accident."

"They think Rudenko cleared the way—or created a need—for himself to get the new job opening."

"Right. But MI5's only got a skeleton crew digging into it, because until they figure out if they've got a mole, they don't know who can be trusted. So what they know is not super useful—yet. It's like the polls on election night. The early returns are interesting, but they may not mean a whole lot."

"When Mossad's tracking signal ended up at the gallery, they didn't know who the recipient of the 'package' was. Turner and his family have a solid, long-standing history in England, very philanthropic. The gallery's been around for ninety-eight years. Paxton's history, however, was a lot more suspect."

"So if they knew where the ricin ended up, they secured it."

"They were preparing an op to search the place and replace the ricin with an inert substance, but it took time to plan because the gallery has video surveillance and they didn't want to spook Paxton in case he was Rudenko. A few days before I got here, it looked like he had started moving the ricin stores when the beacon finally crapped out. So, no. It's still out there. Somewhere."

A chill wind blew, and she wrapped her arms around her body. "You should've leveled with me."

"That's what I'm doing now—I'm telling you the truth—because I need you to back off. Leave Paxton alone."

"Back off? I've uncovered some things about him—"

"Exactly. Because there's a high probability he's a notorious weapons dealer, a cold-blooded killer, and the most prolific bankroller and enabler of war, mass atrocities, and terrorism in the post-Cold War era."

Vail ground her molars. "Did you have anything to do with my kidnapping?"

"Of course not."

She stood there observing him for a moment. "But you knew about it."

"Only after the fact. They told me what they'd done, and why. And where to find you." DeSantos turned away. "There's a lot to this, Karen. A lot you don't know about."

"Damnit, Hector. They scared the crap out of me. I thought they were going to chop my head off!"

DeSantos shook his head. "I didn't know. Honestly—I never would've allowed them to do that. I told you, I wouldn't let anything happen to you."

*That's a nice thing to say, but—* "Who's behind it?"

DeSantos shifted his weight. "You know how this shit works. Need to know. And all *I* apparently needed to know is that they were concerned you'd fuck everything up. Scare away Paxton. Once he's gone, he's gone. The stakes are very high. Obviously."

"Are you being honest with me now?"

"Totally."

"Are you telling me everything?"

"Not even close."

Another breeze. Vail tightened her arms across her chest. "Go on."

"I can't tell you any more than I already have."

"After all we've been through?" She studied his face, but it revealed nothing. "I'm a federal agent, Hector. I took the same oaths you did."

"All due respect, Karen, you can't equate the job you do with the job I do. They're not only in different ballparks, they're in different sports."

"Trust is trust. You either trust me or you don't. And apparently you don't."

"You're taking this personally. It's not. It's the way I have to operate."

She looked off into the darkness, then into DeSantos's eyes, to get a good read. A moment later, she got back into the car.

"Are we okay?"

Vail buckled her seatbelt. "For now. We'll see what tomorrow brings."

# 23

When they arrived back in London, Vail showered in her hotel room while DeSantos ordered dinner for them in the restaurant. The staff was cleaning up and preparing to close, but he convinced them to serve their meal in the bar, which was open till 2:00 AM, another hour from now.

Vail arrived fifteen minutes later, explaining that she would've liked to stay in the shower another thirty minutes, then fall into bed. But she knew she needed to eat.

When she sat down on the barstool, the exhaustion showed in her drooping shoulders. "I look like shit."

"You look great to me."

"Normally, you're a good liar."

"And now?"

"Not so much. I've got abrasions all over my face and I think that episode with the Arabs took ten years off my life."

"Don't be so dramatic. Extreme stress only shaves off a few days."

She looked at him.

"Sorry." The waitress set the two plates in front of them.

"Burgers. Really? After what you put me through today?"

"You were expecting candlelight and caviar?"

"A girl can dream."

"At this time of night, we're lucky to get this. They were closing up. I had to grovel on hands and knees for these burgers."

"I can't imagine you groveling."

"Fine. I asked nicely. The hostess was hot and I promised to repay the favor."

"I'm losing my appetite."

DeSantos gathered up the burger. "Not me."

"Hector, we have to deal with the elephant in the room."

DeSantos stopped chewing, then twisted his torso, taking in the entire bar. "I don't see an elephant, Karen."

"I'm entitled to some answers."

He looked around again. No one was there, and the bartender was in the back restocking glasses.

"What do you want to know?" He held up an index finger. "Be reasonable."

"Let's start with Stonehenge."

"I'm not a historian or anything, but from what I understand, it's really old and there are these big rocks arranged in—"

"Hector. Don't start with me. I'm not exaggerating when I say that I've had a shitty day."

He set his burger on the plate. "Fine. It was staged. You were right."

"Staged, yeah. Any profiler worth her salt would've seen that. But there was a real woman who was sliced and diced."

"A prostitute found dead the night before from an overdose. Her body was...appropriated. No one was actually killed."

"Why the charade?'

DeSantos spread his hands. "For you. C'mon, don't tell me you didn't figure this out."

"I did figure it out. That's apparently what got me in hot water."

"Not exactly. But it didn't help. What caused the problem is that you're too freaking good. You were supposed to be occupied by the sick serial killer who left his victim at Stonehenge. But you saw right through it. A lot faster than they thought you would."

"They?"

"They." He shrugged, as if to say, "Sorry, honey, that's all you're getting."

"Back up and start from the beginning. I may put this all together, but it'll be so much easier if you just tell me. Show me some mercy. I deserve it."

The bartender returned with two large racks of glasses, the loud clinks when he set them on the counter punctuating his return.

DeSantos looked at his food, then lifted the two plates. "Take my beer. We're going to your room. We can't talk about this here."

THEY SAT AT THE DESK, chomping on their burgers as DeSantos mulled the best way of reading her into the mission.

"You've stalled long enough."

"This isn't easy."

"If you're expecting sympathy, you're going to be waiting at least a year."

"Fair enough." He wiped his mouth with a napkin. "So they stole the identities of the MI5 and MI6 agents. I told you that. It presented a huge problem because Rudenko was here in the UK—and so were the chemical weapons."

"So they brought you in. For what? To get close to Paxton?"

"First to verify that he was Rudenko. They only had suspicions that Paxton was Rudenko. Strong suspicions—MI5 believes he's their man. But Six disagrees. CIA couldn't reach a consensus. So we used you to get me close to Paxton."

"Used me?"

"Yeah. Kind of literally, I'm afraid." As DeSantos took a swig of beer, he must have noticed Vail's expression because he swallowed quickly. "This is not the time for you to get angry, Karen. Because if you do, we're never gonna get anywhere. Can we stipulate to the fact that you're going to be upset, that you'd like to throw something through a window—"

"Or someone."

"Right. Or someone."

"Fine. Let's stipulate to that."

DeSantos nodded. "So we're not going to get caught up in who did what to whom, and how you're gonna get revenge."

"I didn't say that. But go on—don't let me stop you."

DeSantos took another drink. "First, this was not my idea. I want to get that on the table to begin with."

"Got it. Stipulations and disclaimers are disposed of. The witness will proceed."

He continued: "The Shakespeare manuscript is a fake. The whole thing with Amelia Bassano Lanier is true, and that guy—what's his name, Hudson?—he's done all the research, he's legit. But the manuscript that was found, that's bogus. A forger working for MI6 put it together. They felt that having concrete proof would blow everyone out of the water."

"Speaking of blowing things up, the bombing at Turner's—"

"Staged, all to deflect attention."

"They blew apart a room, destroyed artwork, and brought me to London all to create a diversion?"

DeSantos grinned. "Exactly. Now you're getting it."

"*You're* gonna get it in a minute. I really *was* used."

"Like I said, I'm just the messenger. And you know the saying. You're not supposed to blame the messenger."

"No. You're supposed to kill him."

"I don't think that's how the saying goes."

"Move on."

"Right. So the plan was to have this groundbreaking manuscript 'discovered,' get the public whipped into a frenzy over the stripping of a British icon, and then bam!—a bomb tries to destroy it, giving the story new life and stirring things up again."

"And they bring me in, why?"

DeSantos squinted, as if it was plainly obvious. "Because you're high profile, and with you on the case, it lends a global reach to it. And because you're a shit disturber. They knew you'd work the case aggressively, turning over rocks and—"

"Bringing even more attention to it."

"Right again. And thanks to all the attention from movies and TV shows, you profilers are like rock stars."

"Go on."

"More importantly, you being on the case would give me an excuse to be there. We know each other, we're friends, and I get close to Gavin Paxton, first to assess, and then to...find out where he's got the chemical weapons. Rudenko doesn't freak and disappear into the wind. We get the ricin and stuff, no one knows anything about anything—except for a bombing intended to destroy a controversial Shakespearean manuscript—and there's no panic. And there's no terrorist attack."

"So that Embankment Underground station bombing was unrelated. Opportunistic."

"Yes, ma'am."

"So who set the bomb that blew up Turner's gallery?"

DeSantos reached for his beer—but Vail grabbed his wrist.

"Look, I'm risking a lot telling you what I'm telling you. You wanted trust? I'm trusting you with everything here—my career, potentially my life. Don't make me sorry."

Vail released her grip on his arm. "So am I supposed to assume that whoever did the bombing and cooked up this plot is also the one who had me kidnapped?"

"Put two and two together. You were getting too close, zeroing in on Paxton. They didn't believe you'd make a connection between the bombing and Paxton, because there wasn't any. But what they didn't figure on is your sixth sense in sniffing out offenders. You zeroed in the guy, but for the wrong reasons."

"So they had to stop me."

"They warned me to rein you in or they'd take matters in their own hands. I tried to warn you off, at lunch. I told you to stay away from Paxton."

"Don't you know that telling me 'no,' or not to do something, is like waving a red flag in my face?"

"What am I supposed to do, tell you, 'Go for it'?"

"At that point, there's nothing you can do. Best not to bring me into a case like this to begin with, I guess. Actually, I have no problem with working a case like this—as long as you read me into it fully, not use me like a dirty rag."

"I told them that. But I don't get paid the big bucks to make those decisions."

Vail leaned back. "Big bucks. Knox was in on this?"

DeSantos flung both hands up. "Whoa. I didn't say that."

"Son of a bitch." She thought a moment, then said, "Am I right?"

"Kinda sorta. Not really."

"What the hell does that mean?"

"It means I can't tell you one way or the other. But this isn't as simple as you think it is."

"I don't think it's simple at all."

DeSantos sighed. "Karen. This is a black op. Total deniability. I get caught, I'm not working for the CIA or the Department of Defense—I'm not working for the US government. And I sure as hell ain't working for the British government."

"Why was I kidnapped?"

"They thought the Stonehenge murder would slow you down enough for me to complete my mission. It didn't. You were on your way to question Paxton, and they freaked. The dungeon op was probably thrown together at the last minute. The idea, I'm sure, was to scare the shit out of you. So much so that you'd be on the next plane out of Heathrow back to DC, to kiss your son and hug your boyfriend."

"Do you see me on the next plane?"

"I didn't say that was my plan, I said it was theirs. I know that Karen Vail doesn't run from things. But the British don't really listen to me. I tell them shit, they say, 'Thank-you very much. Very helpful.' But in fact, they're really saying, 'Get out of our way, you stupid asshole.'"

Vail sat there, fighting anger, trying to sort it out. "So now what?"

"Now you know why it's imperative that you leave Paxton alone. Hands off—completely."

"I can't see any reason for me to stay in England."

"Wrong," DeSantos said. "If you leave now, Rudenko may sense that something's up. That's why they didn't want to have the Legat pull you out. They were afraid it'd spook him. But they were out of options, so they fed the Legat some bullshit story without exposing my op. Apparently, that didn't work, either."

"Montero did text me," she said. "He wanted me to report to him immediately. I thought it was because I was ignoring his phone calls."

"They finally realized that you're like a pit bull locked onto a piece of meat. You can't make him let go."

"Thanks for comparing me to a dog. A male dog, at that." She shook her head. "So now what?"

"You have to 'carry on,' as they say in the UK."

"No."

"No? Karen, consider what's at stake. Put your ego aside and look at the objectives of this mission."

"I feel used." She touched a bruise on her face. "And I definitely feel abused."

"They hurt your feelings, I get it. But this is bigger than you. It's bigger than me. Tens of thousands of lives are at stake. Shit, maybe hundreds of thousands. I don't know the number, but it's a lot. Does it really matter? Those people, innocent people, are counting on us to do our jobs to keep them safe."

Vail sighed deeply. "Of course I'll stay. You knew that. You knew I couldn't say no."

"And you'll stay away from Paxton."

"How about this: since you're already using me, why not use me to the fullest? I can get stuff from him."

DeSantos hesitated. "You're an awesome profiler. But undercover work—no, check that—*dangerous* undercover work…I don't know."

"Hang on a second. How is it that you've known so much about my investigation?" Vail rose from her chair. "Damnit, you have someone on the inside. Hector, look at me." He made eye contact. "Clive Reid."

"Working with you is very difficult for me, Karen."

"You run me in circles and you say that *I'm* difficult to work with?"

"I find it hard to say no to you. I find it even harder to lie to you. Regarding Inspector Reid, let's just say that I can't confirm or deny."

*That's confirmation enough for me.* "So I have an answer to my own question of what we should do now."

"I'm not sure I want to hear it."

"We should have a look around Paxton's flat."

DeSantos chuckled. "Thanks, but it's too risky. He could have watchers, if not surveillance cameras inside his apartment. We did what we could to poke around, but it wasn't anything exciting—or effective. We even went into his neighbor's and drilled through the wall and used fiber optics to get a look inside, but because it's an old building with plaster walls, we were limited in what we could do. Looked like he had a couple of cameras, but it was impossible to be sure."

"So we pose as gas company inspectors—or whatever they have here. And we cut his power in case he has cameras."

DeSantos tilted his head and considered her idea. "Could work."

"Do you have people who can do that?"

"I'll take care of it."

"Anyone we need to worry about?"

"He's got a place in Soho, central London. Lives alone, no dogs."

"We should have Reid confirm that Paxton's at the gallery so he doesn't walk in on us. Or you could go to the gallery and talk Paxton up about that Fregosi painting some more."

DeSantos's face broadened with a wide grain. "That was good, wasn't it?"

"I didn't think you knew anything about art history."

"I didn't. I studied for like three days to be able to pull that off."

"You sold it well. So what about my plan?"

DeSantos drained his beer, then set the empty on the desk. "Still risky, but I don't have anything better. You and I will go in. Reid will keep Paxton busy." He stopped, then said, "I just confirmed Reid's my guy, didn't I?"

She grinned. "Already figured it out."

"Of course you did."

"I thought we first have to confirm that Paxton's Rudenko."

DeSantos slipped on his leather jacket. "Already done. I got a DNA sample when I shook hands with him. I had a special coating on the palm of my hand. The lab analyzed it and compared it to a DNA exemplar we had from Rudenko's younger sibling who was killed in an explosion when MI6 raided one of his weapons storage warehouses. We got a 76 percent match."

"Good. Then tomorrow."

DeSantos pulled a Manchester United baseball cap onto his head. "Tomorrow." He reached forward and gave her a hug. "Remember, you've got my word. And I've got your back."

# 24

Vail feared that she would either lie awake all night—what was left of it—or awaken with terrifying dreams of being imprisoned in the iron cage. She took a Valerian root capsule, hoping it would prevent both, and a short time later fell into a deep sleep. When her alarm rang five hours later, she swung her legs out of bed and felt surprisingly decent.

Later that morning, she met DeSantos a few blocks from Rudenko's apartment. DeSantos had surveilled the building, secured a couple of baby blue British Gas windbreakers, and worked out a plan with Reid.

Owing to the way the building was wired, they had decided against shutting down the electricity because two entire floors would have lost power, which would invite calls to the utility. At the very least, it would attract attention and, if Rudenko found out, it would raise his suspicion.

DeSantos explained that he could enter the flat and remain in the hallway, which was blocked from the view of every room except the kitchen. Before exposing himself, he would use a fiber optic snake to take a good look around the apartment's interior to check for surveillance cameras.

Reid's text message arrived a few minutes before noon indicating they were clear to enter the flat.

Vail and DeSantos had already begun their charade, starting at the apartment several units down from Rudenko's, knocking until they found a renter at home. They went through their spiel of looking for the cause of a gas leak, but once they received Reid's signal, they moved directly to Rudenko's unit. DeSantos picked the lock with efficient ease; an onlooker might think he had a key.

They were careful to avoid any potential issues and made sure no one had eyes on their activities.

DeSantos entered while Vail stood watch out front. Although Rudenko lived alone, there was no stopping an accomplice from coming by. She stood three doors away, down the hall, pretending to take notes on her clipboard.

INSIDE, AFTER CLEARING THE FLAT with the fiber optic kit and finding no cameras, DeSantos searched in a grid-like pattern, taking everything in, absorbing it for future reference. The place was well appointed, with sculptures and paintings that either belonged in Turner's gallery or had once been on sale there. There were two furnished bedrooms, but only one had a lived-in appearance.

He looked for anything that might disclose the location of the chemical weapons or provide indications of who Rudenko was liaising with in London. He was particularly interested in smartphones, tablets, laptops, desktops—anything that might store data he could access.

Problem was, he could not remove devices from the premises. Any investigation had to be done onsite, without leaving trace that he had been inside. Since they had almost zero usable intel on Rudenko's personality, there was no way of knowing if he was a detail person, the type who would notice items slightly out of place. They could not take the risk, so unless DeSantos had reason to suspect that an item could bear fruit, he would leave it untouched.

VAIL CASUALLY CHECKED HER WATCH and then continued to make notes. DeSantos had been in Rudenko's flat for nine minutes—an unusually long period of time given the circumstances. She texted him to hurry up; she was getting nervous standing there in the hall. The longer she remained there, the greater the chance she would look like she did not belong. While it did not seem like Paxton had watchers, the risk grew that someone, a vigilant neighbor or delivery person, would see her—and remember that she was there.

DeSantos responded that he was almost done, that he had found Rudenko's PC and was going to take a look through it.

As Vail was replacing her phone, it vibrated—Montero. Again. *Crap, not now.* She ignored the call, and as she shoved the handset into her pocket, her finger bumped up against the COFEE device she carried on her keychain. Developed by Microsoft, COFEE—short for Computer Online Forensic Evidence Extractor—was a tool kit on a USB thumb drive that she always had with her, alongside a tiny LED flashlight and her Behavioral Analysis Unit office key.

When plugged into a computer, the COFEE automatically downloaded data stored in that PC's temporary cache, or memory, that was lost when a system was powered down. She had forgotten she had the device with her, but the potential benefit was too great to pass up the opportunity.

Vail took the chance of knocking on the door of the flat. DeSantos answered and she told him to switch places with her. He started to object, but she grabbed his jacket collar and pulled him toward her.

"Just do it," she said. "I've got an idea."

He reluctantly took the clipboard and moved outside. Vail stepped in, found the computer, and inserted the drive into a USB port. Ten minutes later, DeSantos texted her:

**we have to get out. whats taking so long**

She wrote back:

**taking a coffee break. be out asap**

When the device had finished copying the temporary files, including Rudenko's internet history, she opened Windows Explorer and dragged as much of the data from the documents folder as she could fit onto the COFEE.

Vail pulled out the device and shoved it into her pocket. She had been at it for eighteen minutes and they had already pushed their luck well beyond reasonable boundaries. She gave one last look around the flat, then joined DeSantos in the hallway.

"Was it worth it?" he asked as they descended the floors in the elevator.

"Won't know till we can get the data to someone who can make sense of it."

The lift doors slid apart and DeSantos led the way out. "I think we know just the person."

# 25

The image of Supervisory Special Agent Aaron Uziel infused Vail with a sense of calm and warmth, even though he was 3,500 miles away. Based on DeSantos's expression, it was clear that Uzi had the same effect on him.

They were seated in the back of a cab, DeSantos having palmed the driver a £20 note as he told him he needed some privacy for ten minutes. The driver smiled slyly—an attractive couple wanting to be alone in the backseat of his taxi conjured only one image for him.

But DeSantos and Vail had something else planned.

DeSantos held his Nokia between them, and the Skype connection was clear and stable.

"Santa," Uzi said. "Long time no see—gotta be, what, five days?"

DeSantos tilted his phone a few degrees and caught the edge of Vail's cheek.

"Hang on a minute—I know that red hair. Karen?"

Vail moved DeSantos's hand to get a more flattering angle on her face.

"Good to see you, Uzi. You have a minute?"

Uzi tilted his head. "I have to say it looks strange seeing you two shoulder to shoulder."

"It's a bit of a story," Vail said. "Let's just say it wasn't my idea."

DeSantos chuckled. "Wasn't mine, either."

Vail leaned back and gave DeSantos a look. *By the end of this mission I may actually figure out who's responsible for getting me into this mess.*

"So how's England?"

Vail didn't quite know how to respond. "Let's just say it's been a blast, and leave it at that."

"We've got this thing we need you to analyze," DeSantos said.

"I'm generally good at analyzing 'things,' but can you be a little more specific?"

"COFEE," Vail said. "Ever hear of it?"

"I assume you don't mean the drink."

Vail smirked. "It's a USB device that's used for—"

"Capturing all the data stored in a computer's cache, encrypted passwords, all that fun stuff."

"Exactly."

"We've got one, and we need the data from it ASAP. Can I upload it somewhere and you can look it over?"

"Won't work, Santa. I need the drive. Some data's hidden."

"Even if we overnight it to you, you won't get it for three days."

"Bring it to the embassy," Uzi said. "If you're lucky, they'll get it on the next military transport and I'll be able to pick it up from Andrews tomorrow."

Vail gave DeSantos her BlackBerry. "See what you can do."

He handed over the Nokia, took her phone, and started dialing.

"Whose data are we looking at?" Uzi asked.

"Can't say over an open line. But put it this way—it's right up your alley, if you get my drift." Vail was certain that Uzi, head of the FBI's Joint Terrorism Task Force in Washington, understood clearly.

"Next time when you go off on a mission like that, give me a heads-up," Uzi said. "I can do things for you like I do for Santa—hook you up with all sorts of cool gadgets. We'd be able to communicate without worrying about eavesdroppers."

"I appreciate the offer, but there won't be another mission like this for me."

"Then I'd better deliver on this now, huh?"

"Hey, you owe me one."

Uzi grinned. "That I do. No worries—I'll get to work on it as soon as I have the flash drive in my hands."

Vail thanked him, hung up, and then turned to DeSantos, who was in the process of ending his own call.

"We're going to meet an embassy messenger. He'll get it over to RAF Mildenhall, the air force base. We keep a large military presence there. It'll be on the next flight out." DeSantos popped open his door and flagged the driver. "Grosvenor Square. Pronto."

The man looked at him.

"It means fast."

The driver's eyes moved from DeSantos to Vail, as if trying to determine what lascivious act this man and woman had done in the backseat of his cab while he was standing a block away.

Vail leaned forward. "What part of 'fast' don't you understand?"

# 26

Vail stood in front of the bronze statue of General Dwight Eisenhower as she waited for DeSantos. Eisenhower, portrayed in a military uniform with his hands on his hips in an authoritative pose, looked out from atop a tall cement pedestal.

Vail had decided not to accompany DeSantos to the embassy security booth, wanting to stay off the radar—and security cameras—of Jesus Montero, the FBI Legal Attaché who had taken such a liking to her on their first visit.

Montero had told her to keep in contact with him, something she had not done. She was surprised she had not received a more urgent message from him when she ignored his calls. Perhaps whoever had put the crunch on his balls when she was in his office had also told him to give her space.

*Unlikely. I'm not that fortunate.*

"You ready?" DeSantos asked, coming up behind her. He considered the sculpture for a second and then said, "Not a bad likeness."

"I'll make sure you're bronzed when you finally bite it."

DeSantos swung his gaze over to Vail. "You'd do that for me?"

"Don't tempt me. Or that day may come sooner than you'd like."

THEY WALKED TO THE NEAREST tube station and descended the escalator. DeSantos glanced around at the handful of passengers milling about, then said, "Are you ready for the next part of our mission?"

"*Our* mission?"

"Let's put it this way, Karen. You're still here. You now know the purpose for your visit to London was a crock. So you could've just gone home."

"I go home when my ASAC tells me to go home. Or the Legat. Not to mention that I haven't gotten my revenge yet on whoever put me in that dungeon."

"I'd be the last one to deny your quest for revenge. But are you ready for me to read you in on the next chapter?"

'You're reading me in?"

"We need to find a guy by the name of Vince Richter."

"And why do we need to do that?"

DeSantos stopped at the edge of the train platform and gave Vail a look. "How about we just say that he's got something to do with...our man?"

"So you're not really reading me in."

"It's need to—"

"Hector, this 'need to know' bullshit is starting to get under my skin."

"Starting?"

"Fine, it burrowed in when we were at Garfunkel's. And it's dug in deeper since then, like an itch that can't be scratched."

"Are you with me?"

Vail closed her eyes. She knew she should beg off this, call Gifford and tell him the entire case was a sham. *I'd leave feeling empty, used. But if we catch Hussein Rudenko and recover those chemical weapons...that'd be a major score.* "I'm in."

"Great. Next stop: Vince Richter's house."

THEY GOT OFF THE UNDERGROUND at Liverpool Street station and ascended to the drizzly, windy streets of East London.

"Which way?" Vail asked.

DeSantos chuckled. "I don't actually know where he lives. We've got a last known address, which I'm pretty sure won't still be good. If it ever was."

"So we just start knocking on doors?"

"Not exactly. Reid gave me a pub and a few names we could start with. We'll lay down some bread crumbs and see what it gets us."

As they walked along Brushfield Street, the rain picked up. DeSantos donned a baseball cap and pulled up the collar on his leather coat.

Lacking an umbrella and getting rained on, Vail asked, "Who is this guy we're looking for?"

"An assassin affiliated with the scumbag responsible for my partner's death."

Vail stopped. "Anthony Scarponi?"

DeSantos whipped his head around. "How do you know that?"

"After our first case together, I looked you up."

"Looked me up? Where? I'm not Google-able. Is that a word?"

"I asked around."

DeSantos nodded slowly. "Uzi."

Vail started walking again, passing the Spitalfields Market on the left. "Yeah. And I know a thing or two about Scarponi. When he was released from prison—"

"That's when Brian and I were brought in. And that's when he got killed. And that's when I made it part of my life's mission to exact revenge. Any other questions?"

"Just what Vince Richter has to do with all this. And what Hussein Rudenko has to do with Vince Richter." She said this in a low voice, though it did not matter; there was no one nearby.

"Reid said MI5 doesn't have a file on Richter, but they do on Scarponi. And there was a known associate whose initials were 'VR,' so I'm hoping they're one in the same. Scarponi had a base of operations for a couple of years in this neighborhood."

"Wait, didn't you mean Scotland Yard has a file on Scarponi?"

"MI5."

"But Reid's with the Met, not the Security Service."

DeSantos crossed Commercial Street but did not reply.

"Hector, answer me."

He stopped on the corner, outside an aged pub sporting rose granite columns. He snagged a look at the sign above him, and pulled the brass handle to open the door. He stepped up to the bar and ordered two real ales.

"I don't want a beer," Vail said.

"Yes, you do. When in Rome…"

"But we're in London."

DeSantos looked at her. "Beer in England dates back to about 100 AD, when Roman soldiers in England relied on Celtic ale to sustain them."

*Oh.* "I still don't want a beer. I need to keep my head clear."

The bartender filled two glasses from a traditional hand-pull, set them on the counter in front of them, and then moved aside to wipe down the counter.

"Take it, Karen," DeSantos said in a low voice. "Drink it."

She took a taste and drew her mouth back. "It's not cold."

"Real ale is cask-conditioned beer, made right here. It's served cool. Not cold, not warm. Tastes good, don't you think? Much better than those processed commercial abominations most people call beer."

Vail held up the glass and examined it against the light. "It is."

DeSantos settled himself on his stool, his back to the bartender, and said, "Anyway, like I was saying before, that wasn't Richard, it was *Vince*." He winked at her.

It took her a second to process DeSantos's intentions. "It wasn't Vince. I specifically remember Richard pulling out his…his big thing and waving it at all the women."

The bartender glanced over at them, listening but trying to appear busy with some other task.

DeSantos cringed, as if to say, "Really? That's the best you could come up with?" Instead, he laughed loud and long. "I remember that too. And I'm telling you, it was Vince. Vince was circumcised. Remember now?"

*Okay, this is my fault. I started us down this path.* "I know a circumcised penis when I see one. And this definitely was not one of 'em."

DeSantos took a long drag from his beer, then pulled open his zipper. "Well, have a look, and you'll see what I'm talking about."

"Whoa," Vail said, jumping off her stool, "what the hell are you doing?"

The bartender came closer. "You two okay?"

"We're fine," DeSantos said, zipping up his pants. "I just—Hey, maybe you can help. Used to be a guy lived around here. Vince. We were buddies with him, partied a lot, but we lost touch a few years ago."

"Don't know a Vince."

"Yeah," DeSantos said, drawing it out, as if he *had* to know the man. "Vince. Vince Richter."

The bartender's face went slack and his eyes widened. "Haven't seen him for a while."

"Vince was like that," Vail said. "In and out of our lives. But we always somehow found each other again. Still owe him some money for a job. A lot of money, come to think of it." She turned to DeSantos. "You remember which one—"

"Hey—quiet. Yeah, I remember." He threw a cautious look at the bartender, then shook his head at Vail before turning back to the man. "Know where we can find him? Anyone who might've seen him lately?"

The bartender busied himself with wiping his hands on a wet rag. "Maybe."

DeSantos deftly placed two £50 notes on the counter. "How about now?"

The man's eyes canted down toward the bills. He palmed them and slipped them into his pocket. "I'll make a call."

DeSantos lifted his ale in a gesture of thanks, then took a pull from it. A few moments later, the man hung up the wall phone and faced them. "Go out, make a left, go one block, turn left on Wilkes. It's a narrow road. Go halfway down and you'll see an alley. Wait right there. Jack'll be on about four."

Vail checked her watch: they had fifteen minutes. They left the pub and followed his instructions, but instead of turning down Wilkes, DeSantos kept walking.

"You're not taking any chances," Vail said.

"This guy is an assassin, Karen. If Vince is 'Jack,' or if Jack's a friend of his, we could be walking into a trap. I want to make sure there's only one of him when we get near."

The rain had stopped, but the charcoal gray miasma was rapidly turning into darkness.

"It gets dark so early in England in the winter," Vail said. "Really shortens the day."

DeSantos did not reply; he was scanning the area, no doubt searching the shadows for nefarious types who could be accomplices of Richter.

They circled back. It was now straight up four o'clock, and DeSantos felt it was safe enough to walk down Wilkes. "Wait here, let me take a look-see."

"Shouldn't I come with you?"

"All eggs in one basket? Nope. Keep your back against the building and your eyes moving."

He proceeded down the narrow street, his footsteps crunching the wet, dirty pavement. She watched as he slowed by the opening to the alley.

"Jack?" he asked as he walked.

Nothing.

He checked in on Vail, then continued on to the end of the block. He gave a look around, turned and headed back.

Ten minutes passed, then another five. Finally DeSantos joined Vail and they returned to the pub. Inside, a different bartender was polishing the glasses.

"The other guy," Vail said. "The one with the beard. He around?"

"Went home. Quits at four."

DeSantos said, "I haven't been in the UK for a few years. I'm looking for a couple of old buddies. Harlan Landley and Pete Aynsley. Seen 'em around?"

"Harlan comes in once a month or so. When, I'm not sure. He just kinda pops in. Pete, haven't seen him in a while. Who should I say is askin'?"

"Rick Trainor." DeSantos pulled over a bar napkin and wrote down a phone number. He slid it over with a £20 bill.

"I'll make some calls." They ordered another couple of ales while the bartender pulled out a cell phone, walked to the end of the bar, and dialed.

"Rick Trainor?" Vail asked.

"One of my cover names. You don't like it?"

"Not sure it fits. Hector Cruz has more style."

"Yeah," he said with a chuckle, "I'm kind of fond of that one, too."

A moment later, the bartender told them he was expecting a return call from one of Landley's friends. Twenty minutes passed before his phone rang.

"No luck," the barman said.

They thanked him and left, headed for the Underground station.

"Well," Vail said. "That was a waste."

DeSantos jerked on her elbow. "Hang on a second." He swung his head left and right, searching for something.

"I know that look. If I had my Glock, I'd have pulled it by now. What do you see?"

DeSantos, keeping hold of Vail's arm, pulled her forward, toward the bright mouth of the tube station. "We're being followed. Keep going, I think we can get inside before they do—and then we can lose them in the maze."

They entered, swiped their Oyster cards, and hung an immediate right down the escalator. They pushed a few patrons aside, weaving their way to the bottom—but the two men DeSantos had seen were keeping up with them, now only thirty feet away.

"Those the guys?" Vail asked. "Gray sweatshirt and black windbreaker?"

"That's them."

They turned left down a narrow tiled hallway, past a tube route map showing the local stops on the line, then right through a short corridor and onto the platform. A train was waiting with its doors open.

"In here," Vail said, pulling DeSantos into the car and then down, below the padded seats.

A second later, the train started moving, the pull of inertia sending them sprawling backward. They steadied themselves, waited until they cleared the station, and then got up onto the plush, thickly padded seats.

"Anything?" she asked, looking over his right shoulder while he peered over her left.

"Nothing. Yet."

An emaciated woman wearing leather pants and a silver ring through her nose had an iPod in her hands and headphones over her ears. She glanced up at them, didn't see anything worth watching, and refocused her attention on the music player.

Once Vail felt confident their pursuers were not on the train, she leaned back in relief. "So what the hell was that back there?"

"Can't be sure," DeSantos said, his glance still sweeping the car from left to right, clearly not as convinced as Vail that they were out of danger. "Asking for those guys certainly triggered a response, though."

"Reid gave you those names."

Keeping his head moving in all directions and not bothering to make eye contact, DeSantos said, "Yeah."

They changed trains twice onto different lines and finally arrived at Charing Cross.

"How do we know that Reid didn't set us up?"

DeSantos rose from his seat, eyes once again working the landscape. "We don't."

THEY EMERGED FROM THE STATION at York Place, past the orange and white striped tiled walls that lined the staircase. There were considerably more people in this area of London—commuters and tourists were buzzing about.

As they turned left around a high stack of bundled *West End Final* newspapers, Vail gestured at the Bistro restaurant off to her left. "We've gotta eat. How about Café Rouge? Or is it safer in the hotel restaurant?"

"Honestly, safest place may be your room. Controlled area."

"All these great restaurants in London and I get meals locked away in my hotel."

"Tell you what. Go get take away in Café Rouge and I'll stand watch."

"Take-away?"

"That's what they call takeout. You've gotta get with the program, Karen."

Vail walked into the red-faced brick building and found the hostess. "I need to order take away."

"Right then. Do you know what you want?"

*Matter of fact, I do. But it's got nothing to do with ordering takeout on the run from assassins.*

TEN MINUTES LATER, Vail walked out of the restaurant with a bag dangling from her right hand. DeSantos was standing across Villiers Street with a panoramic view of the immediate vicinity: one of the tube's exits, the Café Rouge entrance, and a couple of T-shirt and news vendors.

DeSantos walked with her up the steps onto a plaza that led to both the main entrance of Charing Cross station and her hotel.

"Smells good," he said as they passed through the main doors.

"That's probably the Poulet Breton."

"Not sure what that is, but I hope it's for you."

"Yes, that's mine. Chicken, mushrooms, leeks and courgettes, with mash. I think. And don't ask me what courgettes are."

"And for me?"

"Rump steak, aged thirty-five days and less than six hundred calories."

Bypassing the elevator, they took the wide, circular staircase up to Vail's floor.

"You got me something called 'rump steak,' and you're watching my calories? Are you sending me a message?"

"Just looking out for your health. Consider it my way of repaying you for gathering me up in Oxford." As they walked down the hall, Vail pulled out her key and said, "Did I tell you Jack the Ripper stayed in my room?"

"How fitting. Must have a killer view."

Vail chuckled. "Very good."

He pointed at the room privacy card she had hanging from her door. "Someone inside that you don't want me to know about?"

"I wish it were Robby. But no, nothing so romantic. I clean my house once a week, why do I need my hotel room cleaned every day? I don't like my stuff disturbed." She swiped her card and pushed open the door.

They walked in, and just as they cleared the threshold, Vail stopped.

A shadow—on the far wall, created by something standing in front of the lamp she had left on by her bedside. The dark form moved slightly, and DeSantos felt Vail's body stiffen. He shuffled her behind him.

They stood there, waiting.

They didn't have to wait long.

As DeSantos motioned to her to back out of the room, a man came in from the hallway and grabbed Vail from behind.

The shadow DeSantos had seen on the wall morphed into a thick Russian-looking thug—holding a knife. He lunged at DeSantos, who blocked the man's arm, then grabbed his wrist and yanked down, all in one motion. As the knife dropped to the carpet, DeSantos landed a cross to the intruder's cheek.

But in that split second, when the sting of the impact registered in DeSantos's brain, he realized that the blow caused him more pain than it did his adversary.

The attacker grabbed DeSantos's throat, but DeSantos slammed his thumb web into his assailant's trachea, temporarily stunning him. He instantly released his hold.

DeSantos jabbed his neck again, fast and hard, with the intent to kill.

The man's windpipe collapsed and he dropped to his knees, gasping for air that would never come.

THE ACCOMPLICE DRAGGED VAIL backward out of the room and into the hallway. His elbow was pressed firmly against her neck, the blood flow to her carotids slowing. As the oxygen evacuated from her brain, she came to the point of losing consciousness.

*Do something. Now, before it's too late!*

Vail tightened her abdomen and lifted her legs, throwing off the balance of the man dragging her. She slammed her feet against the ground and started walking backward, propelling both of them in an out-of-control lunge to the floor.

He stumbled and fell, pulling her to the carpet with him. She swung her elbows to keep him from getting hold of her again, then rolled and slipped out of his grasp.

*Get away—down the hall—*

She scrabbled to her feet and started forward in a frantic out-of-balance stumble. She heard her attacker growl in anger as he pursued her.

The first door she came to was partially open, and she shouldered it on the run.

But it was a vacant banquet room, with no other exit. She grabbed for the door handle and ran back out, the man only a dozen feet away.

Ahead: more corridor, with a hook to the left. She legged it along the carpet, grateful she was wearing low-heeled boots, hoping someone would appear and scare off her shadow. Then again, a guy like this did not break pursuit; he was the kind who broke the neck of anyone who got in his way—and then finished off his job.

Vail's only hope was to put distance between her and him.

She passed more unoccupied rooms, swung left and then made a quick right through double-windowed doors: a catering kitchen that served the banquet halls.

*Knives. Where the hell are the knives? Who ever heard of a kitchen without knives?*

She threw ladling spoons, pots, pans—anything in her way—across the floor behind her, looking for a sharp weapon of some sort.

And then she froze. The man had entered the kitchen behind her. She turned and faced him. He had a square, firm jaw and narrowed eyes. His hands flexed, no doubt in anticipation of wrapping them around her neck.

"What do you want?" she yelled at him.

He took a step forward. "I will make it so it doesn't hurt," he said with a Chechen accent, his tone steely, fateful.

Vail backed away, moving along the stainless steel trough used to rinse dishes, her right hand dragging along the countertop, near the grill. She touched something cold and grabbed it: a serving spoon. She brought it up and held it out in front of her.

He grinned, not because it was funny but because she would think such a silly weapon had shifted the odds in her favor.

He took another step forward—and stopped, his body going suddenly rigid. His eyes widened and his mouth dropped open. And then he fell forward.

Behind him, DeSantos. And in the man's back, a long, wood knife handle protruded, a circle of blood staining his jacket.

"Saving your ass is getting to be a habit," he said as he reached inside the man's back pocket and removed his wallet.

Vail threw the spoon atop the deceased assassin. And gave him a kick in the skull for good measure.

"He's dead, Karen."

"I know that." She brushed her red hair off her face. "Made me feel better." As she walked past him, she whaled on him again, this time in the ribs. "Definitely makes me feel better. Bastard."

DeSantos removed the pertinent information from the wallet, rubbed it against his pant leg to remove his fingerprints, and then, holding it by its edges, tossed it in a nearby sauce pot. "We need to get your stuff and get out of here. No idea how many others are involved."

"Involved in what? Who's pulling the strings?"

"Don't know that either. C'mon, let's get moving. We'll have time to debate what all this means. But right now, our forensics are all over two murder scenes. Oh yeah, there's a dead guy in your room."

"You just left him there?"

"I thought it was more important to find you."

"You thought right."

"Look at it this way," he said. "We just found another use for that room privacy card."

# 27

After wiping down the room for trace evidence of the man and the scuffle he had gotten into with DeSantos, Vail threw her belongings into a suitcase while DeSantos searched the assailant and took his cash and identification.

Next, they moved the body down the hall into the ice room and propped him against the Coke machine in a seated position. DeSantos opened the top few buttons of his shirt, then splashed the man's face with a few ounces of Gordon's London Dry Gin, which they had taken from the mini bar. Vail set the empty bottle in his right hand and messed his hair.

The hope was that he would look like a passed-out drunk and not be reported until the maids started their morning rounds.

It was an imperfect plan. When the cops started their investigation, they might trace the gin to the missing Gordon's from Vail's room, since those purchases are closely monitored. It would take a sharp inspector and some luck. But it was worth the risk if it fooled a guest or two and deterred them from reporting a dead man in the ice room.

They walked a few blocks, turned west for another tenth of a mile, and then caught a cab. Vail made a point of asking for a hotel recommendation in the area, and the man suggested a couple of places. They chose the

Thistle Victoria, and he dropped them off ten minutes later. DeSantos paid the driver with the cash he had appropriated from his second victim, and they got out across the street from Victoria Station.

Vail waved off the bellman before he could get a grip on her suitcase because she knew that they would not be staying at this accommodation. They moved toward the registration desk, then turned and made their way into the adjacent train depot.

Victoria Station was a major UK transportation hub, being the second busiest center of passage for the Underground, the Gatwick Express train, and various coach lines. It was an ideal place for Vail and DeSantos to slip away to an undetermined, and hopefully untrackable, location. However, the cavernous facility, two stories with restaurants, shops, and vendors of various sorts, did not provide much cover from the ubiquitous closed-circuit cameras that permeated the London landscape.

Hundreds of commuters scurried in all directions, the buzz of conversations, rolling suitcases, and public address announcements coalescing into a white noise common to large transportation venues across the world.

Enormous LCD screens, suspended over the main floor, displayed various bits of information, from travel itineraries to station vendor locations.

Vail burned some of their arrogated cash on a knit wool cap to hide her thick red hair, and a baggy "I Love London" sweatshirt to conceal her figure. DeSantos selected a new baseball hat and a muffler. Though hardly a complete disguise, the two items masked his appearance to some extent. He added a T-shirt and a hoodie, since, unlike Vail, he did not have a change of clothes. He would have to buy underwear and other essentials the next morning, if they had time.

They took the Underground a few stops to Piccadilly Circus and booked themselves into the Savoy Hotel, a ritzy landmark that DeSantos charged to Rick Trainor's Mastercard.

"We're nearly full, Mr. Trainor," the registration clerk said. "We have only a regular room, no suites. King bed. Will that suit your purposes?"

"That'll suit us just fine," Vail said as she took DeSantos's elbow in her hands, trying to like any married couple.

The clerk swiped the room keys, then handed them the welcome packet.

As they made their way to the elevator, Vail said, "So who pays Rick Trainor's credit card bills? This place is several hundred a night."

"You and me," he said. When she tilted her head in confusion, he said, "US taxpayers. OPSIG's budget is black, just like our ops."

"So this is an OPSIG operation?"

DeSantos looked at her.

"Fine. You can't tell me."

They made their way to the room, exhibiting extreme care despite the fact that no one had known they were headed here. The room was clear and they tossed their purchases on a chair beside the bed.

"You're looking forward to this," she said.

"Let me see. I'm in London at a luxury hotel and I get to sleep with a beautiful woman. What red-blooded heterosexual male would not look forward to that?"

Instead of accepting the compliment, she said, "There is an imaginary dividing line in this mattress. Cross it, even to play footsie, and I will do some undesirable things to your balls."

"Karen, I'm disappointed. After all we've been through, do you really think I'd try to take advantage of you?"

"I think that men sometimes listen to the heads below their waist rather than the ones above their shoulders."

DeSantos pursed his lips. "Fair enough. Can't argue with that one. But I would never disrespect you that way."

They managed to get several hours of shuteye without incident before Vail's BlackBerry rang. Without opening her eyes, she felt around for the night table—and instead got DeSantos's shoulder. He picked up the phone and answered it.

"Hey," she said, hitting his shoulder intentionally—and more forcefully—this time.

He feigned pain and shielded his face. "It's Uzi." Into the phone, he said, "Yeah, she's lying in bed right next to me...Yeah, imagine that. I bedded Karen Vail...I know, right?"

Vail plunked him on the head and he handed her the phone.

"Don't listen to him, Uzi."

"I never do. So I've got your COFEE order. Black, with a hint of deception."

Vail groaned. "It's too early in the morning for humor."

"Even good humor?"

"*Good* humor may be okay. But I didn't hear any."

"After working my ass off to get this stuff decrypted and analyzed, you'd think you would show me some love."

"That's what Hector was hoping for last night."

Uzi chuckled. "Okay, so here's what I've got. You pulled some pretty good stuff off our subject's hard drive. I even captured a few of his passwords. There's no smoking gun, but your suspicions about him appear to be right on target. I've been read into the situation by the director."

"You got Knox involved?"

"Turns out he already was. Even if he wasn't, I had no choice. There was something very upsetting in the data. I can't go into it over an unsecure connection. But it's huge and affects us here in DC."

Knowing who their subject was, this was not good news.

"Problem is, you didn't get it all. You need to go back, get the rest of the data."

"Go back there." Vail laughed. "You're joking, right?"

"I tried the joke at the beginning of our conversation. You didn't like it, remember? Right now, I'm dead serious."

"We're going to need details, so we know what we're looking for."

"Can you get a Sat phone?"

"Right now, we're in the shit. We've got assassins after us, and our DNA is all over two crime scenes."

"See, I leave you two alone for a day and look what happens."

"You're trying to be funny again."

"Trying."

"It's not a good time."

"Okay, look. I'll figure something out. You just get over to our guy's place and we'll go from there. But we need that information."

"I'll get back to you."

She rolled out of bed and started getting her things together.

"What's the deal?"

"Back to Paxton's place. Looks like we're right about him. Problem is, there's apparently some stuff we snagged off his hard drive that's incomplete. And it appears to be very important to Washington. Knox is involved."

DeSantos absorbed it in stride, then pulled out his phone. "Let me get with Reid and see if he's got eyes on Paxton. Get your stuff together but only take what's essential. I assume we're coming back here, but there's no way to know."

THEY TOOK THE TUBE to Paxton's apartment building, prepared to enter without their utility company uniforms—or weapons to defend themselves.

"It doesn't take a black ops specialist to know that this is going to be a lot more risky than last time."

"Last time was a piece of cake," DeSantos said as they stood across the street surveilling the area.

"Didn't feel like a piece of cake."

"It will. Compared to now."

*Lovely.*

DeSantos's Nokia vibrated and he checked the display. "Reid's got Paxton. He's in the gallery. We're good to go."

They entered the building and took the stairs to Paxton's apartment. DeSantos waited down the hall while Vail went to the door and knocked. If no one answered, DeSantos would pick the lock and enter while she maintained watch. If someone was there, she would ask to use the phone because of an emergency, get a look around, and assess how many individuals were present. It was less threatening for a woman to ask for entry than a man. Plus, if she ran into difficulties once inside, DeSantos would be in a position to respond.

Vail rapped on the door, listened, and waited. Nothing. She waited thirty seconds, then knocked again. So far so good. She figured it would be best to wait five minutes and try again, in case someone was in the shower and didn't hear her.

She texted DeSantos:

waiting a few min 2b sure

DeSantos noted his smartphone's display and held up a hand in acknowledgment.

Vail banged again, but not hard enough to raise the neighbors' curiosity. After failing to get a response, she motioned to DeSantos, who joined her in front of the door. Seconds later, he had deftly picked the locks.

DESANTOS ENTERED THE APARTMENT, Vail remaining outside as a lookout.

He removed the knife and checked each room, confirming his intel that Rudenko had no roommate.

Seeing nothing that would suggest the imminent arrival of an unwelcome guest, he took a seat at the computer desk, which sat across the room from two large windows that led onto a steel fire escape.

Lacking the means to have a secure conversation—a satellite phone would've attracted attention, and it would not have worked indoors very well—Uzi and DeSantos felt that purchasing disposable SIM cards for each of their cell phones was the best workaround.

A major consideration in communicating via voice was that it gave others the ability to track them. Over the years, DeSantos and his OPSIG team had dropped in on the conversations of more "bad actors" using their cell phones than anything else. Once they identified their target and matched it to his phone and SIM card, they could track him anywhere there were cell towers by bouncing a signal to that phone and then triangulating his position off the towers. To keep that from happening to him and Vail, they planned to switch out the SIM cards so that they couldn't be identified through their telephone handsets.

DeSantos set his knife beside the keyboard and settled himself in front of the screen. After dialing Uzi, he cradled the phone between his ear and shoulder.

"I'm here," DeSantos said, purposely leaving out details because, despite their precautions, it was not a secure line and anyone could be listening, even if they did not yet know who was speaking.

"Go to a command prompt," Uzi said. "Know how to do that?"

"Have you forgotten who you're talking to?"

"Go to the search field and type 'cmd.'" Uzi talked DeSantos through the next several steps, then told him he was ready to give him one of the passwords he had captured using the COFEE device. "He's using TrueCrypt, an excellent open source disk encryption program."

"Can't be that good if you grabbed the password."

"If time wasn't short," Uzi said, "I'd explain how I did it. Not that you'd be interested."

"You're right. Read me the password."

DeSantos typed in the long alphanumeric string, and then hit enter. A previously unseen drive letter appeared, along with a series of folders.

"Holy shit," DeSantos said as he read through the file names. But the first one was all he needed to see: *HD distilled sulfur mustard agent/Yankee Stadium.*

"I'm assuming we're in the right place," Uzi said.

*Yankee Stadium. Fifty thousand people.* "Oh, yeah. That's a fair statement."

"I've set up a SkyDrive account. You're going to upload those files, then we'll erase all traces of you having done what you're about to do."

"Fine. Whatever. Let's do this. I'm late." *Translation: I need to get the hell out of here.*

Minutes later the files were uploading to the cloud storage server somewhere in the world.

DeSantos checked his watch: he'd been in the apartment fourteen minutes. "Hey, man, I'm really, really late. How much more?"

"Another minute and you can start erasing things using the program you downloaded."

Leaving the line open to Uzi, DeSantos pulled the handset from his ear and texted Vail:

> almost done. hows it look

He tapped his finger on the desk while he waited for the last file to finish uploading.

"You're doing fine," Uzi said. "You're almost out."

Vail's text came back:

> quiet. how much longer? pushing ur luck

DeSantos glanced up and saw the status of the last file move from 99 to 100 percent.

VAIL HAD ORIGINALLY INTENDED to stand across the street from Rudenko's building, watching the front entrance. There was a fire exit in the rear, but to reach it Rudenko would have to walk down an alley to the right of the structure. Either way, Vail would see him.

But because Reid had an eyeball on him, it was impossible for Rudenko to mysteriously appear without a warning call, well in advance. Not so, however, for an accomplice.

Vail felt that the greatest benefit would be achieved by hanging out down the hall from Rudenko's flat and watching for anyone exiting the elevator. If he or she turned left, Vail could alert DeSantos and try to stall the individual while DeSantos sought shelter—or a way out.

She wore her cap and baggy sweatshirt—as good a disguise as she could muster—and slouched with her back against the wall. After consulting her watch for about the tenth time, her BlackBerry buzzed: DeSantos, wanting to know how things looked.

*How does it look? Not bad. But you're pushing your luck. How much longer?*

She typed out a reply, shoved the phone back in her pocket, and resumed her ritual of letting her eyes roam the hallway while listening for signs of activity.

A moment later, the elevator bell dinged. Her head swung right, as a splash of adrenaline flooded her bloodstream. She called DeSantos. He answered quickly.

"Elevator alert."

She kept the line open and watched as the doors slid open.

Hussein Rudenko and two other men stepped out.

"Oh shit. It's him," she whispered into the phone. "Three men. Repeat, three. Get out!"

DESANTOS CLOSED THE BROWSER and had launched the eraser program to remove all traces of his movements on the PC when his Nokia buzzed.

"Oh shit. It's him. Three men. Repeat, three. Get out!"

*Him—Rudenko? What about Reid—*

DeSantos disconnected both calls as he shoved the Nokia into his pocket. He moved toward the window—then ran back and turned off the monitor. The program was still running, erasing his digital fingerprint. But Rudenko would know that something had been done to the computer because DeSantos had installed that software, and it wasn't going to uninstall itself.

Key in the door, a click.

DeSantos ran back to the window, pulled it open an inch, and then slipped into the nearest bedroom.

VAIL BURIED HER CHIN against her chest.

Wanted on multiple continents, Rudenko had not survived this long in a dangerous business, striking deals with despots and drug lords, without being smart and cunning.

If Vail revealed herself, Rudenko would ask her what she was doing at his apartment. She had no good answer—at least, not one she could share with him. He would know they had discovered his true identity—and that would not end well for her and DeSantos. While they were not carrying handguns, an infamous arms dealer would almost certainly have something concealable on his person. It would not be much of a fight.

No. DeSantos would have to work this out himself. Hopefully she gave him enough notice to get out or find a place to hide.

# 28

DeSantos concealed himself behind the open bedroom door, eyes searching for a location where he could remain out of sight—or at least maintain a strategic advantage.

The modest room was nearly devoid of furniture: centered on the long wall stood a contemporary, high-gloss mahogany queen platform bed, which eliminated an obvious, though effective, hiding place, and a matching dresser. Nothing offered him a better vantage point than where he currently stood.

Voices chattered in the living room, where the computer desk sat. They were speaking Arabic, and from what DeSantos could tell, the conversation was casual, if not jovial.

*So far, so good.*

But then the man he guessed was Rudenko—based on his memory of Paxton's intonations from the time they met at the gallery—said something that raised the hairs on his neck. "Make sure they're well hidden. I don't want something stupid to trip us up. And make sure the driver doesn't run any red lights."

Had he been in the States, DeSantos would be equipped with sufficient weaponry to challenge Rudenko and his men. Even if it was only a handgun, it would increase his chances of a successful attack to "possible." But at this distance, against three men, and armed with only a knife, taking the offensive was not a winning strategy. Until he knew the extent of Rudenko's network and the location of the chemical weapons, he could not be as aggressive as he would otherwise be: he had to capture Rudenko, not kill him.

But perhaps there was another option.

DeSantos moved the door slowly and peered through the crack below the top hinge. Across the way was the bathroom.

DeSantos pictured the layout of the apartment: the hallway that led to the two bedrooms and bathroom stood perpendicular to another corridor that opened into the living room, where Rudenko and his men were huddled.

"بــك الخــاص الكمبيوتـــــر علــى الـذي الشــــيء هو ما" *What is this on your computer?*

One of Rudenko's men had noticed the program DeSantos left running. He had to act now.

DeSantos moved out from behind the door and took a box of tissues from atop the dresser. Holding it like a football, he tossed it into the tub; it hit and landed with a *thunk!* that was sure to arouse suspicion.

He threw his back up against the wall beside the open doorway. And listened.

"ذلـك تســـمع عمر،هل" *Umar, you hear that?*

"اذهب انظـر ،وليـــد" *Rudenko's voice: Waleed, go see.*

Then the third man: "الملفات،احـــــــذفها بعـض مسـحت" *It deleted some files, erased them.*

DeSantos heard footsteps approaching along the wood floor. He waited, pressed as flat as possible against the wall. A second later, the footsteps stopped.

He knew Waleed was looking in the bathroom and that his next place to check would be the bedroom.

When Waleed ducked his head in, DeSantos was ready. With lizard-like quickness, he fisted the man's hair in both hands and yanked him forward—eliciting intense pain—and then drove his knee into Waleed's face. His head snapped back, a stunned look in his eyes.

But DeSantos did not give him time to clear his jumbled thoughts or tighten his neck muscles. DeSantos slid his hands down to his ears and forcefully jerked the neck in rotary fashion, snapping the second cervical vertebra and effecting what special forces call "a silent death."

He pulled Waleed completely into the room and tossed him on the bed. DeSantos quickly patted down the man's limp body—and found a Tokarev 7.62 handgun.

He press-checked the chamber to be sure it was ready to fire.

If Rudenko's men were anything like the mercenaries he had encountered over the years, Umar would realize his comrade had gone quiet and he would come looking.

DeSantos moved to the doorway and waited. Listened. He heard nothing. Perhaps he had underestimated him. Seconds passed.

DeSantos wondered where Rudenko was—as well as where Vail was. Finally he could wait no longer. If Rudenko had left, he had to find him before he went into the wind.

He swung out into the hallway—and got a face full of boot. He fell backward and landed on the floor, the Tokarev flying from his hand and discharging a round.

Umar kicked away the handgun and pointed his own pistol at DeSantos.

VAIL HEARD THE GUNSHOT. She leaped to her feet and ran toward the apartment door. Tried the knob. Locked.

*Of course. Why should this be easy?*

She stepped back and with all her momentum, threw her right shoulder against the wood panel. It budged, rattled a bit on the frame—but that was about it. *Fuck.*

She did it again, and again—and got nowhere.

*It's loosening. Keep going.*

Was it? Didn't matter—she had to believe she was going to get in. DeSantos did not have a handgun, so the discharged round was not good news. *Damnit, I should've knocked right away; then they would've answered the door. How much of a threat would I have been?*

Three more blows had definitely done some damage—to her shoulder.

Vail shifted her weight and slammed her right foot into the jamb near the lock. It was a solid, square kick, and the wood splintered and finally gave. One more blast with her shoulder and she tumbled into the apartment.

It was at this point she usually leveled her Glock at the occupants and yelled, "Freeze, FBI!"

But she had no Glock.

She had no jurisdiction.

And she was going after assholes who didn't give a damn about those three famous letters.

Along the far wall, the window was open a couple of feet and the curtain billowed in the gentle breeze. *Rudenko.*

"Hector!" she said as she started into the living room.

"I'm fine. Go!"

DeSantos's voice, off to the right. He sounded like he was in distress, but she did as he suggested and headed for the window.

"WHO ARE YOU?" Umar said in British-accented English.

"A friend. I'm here to help. I've got a message for Mr. Rudenko."

Umar tilted his head.

*That's right, fuckhead, makes no sense. You have to figure this out.*

"Mr. Rudenko," DeSantos said, leaning right as if the man was standing behind Umar.

Umar turned his head to look—and that was all DeSantos needed. He swung his left leg in a sweeping motion and hooked his shoe behind Umar's knee and threw him off balance.

He scrambled to his feet and buried his head in Umar's stomach just as the man was turning back toward him. He swiveled his body as DeSantos made contact, minimizing the blow, and then grabbed DeSantos's shirt with his left hand. His right maintained a grip on the pistol, but DeSantos kept Umar's wrist pinned against his thigh, preventing him from raising it and pointing the weapon at him.

The two men wrestled in place to a standoff until DeSantos brought up his right leg and kneed him hard in the groin. Umar recoiled, and the pistol hit the wood floor with a clunk as DeSantos slammed his fist into Umar's nose. The blow stunned him. Umar's head snapped back and his body went limp. Blood spurted from his nose.

DeSantos didn't want to kill him—not yet—because he might have information they could use. And DeSantos did not know how integrated Umar was in Rudenko's network. He could be a valuable asset.

DeSantos spun him around and shoved him up against the wall, then kicked apart his legs. With his left foot, he corralled the Tokarev and brought it close. He bent down and took it in his hand, shoved it into the back of Umar's skull, and said, "Now. You're going to tell me everything that I want to know and I'll let you live. If you don't, I'll pull the trigger and splatter your brains all over the lovely white paint. Understand?"

Umar nodded.

"Good."


JUST OUTSIDE THE WINDOW, a metal fire escape wound its way down the side of the building. And nearing the bottom was Hussein Rudenko, a.k.a. Gavin Paxton.

Vail vaulted through the opening and landed with a thump. Her boots slipped against the slick surface and sent her into the metal balustrade. Her sore shoulder protested.

She started down, feet clanging the steel steps, her weight causing the structure to bounce as she descended.

Seconds later, Rudenko had made street level and began dodging cars as he crossed the road against the light.

Vail was not far behind him, but she knew that when she hit the ground floor she would lose the benefit of the high vantage point. And since she didn't know London, Rudenko could easily slip into an alley, a tube station, a coffee shop—and she would run right by him.

Vail jumped to the pavement and started in Rudenko's direction, passing a kiosk vendor selling "Magic Corn" for £2 a cup, in multiple flavors. She didn't stop to order but definitely could have used some magic right now—because she'd lost sight of the man who had eluded law enforcement the world over for decades, who had single-handedly caused so much death and destruction.

*How can I be so close, and yet so far?*

Sirens, a block or two away. She made a quick visual search of each shop as she passed by. But as the moments ticked by, she realized her efforts were fruitless.

Two white Metropolitan Police cruisers pulled to the curb, their flat, low profile light bars whipping blue and red lights, a fluorescent orange and blue stripe running the length of the vehicles' side panels.

*Probably responding to the gunshot.*

AFTER TAKING ONE last survey of the area, Vail texted DeSantos. She gave him her twenty, and a moment later he came running down the block. He had a large red bruise on his chin.

She gave him the bad news that Rudenko had escaped.

"Son of a bitch." DeSantos kicked an empty beer can down the sidewalk.

"If he goes underground, we're totally screwed."

"He won't go underground," DeSantos said. "He's got an attack to launch. But that doesn't mean he'll be easy to find." He slammed his toe against the can again and sent it under the tire of a passing cab. It crushed pancake-thin with a crunch.

"Let's get out of the street," he said. "More of his men may be around. Not to mention the police."

"The police?"

"My DNA's all over that place, not to mention prints, hair, fibers. I left them a treasure trove of forensics."

"Do they—or Interpol—have your prints?"

"If our people have done their jobs over the years, no. But after that business at our hotel, if we were captured on film, they'll eventually start putting a face with all the forensics I've left behind. I've been sloppy."

They slipped into a Starbucks and moved to the back of the crowded café; surprisingly, there was no wait at the counter. Vail bought a couple of espresso brownies and handed one to DeSantos.

"You gonna tell me what happened back there?"

DeSantos took a large bite. "I had to get creative. And I left behind more than just some forensics." He whispered by her ear, "Another body or two."

"That's becoming a habit."

"It became a habit a long time ago," he said, staring off at the busy streetscape through the storefront windows.

"In another context, I'd be drawing up a profile on you."

DeSantos frowned, then watched as another police cruiser sped by the café. "We shouldn't stay here. Let's get moving."

They left Starbucks and started down the street.

In a low voice, Vail said, "How did that happen? Rudenko showing up."

"You mean because Reid was keeping tabs on him."

"Exactly."

DeSantos chewed on that one—his jaw muscles literally got busy working. "Let's go find out."

# 29

Vail and DeSantos emerged from the Bond Street tube station and headed up the busy avenue.

"Before I leave England, I'm going to buy a pair of boots in that shop," Vail said, nodding at the Russell & Bromley store across from Turner's gallery.

DeSantos did not reply. Vail knew that his mind was on Reid's failure to warn them that Rudenko had left the store. Vail had the same thoughts, but had a difficult time believing that Reid's screw-up was an intentional act. Then again, what did she really know about him? She knew what he told her, so if his intent was to deceive, other than her ability to evaluate violent human behavior, she was not in a strong position to determine his veracity.

As they ascended the steps, Vail silently hoped that they'd walk in and see Rudenko busying himself in the gallery, as if nothing had happened. *No chance of that.*

When they entered, Reid was seated on a chair in the office doing paperwork.

"Just about to call you," Reid said. He slid off his seat and glanced at the back room.

"Where is he?" Vail asked.

Reid frowned, clearly realizing that something was wrong. "In the other room working on a restoration. Why?"

Vail held his gaze a long moment, but got nothing from his expression. "Let's go see. We've got some questions for him."

"Mr. Paxton," Reid called as he led the way down the short corridor. He pushed open the door from its half-closed position and stepped into the long, narrow room. He continued toward the far wall, passing rows of canvases propped at random angles. "Mr. Paxton," Reid called again, his pace quickening.

When they reached the last easel in the room, where a large oil painting was resting, Reid stopped short. The stool was empty.

"Oh shite." Reid's head whipped from side to side, eyes scanning the space in front of him. "He's not here."

"No," Vail said, "he's not. In fact, he and his goons just tried to kill Hector."

Reid's eyes shifted to DeSantos.

"What the hell happened? You were supposed to—" DeSantos lowered his voice. "Is Turner here?"

Reid wiped at the flop sweat on his forehead. "He left. Had a meeting with a dealer."

"You were supposed to keep an eye on Rudenko, let us know if he left the building. And give us a heads-up."

"Bollocks." He rubbed his temples. "I—I fucked up."

"Did he just walk right past you?" Vail asked. "I mean, really, Reid, what are we supposed to think?"

Reid's eyes shot over to Vail. "What the hell does that mean?"

Vail stared at him. "You know what it means."

The inspector shuffled his feet. "I'm less concerned with assigning blame than I am with figuring out how he got past me. I rather think that's more productive."

"I'm interested in both," DeSantos said. "You don't want us questioning your veracity, but a highly prized asset walked out of this place without you seeing him. That requires an explanation—because right now, you're looking like a conspirator."

Without a word, Reid walked toward the opposite end of the restoration studio. He weaved past a number of easels that held large canvases in various stages of repair. His voice suddenly emerged from behind one of the paintings. "Oh shite."

Vail folded her arms across her chest. "I'm getting tired of hearing you say that."

"Come see for yourself."

Vail and DeSantos joined Reid along the side wall beside a gray metal emergency fire door.

Vail frowned. "Oh shite."

"That's what I was saying. He must've slipped out the back."

"And you didn't know about this door?" DeSantos said, making no attempt to mask his incredulity.

Reid's face shaded red. "Not this one, no." A moment later, he said, "Still, it's alarmed. How'd he get out?"

"Rudenko disabled it," DeSantos said. "Who knows how many times he slipped out without you knowing?"

"You think he made you?" Vail asked.

"Made me?"

"Realized that you were watching him, that you'd figured out who he really was."

Reid thought a moment. "I gave him no reason to suspect anything. I did nothing different."

Vail glanced around at the easels, cleverly arranged to provide an effective screen to the emergency door from multiple angles. "This was purposeful, the way he's positioned everything. It's a shield."

"So he did know something was up," Reid said.

"Not necessarily," Vail said. "When the gallery exploded, with law enforcement now all around him, he made sure he had the ability to slip away for a while without the police knowing, to conduct his real business. No prying eyes and ears."

DeSantos lifted one of the paintings from the easel and examined it. "And he created this 'screen' in case one of the cops keyed in on who he was. He had an escape route planned."

"Sounds right to me," Reid said.

*Yeah, no shit. Of course it would. And it better be right, 'cause if I find out that you're screwing with me, I'm gonna kick you in the bollocks.*

DeSantos set the canvas back on its stand. "When we got here, you said you were about to call us. What about?"

Out of habit, Reid glanced around the empty room. "The director general wants to see you. Do you know where the Aldwych tube station is, in the Strand? The sign now actually says, 'Strand Station.'"

DeSantos squinted. "Near the London School of Economics. Yeah. But that station's been decommissioned, or whatever you call it."

"Disused."

"Disused?" Vail asked.

"When they stop using an Underground station," Reid said, "they just lock down the doors and shut off the power. Otherwise, the thing's intact, like a time capsule. You'll be meeting Director General Aden Buck in a little known part of the station that was never actually opened."

"Where's the entrance?" Vail asked.

"There isn't one, not really. Not to this part of the station. Sometime after they buttoned the whole thing down, they filled the old entryway with cinderblocks to prevent people from getting in. But there's a way in if you know about it."

"And you know about it."

"The director general uses it for highly sensitive meets. There are only four of us who've been read in."

"Where's the entrance?" DeSantos asked.

"A local pub."

Vail canted her head. "Come again? A local pub?"

"It's well disguised. The George IV, it's owned by the school. Mostly grad students use the place. Go in, hang a left in front of the bar, through a side door, and down a few steps. Next to the loo you'll see a short brown door marked "private." There's a keypad on the knob. Enter 938483. One of his men will fetch you there and escort you the rest of the way. It's dark and the stairwell's in a bad way, so it can be a bit dangerous."

"Why don't you just take us?" Vail asked.

Reid consulted his watch. "Can't. Have a meeting with Grouze at the station." He dug into his pocket and pulled out a ring of keys. "Take my car."

DESANTOS GAVE A LOOK AROUND from a second floor window before they ventured to street level. Although he told Vail that he couldn't be sure their hit squad would not be waiting for them, he was trained to pick out covert operators, particularly professionals.

As they walked toward Regent Street to pick up Reid's sedan, Vail turned to DeSantos. "He said 'us.'"

"Can you give me an idea of what you're talking about? You're the one who reads minds, not me."

"I don't read—You're just trying to piss me off, aren't you?"

"Trying."

"Reid. When I asked him if he knew where this secret Underground meeting place was located he said, 'There are only four of us' who know. But that makes no sense."

DeSantos did not respond.

*No, it doesn't make sense. And if Hector's not talking, it means I'm on to something.* "Because," she said, "Reid's a Scotland Yard detective and he was talking about a place that the director general of MI5 uses for clandestine meets."

"Why is this important?" DeSantos asked as they approached the car, his head rotating in all directions, scanning the area.

"I knew he was MI5."

Satisfied it was safe to approach, DeSantos extended a hand. "Keys?"

Vail stopped a few feet short of the car. "It's important. You know it is, which is why you're not answering me."

"That's right. Keys?"

"Who said you're driving?" she asked as she hit a button on the remote and unlocked the door.

"You're punishing me because I'm not telling you what you want to know." He sat down in the passenger seat.

"Not at all." She turned over the engine and pulled away from the curb. "I just want to drive. I need to be in control of something on this mission."

"You realize you called this a mission."

"What should I call it?"

DeSantos grinned. "Mission's fine. I just—It's just that you're usually parked behind a desk. It's been so long since you've been out in the field on a tactical op that I didn't think you even still remembered the lingo."

"Haven't you learned by now that using diversion doesn't work with me? Tell me about Reid. He's not really an inspector with the Met, is he? He's MI5."

"I'm not sure how to answer that." He glanced around. "Do you know where you're going?"

"Not at all. I figured I'd just drive and you'd get around to directing me sooner or later."

"I have a new appreciation for Robby. You're exhausting, Karen."

"*That*," she said, "is something you already knew. Now, about Reid."

"Take this to Haymarket and hang a right."

Instead, she hit the automatic door lock and pulled to the curb. "We're not going anywhere until you answer me."

He craned his neck in all directions. "We shouldn't stay here, out in the open. Keep moving."

"Tell me what I want to know."

He unlocked his door, but Vail immediately locked it.

"Damnit, Karen."

"Tell me!"

"Fine. You're right. He's MI5. But he's also with the Met."

"Scotland Yard's his cover?"

"Get moving, will you? You're putting us in jeopardy. If you know *anything* about running covert ops, you know I'm not bullshitting you."

Vail pulled back into traffic and resumed their heading.

"It's kind of screwy," DeSantos finally said. "And irregular. But MI5 has their reasons—which, by the way, they haven't shared with me, because I don't need to know. What I do know is that he's been with the Security Service a long time, one of their most trusted agents. But he 'left' about seven years ago so he could have deniability and operate out in the open, even though he's working covertly."

Vail turned onto Haymarket as she thought through Reid's cover. "Actually, that's kind of brilliant."

"Whether it is or not doesn't matter much. Important thing is that you keep it to yourself."

Following DeSantos's instructions, she turned left on Pall Mall East and followed it around Trafalgar Square onto Strand.

Once she was through the complicated maneuvers, DeSantos said, "Let's park. Over there." He pointed to an empty curb space on the left, along Melbourne Place, and Vail pulled into the spot.

"That was very disorienting. Driving in London, I mean. On the wrong side of the road."

"You're actually driving on the right side of the road."

"Don't start with me." She chirped the remote to lock the doors, then joined DeSantos on the sidewalk. But she realized his body had tensed, his eyes suddenly scanning the area.

He grabbed Vail's arm and pulled her left. "We've got a problem."

"Where?"

"Behind us, five o'clock. Don't look. A man in a suit, blue tie."

"Suit? Who the hell are these people?"

"Professionals. Most people tend to trust well dressed businessmen."

"There's only one?"

"Hard to say. Right now, that's all I see. But if I'm right, there are others. Do you know where we're going?"

"I've got the address."

DeSantos released his grip. "Go there. Not directly. Think angles, diversions, and distance."

"What about you?"

"I'm good with diversions, remember? I'll meet you there." He turned and met her eyes. "Be careful. Stay in populated areas and—"

"I know how to do this."

DeSantos's look suggested that he doubted her statement. But that only made her more determined to prove him wrong.

# 30

Vail continued to the corner of Melbourne and Strand, crossed Strand, and then turned right. To her left was apparently one of the old entrances to the disused tube station in Aldwych—where she would be ending up, though she would be accessing it from a different location. A metal gate with a Squire padlock prevented entry; an adjacent cinder block wall abutted a portion of well preserved tile and the first couple letters of the old "Strand Station" sign.

As she casually checked over her shoulder, she saw a suited man who looked like a run-of-the-mill banker—with one exception: the handgun-sized bulge beneath his lapel. *Hector said there'd be others.*

Vail continued down the street past a series of windows filled with portraits of what appeared to be scholars, artists, or luminaries of some sort: they were emblazoned with the likes of Morpurgo, Ramphal, Owen, Auld. She kept the same pace, not letting on that she had seen the man following her.

To her right, a narrow church building—St. Mary le Strand, according to the sign—split the avenue on a traffic island, a wrought iron fence rimming the front.

The sound of a revving motorcycle snapped her head away from the structure and toward the entrance to King's College, where a couple of London's ever-present closed-circuit cameras were supplemented by a guard dressed in a short yellow fluorescent jacket. He stood behind the security gate, a woefully inadequate red-and-white striped beam blocking the driveway.

*Wonder if the campus cop sees the assassin who's following me. Probably doesn't know a suited killer from a foundation donor.*

Vail passed the steel-gray metal gate that proudly displayed the King's College crest and continued down the block until reaching the majestic arched entryway of Somerset House. Closed circuit cameras stared down at her from above. She turned left through a blue pedestrian gate, daring the man following her to continue his pursuit under the watchful eyes of Big Brother.

She emerged in a voluminous cobblestone quad bounded on all sides by sizable, columned, Portland Stone-and-brick buildings. On her left was an A-frame sign with arrows pointing toward The Courtauld Gallery. Vail knew The Courtauld was famous for, among other things, its collection of Impressionist paintings—something that figured prominently in her Dead Eyes case.

Vail thought of exploring the courtyard's nooks for an alley where she could disappear. She didn't see anything promising, so she stayed in the open, walking straight ahead toward a large, raised sculpture of a man and a lion, headed for the glass-domed building directly in front of her.

After coming around the other side of the charcoal-colored, platformed statue, a concrete courtyard came into view, with dozens of rows of fountains spurting tall streams of water. A few people were walking among them under umbrellas.

*Great place for kids—in bathing suits—during the summer.*

It was not summer, Vail was not wearing a bathing suit, and she was not concerned about getting her clothing wet. But the suited man behind her might look a tad out of place if he followed her in, and whatever drew attention to him was to her advantage. There had to be CCTV cameras recording their movements in here.

Vail jogged forward, her boots sloshing through the puddles, eyes squinting as the joltingly cold water struck her hair and scalp.

She planned to go through the building and exit onto a street that would take her back toward the George IV pub, her destination. She needed to lose the thug along the way—not an easy task, since she was certain he would not break off pursuit until he finished his job: eliminating her.

But as Vail approached the entrance, she saw the reflection of the suited man behind her, no more than fifty yards away, walking determinedly, and confidently, through the sprouting fountains.

DESANTOS CROSSED ALDWYCH and neared the London School of Economics, or LSE, a limestone-fronted edifice with four massive Ionic columns at the corner entrance and a number of smaller ones abutting the building's face. A couple of classic London-red phone booths poked out at him against the gray facade. Two naked, helmeted warrior figures stood poised to strike above an arched, secondary doorway bearing the sign "Clement House."

He continued along the block-long LSE structure, toward Columbia House. The man jogged across Aldwych thirty seconds behind him.

DeSantos hung a right on Houghton Street in front of the "Pedestrian Zone" sign and stepped onto the cobblestone road. He walked past the line of bicycles on his left, cutting through the campus in the direction of the overhead bridge.

DeSantos continued past the Old Building and hung a left at Clare Market in front of St. Clement's. He turned right and right again, down a narrow alley, headed toward John Watkins Plaza. If memory served, that's where the LSE library was located.

He gave a quick glance over his shoulder. His pursuer was a few dozen feet behind him.

He quickened his pace and walked up the plaza's ramp, past a number of students seated at the aluminum tables to his right. Ahead, as he had thought, was the entrance to the library.

Knowing it would be more difficult for his adversary to take out his target in a building with an open floor plan and many people present, he pulled on the handle of the glass door and walked inside.

VAIL EXITED THE MUSEUM and looked out across a four lane divided road, beyond which the choppy River Thames flowed, tour boats moored along its edge and pedestrians strolling along the tree-lined frontage. The posted sign told her this was Victoria Embankment, and she turned left, down the sidewalk that ran along the Courtauld Gallery buildings and art institute.

Vail passed a worker in an orange maintenance vest who was pushing a broom along the pavement and saw, up ahead, an archway of some sort. She thought of ducking in, but a bit farther down was a street that led in the direction that she needed to go.

But as she approached, she realized it didn't make a hard turn, as she had thought. It more or less curved left off of Victoria Embankment; the street sign indicated it was Temple Place. She followed that until it crossed Surrey Street. She hung a left again and within about fifty yards the area turned into mixed residential and commercial. But there was no one in the vicinity—not even the suited man.

Vail wanted to think that she had lost him, but she knew that his drive to kill her was as powerful as hers was to stay alive.

She continued along Surrey, past an aging, once-elegant apartment building with bay windows and faux terraces. A few hundred feet later, as she approached a striped rust-colored brick and cream-toned block edifice, the suited man stepped out from a fenced-in alley.

And he was ten feet away.

# 31

DeSantos looked out at the cavernous room. It featured a central spiral staircase that corkscrewed five stories toward a transparent ceiling, with two glass elevator cars running along a track in the middle of the curving stairway.

To his left by the service counter was a security station staffed by three guards. How many others there were, he didn't know, but there had to be enough to make their rounds at the appointed times. It was impossible to determine what weapons, if any, they possessed. The safe assumption was that they did not carry handguns. But batons or Tasers could not be ruled out.

Two of the men were chatting along the back wall and the third was studying his computer monitor, which sat adjacent to a series of turnstiles that required keycard access to enter the library; the one at the far left was a short glass door that, according to the posted sign, was an entrance for people with disabilities. DeSantos saw a young woman in a wheelchair approaching it; he quickly made his way over to her and grabbed the handlebars as the door swung open.

"I got it," he said as he gave her a gentle push.

The woman glanced over her shoulder. "Thanks."

"No, no," DeSantos said with a laugh. "Pleasure's all mine."

He stepped aside and kept moving forward, his objective being to create space and distance between him and his assailant. An elevator would not accomplish that—he would be rendered imprisoned once he stepped inside—so he jogged to the blue-carpeted ramp leading to the staircase and started climbing.

Below, and all around him on all sides of the trapezoidal room that stretched as far as he could see, students occupied every available seat, staring at their computer screens or chatting with one another. Apparently talking was tolerated on these lower floors of the library.

After he reached the third level, he found the student body thinned out. It also became noticeably quieter. This was the area for serious study.

DeSantos glanced over the metal railing at the entrance but did not see his pursuer; a disadvantage of being the one chased was that unless you constantly checked behind you, there was no way to keep track of your adversary. Had he watched DeSantos enter the library? Worse, was he familiar with the building and did he know a shortcut that would have beaten DeSantos to his current location? As he moved along the circular path, he pulled his eyes away from the library entrance and did a quick survey. All clear.

He scouted the general layout of the interior and formulated a plan—but it required the assassin to see him. He glanced back at the ground floor and saw the man looking left, right—and up. He locked eyes with DeSantos, then DeSantos backed out of his line of sight.

DeSantos left the twisting staircase and stepped onto the third floor, where rows of tall bookshelves formed a maze of hiding places. With his UK body count already too high, he preferred not to add to it—if possible. But left alive, this man would keep coming after them. No. He had to dispose of him—without noise and blood. The more time that elapsed before the corpse was discovered, the better.

DeSantos moved about the reserve periodical stacks, using them like a running back uses his offensive line, keeping the shelving between himself and the staircase—and the hitman.

The assassin came onto the floor still jogging, but stopped abruptly and scanned the vicinity. DeSantos noticed that his breathing was not labored, meaning that he was fit; about what he had expected from a professional.

That begged the question of who this guy was and, more importantly, who he was working for. The logical assumption was that his boss was Hussein Rudenko, but little was known of his organization. It had long been posited that Rudenko worked with foreign nationals from a variety of countries, either men who belonged to his network or support personnel supplied by a colleague. If the latter were true, Rudenko's group might be one with many supplementary tentacles. It was crucial to identify those players as well.

If he could get a good look at this mercenary, he could potentially determine nationality, and that might give him a clue as to who he was dealing with. DeSantos inched around the bookshelf and spied his adversary: something about him said Chechen.

The man passed the printers and was moving alongside the computer workstation desk, occupied by a couple of students. He then turned right, down the aisle adjacent to the one where DeSantos was standing.

DeSantos moved to the end, then prepared to engage him as he rounded the corner.

But after counting off the seconds it should have taken for the assassin to reach his location, DeSantos realized something was wrong. He waited another five and—nothing.

As he inched forward, taking care to remain concealed, a wire snapped around his neck from behind and he was jerked back against a taut body.

DeSantos did not make the common error of trying to dislodge the garrote; instead, he focused his energies and remaining seconds of life on defeating—or at least disabling—the man attempting to kill him.

He swung, writhed, grabbed—but he was unable to make any headway.

This guy knew what he was doing.

DeSantos felt the first effects of diminished oxygen to the brain—lightheadedness and dizziness—and knew he had to do something.

He planted both feet firmly on the dense industrial carpet and drove his legs backward, into the Chechen's body, throwing them both into the bookcase behind them, boxes of periodicals raining down on their heads and shoulders. DeSantos kept driving, pushing, until the rack gave way and tipped over. It slammed into the one behind it, and it went toppling as well, like dominoes on a board.

As they fell, the assassin's grip loosened. DeSantos grabbed the wire and tugged it off his head, as if he were removing a tight sweater.

Knowing he had only a small window with strategic leverage, DeSantos twisted his body and swung hard with a left hook, catching the man in the eye. The Chechen landed his own blow, but it glanced off DeSantos's cheek.

DeSantos grabbed him by the neck and put his weight behind it, cutting off the hitman's airway. The assailant brought his knees up and struck DeSantos in the back, but that only increased the weight on his own windpipe.

In his peripheral vision, DeSantos became aware of a number of students who had gathered nearby—as well as three security guards, who were approaching on the run. They were blowing their whistles, headed in his direction from one of the fire escape stairwells located at the building's corners.

"WHO ARE YOU and what do you want?" Vail yelled, mustering as much authority as she could with her heart thumping against her chest, her breath suddenly short.

The man advanced a step—and Vail took the advice of dozens of perps she had encountered over the years. She turned and ran.

Her eyes rolled left and right, looking for a way out—but there was none. *C'mon, Karen. Outrun this guy.*

But the moment she had that thought, a thick hand clamped around her mouth.

As he pulled her closer to the mouth of the alley, she drew her knees up, forcing the man to bear her full weight as he simultaneously yanked her backward.

But he was strong, and he repositioned his grip around her body and swung her onto his side like a potato sack.

*He's gonna kill me—*

*gotta get away*

*before he gets me in there*

He flung her weight through the opening in the fence—but she hooked her foot on the metal post. It threw him off kilter and he stumbled back into the opposing pole of the gate's entry.

Vail managed to free one of her arms and she swung it wildly, striking flesh.

The man pulled her closer, squeezing the air from her lungs—

*Constricting*

*Can't breathe*

*Need air—*

He gave a final yank and pulled her into the alley.

The gate swung closed with an echoing clank.

DESANTOS NEEDED TO FINISH this guy off, to make sure he did not have an opportunity to come after him again. But he could not risk getting arrested. He had seen three guards, but there could be more—and they could be carrying Tasers. They were also likely required to alert the Met, so the police would be on the way, as well.

With no choice, and with his task incomplete, DeSantos released his grip on the man's neck and fled, pushing through the line of students who had gathered in the study area to watch the melee.

He passed the Russian Collection stacks and circled around and through another computer workstation area in the corner of the room. As the guards went after the assassin, who had gotten up and fled in the opposite direction, DeSantos slipped into the fire escape stairwell and hurried down the steps. He hit the ground floor quickly, but when he yanked open the door, he realized that he was in the lobby, right near the security desk. He gambled that all the guards were deployed, chasing the man they had seen fleeing.

DeSantos took a deep breath, gave a quick survey of himself, and adjusted his disheveled clothing. The red mark that was undoubtedly—and for the foreseeable future, indelibly—encircling his neck was unfortunately going to be visible.

He pulled open the door and walked out of the stairwell.

THE MAN KEPT HIS HAND clamped over Vail's mouth as she attempted to dislodge her left arm while swinging her right elbow in his direction. He fended off her attempts and then brought his free hand forward.

A garrote dangled from his fist.

Vail's eyes widened. *I've been kidnapped by serial killers and lived to tell about it, but some goddamn assassin in London is gonna be the one to end my life? How ironic is that?*

Vail twisted her torso, tucked her chin, and tried to keep him from getting the wire around her neck. He head-butted her, then slipped the cold metal cable against her trachea.

Vail slammed her boot heel onto his foot, then swung her elbow down toward his abdomen and landed a solid blow, driving him back. She spun and kicked him, her shoe slapping against his cheek and slamming him against the brick facing.

He struck the wall hard but scowled and came at her, slapping away her punch and landing a blow to her chin.

It straightened Vail and stunned her, and she hung in the air a second before her knees buckled and everything started spinning. She reached out, trying to regain her balance—

But another blow to her face sent her to the pavement.

Off in the distance, a gunshot.

The suited man dropped in a heap by her side. She struggled to focus her eyes, and a moment later was able to clear her head and sit up.

Walking toward her was Clive Reid. He extended a hand but she shook it off, rolling onto her knees and slowly pushing herself off the pavement, avoiding the puddle of blood that was spreading outward from the assailant's chest.

"I could've taken him."

Reid raised an eyebrow. "Unless you have some kind of levitation weapon, I don't think so. You were flat on the pavement. It didn't look very promising."

Vail straightened her clothing. "Think what you want. I didn't need your help."

"Strange way of saying thank-you."

She felt her face, which she was sure had a couple of sizable welts—and said, "That's because I didn't."

Feeling more steady, she knelt in front of the man's body and patted down his pockets. Other than some cash and a credit card, there was nothing. She turned the Visa over and snorted: "Kevin Smith. Yeah, I'm sure that's his real name."

"Not much chance of that, I fancy."

Vail gathered up the garrote and pocketed it. "I was sure he had a gun." She slapped at the man's torso again but did not find it.

Reid swung his body around, checking the dim alley. "Forget it. We have to get out of here before the Met shows. The camera." He gestured above her at a grimy, white CCTV device.

Vail canted her head to look but felt a pinch in her neck. *Lovely. I need this like a pain in the neck. Can I slap myself for a bad joke? No. Two shots to the jaw were quite enough.*

"And you've to get to your rendezvous point. Let's go." Reid shoved his pistol in the back of his waistband, and they walked out of the alley. There was still no one on the street—or they took cover once they heard the gunshot.

"I thought you had a meeting with Grouze," she said as they headed up Surrey.

"I did. But then I realized that Grouze can wait, that you two might need my help."

"Very intuitive."

"Not really. I didn't want to screw up twice in one day. Once was bad enough."

She glanced at Reid as they crossed Strand; she had parked their car ahead on Melbourne Place. "I've had my doubts about you."

"I've gotten to know you a bit, Karen. And I'd say you still have doubts."

Vail couldn't help but smile. She rubbed her sore jaw. "Keep saving my life, and I may have to reevaluate."

Reid lifted his brow. "You admit that I saved your life?"

"Of course I admit it. I'm not an idiot."

"But you said—"

"I thought you said you were getting to know me."

A siren wailed in the distance—and seemed to be getting closer.

They shared a look.

"We've got a problem, don't we?" she asked.

Reid swung his head around, surveying the area. "Yep. But I know a place where we might be able to get some help."

# 32

DeSantos stood on John Watkins Plaza, approximately thirty yards from the library entrance. He had walked down the ramp and parked himself behind the brick wall along Saint Clement's Lane, an alley-wide pedestrian walkway that, at the moment, was clear of foot traffic.

If his assailant exited, DeSantos would follow him and finish the job, assuming the man managed to escape the guards. He would give him five minutes; more than that, and either he had been taken into custody—which DeSantos could not fathom happening to a professional assassin with his demonstrated skill-set—or he had gotten out of the building via a doorway DeSantos was not aware of, or he had found a safe place to hide. Either way, DeSantos did not have time to wait.

But a minute later, the Chechen left the building. He could turn right to Portugal Street or go down the ramp, straight ahead, toward DeSantos. Regardless of which way he chose, DeSantos had formulated a plan of engagement.

When the man decided on the ramp, DeSantos headed down Saint Clement's to a recessed cement staircase with a small wrought iron fence. It was hardly the perfect hiding place, but it would have to suffice. Worst case scenario, the man would see him and they would have to fight for control.

Seconds later, with DeSantos coiled and hidden, the man strolled past, more concerned about being spotted by police than suspecting that his target was poised to turn the tables on him.

As he passed, DeSantos lunged forward and cracked the man across the back of his neck with the knife edge of his hand.

His legs buckled but he regained his balance and started to turn. DeSantos was ready with a blitz-quick attack, grabbing his wrist and breaking it with a sharp downward twist. In nearly the same motion, he spun the killer around and delivered a blow to the man's nose with the palm of his hand.

The impact drove the stunned mercenary into the brick building—but he did not go down. DeSantos finished him off by driving his thumb web into his Adam's apple. The man's eyes opened wide as the air left his lungs and he dropped to his knees, unable to breathe.

To leave no doubt, DeSantos drove his shoe repeatedly into the man's skull until he stopped moving.

Sirens wailed. Whistles blew. And several Metro bobbies approached on the run.

A larger problem, however, was that the cops were backed up by CO19, the elite firearms unit of the Metropolitan Police—the British equivalent of SWAT—which was coming at him from the opposite direction.

# 33

"I can't believe all these closed-circuit TV cameras," Vail said as they passed beneath another mounted device on Portugal Street.

Reid shoved his hands into his pants pockets. "You know they're not all controlled by Scotland Yard. Or MI5, for that matter. Most are private."

"But law enforcement can tap into them if needed."

"Kind of, yes. It takes some doing. Not as easy as you might think."

"*Legally*, it takes some doing. Hacking in, not so much."

"Right," Reid said with a laugh. "Legally. But we aren't hackers. We take the proper route."

"When you say, 'we,' are you talking about Scotland Yard or MI5?"

Their eyes locked. "You know?"

"I know. I just found out, if that makes you feel any better."

"Feel better? How would you feel if *your* cover was blown?"

"Your cover isn't blown, Reid. Your assignment is safe with me. In fact, it explains a lot. Like why you lied to me."

"I didn't lie to—" He stopped himself and said, "Guess I did, didn't I? It was necessary. I'm sure you understand."

Vail made a face. "Whatever. Now that I know, it's not important."

"We're here," Reid said, stopping on Portsmouth Street, in front of an oddly shaped white and green building.

Vail craned her neck to look at the hand-lettered sign that read:

## The Old Curiosity Shop Immortalised by Charles Dickens

She turned around in a circle, as if looking for a lost item. "We're here...where? All I see is an old store."

"Oh, it's much more than that. It's old, yes—about five hundred years. More recently it was a custom shoe shop, and then an antique and modern art gallery, but its owners now lease it out. They sometimes do book launch parties, art exhibitions. A friend of mine set up shop here about nine months ago selling specialty costumes."

Reid reached for the door handle of the green-painted wood door. Vail stopped him.

"Costumes. You're kidding, right? You said you knew a way out of this mess."

"That's not what I said. I said I thought I knew a place that might be able to help, and that's what this is. Like it or not, you've been photographed all over the city from just about every angle. Your location can now be tracked. You need some kind of disguise or these people are going to keep finding you. They may anyway, but at least we can take away one of their tools. You said it yourself—we're the only ones who *legally* tap into the closed-circuit network."

The unmistakable scream of sirens blared a few blocks away. Vail shared a look of urgency with Reid, and she removed her hand from the door. Reid pulled it open and they walked inside.

Wide dark brown wood plank floors, recently refinished, dominated the room. A subtle mustiness tickled Vail's sensitive nose, but it was not bad for a structure that has been around since the 1500s. Off to her left, a wood staircase rose to the second floor, while a red brick-mantled fireplace stood several feet to her right.

A middle-aged woman with brunette hair pulled up in a bun descended the stairs. "Well, if it isn't Scotland Yard come to pay us a visit. Looking for a Halloween costume now, inspector? Your timing's a little off."

"Elizabeth, always nice to see you." Reid hugged the woman, then stepped back and gave her a once-over. "You're looking good."

"Nice of you to notice." She glanced at Vail, lingering on the welts on her face, then turned back to Reid. "I'm guessing there's an official reason for your visit."

"As a matter of fact..." He hesitated a moment. "Anyone else in the shop?"

Elizabeth put her hands on her hips. "Just the three of us. Why?"

"We need to do a little undercover work, I'm afraid. So we'll be counting on your discretion."

"You're talking to *me*, Clive. You needn't ask."

Vail caught the "Clive" reference. *These two were clearly friends, perhaps more.*

"You haven't been around in a while."

"No," Reid said, examining his shoes. "Sorry about that."

"And you haven't returned my last couple of calls."

"Guilty again." Reid managed a weak smile. "Things are complicated, Liz, and quite frankly, now isn't the time. But how 'bout we grab a round next week? Or dinner."

"Dinner sounds smashing." She gave a quick glance at Vail. "So tell me what you had in mind. For you—or your colleague here?"

Vail stepped forward. "My friend and I need to change our appearance. He's big, about six-three. Extra-large, I'd guess. We need something simple but effective. Something that can hide our faces. My red hair."

"The cameras," Elizabeth said.

"Yes, ma'am."

"Ma'am," Elizabeth said as if it was a sour lemon. "This really is official." She appraised Vail a moment, then said, "It's gotta be a crime to hide that beautiful hair of yours. But let's see what I can do."

DESANTOS HAD ONLY ONE option. He had to get to the ramp before the bobbies and CO19 did—because it'd give him a chance, slim though it may be, of getting to Portugal Street, where he needed to end up. Unfortunately, there weren't many places along the way to hide from the officers deployed to corral him. At least, not without some kind of head start.

He would worry about that later. Right now, he had to put some distance between himself and the police before they drew down on him. Once that happened, his entire mission was in jeopardy.

DeSantos hit the ramp as several coppers began screaming at him, and just as the three security guards poured out the LSE Library doors. Two stepped in front of him—if they used Tasers he was in trouble—so he lowered his shoulder and bull-rushed them, sending both men sprawling.

DeSantos lost his footing and nearly took a header on the pavement, but regained his balance and hung a right onto Portugal Street. This is where it got dicey—as if it wasn't before—because he was completely exposed. Although there were multiple alleys, he didn't want to get in a foot chase through the streets because the area was maze-like and he was afraid he would get turned around.

He had to get to the pub.

The good news was that it was only a block away. The bad news was that it was a block away. If he didn't do this right, he could lead his pursuers to Vail.

He broke into a sprint down Portugal and, eschewing the bar's entrance nearest him, planned to hang a left at the light post ahead and enter the establishment on Portsmouth, through the wood and etched glass side doors.

VAIL AND REID WALKED into The George IV Pub and found a handful of patrons—primarily graduate students watching a football match, or soccer game in American parlance, on the television. Reid shared a laugh with the bartender, who apparently recognized him. Vail jabbed him with an elbow. "Small talk later. We've got an appointment, *Clive.*" She forced a smile.

"Right. Right you are. Excuse me," Reid said. "We need to use the loo."

*We? Jesus, man, can you sound more suspicious?*

He led the way to the brown metal door as the approaching police sirens wailed louder.

"That can't be good," Reid said. "Hector?"

Vail clenched her jaw and looked over her shoulder, through the spacious storefront windows. "Hope not."

"What do you want to do?"

"Follow the plan. Let's get inside. Hopefully he'll find his way."

They descended the three steps and as Reid started to enter the code into the electronic keypad, DeSantos burst into the pub through the side door.

*Thank God.*

"Now would be a good time," DeSantos said as he approached. He came up behind Vail and said, "Gun squad's hot on my tail along with a bunch of very angry bobbies."

"Christ." Reid fumbled with the keypad, cursed, took a deep breath, and then started over.

DeSantos crouched low to prevent officers from seeing him—and noticed Vail's stuffed Old Curiosity Shop bag.

"Tell me you didn't go shopping. Are you out of your mind? This is your idea of evading trained assassins?"

Before Vail could respond, Reid pulled open the short door, revealing a serious-looking man in a dark sweater. "Get in here. Quickly."

They shuffled inside the dark stairwell, Vail nearly slipping on the narrow, grimy steps.

"Walk with care," their guide said.

*Yeah, no shit.*

"Here's a torch," the man said as he handed back an extra flashlight. "There'll be electricity in a bit. Don't want any light seeping through the doorway into the pub."

Vail held her light so that Reid and DeSantos could catch some of the beam's expanse. "When was the station closed?"

"Depends on what section you're talking about," Reid said. "There are three different parts. You've got Platform A and its connecting areas, which were shuttered in '94. Those are in pretty decent shape, and they get used once in a while for filming movies. Then there's Platform B. Those sections opened in 1907 and closed in 1917—fascinating to visit in their own right. You'll see some of it as we go through.

"But we're going to a section not too many know about, unless you're an Underground archivist—because it's a section that was never completed. Most of it's pretty rough, because, well, it's old, and because they just stopped building those areas in the middle of construction. It's like the boss blew the whistle, the masons shuffled out, and that's how it stayed till the Security Service walled it off and fixed it up to use as a safe house of sorts."

As they followed their guide, they reached an area brightly lit by fluorescent fixtures. Vail shut her flashlight and said, "Just a guess. This is the section closed in '94."

"You must be a detective," Reid said. "Right you are."

They continued on, moving into another section that looked like it was from an earlier era—because, as Reid had explained, it was. The corridor was well lit but narrow, and they had to walk single file. Vail felt a damp sweat blanket her forehead and neck. *Another claustrophobic dungeon. How many of these does England have?* She stopped and Reid bumped into her.

"What are you doing?" he asked.

*You can get through this. Keep moving, keep your mind on the objective. What's the objective? The director general.* "Nothing."

"She's got a problem with tight spaces," DeSantos said.

"I'm fine," Vail said between clenched teeth, pressing forward, keeping her mind off where she was. *A hundred feet below the surface, in a tomb of cement and masonry—stop it!*

Bare brick poked through crumbling rust-colored walls. They passed a half dozen doors on both sides of the corridor; a couple were open and revealed small rooms.

"What is this place?" DeSantos asked.

"Old offices," Reid said, "from World War II. Parts of the station were also used as a bomb shelter when we were being attacked. I think they even brought some exhibits from the British Museum down here to protect them from being destroyed."

"That's correct." This from their guide, who had fallen silent for most of their journey.

They passed into an area that still bore remnants of the original platform décor, a cream and green tile motif, with hand-painted maroon and tan signs.

The corridor expanded into a platform-wide cavity with an arched roof. But before Vail could express relief over getting out of the cramped tunnel, they stepped into another narrow hall and descended steps littered with loose electrical wiring and chunks of cement.

The man led the way through a locked door that brought them to the terminus of the platform, where the train tunnel began. The railway stretched into the distance, beyond the reach of Vail's flashlight. Electrical conduits snaked along the brick facing above the mouth of the bore and disappeared inside, along its curved walls.

"How much longer?" Vail asked.

"Almost there." Reid motioned to her flashlight. "Keep it on. We're about to enter the section that was never finished. Until we get to the area the Service uses, it can be a little dangerous."

*A little* dangerous? *That'd be an improvement over this entire UK trip.*

They walked up a flight of stairs, avoiding the discarded construction debris, layers of decades-old dirt, and thick grime that lined the sides of each step.

They emerged in a tunnel that was conical in shape, its walls roughened, unfinished concrete. It appeared as if the next step in the build-out would have been the installation of hundreds of yards of green and cream tiles—something that never occurred.

The man led them to an area where the room opened up into a large chamber. Several desks and chairs were set against the wall, and a laptop sat on two of them beside a stainless steel equipment box placed in front of a man with a full head of silver hair, combed back. His suit was dark and impeccably pressed. The red tie screamed "power."

*Aden Buck, MI5 director general.*

He rose from his seat and moved out in front of the desk. Two large men joined their circle—agents, guards, Vail didn't know. But their roles were clear.

"You're late," Buck said.

"They encountered a bit of resistance," Reid said.

"Have they been compromised?"

"I don't believe so—nothing that can't be remedied. But there are risks."

"Yes, well, if we had an alternative we'd use it. We don't." He stepped to the right, where Vail was standing. "This young lady certainly needs no introduction—the source of my pain and suffering. Karen Vail."

Vail tilted her head. "Excuse me?"

Buck frowned. "Let's just say that you ruined a perfectly good operation."

Vail looked to DeSantos.

"Hussein Rudenko," Buck said. "The Shakespeare manuscript."

Vail snorted. "It might've been a 'good' operation if you hadn't forgotten one key thing—telling me that you were *running* an operation."

*Please don't say it. Please don't say that I didn't need to know.*

"Very few were read into that mission," Buck said. "And you were not one of those select few we deemed necessary to inform."

"Surely there were better ways of carrying out the objective of—"

"Since you are not an expert on British intelligence or on the vagaries of British society, I suggest you keep your trap shut."

Vail stepped forward. "What?"

"You heard me. You're here because I wanted you here, Agent Vail. You are a tool at my disposal. That's it. If I swing you, you strike the nail. You don't get to have independent thought."

Vail put both hands on her hips. "Is that right? Well, to hell with you, director general. This *tool* is taking the express train to Heathrow. Is that independent enough for you?" Vail turned to leave, but the two beefy men blocked her path. "Move it, assholes." But the men stood erect, hands clasped in front of them, daring her to make a move and doubting she could do anything to challenge them.

"Karen," DeSantos said evenly. "Karen, let's not lose sight of the bigger picture. We need to turn our emotions off. Facts and the greater good."

Vail turned to face him. "Facts and the greater good?"

"Yes. We've got a chemical weapon loose. And terrorists trying to deploy it. First here, and if we don't stop them, in the US. Aden Buck is not our enemy."

Vail snorted, then turned to face Buck. "Were you responsible for that kidnapping stunt?"

Buck looked at her but did not answer.

"You son of a bitch. I thought I was going to be decapitated!"

"Agent Vail, I thought you were smarter than that." When she did not answer, he said, "That was the point, you daft fool! You'd served your purpose, and you played your part well. But you were becoming a problem. I couldn't just have you eliminated, and I couldn't arrest or deport you without causing a stir—because it'd tip off the very terrorists this operation is designed to capture. You left us no choice but to scare the living daylights from you. And have you decide on your own to go back home."

Vail felt DeSantos's grip around her bicep. It tightened as Buck continued. *And it's a good thing, because right now I think I could strangle the bastard. Now that would be for the 'greater good.'*

"C'mon," DeSantos said by her ear. "We need to get out of here. Before one of us does something we'll both regret later."

He gave a gentle nudge and she submitted to his advice. At the moment, she was not exactly thinking clearly.

"Mr. Cruz," Buck said. "You mustn't leave before we conduct the business purpose of our meeting. I have something for you."

One of Buck's companions handed him a smartphone-type device. The top half of the vertical face was a small screen, with a physical keyboard beneath it.

"To reduce the risk we face by meeting in person, you'll use a highly secure mobile that sends text messages using a microburst architecture. It's called CLAIR, though don't ask me what it stands for because I'm not a tech guru and I wouldn't remember even if they told me. Suffice it to state that it's a high bandwidth, low power device that will only transmit a message between my handset and yours. Both units share the same hardware key so the encrypted messages sent between them can only be decoded by them."

"So even if someone could intercept the messages," Reid said, "they'll be unreadable."

"Precisely."

"Does it keep a log of the texts?" Vail asked.

"No. Thirty minutes after receiving or sending a message, the flash memory self-erases by writing over itself repeatedly with random bytes. The log and the messages are electronically shred. In brief, it's safe to use. Just be sure to leave it on at all times so it can make full use of its security features."

"Do you want manual confirmation of sent messages?" DeSantos asked.

"Not necessary. There's an encryption protocol built in for the devices to confirm that the text was received."

DeSantos looked at the handset and shoved it into his pocket. "Charger?"

"It's a low power device. The battery will last three weeks, well beyond the duration of your assignment. I will make arrangements to get it back from you when you have completed this mission. You will not see me again. It's too risky."

*Yeah, considering what we went through to make it here alive, I agree.*

"Only your handset and mine can communicate with each other?" DeSantos asked.

"Correct."

"So," Vail said, "If I texted that number, he wouldn't receive it?"

"Precisely."

Vail pulled out her BlackBerry.

"You don't believe me?"

"Trust has to be earned. And you haven't earned mine. Just the opposite, in fact," she said as she typed out a test message to both DeSantos's real phone and the MI5 device. After Buck gave her the number, she hit send. Nothing happened.

Buck, wearing a self-satisfied grin, said, "You won't get service down here. We're quite deep underground, and we've installed signal damping devices to prevent hackers and other unwanted malfeasants from eavesdropping."

"We're lacking some key intel," DeSantos said.

"Right you are. Here's what we know." Buck nodded at one of his men, who switched on a handheld LCD projector and aimed it at a square of the wall that had been painted white. An array of five faces splashed across the makeshift screen.

"There are multiple targets. Rudenko is not a target; I repeat, he is not a target. We want him captured alive. We, the US, and Interpol have an array of questions for him."

Vail had to keep herself from laughing. "You really think a guy like that is going to talk?"

Buck tightened his jaw. "Leave that to us. He is to be captured, not killed. Is that clear?" His gaze touched on the eyes of the three of them.

*Clear to me.*

Obviously believing that he had made his point, Buck turned his attention back to the faces on the wall. He activated a laser pointer and aimed it at the images on the right. "We've identified three lieutenants: Ratib Morsi, Emir Dhul Fiqar, and Nikola Hačko. They're to be taken alive, if possible. The other two, Malik al-Atah and Farkhad Gogun, are expendable and are to be eliminated, as they're likely the triggers. If we dispose of al-Atah and Gogun, we may be able to put off the attack, at least until we grab up Rudenko. They're pawns and will not know anything of value. They're given their instructions at the last moment." He pointed at DeSantos's pocket. "I will send you a secure message as soon as we have locations on any of these people. As well as any collaborators that we learn of. So be aware."

"Nikola," Vail said. "A woman?"

"Croatian," Buck said. "We think she was a love interest of Morsi or Fiqar, but we don't know for sure. However she hooked on with Rudenko's group, what we do know is that she's now intimately involved in the deployment of the weapons. She holds a degree in chemical engineering. One of her specialties is water processing and food treatment. Ideal for ricin." He turned to Vail. "Are you aware that we're looking for ricin stores appropriated from Libya?"

"That's one of the few things I do know."

"What do you know about weaponized ricin?"

"It's made from castor beans and it's a stable toxin. That's about it. Well, that and I should avoid it at all costs."

"Yes, well, this is not our first run-in with ricin. Arab terrorists were captured with it in London some years back. If you're a terrorist, the advantages of ricin are clear: it's extremely toxic and you can do your damage through multiple vectors: inhalation, ingestion, or injection. As I said, Nikola Hačko's expertise makes contamination of water or food supplies an obvious threat. But the toxin can also be aerosolized as a liquid or a powder."

"So it's nearly impossible to guard against," Vail said.

"Precisely. And since it only takes one milligram—a grain of salt—to kill an adult, the problem is not to be understated. I fully expect them to announce their attack, but if they don't, symptoms we'll be watching for are bloody diarrhea, nausea and vomiting, abdominal cramps, internal bleeding, liver and kidney failure, heart failure, and, well, death."

"Have you put out a public health notice?"

"Can't, not without instilling panic—and tipping off the very people we're trying to apprehend. The National Health Service has put hospitals on alert, but the home secretary classified it as a potential infectious disease of unknown origin. It kills in less than an hour—or overnight—depending on a number of factors. Bottom line, if we're not diligent, if we don't do our jobs, this will be disastrous. There's no vaccine or prophylactic antitoxin, so you people are our one and only front line in this battle."

*Nothing like a little pressure.*

"Other than securing the ricin stores," DeSantos said, "what are our mission objectives? And what kind of support can we expect?"

"You are to capture Rudenko and at least one of his two lieutenants. Dispose of the trigger men. Equally important, after you secure the chemical weapons, obtain any intel on a US attack they've reportedly been planning."

"That's all?" Vail asked. "I mean, where's the challenge? We should be able to wrap all this up in a couple of hours."

Buck squinted and stepped forward. "I don't like you, Agent Vail."

"Understood, sir. Not all men are good with tools."

"As to backup," Buck said firmly, keeping his eyes on Vail but addressing DeSantos, "you've got a skeleton crew. Reid here. Carter from our Joint Terrorism Analysis Centre. I might be able to bring a couple more assets on board, but the fewer we read in, the better for everyone involved. We've got a serious compromise of the Security Services, and we've been unable to identify the individual or individuals responsible. We're making progress, but it's been slow. It's being done by a select number of trusted men and women."

He walked to the desk on his left and opened an envelope. He turned it upside down and dumped several small digital cards into his hand. "SIMs, for your phones. Four for each of you. Use them wisely."

Vail took them and distributed the small, plastic-encased devices to Reid and DeSantos.

Buck dropped the envelope back on the desk. "Now, time to get you three back out there. You're not going to solve these problems standing around in a disused tube station, are you now?"

"We have a slight problem that's gotta be dealt with," DeSantos said. "I've left a body count behind me and my—*our* forensics are all over every crime scene, not to mention that one of Rudenko's men had to be disposed of in Agent Vail's hotel room."

Buck chewed his bottom lip as he considered this. "Because of the infiltrators, the manpower I'm able to devote to this is slim. And I have to be extremely discreet in who I share your mission with. So there's only so much I can do. I'll see if we can run a counter op to divert the Met's investigation. Or at least slow it down. I'll see if the home secretary can play a role." When there were no other questions, he said, "Now, be gone."

As they turned to leave, Buck said, "Except for you, Mr. Reid. I have some internal files to review with you. If we can root out this mole—or at least narrow it down—I may be able to free up some assets." He looked at Vail and made a shooing gesture with his hands. "Go on."

# 34

DeSantos put on the dark-rimmed glasses and Lundberg Stetson hat Vail had gotten him, and Vail pulled on her wool cap, carefully tucking in all of her red hair. She slipped on a pair of sunglasses.

DeSantos's jaw was tight as he fingered the communication device Buck had given him. He was silent as they walked along Lincoln's Inn Fields public square, and Vail could tell something was bothering him.

"What is it?"

"Nothing."

"You realize trying to put one over on a profiler isn't usually a very successful strategy."

"Believe me, Karen, you don't want to know."

"See, that's where you've got it wrong. I do want to know. But you don't think I need to know. If there's one thing you should know about me, it's that I always want to know."

"If you're trying to make me laugh, to make me feel better, it's not working."

She pulled him through the glass door entrance of the Starbucks on High Holborn Street and ordered two lattes. When she rejoined him at the table, as far from the window as they could get in the small café, his brow was hard and he was shaking his leg.

"I got you decaf. Looks like you're amped up enough." She looked around to make sure no one was picking up on their conversation. It was loud and the coffee grinder groan echoed off the walls, so she figured they were safe to talk.

"Enough brooding. What the hell's crawled up your ass?"

DeSantos took the drink and sipped it. He looked at her over the top of his mug, as if deciding what to tell her. Finally he set it down and leaned forward, across the table. She joined him somewhere in the middle. To anyone observing from outside, they would look like lovers sharing an intimate moment.

"My orders are to take out our man."

"As in kill?"

DeSantos looked at her. "What do you think?"

*Would've been nice to know.* "Go on."

"There was a standing order issued by President Whitehall years ago to eliminate him using any means possible. Kind of like bin Laden, but much lower profile. Whereas we announced we were going to hunt down and kill bin Laden, we kept this a tightly guarded secret. Two years ago, the Agency got rare intel that our guy was at a meeting in a desert villa in Syria. We launched a drone strike, but he narrowly escaped and went deeper underground. We talked about numerous missions to hunt him down, but President Nunn rescinded the order."

"Why would he do that?"

"No idea."

"And now? What's changed?"

"The Middle East. The Arab Spring, Libya's fall. Assad's collapse. Chemical weapons, missiles, grenade launchers, all sorts of sophisticated munitions that were once under tight control were suddenly available for the taking. Knox, Tasset, and McNamara knew this meant that our man would resurface—and be on the hunt for whatever he could get his hands on. So they met for five weeks hammering out a plan."

"But?"

"But the president said no."

"Nunn refused to reinstate the kill order?"

"Right. That's why OPSIG's involved. That's why I'm here. That's a big reason why this is a black op."

She looked down at her latte. "Again, you haven't been honest with me."

"Need to know. Are we going to go through this again?"

She took a drink, trying to sort through her emotions. "Fine. Go with me on this. What happens when you kill him, and Buck tells the home secretary that you were the one who did it, and then it gets back to those people in the government who don't know about your black op—like President Nunn? Isn't the idea of a black op that those in charge—even the entire country—has deniability?"

"More or less."

"You'll be hung out to dry." *And so will I.*

"Sometimes that's what you have to do. Greater good, remember? Those weren't just hollow words, Karen. I meant them."

"Don't you think you should've leveled with me from the start?"

"No."

Two large men in suits entered. Though they didn't give Vail and DeSantos so much as a once-over, Vail now had a visceral reaction to a well dressed man—something she hoped to get over before returning home.

She set her latte down. "Let's get out of here."

They walked in silence toward the Holborn Underground station. After making their way to the platform, the train pulled to a stop in front of them. "Mind the gap," the female voice said.

They got onto an empty car. "You've drawn me into this mess," Vail finally said. "I'm risking my career—not to mention my life. I didn't sign on for that."

"When you became an FBI agent, you swore to protect and defend the United States of America. Yeah, fine, you now chase serial killers rather than terrorists. And you've saved dozens of lives over the years. But I'm talking about something on an entirely different scale: the lives of thousands, hundreds of thousands, if not millions, of people. All hinging on what we do, or don't do, next."

*Don't you think I know this?* Vail sat down in resignation. "You should've given me that choice. Wouldn't that have been the fair thing to do?"

"Fair? Life isn't fair, Karen. But I know you. You wouldn't have done anything different. Even if I'd told you everything up front, you still would be at my side looking to find these WMD and taking Hussein Rudenko out of circulation. Tell me I'm wrong."

"I don't know."

"Bullshit."

She sat through a couple of tube stops before answering. "It's not as simple as that for me. I applied to the BAU because I wanted to be off the streets so there'd be less chance that I'd be involved in gun battles and bank robberies and terrorist attacks. I had a young son." She laughed. "And I ended up chasing serial killers, almost getting killed by one of my own, tangling with drug cartels—" Vail looked up at him. "Not exactly safer than being on the street, is it?" She began to realize she was reminding herself of this as much as telling DeSantos of the resulting absurdity of her career decisions.

DeSantos grabbed the overhead handrail to steady himself. "Hey, you're the shrink here, but I have some decent training and insight into people's motivations, too. And I know that you care deeply about what you do, about keeping the public safe and catching the bad guys. That disease afflicts a lot of law enforcement officers, no matter what agency they're with, no matter what city or government they work for. We all have different reasons for how we got where we are, but bottom line is, maintaining law and order, rounding up the vermin, working for the betterment of the good people on our watch—it's in our DNA."

Vail thought a long moment until the train lurched as it approached a station.

"I've got a son who's fatherless. What about him?"

"He's got Robby."

Vail nodded. "And that's been huge. But..."

"But." DeSantos thought a moment, then squatted in front of her. "Maybe it wasn't totally fair that I didn't tell you the whole story. That's the way I've operated almost my entire DOD career, and sometimes I forget that's not what you're accustomed to. So you're free to go. If you want out before we get any deeper, I'm good with that. I understand. No hard feelings. And I'll do my best to shield you. Tell them I forced you into it, blackmailed you, whatever. I'll support your story. I'll handle it on my end." He stopped and waited a moment for Vail to respond. She sat there, unmoving, staring at the ground, tears straining her lower lids.

DeSantos stood up. He touched her shoulder and said, "Like I said, no worries. Thanks for all your help. I enjoyed running from the cops and chasing down the bad guys with you. But be careful. They're still out there and still have you in their sights." The tube car stopped and the doors opened. In the far reaches of her thoughts, she heard, "Mind the gap."

When Vail finally looked up, DeSantos was no longer in front of her. She saw the back of his head through the window as the doors slid shut and the train pulled away from the station.

# 35

Vail stood outside the American Embassy staring up at the humongous eagle mounted five stories above the entrance. She felt a pang of patriotism in her heart as she considered DeSantos's words about duty, the greater good, and about why she went into law enforcement in the first place.

She stepped up to the security booth window and showed her identification. "I need to speak with Jesus Montero, the FBI Legat."

The armed officer, whose name tag read, "Lewis," examined her ID. "Do you have an appointment, Ms. Vail?"

"No appointment. But I'm operating under Mr. Montero's orders." *Or at least I'm supposed to be.*

A block from the embassy Vail had removed her hat and glasses and shoved them into her pocket. She would no longer be needing them. She felt as if a weight had been removed from her chest—but had a sense of foreboding that she had started in motion something that was terribly wrong.

She could not recall a situation in her career when she'd experienced such intensely conflicting emotions.

Lewis stepped from the window and lifted a phone from the wall. While he chatted with the operator, Vail paced, slowly, in front of the large security structure. The sun had broken through the clouds and she looked up at the overcast sky, a brave patch of blue fighting for significance.

After a prolonged wait, Vail checked in on Lewis. The man spoke several words, nodded tightly, and then brought his shoulders back. His eyes shifted to Vail as his hand disappeared beneath the counter.

She knew what was about to happen, and she was not looking forward to it.

Finally Lewis hung up the phone and said something to a colleague, who in turn signaled a soldier holding an MP5 submachine gun and patrolling behind the wrought iron fencing.

"Ms. Vail," Lewis called through the window. "Please come in. The Legal Attaché will see you."

Vail hesitated a moment, then stepped through the metal and bulletproof glass door. After removing her jacket and emptying her pockets, she walked through the magnetometer, smiling at her foresight when she had wiped down the garrote and dumped it in the bushes of Grosvenor Park across the way from the embassy.

As she retrieved her belongings and slipped into her jacket, Lewis explained that he would need to secure her passport during her stay. He then turned her over to two guards, who ushered her up to the Legat's office.

*So far they haven't arrested me. Maybe this won't be so bad after all.*

After delivering Vail to Annette Winston's desk, the men returned to the elevator, headed back to their posts.

"Mr. Montero is waiting for you."

*I'm sure he is.*

"Can I get you something—coffee, soda, water?"

*Kind of like a last cigarette before the firing squad?* "Cappuccino, if you've got it."

"All we have is plain coffee," Winston said. "This isn't Starbucks."

*Oh, really? Dipshit.*

Vail knocked on Montero's door. She heard him call her in, so she entered, expecting a grim-faced man with a sour disposition.

He motioned her to the chair in front of his desk. The last time she was here she had just gotten out of hot water in Madrid. Now she was hoping for a similar resolution so she could just get the hell out of England.

"So, Agent Vail. Sounds like you've had quite a stay in the United Kingdom."

"Quite a stay, yes sir."

He rocked back in his chair, studying her face. "How come you didn't report in or answer your phone when I called?"

"You called?" She feigned surprise and pulled her BlackBerry and made a convincing show of checking the call log. "Sir, my apologies. I see that you did." *Wow, nine times? Oops.* "Please accept my apologies. I'm truly sorry for missing these calls, sir."

"Sorry?" He sprung his chair forward. "What kind of bullshit answer is that?"

"Pretty bad, I have to admit. But I am sorry."

"Do you know what I received this morning?"

Vail thought back to her initial meeting with Montero and her discussion with Gifford. "A phone call?"

Montero drew his chin back, as if he couldn't believe that Vail had guessed correctly. "Yes, a phone call."

*Great. That means I'm really in trouble.*

"Along with several video clips transferred over secure email from CCTV cameras of you engaged in a fight with a man near the London School of Economics. And a lab report from Scotland Yard that claims their forensics crew found your DNA on two men who were murdered in the hotel you were staying in."

Vail swallowed. *I guess this is what it's like when the shit hits the fan.*

"Well? What have you got to say for yourself?"

"Do I need my FLEOA lawyer here, sir?" she asked, referring to the Federal Law Enforcement Officers Association.

"Only guilty people call their lawyers. So you tell me. Do you need to call him?"

*Is this the part where I start bawling about Hector DeSantos and how he forced me to do all these bad things? How he blackmailed me and threatened my son's life?*

"By the sound of this conversation, I think it'd be a good idea."

Montero threw up his hands. "Okay, hang on a second. I'm sorry for how this is coming off. Let's back up a second and start over. Totally off the record. As your boss—as your best friend and sole advocate in the UK—I'd like to know what the hell's going on. I know you've had issues over the years, insubordination and God knows what else. But I also know you're a terrific agent who's made a lot of key arrests. Your ASAC is particularly protective of you."

*Why do people always wait to say the nice things about you after you're dead—or disgraced?*

"Thing is, I don't buy what Scotland Yard's selling. Just tell me what's really going on and I'll back you."

*Does he think I'm an idiot?*

"Sir, if I knew what was going on, I'd tell you. But I think we've got a case of mistaken identity. Someone made...an error in processing the evidence. As to the video, yes. I was attacked near LSE. I was lucky to get away alive."

"Looks like you had some assistance. The Yard's currently looking for one of its own. Clive Reid. You, they just want for questioning. Reid, they've got an arrest warrant out for him."

*Shit, this is bad. I've got to warn him.*

Vail clutched her abdomen and leaned forward, let out a muted groan. "Sir, would you mind if I use the restroom? I suddenly feel...a little sick." *C'mon, Karen, sell it! Don't give him time to think it through.* She rose quickly and looked around as if she had better find a toilet—fast.

Montero frowned. "Go ahead. It's down the hall, make a right past the elevator bank, women's on the left. We'll figure out this mess when you get back. Be quick."

Clutching her lower abdomen, Vail practically ran out of the office. She followed Montero's directions, but instead of passing the elevators and making a right, she hit the fire door to the stairwell and ran down the flights while simultaneously trying to dial her BlackBerry.

Reid answered on the first ring. "Where in arse's hell are you? I've tried reaching Hector—"

"You're in trouble," Vail said as she hit the ground floor. "Met's issued an arrest warrant for you, the guy in the alley. Meet me in Trafalgar Square. Get two new SIM cards, pay cash, so we can't be tracked. What the hell am I saying? You're MI5. Do your thing. Good luck."

She hung up and pulled the wool cap and glasses from her pocket, tucked in her red hair, and walked out of the embassy.

# 36

Trafalgar Square dated back to the mid-1800s, and aside from various improvements, the general layout remained unchanged. Its large central area, bounded by roadways on three sides and a terrace for the National Gallery to the north, had served as a public meeting place for Londoners since its completion.

Despite two fountains and four statues mounted on stone plinths, its most enduring—and dominant—feature was Nelson's Column, a 170-foot-tall Corinthian pillar guarded by four colossal bronze lions at its base and supporting a stately depiction of a war hero from England's historic Battle of Trafalgar.

Vail remembered reading about the square in a travel magazine on the plane from Madrid. Little did she know that a short time later she would be standing at the famous tourist attraction, wearing a disguise and running from local law enforcement and foreign assassins, tracking down a notorious weapons trader and trying to avert a chemical weapons attack. *How do I always get myself into this shit?*

Darkness had fallen. The city lights from the surrounding office buildings and the bustle of people navigating rush hour gave the area a festive, vibrant feeling. *And hopefully, if we're successful, it'll stay that way for years to come.*

Vail found Clive Reid standing beneath an enormous ship in a bottle, the largest one she had ever seen. Several birds perched on its stone platform, and the noise of rushing water from the two adjacent fountains allowed them to talk freely without the danger of parabolic microphones picking up their conversation.

Reid wore a faux beard and mustache and an "I Love London" ball cap pulled down over his forehead.

"Like the cap. Makes you look like a tourist."

"Grabbed it at Cool Britannia in Piccadilly Circus on the way over. Facial hair I had in the trunk."

"You should leave it there."

"Oh, yeah?" He gestured at her face. "Well, newsflash, Miss FBI agent: sunglasses don't really work as a disguise after sunset."

"You think I look a little conspicuous?"

Reid made a point of stepping back and looking her over. "A bit." He reached into his pocket. "Put these on." He produced a pair of horn-rimmed frames.

Vail made the switch.

"So they've got a warrant out?" he asked. "The cameras on Surrey caught my one-round kill shot?"

"Apparently. The legal attaché told me."

Reid lifted his brow. "That was nice of him. He wasn't worried about you warning me?"

"He doesn't know. I told him I had to use the bathroom and walked out of the embassy."

"Oh, cack. This is just getting better."

"No, what's better is that they have my passport."

Reid spied a Metropolitan Police car cruising by; he turned his body and, out of the corner of his eye, watched it pass beneath the majestic Admiralty Arch. "Let's get going. Being out in the open for too long isn't safe." He placed a hand on the small of her back and propelled her forward. "Hopefully we'll get everything sorted out, carry out our mission, and be lauded as heroes. All transgressions forgotten."

"Yeah, and have our likenesses reduced to stone and displayed on a pedestal in Trafalgar Square."

They passed the lions and waited for the light to change, the white lettering at the curb reminding them to "Look right"—an obvious aid to

Americans and other foreigners who don't expect the cars to be coming at them from that side. Vail was sure that simple painted phrase saved lives on a daily basis.

"Hector will be waiting for you in The Sherlock Holmes—it's a pub a couple of blocks down Northumberland—that's that street right there," he said, pointing straight ahead. "I've got something to set up for us, and then I'll meet you."

"At the pub?"

"No. Hector will explain. Two blocks down on the left. Black and gold storefront with chairs out front along the sidewalk. I'll meet up with you in a couple hours."

*Something tells me it's not going to be that simple.*

# 37

I t was a straight shot down Northumberland, like Reid had said. Before Vail stepped inside The Sherlock Holmes, DeSantos emerged. "I didn't think I'd see you again," he said as he led her to their car.

"I kind of walked out of the embassy. They know about the bodies in my hotel, and the shit that went down near LSE. The Met's got an arrest warrant out for Reid."

"None of this is surprising, Karen. But I know it bothers you."

"Don't take this the wrong way, but it would bother any sane person."

"It's part of the stuff I do, the challenges I face. Normally, things are a lot cleaner and I'm in and out and no one knows I've been there. But sometimes things go to hell and the FUBAR scenario comes into play."

*Fucked Up Beyond All Recognition. Now there's a military acronym I'm all too familiar with.*

DeSantos chirped the car remote. "Well, it's in play now, full tilt."

"What's the plan?"

"The plan is that we get in and drive for about ninety minutes."

"Where?"

"The Cotswolds."

"The what?"

"A range of hills in west-central England with quaint villages, craft shops, historic churches. Typical English countryside. Most of all, for us, it's the location of an old, abandoned MI5 safe house."

"And why do we need an old, abandoned MI5 safe house?"

"Not so fast. I've got some stuff to tell you first."

Vail was in the process of buckling her belt but stopped and looked at DeSantos. "Are you actually reading me in?"

"You want to hear what I've got to say, or not?"

She clicked the restraint closed and twisted her body to face DeSantos.

"I'm going to level with you. You sure you can handle the truth?"

"Our problems have usually come about when you don't tell me the truth. Or at least the whole truth."

He navigated his way through the London streets like a pro, heading toward the M40 motorway.

"Remember when we were talking about Anthony Scarponi? How much do you know about him?"

Vail snorted. "The Behavioral Sciences Unit spent months studying his case because of the drugs they used to control him for such a long time. It was an extraordinary case. We petitioned the Department of Defense to interview him, just like we'd done so many times in the past for convicted serial killers."

"Let me guess. You got a big, fat no."

"Right. We explained that this was an unprecedented opportunity to gain insight into the human mind on a scale we'd never encountered."

"And they didn't give a shit, right?"

"Right."

DeSantos chuckled. "I tried getting in to see him, too. Of course I wanted to kill the guy, and Knox knew it. That probably had something to do with denying me access."

"Can't say they were wrong on that one, Hector."

DeSantos ground his jaw. "Yeah. Maybe. Whatever." He waited a beat, then said, "An NSA buddy of mine tipped me on something they picked up while reviewing intercepted communications. Hussein Rudenko appeared to be surfacing. I asked Uzi to check with his Mossad connections to see if they'd heard something. And they had. The intel on those intercepted communications came out of Israel. So it got a little dicey, spying on an ally, but Knox asked Uzi to talk with Director General Gideon Aksel, to informally ask what they knew about Rudenko."

"And that's when you got the news about the chemical weapons tracer Mossad had put on the shipment they'd intercepted."

"Yes." DeSantos turned onto the M40 and entered the motorway. It was wide and looked like any US highway.

"A few months later, Logan Harwood passed some info to MI6 that China was negotiating to buy chemical weapons stores from Libya."

"Harwood was the guy murdered by the wife of that Chinese politician."

"Yeah. The spy who wasn't a spy. Anyway, China claimed that their overtures to the Libyan forces were intended to get the WMD off the market, because they were concerned they'd fall into the wrong hands— like Rudenko."

"MI6 had a different interpretation, I take it."

"As did the CIA. They were worried that China wanted the weapons to add to their arsenal. Kind of like the stealth bombers and drones and mammoth aircraft carriers they're building. Bang—make a purchase and you've got chemical weapons at your disposal. But once I heard that China was involved on some level, I started thinking that Scarponi, or his people, might be connected somehow. Scarponi and his crew had deep roots in China."

"And you explained this to Knox, hoping he'd give you access."

"Not yet. I started working on it, off the books, with my OPSIG team. But we couldn't come up with anything other than a tenuous connection between Scarponi and Rudenko—like they'd been in the same city when some big deals went down, leading us to think that Scarponi wasn't just an assassin. He also might've been working with Rudenko on some level closing illegal weapons sales."

"But you couldn't bring any of this to Knox because he would've told you to find a more solid connection before you approached Scarponi."

"It was even more complicated than that. There was concern that talking with Scarponi about his past might trigger something and cause a regression in his treatment. They were trying to 'rehabilitate' him so that he could provide them with intel on the brain research program China had used on him, and so that they could eventually return him to the field. With his knowledge and network, they thought he could be an invaluable CIA asset."

"So you had to convince Knox that this would be a good test of their progress."

"Problem was, they wanted to wait until the doctor gave his blessing. So I lobbied Knox and he got together with my boss, SecDef McNamara, and they—"

"Your boss is the secretary of defense? Are you shitting me?"

"I didn't say that."

"You just said—"

"No, listen to me. I did not tell you that. OPSIG is black, Karen, so details about it aren't known. Lose that information from your brain."

"How do I do that?"

"How the hell do I know? Just, you know, forget it."

"Forget what?"

DeSantos gave her a slight nod. "Thank-you."

"So you got in to talk to Scarponi."

He turned his attention back to the road. "Yeah. I wanted to get the names of his accomplices. This is hard to explain, but I promised Brian—Brian Archer, my partner—that I'd find the guys who killed him."

"Did Knox know you wanted to off Scarponi and his men?"

"He's worked with special ops guys, black operators for decades. He knows the deal. When I told him about the Rudenko connection, he was intrigued. But not convinced. So I didn't press it. My strongest play was to tell him I needed to get the names of the men in Scarponi's network. That was true. I'd waited a long time for a chance to pursue those guys, and I had to put the matter to rest. It was destroying me inside knowing those guys are still out there.

"Anyway, I suspected a trained killer like Scarponi could put up a convincing front for medical researchers who aren't skilled in dealing with people like him. And as soon as I started questioning Scarponi, I could tell he was bullshitting the doctors, manipulating them. He was no different from the day he entered the facility. He was the same trained assassin who'd killed Brian. And if they set him free...Only bad things would've come from that."

"You felt compelled to prove to Knox and McNamara that he wasn't safe to be released." Vail smiled when DeSantos glanced over at her. She shrugged. "That's how I would've felt."

"I wanted them to see it, I wanted to expose Scarponi for what he was—still is."

He fell silent, the oncoming headlights from the other side of the motorway flashing across his face at regular intervals.

Finally DeSantos said, "But I blew it. He did a passive resistive act, which I should've anticipated—but didn't. I had no alternative but to threaten his life. Even then, I wasn't sure he'd give me those names. I admit that I lost control. Being in that room with him, that smug asshole...knowing he killed my partner...honestly, Karen, I just wanted to pummel him. For Brian. So I did."

Vail placed a hand on DeSantos's forearm. "I understand."

DeSantos's face remained set and stern. "I know you do." Suddenly he smiled. "I've seen you in action."

Vail grinned as well. "As different as you and I are, I guess we share a few similar character traits."

"I think your ASAC is a little more understanding than the secretary of defense. While I was working over Scarponi, the MPs broke in and, well, they suspended me. I wasn't lying when we first ran into each other. I really did get into hot water."

"Looks like you came out of it okay."

"They let me stew for a while, reduced my security clearance, kept me on a tight chain. Everything I did—office work, phone calls, email— everything was closely monitored. I'd never been in Knox's doghouse before. Can't say it was a pleasant experience."

"Obviously at some point they started trusting you again."

"I brought them some really important intel that changed the game. The communication NSA intercepted from Mossad. Once Uzi was involved, he started looking for any indication Rudenko and his crew were going to use these weapons on US soil. He finally found it and I renewed my case for interrogating Scarponi. They said no. But a few days later, the Security Services' database got hacked. This time they came to me."

"What about Scarponi? Did you get anything out of him before they shut you down?"

"Names. I asked him about Rudenko, too. Didn't get anything tangible, but I could tell by his reaction that I was on to something. And it looks like it's paid off."

"How so?"

"Remember Vince Richter?"

Vail thought a moment. "The guy we asked about in that bar. Scarponi's associate."

"Right."

"That was one of the names Scarponi gave me. Richter and his buddies, Mike Hagel and Kyle Walker. We looked for them all over the globe. Interpol had nothing recent, Mossad had nothing. Even the Russians—the FSB surprisingly cooperated—they had zip. Everything had been quiet for the past six years. Some felt they'd been taken out somewhere, somehow, by someone. But I had a feeling they were still around. Ultimately we decided Richter was the one we had the best shot at finding.

"Once we put out the feeler at the bar, MI5 picked up some activity. It set things in motion, made Richter surface, put him back on the grid. Some Met-controlled CCTV cameras have been fitted with new facial recognition software. They'd talked about it for years, but they're finally starting to roll it out."

"So we have a fix on him?"

"You could say that. Carter's got him in custody at a safe house in the Cotswolds."

"You think he'll give us anything that could help us?"

"Even if he's not directly involved—which I think he is—he knows stuff, I'm sure of it. Assuming I'm right, he could be our 'in' for penetrating Rudenko's network."

"Just remember that we need to find those chemical weapons stores before they're used."

"What's your point?"

"Promise me that this visit with Richter isn't going to be about vengeance."

DeSantos snorted. "Would I do that?"

"It's human nature, Hector. I may not know about black ops and covert missions, but I do know behavioral tendencies."

DeSantos considered that a bit. "Well, maybe we'll both get what we want. Two birds, right?"

Vail gave him a dubious look. *That remains to be seen.*

# 38

Vail craned her neck to get a look at the stone house that was illuminated by the car's headlights. Given the countryside's suffocating darkness, the contrasting brightness was stark.

According to DeSantos, the structure's low roofline and row of gables made it a prime example of Cotswold architecture.

"This is the safe house?" Vail asked. "Looks like it's a couple hundred years old."

"Maybe more. Its virtues are pretty obvious—it's well isolated, it's only got a few small windows on the main floor, and it's made of rock. Pretty easy to defend against an incursion."

They walked up to the front entrance and knocked. A halogen porch light came on, and a moment later Reid pulled open the arched wooden door.

"How'd you get here before us?" Vail asked.

"I know a short cut. Follow me."

He led them to a bookcase in the living room, which featured roughhewn kiln-dried beams and a creaky wood floor. He removed a copy of Don Quixote and pressed a button. A latch released and he pulled the furniture toward them; it moved smoothly on a piano hinge mounted along its left side.

They descended two stories down a tightly-wound metal spiral staircase into a subbasement that appeared to be from another century: modern glass walls stretched the entire length of the house.

*This doesn't look like a safe house; it looks like a black site.*

"Black site" was a military term more recently associated with CIA-run covert rendition locations in foreign countries where enhanced interrogation techniques were employed on high value prisoners acquired in the War on Terror. Vail did not know of any on UK soil, but this bore the hallmarks of a rendition site designed to extract information outside the traditional law enforcement environment.

Ethan Carter stood in an area directly ahead of them, rummaging through a drawer in a Craftsman tool chest.

In one of the glass rooms sat a man of about forty, disheveled black hair and day-old stubble his most distinguishing features. He was seated on a metal folding chair, his manacled wrists resting on a small table in front of him.

"That our guy?" Vail asked.

"Vince Richter," Reid said. "Hector briefed you?"

"I did." DeSantos stepped beside Carter and examined the items he was sorting through. "Is this what we've got to work with?"

"Some of it," Carter said. "What did you have in mind?"

Vail stole a look at the spread of devices and shook her head. "No, this is not the way to go."

DeSantos snorted. "Who labeled you the expert and put you in charge?"

"I *am* an expert in interview techniques. And I put me in charge."

"This isn't an interview, Karen. It's an interrogation, a plain, old balls-to-the-wall interrogation. You don't have to be PC here."

"I can't be here, period. If I'm a party to a coercive interrogation, I have to report it. It's against FBI regs. I could be fired."

"Report it?" Carter asked. He exchanged looks with Reid and DeSantos. "Do you not understand what we're doing here? What you're doing here? The Security Service has entrusted us with an extremely sensitive operation. Our ranks have been compromised. What we're doing here isn't happening. So no matter what comes out of this, no matter what's done or what interrogation techniques are used, it's not happening. There's nothing to *report*."

"That's a nice thought, but—"

"This isn't a negotiation, Karen." DeSantos checked his watch. "And we don't have a lot of time."

Vail set her jaw, realizing that her need to follow FBI regulations probably went out the window once she agreed to work with Buck. Then again, maybe she crossed that threshold when she landed at Heathrow. She folded her arms and asked, "How aggressive do you plan to get?"

"Let's see. There's a notorious weapons dealer out there with a small cadre of ready and willing soldiers preparing to release a lethal toxin on the city of London. How aggressive should we get?"

*Smartass.* "You know about the Senate Intelligence Committee report on enhanced interrogation?"

"It's classified, Karen. And it's six thousand pages long."

"Enough of it's been leaked. And from what I've read, forcing a prisoner to divulge information under duress doesn't work."

"It depends on the prisoner. It depends on the interrogator. And it depends on a number of other factors that we don't have time to sit here and discuss."

"I'm just saying there are more effective ways of getting the information that we need." She looked at Carter and Reid, who turned to DeSantos, a look of deference penetrating their gazes.

Vail understood the dynamic: she was DeSantos's colleague; he should be the one to deal with her—first. If they didn't like where it was going, they would then intervene.

DeSantos pulled over a metal stool and sat down. "Okay, what's your plan?"

"I'll go in and talk with him. I may be able to get him to give us what we want without resorting to torture."

"Enhanced interrogation."

"Fine, call it what you want. Torture."

DeSantos cocked his head. "I'm curious. Why do you think it's okay to get...aggressive when your loved one's life is on the line, but in this case you're willing to back off and follow the letter of the law?"

Vail ground her molars. "If we were following the letter of the law, we wouldn't be in a black site in the middle of the English countryside with a bunch of...*tools* in our possession, now, would we?"

"That's not an answer."

"No," Vail said, "it's not."

VAIL YANKED OPEN THE GLASS DOOR to the room where Richter was seated. To properly conduct the type of "rapport building" interview she was attempting, she would need at least two weeks, multiple visits, and a host of other conditions she did not have at her disposal. In fact, the imminent threat posed by the men standing behind her—in full view because of the glass walls—doomed her efforts before she would speak her first word.

Ideally, Vail's goal would be to treat the prisoner with respect and dignity, and to make him understand that she was going to be truthful with him. She would explain that she was his advocate and would help him obtain whatever it was he wanted, short of freedom—though even that could potentially be dangled as a benefit depending on his level of cooperation and the nature of his past transgressions.

Establishing rapport, building trust had worked with captured al-Qaeda terrorists, so there was some hope that it could work with a guy like Vince Richter. Hardened though he likely was, having almost assuredly received resistance training, it might be their best approach. In this case, Vail would not even start discussing Rudenko, ricin, or his colleagues for at least a couple of interviews. She would ask him about his needs, his views on what he did for a living, his family life, the hardships he faced as a child...topics that built a relationship—not to be friends, but to be negotiating partners. You give me what I need, and I'll give you what you need.

This approach required weeks to be effective.

But Vail did not have weeks. She had minutes.

Equally important, the threat of aggressive coercive techniques—so-called enhanced interrogation—presented an insurmountable obstacle. It was impossible to build rapport with Richter when three men stood in the adjacent room making no effort to hide their desire to get their hands around his neck.

What she really needed was a one-time dump of information from Richter—names, places, times. But he had no motivation to do this, and Vail had no basis for being in a position to help him get what he wanted. In fact, he would probably step in front of a moving train before giving up information that would endanger his comrades.

She knew all this as she entered the room, yet she felt the need to try.

"Mr. Richter, I'm Karen Vail."

"Is that supposed to mean something?"

"Not in the least. I was just introducing myself. I like to know who I'm talking with, so I wanted to afford you the same courtesy."

He sat up straight and tilted his head slightly, as if wondering if she was being truthful. This clearly was not what he was expecting.

"I know what you're thinking. You were waiting for those guys to break out the pliers and start pulling out your fingernails. Or smash your testicles with the hammer they've got out there."

*Yeah, that got his attention.* His eyes were riveted to hers. They widened slightly at the first part of her comment and his pupils dilated when the most sensitive part of his anatomy was mentioned.

"I'm not going to lie to you, Mr. Richter. That's what they intend to do. And I think you know that. But I was hoping we could chat a bit and avoid all that. Because I know those guys, one of them really, really well. And let's just say you owe me big time for coming in here first. He was chomping at the bit."

"I know all about Hector Cruz."

*Good move on his part; he's trying to throw me off my game by showing me he has information that he should not have.*

"Do you, now?"

"I do."

She spread her hands, palms up. "Excellent. Then you know he's like you, a trained assassin. And you know that he's not bluffing. Neither am I. I'm your best chance at avoiding a very, very bad evening. So help me to help you. Make it easy on both of us."

Richter looked at her a long moment, his eyes moving left to right. Assessing her, sizing her up. "What do you want to know?"

"Where can we find Hussein Rudenko?"

"No idea."

REID LEANED BOTH HANDS on the glass. "I like Karen, but she's out of her league."

"This isn't gonna work," Carter said.

DeSantos did not remove his gaze from Richter. "I'm not so sure of that. She's gone nose to nose with serial killers and drug cartel lieutenants. In a way, she's in her element."

"Sounds like you support her nice guy approach," Carter said.

DeSantos lifted a shoulder. "I respect her abilities. But I'd rather hook up a battery to Richter's balls, if that's what you mean, because we don't have time to do a dance with this guy. That's why she's on a short rope. Five minutes. She doesn't produce, it's my turn."

VAIL NODDED SLOWLY. "You have no idea where Hussein Rudenko is. Well, that's not a good start to our conversation, Vince. But that's okay. There's lots of other stuff I need to know. Like, where's the ricin being stored?"

Richter hesitated a moment. His gaze drifted over to where DeSantos was standing, legs spread, arms folded across his chest, staring intently at him through the glass walls.

"Also no idea. But a guy like Rudenko, the way he'd work is he'd sock it away in multiple places. Makes it harder to stop the attack. Kind of like not putting all your eggs in one basket."

"Good analogy," Vail said. "So where are these places?"

Richter pushed the palms of his hands down along his legs. "Only Mr. Rudenko knows. He doesn't tell us information we don't need to know."

*You've gotta be kidding me. If I hear that one more time, I'm gonna scream.*

"Is there anything you want that I can get you?"

"How about letting me walk out of here."

Vail smiled. "What I asked was, is there anything you want *that I can get you.* I can't let you go. You know that."

"You mean like a beer?"

"A beer. A steak. Something like that."

"Nope."

*He's not making this easy. Then again, where the hell would I get a steak in the middle of nowhere?*

"Any idea how we can go about finding Mr. Rudenko?"

"He's on the move, not staying in one place more than a day."

*Figured as much.*

"Do you have a way of getting in touch with him?"

Richter rolled his eyes toward the ceiling. "He contacts me, not the other way around. I'm not part of his organization, I'm just a contractor. He pays me, I do my job, and I disappear like a good contract killer until the next time he needs me. And I'm not involved in the ricin deal. I know of it, because one of his guys talked."

"Which guy—what's his name?"

Richter narrowed his eyes as he looked at Vail. "Don't know his name. But he wouldn't do you no good, anyway."

"And why's that?"

"Because he's dead."

"You sure?"

"Killed him myself. A .40 round behind the ear. Yeah, he's dead."

*That was the easiest confession I ever got. Too bad it can't be used against him. This place doesn't exist and this discussion isn't really happening.*

"What about Mike Hagel and Kyle Walker? Where are they?"

Richter turned his head away and stared at the floor.

"How about Ratib Morsi, Emir Dhul Fiqar, or Nikola Hačko?"

"I don't know those names," Richter said.

"What about Malik al-Atah and Farkhad Gogun?"

Richter shook his head. "Those either."

Vail waited a few seconds, then stepped in front of him. "Look. Vince. I told you that if you don't tell us what we need to know, the guys out there are gonna be your next visitors, and they're not as nice as I am. Definitely not as attractive." She waited. No reaction. "C'mon. Give me something."

Richter, wearing a dour frown, said, "Hagel's in Hackney, renting a bedsit at Graham and Mare, by the train tracks. Two-B. Walker's got a place on Battersea Park Road, by Albert Bridge. He rents a room in the back of the old gray house. That's all I got. Don't know any of those other names."

Vail took a long look at him. "You're sure about that. Because once I walk out, I'm not coming back in, even if you scream for me. I won't be sticking around here. Besides, I think I'd vomit if I watched them smash your balls." She shivered—a genuine shudder.

"Like I said."

The door opened and DeSantos gave Vail a sideways nod. He wanted her to leave.

Richter rose from his seat. "I told her what I know, DeSantos. I'm serious—that's all I got."

DeSantos held up a pair of rusted needle nose pliers. "These do the job on fingernails, as Karen pointed out. But I've found they work well on teeth, too. Both hurt. A lot."

"This is where I say good-bye." Vail glanced at Richter, giving him one more chance before the hungry lions were unleashed.

"Don't let the door hit you in your very *attractive* ass on the way out," he said, leaning in his chair to get a look.

*Asshole. I tried to save your life.*

OUT OF RESPECT FOR VAIL, DeSantos waited for the door to close before continuing.

"I'm sure you're well schooled in SERE," he said, referring to the Pentagon's "Survival, Evasion, Resistance, Escape" program that trained its soldiers how to repel efforts to extract vital information under duress. "And I'm sure you know that I've been taught how to get what I need in situations like this."

DeSantos examined the pliers. "See, the thing is, Vince, when I was in the SEALs, we also had rigorous training. Just about every scenario you can imagine, in impossibly tough physical and mental conditions. But like so many of the guys who came before and after me, no one knows how he'll react when he's put in the situation he's trained weeks, months, years for. He doesn't know if he's really going to be any good at it, how his brain will respond to the fear, the intensity, the life-or-death pressure.

But once the bullets start flying, when the adrenaline's surging, that's when you find out what you've got. And how good you are."

DeSantos sat down at the table and waited, studied Richter's face. "I don't know if you've ever been in a situation like this out in the field. I have, and it was probably one of the worst times of my life. I still have the scars to show for it. Physical. Mental." He rested the pliers on the table in front of him, inches from Richter's fingers. "But, see, that's what makes me so good at what I do.

"So, Vince. From one man to another." He leaned forward. "From one killer to another. Tell me where I can find Hussein Rudenko."

Richter stared at DeSantos a solid two minutes. DeSantos was on the verge of abandoning his last attempt at using reason when Richter cleared his throat.

"Rudenko's got a flat rented out under the name of Bassioni."

DeSantos lifted his brow. "Where?"

"Lambeth. Stangate apartments."

"I hope you're being honest with me, Vince, because if not..." He let that thought ride on the air and walked out, closing the door behind him.

"Searching databases for those names," Carter said as he struck the onscreen keyboard of his tablet.

"I know the Stangate," Reid said, huddling with Carter over the screen.

"Let me know as soon as you have something," DeSantos said as he made his way up the winding stairs to the main house.

DeSantos pulled out the CLAIR communications device that Buck had given him. There was no reception, most likely because of the stone walls. DeSantos did not fully understand the technology behind the CLAIR, but he knew that sometimes handsets like this, at extreme distances, required either satellites or relay towers to transmit the signal, or some other method of reamplifying it.

He headed for the front door and then stepped outside, where Vail was pacing.

"Normally, I need a couple weeks to establish rapport, do it the right way," she said.

"And to do what I'd normally do, those 'enhanced' techniques, there's a method, a process to them. They require time to work, too. Time we don't have."

"Considering the circumstances, I think we got some potentially good info. The stuff he said seemed truthful. Organizations like Rudenko's operate like traditional terrorism cells, insular and separate. So that if one person gets grabbed up, he can't damage the entire org—"

"Yes, Karen, I know."

"And if he's only a contractor—"

"Yes, Karen, I know."

"You weren't in there very long. Did you get anything else from him?"

DeSantos walked in front of their car while examining the CLAIR's screen. "We've got service." He started tapping out a message. "He gave us a potential location of Rudenko. Lambeth. Assuming he wasn't jerking my chain."

"Did you— Forget it, I don't want to know."

"No, I didn't. But he understood what was going to happen if he didn't cooperate."

*Let's hope that won't be necessary.*

A light breeze ruffled her hair. "Freaking cold out here." She hugged herself and walked in place to get her blood moving. "Are you asking Buck to confirm what Richter gave us?"

"Exactly."

He shoved the device back in his pocket.

"Where's Lambeth?"

"A borough in south London." His answer was short, his voice taut.

Buck's reply came through surprisingly fast. "They're sending CO19 over to those locations," DeSantos said. "We'll know in a few minutes if the info was good."

"A few minutes? How—"

"CO19 units are mobile, located all around London. When a situation hits, one of them's never that far away."

Vail thought a moment, then said, "We haven't given them much to go on. How're they gonna be able to verify whether or not these guys are there, or if it's all just a bullshit exercise?"

"It's all we've got," DeSantos said.

"But—"

"What do you want me to say, Karen? I'm doing the best I can."

"I know." Vail turned around and stared into the darkness. A light drizzle began falling and tickled her face. Judging by the freshness of the air, she had a feeling the surroundings were lush and picturesque. But it was so pitch dark that she might as well be staring at a concrete wall.

"You don't have to wait out here with me. Go inside, get warm."

"I'm fine." She turned around to find DeSantos pacing. He could've been cold or nervous, but Vail sensed it was something else. "What's bothering you?

He kept walking, hands shoved in his pockets. "I'm not sure. Something. Something's not right."

Vail trusted his intuition, so she started replaying the interview with Richter in her mind. Everything appeared to have been above board. He answered truthfully, she thought. She didn't pick up anything out of the ordinary. Where he held back, she called him on it.

Fifteen more minutes passed. Her toes were getting numb and her hands, even though they were tucked away in her pockets, were starting to lose feeling, too. "How much longer do—"

The CLAIR vibrated.

DeSantos pulled it out and read the display. "Checked twenties for Hagel and Walker. Negative on Walker. There's no one in the back room of the house—hasn't been rented out for two years. It's filled with junk." A second later, another message arrived: "As to Hagel, the flat mates at that location are all college kids. Haven't shared the place with a middle-aged guy. Just in case, CO19's doing a general sweep of the building, but so far, negative. They need more time." He looked up from the device as the front door opened and Reid emerged.

"No records of these guys where he said. No records of anyone by those names living in those boroughs."

Vail blew on her hands. "Aliases."

"Possibly. Ethan's checking, but where the hell do you start with that? It's a long shot."

*This whole thing's a long shot.*

"Between a records search and visuals, we should have a pretty decent idea if the info's good," DeSantos said.

"We don't even have a physical description of these guys," Reid said. "They could be looking right at both of them and not know it."

"They were given a general description," DeSantos said. "Caucasian males, between thirty and fifty. Anyone residing at those locations who fell in that category was to be questioned."

Reid rolled his eyes. "It's a shitty way of going about this. Assuming Richter told us the truth, it's easy to miss the prize. We can't be back there searching ourselves, and we can't trust anyone with the Met or MI5 with full information because we don't know who's the mole and we can't let 'em know what's going down." Reid shivered, then pulled up his collar. "Cold out here."

"Really?" Vail asked as she stamped her feet. "Hadn't noticed."

The CLAIR vibrated again. DeSantos read the display. "The Rudenko lead's bogus, too. They're questioning the Stangate landlord. No one living there matching the description. No tenant by the name of Bassioni. They're showing around a photo array of Gavin Paxton that Buck pulled off the Turner Gallery security camera footage. They're doing a door to door, but it's a big building. Gonna take a while."

"And there's no record of a renter with the name of Bassioni or known aliases," Carter called from the doorway. "Not in the Stangate, or anywhere in Lambeth. Unless we're missing something, it looks like Richter was making us butcher's fancy a fool."

*I have no idea what he just said, but I'm sure it's not good.*

DeSantos looked hard at Vail.

"Look," Vail said, "like you, I did my best with what I had. But I've been over it in my head, and it didn't look to me like he was hiding anything."

"Oh, he was definitely hiding things. And it looked to me like he was downright lying."

"What makes you say that?"

"His body language, his eyes, his hands, his—It was a combination of things."

"Like what?"

DeSantos let his shoulders drop. "Like rubbing the palms of his hands on his legs when you asked him where the ricin was. I knew then that there was a good chance that at least some of the stuff he was telling you was suspect."

"Why didn't you say anything?"

"Because it's very difficult to accurately conclude that someone's lying based on nonverbal clues. In retrospect, you realize you were right. But it's far from foolproof."

*How could I have missed these behaviors?* She again played the interview through her mind. "I don't remember seeing anything that...Wait a minute." She thought a moment, then grabbed DeSantos's arm and pulled him aside. In his ear, she said, "Richter called you 'DeSantos.' But you're only known here as Cruz."

DeSantos locked eyes with Vail for a moment.

"Christ." He ran back toward the house, headed for the subbasement.

# 39

Richter was grinning as they entered the interrogation suite.

"The asshole knew he gave us a load of bullshit," DeSantos said.

Vail moved in front of DeSantos. "Forget that. How could he know? How'd he know your name?"

DeSantos did not acknowledge her. He was locked in on Richter's face. Finally he turned around and went over to the toolbox.

"Hector," Vail said, grasping his arm from behind, "don't do this."

"Let go," he said, shaking her hand loose. "I've had enough. We don't have time to waste with this jerk-off."

He started toward the room but Vail grabbed him again. He flung her aside and she slammed against the glass wall behind her.

DeSantos yanked the door open and went inside.

Vail gathered herself and took a step toward the room, but Carter and Reid stopped her. "We tried it your way. Now it's our turn."

THE DOOR SWUNG WIDE, the rubber stop slamming against the opposing pane of glass. DeSantos's chest was heaving and he was hyperventilating.

He had to calm down. Breathe. Think.

Richter did not flinch. He did not cower—but he did start laughing.

"You finally figured it out, Hector *DeSantos*. Took you long enough."

"Too long." As he stood there, studying Richter's smug face, he decided that they had given the man enough opportunities to make things right. He had made his choice.

"I want answers."

"And I want to walk out of here, but that's not going to happen because you're not gonna get your answers. See, here's the problem, my friend. You're gonna kill me anyway, revenge for your partner's death. I get that. So why would I tell you shit?"

DeSantos slapped both palms on the table in front of Richter. "Because I'm not going to just kill you. I'm going to make you hurt. But—you give me the right answers, and I'll make it quick. No pain. That's where we're at, that's the place you've come to. This is how you're going to spend the last minutes of your life."

"I knew it'd come to this eventually. I've had a great life, I'm in a good place. Do what you need to do."

This was not how DeSantos pictured this moment going. He took a deep breath. He had to focus, forget about his vendetta. He had to do his job.

He cleared his throat, more in control—but just barely. "How do you know my name?

"After Scarponi found out who we'd killed—and who Brian Archer was—he got a message to us. He knew the score, so he set up a simple warning. Anyone comes around asking for Vince Richter, he's looking to off us. You and Vail came looking, so—"

"But that's your name. I don't get it."

"My legal name's Vince, but no one calls me that. *No one.* I go by Cam. Get it now, Hector?"

Oh yeah, he got it. Scarponi wasn't merely giving him names when he questioned him. He was setting him up, using "Vince Richter" as a code word, a booby trap. Brilliant move for Scarponi. Blatantly stupid for DeSantos. How could he not see this? What the hell was wrong with him?

"Yeah," Richter said, "I can see you're starting to put it all together. Take another minute, and maybe you won't need to ask me anymore questions." He laughed, a raspy chuckle.

DeSantos was, in fact, putting it together: those mercenaries by Aldwych and Strand weren't working for Rudenko. They were Scarponi's men.

DeSantos took the pliers and swung them, slicing a jagged gash across Richter's forehead. He fell off the chair, shook his head, and laughed. "I thought you were gonna use those to pull out my fingernails. They work a whole lot better that way." He got back on the seat and slapped his cuffed hands on the table, splaying the digits wide. Daring DeSantos to do it.

DeSantos tightened his grip around the tool, wanting desperately to inflict unending pain on this man. For Brian. For himself.

He raised the pliers and jabbed them through Richter's hand into the wood table.

The scream was deafening.

# 40

"Jesus Christ." Vail started for the room, but again Reid and Carter held her back. She turned and punched Carter in the jaw and was about to hit Reid when DeSantos yelled, "Enough!"

Richter, writhing in pain but unable to extract the pliers because of the flexcuffs, whimpered loudly in the background.

DeSantos set his jaw. "Get her the hell out of here."

Carter, sporting a red blotch over his cheek, was a bit rougher than Reid as they took Vail by the arms and dragged her back toward the staircase.

"Hector," Vail said, "don't do this. You'll regret it later. You'll have to live with it."

DeSantos stopped them and approached Vail. She stood quietly in their grasp.

"I'll have to live with it?" He snorted. "Do you know the pain that I've lived with since they killed Brian? The pain of knowing his beautiful young daughter's growing up without her dad? That Brian never even got to meet her?" He closed his eyes. "We had an agreement." He sighed, looked up at the ceiling. "That's what kept us going, knowing that if one of us went down during a mission, the other would make things right. When you've been through the kind of shit Brian and I have been through, a pact like that means everything. It makes it possible to complete your mission. Our whole team operated that way." He shook his head. "I can't expect you to understand. But yeah. You bet I'll have to live with it. I'm counting on it."

For the first time in a long time, Vail had nothing to say.

DeSantos turned and headed back to the toolbox.


THEY SHOVED VAIL THROUGH the wood door and onto the wet grass. Carter disappeared back inside the house. Reid remained there with her.

"This is wrong, Reid. You know it's wrong."

"Richter's scum. Why do you care what happens to him? He admitted being a murderer. To your face."

"That's not the point." *Am I more concerned with Richter's well-being, or Hector's? I shouldn't have been there to begin with. I should've left when I had the chance.*

Vail sat down on the stone curb by the front door. She knew the human mind, she understood what DeSantos felt—but she was unconvinced he would feel better after he settled his score. In some ways, yes. But in practice, things aren't always what you think they'll be.

Vail looked up and realized Reid was waiting for her to elaborate. "I've been on the edge, I've threatened offenders at gunpoint to get information. I know what it feels like, being out of control, willing to kill for your loved one. I get that. I know that look in Hector's eyes because I've had it." She collected her thoughts a moment. "It changed me, affected me in ways I never could've appreciated if I hadn't lived through it."

Reid looked out into the darkness. "I've been there, too."

Vail waited for him to explain. When he didn't, she asked, "On the job?"

He pulled a lighter and cigarette from his pocket and set it aflame.

"You smoke?"

He leaned back against the stone column of the entryway. "Only in times like these."

*I can understand that.* She thought about asking for one but decided against it.

"That picture you saw in my car, of Brant? None of what I told you was true. Well, except the divorce."

"What the hell? Why lie to me?"

"To give us something in common. To gain your trust. We have a file on you, Karen. We know about Jonathan."

Vail shuddered, and it had nothing to do with the chilly air. She felt violated. "We? MI5?"

Reid took a drag and then launched the smoke into the damp air. "Brant was real. He was my son. Murdered in the park by a gang. He found himself in the wrong part of town with a group of friends on holiday. He wouldn't give up his iPod. It was his Christmas present, and—and it was my idea to get it for him." Reid gathered himself, fought back a tear. "He was stabbed."

"I'm sorry."

"I went down there to East London every day, working that case. Until I found the fucker who killed him."

Reid stopped and fell silent. He examined the butt, watching it burn through the edges of the paper.

Vail could make a pretty good guess about how that story ended. Deciding it was best to change the subject, she said, "I'm not convinced that torture is going to get the information Hector wants. Richter can't give us what he doesn't have. And I can't stand by and let it happen. My oath as an FBI agent—"

"Stop right there." He pushed away from the stone column. "You operate by a different set of rules than someone like Hector does. He's a black operator. What he does...one of the rules he lives by is that there *are* no rules. Mission success is the only acceptable result, because if he fails...he or people in his unit will die. People he's there to save will die. There is no safety net, and usually very little margin for error. The only option is to win, at all costs."

Vail looked away.

"Don't be so hard on him. I can tell he's a good man—because he cares. You may think the killing doesn't affect him. It does."

"You talk like you know firsthand."

Vail regretted saying it the moment it left her mouth, for fear that he was talking about Brant's death. But he surprised her.

"I'm a spook. Always have been." Reid shook his head. "I've said enough."

Vail sighed deeply and realized she had some thinking to do before DeSantos emerged from the basement.

DESANTOS CONSIDERED EACH of the devices arrayed in front of him.

He lifted a syringe of clear liquid and looked at Carter for explanation.

"SP-117."

"No shit."

"We got it off the Russians, so it doesn't have the Security Service's fingerprints on it. Or the CIA's, for that matter."

DeSantos looked at Richter, who had stopped writhing. He was pounding his free fist on the table, no doubt trying to take his mind off the pain.

"Go remove the pliers," he said. "I'm going to use the drug."

"It's old," Carter said. "It's been here for years. Don't know how effective it'll be. Heck, it could kill him. And then we won't get anything, if there's anything to get."

"Understood."

DeSantos knew that SP-117 was a Russian invention, a potent psychoactive medication used to obtain information from unwilling participants. It was, in effect, a truth serum.

Although there was no US law that prohibited the use of such drugs, international law considered them a form of torture. Oddly, however, psychiatrists could use the pharmaceuticals legally on psychotic patients. A convincing argument could be made that Vince Richter was indeed psychotic. But DeSantos was not concerned with legalities. Masses of people were in danger of being killed by the release of a deadly toxin, and if he had to drug a guy to find out where the ricin was being held, or where the attack was going to occur, he had no problem with doing that.

Carter joined him, bloody pliers in hand, and said, "Smug asshole's not laughing anymore."

"Pain has a way of doing that."

DeSantos walked into the room and then folded his arms as he leaned against the glass door. "How ya doin', Vince? Or should I call you Cam?"

Richter drew himself up in his chair, cradling his swollen and bloody right hand. He wiped the saliva from his chin with his other shoulder.

"I'm going to show you some mercy. Why? No goddamn idea. Vail guilted me into it, I guess. Whatever the reason, it's your lucky night." DeSantos chuckled. "Then again, maybe 'lucky night' is a poor choice of words." He held the syringe up to the light and examined the fluid. "Years ago, a defector from the KGB's biological weapons directorate gave the CIA a truth drug codenamed SP-117. He claimed it had been used as a remedy to break down one's defenses. Officers of the directorate used it to check the veracity of their own agents on assignment in foreign territories."

DeSantos stepped around the table to Richter's right. "I've never actually used this stuff, so I'm curious to see how effective it is."

He jabbed it into Richter's neck and pressed the plunger part way. He had no idea what the proper dosage was, and he didn't want to overmedicate him. He'd either have a heart attack or fall asleep. Better to start with a lower dosage and increase it if needed.

Richter cringed. "Bastard."

"I've been called a whole lot worse," DeSantos said matter-of-factly. "By people a whole lot tougher than you."

He recapped the needle, placed the syringe in his pocket, and then joined Carter outside the room.

"Any idea how long I should give it?"

"Never used it. Too many variables. And that's assuming it's still got some potency left."

"I hope it works. I don't know about you, but I don't particularly enjoy inflicting pain to get information. I'm good at it. And I'm good at selling it—I have to look like I get off on it, so they believe I'll do whatever needs to be done. They have to buy that I'm a sadistic nutcase who'll chop off their hand."

"I know."

"You?"

Carter shrugged. "It's a tool. I can take it or leave it. Depends on the bloke, I guess. I won't say I never enjoy it. I tuned up a child molester in my sister's neighborhood a few years back. The law failed and they cut him loose. I felt I had to do something. So I did." He fiddled with the metal instruments in the drawer. "I quite enjoyed it." He looked up at DeSantos. "I've never told anyone that."

"I imagine you've never lost any sleep over it."

"Not a wink."

DeSantos gave his shoulder a slap. "I'm gonna go see how helpful our friend is."

He reentered the room and sat down. Richter was sitting there, staring ahead. His eyes followed DeSantos's movements.

"Cam, I need to know about the ricin. Where's it being stored?"

Richter blinked twice, tilted his head back a few degrees, and said, "I'm not sure."

"Why don't you tell me what you know."

"It's in three different places. Two have the liquid drums. The other, it's got powder, that's the big one. But I—I never saw it myself. One of the guys I was working with, he told me."

"His name?"

"Wally-D, or something like—"

"Waleed?"

Richter nodded animatedly. "That's it."

*Shit. That's the asshole I killed in Rudenko's flat.*

"And where did Waleed say it was being stored?"

"On a ship somewhere, on the Thames. But that one they may've moved. Where, I don't know."

"The others?"

"One's in storage somewhere."

"That's not very helpful, Cam. Storage, where?"

"I didn't ask."

DeSantos clenched his fist. Based on his lack of distress-based hand and facial movements, DeSantos believed Richter was being truthful with him. The drug appeared to be working. But that kind of nondescript answer was not going to help them. "Where else is the ricin?"

"A church."

"Which church?"

Richter giggled. "It's a good one."

DeSantos had to restrain himself from reaching across the table and shaking him. "How good? What church?"

Richter laughed again. "St. Paul's."

"Holy shit."

"Exactly, right? See, I told you it was a good one."

DeSantos knew that St. Paul's cathedral was one of the most recognizable landmarks in London, having been around for centuries. He had only been there once, but lavish did not begin to describe its grandeur. There might be other significance to storing the ricin there, but at this point it did not matter.

DeSantos wanted to run out and send a secure text to Buck, but he had to finish this interrogation while the drug was still effective. He had no idea how long it would last.

"You and your buddies—Hagel and Walker. You work for Anthony Scarponi or Hussein Rudenko?"

Richter blinked a few times, and his head swayed a bit to the side. "We're loyal to Scarponi, but, you gotta understand, he's indisposed right now. How long, who knows. So we take contract jobs, yeah. But Rudenko offered us the kind of money you can't say no to."

"You're part of Rudenko's crew?"

"For now."

"Where can we find Rudenko?"

After asking the question, DeSantos detected the first hints of resistance. Richter's pupils quickly dilated, and then, in the next instant, constricted.

"I don't think I should tell you. I don't think that's a good idea."

"That's totally understandable. But I need to know, Cam. I need you to tell me where Hussein Rudenko is."

Richter bit his lip.

DeSantos removed the syringe from his pocket and uncapped it. He squeezed off another few cc's of the drug into Richter's arm and sat back in his chair. Richter asked why he was giving him "medicine," and DeSantos told him it was to make him feel better.

Five minutes later, DeSantos tried again.

"I'm trying to find Hussein Rudenko. He's an old friend and I want to grab a beer with him. Where is he?"

Richter's eyes darted around the room, and his movements were slow, exaggerated. DeSantos was concerned he had overdosed him.

"Where can I find him?"

"He has a few places. One in Soho—"

"I know about Soho. Where else?"

"Woodford Green, and, uh…Battersea."

Battersea was a dead end. Unless the area was genuine and the specific flat he had given them earlier was bogus.

DeSantos placed his elbows on the table. "Addresses. I need addresses, Cam. Otherwise I won't be able to find him."

Richter looked DeSantos in the eyes. "I don't know the addresses. I never went to these places. I just know because of Wally-D. What he told me."

"I've also got some money for Ratib Morsi and Emir Fiqar. Any idea how I can find them?"

"Nope. Don't know 'em."

"They're friends of Nikola Hačko. And Malik al-Atah. Do you know either of them?"

"Never heard those names."

DeSantos intertwined his fingers, squeezing, trying to control his building frustration. "When are they going to release the ricin?"

"Soon. I asked when, but that's all he said."

Rudenko did not exhibit any tics indicating distress or deception, so DeSantos pressed on.

"What are the targets?"

"People. Lots of people. Crowded areas."

"Where?"

Richter slowly blinked. "I had no reason to know, so he didn't tell me. Air—Air."

DeSantos sat forward. "You need some air?" He grabbed his wrist and checked his pulse. It was slow but otherwise normal. His skin, however, felt clammy and DeSantos noticed perspiration appearing on his forehead and cheeks.

"Cam." He gently slapped the sides of his face. "Just tell me where they're going to release the ricin."

"They…" His lids fluttered open, closed, and open. And then he laughed.

DeSantos leaned back and sighed deeply. He had reached the end of the interrogation; nothing further was to be gained. He twisted in his seat and looked at Carter, who shrugged his shoulders.

Richter lifted his hand and looked at it, as if he had just discovered the limb. "This hurts. A lot."

"I know it does," DeSantos said.

He thought of Brian. And he thought of this mission. Vince Richter had been reduced to trash. He had given all he had to give and was of no further use to them.

The sole remaining issue was his commitment to his former partner.

DeSantos glanced at Carter, who stood there, waiting. No words were exchanged, but none needed to be.

A moment later, Carter tapped his watch, then nodded. DeSantos rose from his seat and walked behind Richter.

# 41

Vail had resorted to pacing—whether it was due to her nerves or the cold, or both—all that mattered was that it helped pass the time.

Reid had fallen quiet, periodically checking his watch.

DeSantos emerged from the house a little past 9:00 PM. His mood was subdued as he pulled out the CLAIR and typed a message.

When he was done, Vail said, "You get anything?"

"Some actionable intel," DeSantos said. "I'm confident at least some of it's real." He pulled the car keys from his pocket. "Richter gave me everything he knew."

"He willingly cooperated?"

"Depends on how you look at it."

*What the hell does that mean? Do I really want to push this? Do I really want to know?*

"Did you kill him?"

DeSantos looked at her for the first time. He did not answer her verbally, but the set of his jaw, the intensity of his gaze told her all she needed to know.

"You didn't need to do that."

DeSantos headed toward the car. "If the situation were reversed, you would've done what I did."

"I would've wanted to. I don't think I would've done it."

"That's the point, isn't it? You don't really know. Until you've walked in my shoes, don't judge me."

"I'm not—Yes, fine. I'm judging you. And maybe that's not fair. I'm, I'm just conflicted. I understand the emotions you're feeling, but it goes against my training, what I believe in."

"Karen, don't take this the wrong way. But I'm not interested in your opinion. And I'm not interested in discussing it."

"I've had some time to think out here," she said.

"He said he's had enough," Reid said. "Leave it be."

His voice came from nowhere; Vail had forgotten he was still there.

"Carter will bring you up to speed," DeSantos said to Reid. "The ricin might be in three separate places. St. Paul's is a possible twenty. I told Buck." He gestured toward the house. "Would you help Carter finish up down there?"

Reid gave Vail a long look—of caution? of pleading?—she wasn't sure.

But he did as DeSantos requested, and when the door closed, Vail said, "Killing comes too easily to you, Hector."

"It's my job, my way of life. A matter of survival. I only kill the people I'm assigned to kill. I carry out my mission."

"Are you sure about that? Vince Richter didn't need to die. You didn't *need* to kill that man. It wasn't part of your mission."

"And what should we have done, huh? We couldn't arrest him because we had nothing on him. He's a trained assassin and he's part of Rudenko's crew. What he *isn't* is an upstanding citizen who contributes to society. Letting him go meant more innocent people would've died. Not to mention if we cut him loose, he would've joined back up with Rudenko to finish the job—with key intel on us. What we know, what we *don't* know. All of that's in direct contradiction to our mission."

"No," she said. "If you look inward, if you see this objectively, you'll admit to yourself that you killed him because you wanted to do it. Out of revenge."

"I did it because I had to," he said through clenched teeth. "And yes, it was also a promise I made to my dying friend. I had no choice. It was my duty."

He got in the car and turned over the engine. Vail joined him and sat down hard.

"Your thinking's polluted."

"This is my world, Karen. You have to trust me to do things right, the way they're supposed to be done. The way they have to be done in order to survive."

"Trust you? You've done nothing but lie to me the whole time."

"Because it's my job." He pulled onto the dark road, and neither of them spoke for a mile.

"I don't expect you to understand. But I do expect you to trust me. Because when you peel away Hector DeSantos the black operative, you've got Hector DeSantos, a guy who cares about you and would never let anyone hurt you. So think what you want. I know in my heart who I am. And I'm able to live with that."

She didn't want to keep pressing him because he was too close to the situation, too passionate and emotional. He could not see it objectively and might never be able to. Then again, he was right that she could not know what he was feeling. She'd come close, but as close as that was, it did not reach the depth of pain DeSantos had experienced. She had to respect that.

And she certainly did not know the "rules" of black ops engagement and the oaths those operatives shared, the methods and tactics that were customary. Or necessary.

"I'm sorry," she said.

"It's done. We move on. Fresh page."

"Because we have to complete our mission. At all costs."

"That's right," DeSantos said with a hint of surprise in his voice. "At all costs."

# 42

They had passed Northolt on the way back to London when a secure message came through from Buck.

With no place to pull off the road, DeSantos handed Vail the CLAIR. "What's it say?"

"They've located one of the trigger men. Where's Edgware?"

"Northwest London, maybe fifteen, twenty minutes from here."

The device buzzed again.

"They have a positive ID. Thermal imaging shows he's the only one in the house, but he's moving around from room to room, as if he's packing. Buck says we need to hurry, he may be on the move."

"Address?"

"And GPS coordinates."

"Perfect." DeSantos handed his Nokia to Vail. "Use the GPS app Uzi loaded. It's the logo on the home screen with the big 'LR.'"

"LR?"

"The initials of his shrink, Leonard Rudnick. Because he helped Uzi find his way."

"He helped me, too. I miss that old man." After entering the coordinates, she handed the CLAIR back to DeSantos. A moment later, the LR app had mapped out the entire route.

"Up ahead, left on Greenford Road."

DeSantos accelerated. "I'll get us there as fast as I can, but this ain't my 'vette."

She grabbed onto the door handle as he deftly turned the corner at forty miles per hour. "Judging by the way you drive, that may not be a bad thing."

"How's that?"

"If we were in your Corvette, you would've taken that turn at sixty."

DeSantos allowed a smile to tease his lips. "Damn straight."

"THIS IS IT," Vail said, struggling to get a look at the house and her surroundings. "It's so freaking dark around here."

"You're sure this is the right place."

"This isn't a regular GPS that takes you to a location half a mile away from where you're supposed to be. I used the actual coordinates. And I checked them three times. Yes, I'm positive." She pointed ahead. "Three houses up, on the right."

They were in a residential neighborhood of mostly older, well kept homes, modest lawns with driveways and garages. Aside from minor variances in architecture, they could have been in any upper middle-class suburban community in America.

DeSantos drove past the target's house and cut the engine. He reached into his jacket and pulled out a P220 SAS compact SIG Sauer. "You good with this?"

Vail's eyes widened. "I don't think I've ever been so happy to see a handgun. Where'd you get it?"

"Safe house. Figured these SIGs might come in handy. No suppressors, but beggars can't be too picky."

"That's not the saying."

"Do you really care?"

Vail pulled open the slide and press-checked the chamber. DeSantos did the same.

"Six round mag. And I don't have any spares, so make your shots count."

"How many do you think we'll need?"

"Hopefully no more than one." He tilted his head as he studied her face. "You going to be able to do this, take this guy out?"

Vail looked ahead, out the windshield, struggling with the answer.

"I need to know, Karen. Doubt, conflicting emotions, that won't cut it. If you're not sure, if you have any reservations, I'll go in myself."

"You can't do this yourself."

"That wouldn't be my preference, but we've got our orders and there's a lot at stake. I'll get it done."

Vail looked down at the SIG in her hand.

"Okay," DeSantos said. "Here's the plan. Hang out here, keep a watch on the street, and buzz me if we get company."

"I'm going in with you."

DeSantos twisted his torso and faced her square on. "You don't have to do this. I'll take care of it."

"I'm fine."

"You're not just saying that because you feel like you have to prove yourself, right? Because you're a woman?"

Vail stared him down. If she were standing, she might have kicked him in the balls.

"Let's go. And don't ever say that to me again." She reached up and turned off the interior dome light.

DeSantos nodded. "Very good. Nice tradecraft."

"Don't patronize me, Hector. What's the plan?"

"I'll go in the back. You watch the front in case he comes out. If he does—"

"I'll handle it."

"This is a known terrorist. His mission is to release ricin on the British population. *Our* mission is to make sure he doesn't get the chance."

"I get it. I was at the briefing."

"He may be armed."

She gave him another stern look.

"Right. Let's go."

Vail pushed open her door and got out.

They used the short brick wall for cover as they approached the house—handguns hidden, in case they encountered someone taking a dog for a late night walk.

Vail nearly tripped on a raised fissure of broken sidewalk. *Don't these people believe in streetlights?*

They reached the perimeter of the house and separated, Vail taking the front door and DeSantos the rear.

Vail settled herself on the porch, her back against the front wall, facing out, eyes straining to scan the area ahead of her, ears tuned to any unexpected noises emanating from the interior.

DESANTOS MADE HIS WAY through the yard to the backdoor. He would have preferred to be wearing night vision goggles, but this was an unorthodox op. He had made do with minimal equipment and a paucity of information in the past.

He quickly picked the door locks and stepped inside. It was completely dark. He stood a moment, allowing his senses to adjust to the surroundings. He needed to learn the normal sounds so that if he heard something else, he could react appropriately—a measured, efficient response. Disable his target as swiftly and as quietly as possible, with minimal struggle.

Although he had the SIG in his waistband, he drew a Black Raven tactical knife from a sheath in the pocket of his 5.11s. This was likely going to be a close-quarters fight, and a handgun would not be his first choice. Normally he would have brought a favorite brand from his SEAL days, an Ontario, but the MK3 was a government-issue blade, and he did not want to carry any identifiable equipment that could place him in a US-sanctioned operation.

The Raven was no slouch, however: its Tanto-shaped tip was as lethal as any other knife. In truth, however, a skilled operator had to be able to fight with no weapons—just his hands.

He advanced through the kitchen and into the dining and living rooms. Nothing; if this guy was getting ready to flee, it was the most sedate exit he had ever seen. Perhaps the intel was flawed.

Odd—the interior of the house was completely black. No lighted microwave clocks, no cable box power LEDs.

He headed up the stairs to the second floor and took a right into the master bedroom. As he cleared the adjacent bathroom, he heard a noise back out in the hall.

He emerged and saw a shadowy figure draw back.

"Who are you?" the voice asked. He shone a flashlight in DeSantos's direction.

The man was part of Rudenko's network, which automatically made him a threat; and DeSantos's mission was to terminate, not interrogate. Too far away to use the knife effectively, he instantly drew the SIG.

As he cleared his waistband, the man turned and ran down the steps, yelling. DeSantos was not sure what he was saying, but it didn't matter. DeSantos drew down and squeezed off a round. It struck the large wooden knob at the bottom of the staircase just as the man yanked open the front door.

VAIL HEARD VOICES, WHICH was not a good sign. She raised her handgun and moved back a few steps, facing the house.

A gunshot—and then the front door opened.

A man ran out and Vail yelled, "Freeze!"

The man turned, clearly startled at hearing a female voice—and DeSantos drilled him. Twice in the chest and once in the forehead: the lethally effective "failure drill" technique.

DeSantos did a quick assessment of his target, then grabbed both his arms and started pulling him back into the house.

"'Freeze?' Are you kidding me? That was not the plan."

"I wanted to see if we could ask him some questions, see what he knew."

"Nice idea," DeSantos said as he dropped the man's arms and then kicked the front door closed with his foot. "But those weren't our orders."

"I was never any good at that part of the job."

DeSantos turned the guy over and froze. He pulled out his phone and turned on the flashlight. "Shit. This is not good."

"What's wrong?"

His hands moved quickly, patting down his target's pockets and finding nothing.

"He's in sweats," Vail said. "No socks. Doesn't look like he was on the run."

"We've gotta search the place." He stole a look at his watch. "Three minutes, max. Go!"

DeSantos took the upstairs, Vail the ground floor. She found a name and address on a utility bill by the telephone. The name meant nothing to her. She continued through the rooms and found a family photo album on the coffee table—the man DeSantos had shot was pictured with a woman and two children. Judging by the woman's hairstyle, Vail estimated the photo at perhaps fifteen years old. The kids were now likely grown and out of the house. But this guy was a terrorist, preparing to let loose a chemical weapons attack on London in concert with one of the most notorious gun dealers and money launderers in history.

Not unheard of—an example from this very region, Northern Ireland, was proof enough that revolutionaries could have wives and children and look like perfectly harmless family men. Hell, many notorious serial killers could make the same claim.

Still, she could not shake the sense that this did not add up.

Vail turned a few more pages of the album and froze when she hit the glossy 5 x 7—the last one in the book. Her heart skipped a beat, and she felt the uneven rhythm in her chest.

Whatever Hector had seen when he looked at the man's face, she was now having her own "oh shit" moment.

DeSantos came bounding down the stairs. "We've gotta get out of here. Now."

"But—"

"Now, out the back!"

Vail grabbed the 5 x 7 print from the album and shoved it into her pocket, seconds behind DeSantos.

They made it to their car and DeSantos sped away as quickly as possible without spinning his wheels and calling even more attention to themselves.

In the distance, sirens.

When they had navigated a safe distance from the house, Vail cleared her throat. A feeling of dread enveloped her, and a sense of claustrophobia gripped her throat as if she had been in a tight elevator stuck between floors with fifteen other passengers crammed in front of her.

She rolled down the window and the cold late-night air blew in her face. As the panic waned, she rolled it up and looked at DeSantos. His jaw was set and his eyes were wide.

Vail could not help but think that this was definitely not the way she had seen her evening going. Actually, she hadn't thought much about how things were going to unfold. Maybe if she had, if she hadn't been kept in the dark and if she'd had a full mission briefing, she could've prevented them from doing whatever it was that they had just done.

After they had driven several miles, DeSantos pulled over to the curb. He rooted the Nokia out of his pocket and pried off the back.

"Remove the battery from your BlackBerry."

While Vail did as instructed, she said, "What happened back there?"

"Best guess?"

"You don't know?"

"I'll tell you what I know: we fucked up. Big time. We're in real trouble. We just—Do you know who we just killed?"

"I've got a name, but I have no idea who—"

"Basil Walpole is an up-and-coming member of Parliament, a very prominent politician, someone widely expected to be prime minister in the near future. That is, before we broke into his house and murdered him."

Vail's mouth was desert dry. She managed to scrape, "What?" from her throat, followed by, "How?"

"I don't know, I have to—I have to think this through." He rested his forehead on the steering wheel. "Walpole was pushing legislation for the UK to have one fiscal policy and one foreign policy—essentially, they'd become the United States of Europe. That obviously runs counter to the BHP and their more radical right-wing friends."

"So we just assassinated a prominent politician? We did the dirty work of a rival political party?"

"Right now that's the best explanation I've got."

Vail pulled the photo from her pocket and looked at it in the stray light streaming in from the headlights of a car passing from behind them. It was a shot of Walpole shaking hands with former US President Jonathan Whitehall—in the Oval Office.

DeSantos sat back in the seat. "He was also spearheading efforts, with the US, to pass legislation to make money laundering a whole lot more difficult."

"Which would be bad news for despots in the Middle East and Africa, Russian organized crime, Iran, Hezbollah. The list of those who'd want him out of the way is ridiculously long." *Just when I thought it couldn't get any worse.*

"Our friend Hussein Rudenko is on that list."

She shoved the picture back in her pocket. "We need to clear our heads, look at this logically. Not what's possible but what's feasible— what's most likely. Agreed?"

"Works for me."

"The kill order came from Aden Buck. He used the CLAIR device; it was a secure message. Let's start by explaining that."

DeSantos checked his watch. It had been twenty-four minutes since he received the text from Buck. He removed the CLAIR from his pocket and reviewed the messages. "Everything's right." He powered down the handset and removed the battery, as they had done with their phones. "We can't take a chance they'll be able to use it to find us. I have no idea how it works. For all I know, it could be outfitted with a microphone."

"That's being a little paranoid."

"Is it?" DeSantos asked. "I used to have that healthy dose of paranoia. Somewhere along the way I lost it. I've lost my edge." He slammed his hand on the steering wheel.

They were both alone with their thoughts for a long minute.

"No matter how I look at it," he said, "there's no way out of this. We're black, no one will step forward and acknowledge what we're doing, or why. And we can't come forward and explain it because if Rudenko thinks we've keyed in on his plans, he'll hit the wind."

"If he hasn't already."

DeSantos closed his eyes. "We've irreparably altered British politics. And the very man we were relying on to watch our backs and feed us intel on how to stop the ricin attacks has set us up."

*Think of something, Karen. Think! There's gotta be a way to fix all this.*

"The lights," DeSantos said.

"What lights?"

"Everything was off in the house, the power. Someone cut it. Walpole probably looked out his window and saw that his neighbor had electricity on, so he grabbed a flashlight and went down to the circuit breaker to see what the hell was wrong."

"But I walked in and scared the crap out of him." He slammed the steering wheel again, then took a deep breath. His demeanor changed; his brow hardened and his eyes narrowed. "Okay. We can't worry about Basil Walpole. So—"

"What are you talking about? We just killed an innocent man. We murdered him. How can we just push that aside?"

"For now. We compartmentalize it, lock it away, because we can't fix it and we've got a job to do."

Vail turned away.

"What would you have us do, walk into the nearest Met station and confess? Sorry guys, it was all just a misunderstanding. Now we'll be on our way to head off a ricin attack that you know nothing about."

"Of course not. But how can you just forget that we killed that man. He's got two kids—"

"I know, okay? We fucked up." He sat there a long moment. Finally he said, "Right now, Karen, we have to shove our feelings in a drawer so we can complete this mission."

Vail sat up straight. "You're right. I'm sorry. I'm tired, I'm—I'm being emotional." *Did I just admit that?*

DeSantos pulled away from the curb.

"We need to radically alter our appearance. Caps and glasses won't cut it."

DeSantos checked his mirrors to make sure they were not being followed. "How do you figure?"

"Whoever set us up is going to leak to the press and the police, or both, that we kil—that we were seen leaving the scene. This wasn't some last minute frame-up. It was well planned, well timed, and well executed."

DeSantos nodded. "You're right. Fine. We'll find a place to crash for the night. We'll need to get new SIM cards because the ones that Buck gave us are likely in their system by now and they may've voice ID'd us to those cards."

"And that brings us back to figuring out what the hell's going on. The most logical person behind this is not the Russians, or the BHP, or other radical far right groups. It's Rudenko. He'd be hit hard if money laundering rules were changed and he suddenly couldn't move his funds around—or hide them."

"Agreed. So, what? Buck's been working with Rudenko all along? Is he the mole who exposed all the security service agents? Why?"

Vail considered the question a moment. "Because if he takes out his entire domestic and international spy network, or disables it for a bit, then Rudenko is free to operate as he sees fit, giving him enough time to launch his attack."

"But why bring you and me here?"

"To make a good show, to stall. I'm sure he got pressure from the prime minister to take action, to track down Rudenko and find this ricin shipment that landed on their soil. And he probably didn't see you as a threat. He was definitely surprised when you keyed in on Paxton."

"There's only one person involved in this thing that we can find, right?"

"Yeah," Vail said. "Buck." She turned to DeSantos. "No."

"It's the fastest way to answers."

Vail shifted in her seat. "That's a mistake."

"Kidnapping the director general of MI5 isn't a whole lot worse than anything else we've done the past few days."

"Don't remind me." Vail rubbed both hands over her cheeks. "You're serious, aren't you?"

DeSantos pulled the car over again. "I am." He assembled his phone, powered it up, and typed out a text. When it had sent, he removed the battery again.

"What was that?"

"I just sent Knox a coded message."

"What kind of coded message?"

"An electronic SOS."

# 43

Douglas Knox, seated with Earl Tasset and Senator Tom Hendricks as they polished off their after-dinner drinks, stole a look at his BlackBerry. The screen had lit up and the handset was vibrating on the table in front of him.

He puffed on his Hoyo de Monterrey Double Corona, which was perched between his teeth, and tilted his head back to read the message.

"Shit." He removed the cigar and set it on the edge of the crystal ashtray.

"Everything okay?" Hendricks asked.

"The usual. I'll be right back."

Knox donned his wool overcoat and walked outside. He dialed a number and waited while it rang.

"Agent Uziel, this is Douglas Knox."

"Good evening, Mr. Director."

"We have to meet. Fifteen minutes, at the Pennsylvania pillar of the World War II memorial."

"I'll be there."

UZI, LEANING AGAINST the stone wall, looked out at the brightly lit Washington Monument. The wind was chilled and strong, and the vapor escaping from his mouth obscured his view.

Douglas Knox cleared his throat and Uzi pivoted around.

"Mr. Director."

Knox gave a quick survey of the area—which immediately set Uzi's senses on edge—and he, too, started taking note of who and what was nearby.

"I received a message from Hector."

He swallowed hard, expecting the worst. "What did it say?"

"It was in code, but the gist is that he's in trouble and needs help. If I interpreted his code properly, he wants you and Troy Rodman to get to London ASAP. Do you have a go-bag in your trunk?"

"Always, sir."

"Go directly to Dulles and grab the United flight at ten. I'll have whatever equipment you need from your office or house brought to you. Rodman will meet you there and bring your kit and boarding pass."

"Have you gotten a SitRep from him?" Uzi asked, referring to a situation report.

"He's dark—and black. So we're not having this conversation. And no, I don't know what the problem is. I've told Rodman to prepare for a real shit storm. I suggest you do the same."

# 44

Vail and DeSantos switched license plates with another vehicle, and then drove around for an hour until they located the same make and model sedan as the one they were driving. They then repeated the process, several miles away.

Finally, around 2:00 AM, they pulled into a dark, secluded neighborhood and spent the night in the car; it was safer than attempting to find a hotel and taking the risk of being identified. Until they devised better disguises, each minute they were out in public, the greater the chance they would be recognized.

They awoke at dawn and moved the vehicle to another suburban area, where Vail found a drugstore. The plan was for her to buy various accoutrements, including hair coloring, disposable razors, hats, and Adonis Bronzing Spray. DeSantos, meanwhile, went in search of a mobile accessories store to purchase SIMs or throwaway phones.

They had to conserve their cash because using a credit card was out of the question: their electronic footprint would be located in seconds.

Once back in the car, DeSantos put the battery into his Nokia and powered it up with a new SIM and swept the vehicle for electronic tracking devices using an app that Uzi had preloaded on his phone. He had wanted to do it last night but could not risk using the phone more than he already had. It would have acted like a beacon straight to their position. He decided to take the risk that the vehicle was clean, and his sweep now indicated that was the case.

Hoping that Knox had understood his message, DeSantos texted Uzi and told him this was now his number for the near term, and to contact him when possible.

He walked back to the car, waiting for Vail to return...and for his phone to vibrate.

WHEN VAIL KNOCKED on the car window, DeSantos hardly recognized her. She had cut her hair short and colored it.

"Not bad as a brunet," he said. "I'd definitely be checking you out if you walked by my park bench."

She pulled down the visor and examined her handiwork in the mirror. "I haven't had short hair in twenty years. My mom had a brilliant idea that it'd be cute. I hated it." She thought about her mother, now in a home with Alzheimer's. Realizing DeSantos was staring at her, she pulled her thoughts back to the present. "What?"

"You look so different."

"Good. Now you." She handed DeSantos the bag containing the scissors, razors, and spray-on tan.

"You know this is only a partial fix," he said.

"Why is that?"

"We've got two problems: physical visual identification and CCTV identification."

"Do their cameras use facial recognition?"

"Some are outfitted with it, some aren't. And it depends whether we're talking about government cameras or private security. Bottom line, it's best to stay off them or give them a bad look at us. We're at risk, there's no way around it. A hat, a pair of eyeglasses, a different hairstyle—all that stuff will prevent a cop from picking us off the street from a photo array he saw in roll call. And it'll help prevent a guy from watching a screen at the Met's Communications Division from recognizing us. But it's not going to help us much with cameras that have facial recognition."

"They compensate for different hair styles?"

"The technology is always improving, and I don't know where the UK falls on that spectrum."

"Then we'll have to settle for defeating two of the three systems."

"Except that there are a ton of cameras in the UK—anywhere from several hundred thousand to four million, last I heard. The average person is photographed dozens of times every day."

"Thanks for making me feel better."

"Just pointing out what we're up against."

"We can only do what we can do. And right now, that means you taking the stuff in that bag and going at it. But I am sorry."

"About what?"

She reached over and ran her fingers through his thick hair. "I look kind of cute this way. I'm not so sure you're going to get the same result when you shave your head."

He frowned and grabbed the bag. "We'll see. I've always wanted to try the badass look."

"Don't you mean *bareass*?"

He slammed the door, leaving without a word.

# 45

The Nokia buzzed at 9:49 AM. DeSantos snatched it up and, reading the display, said, "Uzi just landed."

He handed the phone to Vail. "Tell him we need a live drop, and warn him."

She typed:

have something for you. we're very hot but need an LD.

"Any ideas where? Does Uzi know England?"

"Pretty well," DeSantos said. "As to where, we need to head toward London and keep off the cameras."

"You've got to be kidding."

"It's gonna happen; nothing we can do about it. But the longer we can put it off, the better."

"Then where? Where can we go to get away from the cameras? They're everywhere."

DeSantos thought a moment. "Cranford Park. It's near Heathrow, right off the M4. Tell him to take the road across the river and meet us in the parking lot. Our hood will be up."

Vail sent off the message. "Anything else?"

"Tell him to check things out before he approaches. And ask him if he remembers our buddy Tad Bishop."

Vail stopped typing. "Bishop. The informant you were working with who was ultra-paranoid?"

"*Uzi* was working with him, not me. But yeah, that's the one. He also happened to be bald."

"Got it." She typed out the second message.

careful. survey b4 approach. oh I look like tad bishop now ;-)

Seconds later, Uzi texted back:

copy. c u soon

DeSantos took the phone back and did a double take. "You're staring at me."

"I like it more than I thought I would. You used the bronzing spray."

"Of course. My scalp hasn't seen sunlight since I was a baby."

"And your scalp still hasn't seen sunlight. You're in England, remember?"

THEY ARRIVED AT Cranford Park and pulled into the parking lot, which was already occupied by half a dozen vehicles. DeSantos pointed the car's nose in, against a stand of trees that formed the western side of the park.

DeSantos had dropped Vail off along the road, about fifty yards away. She gave a look around to make sure no one was following them, and that it was safe for the meet to take place. She saw nothing untoward—and equally important, no CCTV cameras.

As Vail approached, DeSantos got out and opened the hood. Although they felt reasonably sure that they were not being watched, DeSantos made an effort to look like he was working on the engine.

A few moments later, a panel van containing two men pulled into the lot.

The large black dude—Rodman—remained in the passenger seat. The large white dude—Uzi—got out and made his way over to the "disabled" vehicle.

"Boychick," DeSantos said, using his nickname for Uzi. "Good to see you."

"Same here. Need a hand?"

"You have no idea," Vail said.

DeSantos removed the CLAIR from his pocket and placed it atop the battery. "That's yours. It's a comms device given to us by Aden Buck."

"Buck. Really?"

"It's set up to transmit a secure message only between this and another identical handset. It's a high—"

"High bandwidth low power reprogrammable SDR with a full-duplex RF transceiver. Microburst architecture."

"You know," Vail said, "I love it when you talk techy."

Uzi winked. "Now—to your problem." He reached into the engine compartment, palmed the CLAIR, and slipped it partially up his sleeve. "I'll get to work on it. I brought my 'mobile lab' with me, so that should give me everything I need. I don't know how long it'll take. It depends on how strong the MI5 firewalls are. I'm assuming they're pretty damn good."

"No match for your skills."

"Let's hope not."

"Once you turn it on, work fast. The thing self-erases."

"Nothing like a good challenge." Uzi stuck a hand into a pocket of his 5.11 tactical pants and pulled something out. He reached forward and touched the engine. "Here's the problem. Clogged air filter." He tapped twice on the metal housing. "Much better. That should do it." When he removed his hand, an iPhone was nestled on the crank case. "Latest model, specially outfitted. It should allow us to communicate securely."

"Should?" Vail asked.

"Hey, I'm good but I'm not perfect."

"I'm going to use that against you someday."

"I'll deny I ever said it."

"I have a witness." Vail tilted her head left, indicating DeSantos.

DeSantos squinted. "I didn't hear anything."

"Before I forget," Uzi said. "That document we found on Rudenko's PC, the mustard agent attack on Yankee Stadium. Looks like it wasn't an actual plan. They were just brainstorming on how it could be carried out and where to get the mustard agent. NSA's still working on decrypting the other docs, but so far, it looks like the ricin's the only clear and present danger." He bent slightly at the knees. "I'm dropping a gift bag by your feet, Santa. Pick it up before you head out."

DeSantos did not look down. "Got it."

Uzi turned to him and gave his face a once-over. "You are gonna grow back your hair, right?"

"You don't like the badass look?"

"I do. But yours looks more *bare*ass than badass."

Vail slapped the fender. "That's exactly what I said!"

Uzi suppressed a smile. "Good luck. I'll be in touch as soon as I've got something." After he'd walked a couple dozen feet, he turned around and pointed at the vehicle. "Go ahead and give it a try. I think it'll start now. I'm really good with car engines, too."

# 46

DeSantos and Vail headed into the city, glasses on, sporting their new coiffures and, for DeSantos, the new beard and moustache Uzi had left for him. They hoped it was enough to defeat London's ubiquitous camera network.

"I have to say," DeSantos said, rubbing his cheek, "I don't care for Uzi's taste in gifts. The adhesive on this beard itches."

Vail glanced around at the masses of workers and tourists on the streets. "Are we really going to do this?"

"Fastest way to get answers."

"It could also be the fastest way to a cold cell in a UK max security prison."

"Got any better ideas?"

"Nope."

"Didn't think so."

THAMES HOUSE, MI5'S headquarters in Millbank, consisted of an uninspired and unremarkable rectangle of a building that sat on the north bank of the Thames. It was an architectural eyesore with a million dollar view.

An effective strategic plan would have required days of preparation and the subsequent placement of an operator at each entrance/exit point. But the circumstances were far from ideal, and they had no such manpower, so they had to rely on logic, short-term observation of the facility's flow and traffic patterns, and their general knowledge of how high-security buildings were designed.

Although a brief exchange with Clive Reid brought a few details, including Buck's car make and license plate number, DeSantos did not want to get into why he needed the information. At this point, the less Reid knew, the better.

Working on the assumption that the vicinity was under constant surveillance, they donned their caps and scouted the area by car to determine the CCTV locations. After completing their assessment, DeSantos dropped her off and she strolled up Thorney Street, stopping across from the building's parking garage. She placed herself at the most undesirable angle for the nearest lens—by a fenced-in Caterpillar backhoe—hoping that her low tech solution would provide her sufficient cover while allowing her to casually watch for Aden Buck's car.

Like federal buildings in the US, parking was prohibited anywhere along the periphery; in the case of Thames House, black metal pillars rose from the sidewalk every few feet, preventing a van or truck from driving up to the structure and rendering it so much rubble, Oklahoma City-like in its level of destruction.

Meanwhile, DeSantos circled the block, hoping to be in reasonable proximity to Vail when Buck's vehicle emerged. At 6:26 PM, two hours after darkness fell and ninety minutes after they took their positions, Buck's BMW appeared behind the massive black metal gates that almost looked stylish with their sectional design and diagonal slats.

Vail lifted the BlackBerry to her lips. "In ten seconds, he'll be turning right onto Thorney. His driver's waiting for the barricade to retract into the pavement. How close are you?"

"Coming down Thorney now. Looks like there's construction near you."

"Yeah, half the block's got equipment and fencing. Gave me some really good cover. I'll be by the orange cones."

Buck's vehicle swung onto Thorney and turned in front of Vail. A second later, DeSantos pulled to a stop and Vail jumped in. They followed the BMW a few blocks as it turned left on Horseferry Road. It pulled to a stop and Buck got out.

"Are you serious?" Vail asked. "He took his car and driver to go, what, three blocks?"

"Safer than walking these days when you're the director general of MI5. No way of knowing how extensive that data breach was."

DeSantos dropped Vail at the corner and she followed Buck into the Firecracker oriental restaurant.

She waited for Buck to be seated, then asked for a table in the same room. Red was the prevailing theme, with blood-colored vinyl benches and black-and-white marble-grained granite tables. The light cream wall at the end of the aisle of tables featured dark diagonal floor-to-ceiling lines. In a word or two, the restaurant was contemporary chic.

DeSantos joined her seven minutes later. He sat down and casually hid behind his menu.

"Anyone with him?" he asked.

"Not that I've seen."

"There are two men in suits outside the front entrance who look like they may be Security Service agents."

"So we go out the back."

"Is there a backdoor?" DeSantos asked.

"Doesn't there have to be?"

DeSantos lowered his menu. "No, Karen, there doesn't have to be. But we can't worry about it. We're committed. We'll make it work." He filled her in on his plan and told her he had formulated it on the fly less than two minutes earlier. It was full of uncertainty and risk, but it was their best, and only, shot.

Vail glanced over and watched as Buck perused his menu. "Do you usually carry out your missions like this?"

"Like what?"

"Seat of your pants."

"Usually things are prepped well in advance, with intel and diagrams, floor plans and dossiers. Sometimes they're last minute things, with very little notice. A known target is in a particular place for an hour, and that's your window because a chance like that may not happen again for weeks, months. Sometimes years. But you've got your training and you've got your instincts. You find ways to get the job done." He gave a final look around the room. "You ready?"

"As ready as possible without any preparation, intel, diagrams, floor plans, or dossiers."

"Nonsense. I had 120 seconds to put it together. Plenty of time. Now—do as I said."

Vail pulled out a pen and scribbled something on a piece of paper. A moment later, she walked by Buck's table and casually dropped the folded note to the left of his plate, then continued on toward the restroom.

DESANTOS WATCHED BUCK pick up the note and then snap his head upright as he attempted to get a look at the person who had deposited it on his table.

As Vail moved out of the room, Buck unfurled the paper and read it. He stiffened, then rotated his head left and right, scanning the vicinity.

DeSantos dropped his head a bit lower, closer to his plate. He was not sure if Buck would recognize him, shaved bald with a beard and mustache, but it was not worth taking the chance.

When Buck looked down to reread the note, DeSantos casually rose from his seat and left the room, headed in the same direction as Vail.

Vail's missive informed Buck that they had vital information on the case, and instructed him to meet DeSantos in the restroom. But because of the circumstances, he would not wait there more than two minutes.

The route Buck had to take would bring him down a narrow corridor, and if their stars were aligned, no one else would be there. If there was someone present, Vail would attempt to explain that she was engaged in police business and needed to clear the area. If that didn't work, they would have a witness—clearly a scenario they wanted to avoid.

Vail stood at the end of the hallway, near the restroom entrance. At the moment, it was clear. When Buck appeared in the corridor, he saw her—recognition registering on his face but with a dose of hesitation. The dominant locks of curly red hair were gone, and she looked substantially different.

He stopped, trying to work this through his brain. But DeSantos came up behind him and placed his pistol firmly in the small of Buck's back.

"We have to talk," he said into the director general's left ear. "Alone."

# 47

Vail remained with Buck while DeSantos brought the vehicle forward.

"Call your men and tell them to meet you in the Function Room, at the large round table."

Buck did not move.

"Now, sir. We don't have a lot of time."

"After what you did to Basil Walpole, why should I listen to you? Why should I trust you?"

Vail clenched her jaw. "We're not the bad guys here. But I'm not going to get into that with you right now. Make that call and get your men inside the restaurant." She gave the SIG a not so gentle push into his spine for emphasis.

Buck removed his phone and started to dial.

"Careful. DeSantos is near them, and if you set off alarms, he's going to be forced to take them out. We don't want that to happen. Hector's really good at what he does—which is why you brought him to England."

Buck did as Vail instructed. They watched from the deep reaches of the corridor as his two agents were led across the room through the restaurant by one of the wait staff.

When the men had passed, Vail took Buck's cell phone and then ushered him outside, where DeSantos was waiting with their car. She directed him to the rear seat, then slid in beside him.

As DeSantos accelerated, he glanced in the rearview mirror at Vail. A slight smile teased the corners of his mouth.

UZI AND TROY RODMAN sat in the back of their rented Ford van, parked at a curb outside a cyber café in Surrey Quays, "borrowing" the establishment's wireless signal.

"You want me to get GQ on the line?" Rodman asked.

Uzi squinted. "GQ. You talking about Santa?"

"Who else?"

Uzi grinned, but he did not take his eyes off the laptop's screen, did not still his hands. "I'm not gonna let him live that one down." Uzi read the data on the monitor as Rodman checked his watch yet again.

"We've got to give them something soon."

Uzi struck another key, sat back, and nodded. "Then it's a good thing I actually have something useful to tell them. Okay. Get GQ on the line."

Rodman pulled out his phone. "GQ's *my* thing. Don't be calling him that."

Uzi tapped the keys, then paused. "You're right. Without his hair and cool glasses, he's no longer worthy of the nickname. I'll get him an earring and call him Mr. Clean."

Rodman rolled his eyes as he handed Uzi the handset.

Uzi waited three rings before DeSantos answered. "Santa, listen. I've got something for you, but it's incomplete."

"Right now, I'll take anything I don't already have."

"I examined the device and downloaded the data before it could be deleted. Shutting it down was the right move. Good thinking."

"Would you expect anything less?"

"You don't want me to answer that. So here's the deal: the transmission checks out. The two handsets—yours and Buck's—did execute a handshake, essentially confirming the encryption algorithm and verifying each device in the data stream. It basically tells them it's okay to communicate with each other. If there's no handshake, the message doesn't get authenticated, and the message isn't delivered."

"A bit over my head, but I think I got it. Bottom line?"

"That the message went from point A to point B, as it was designed to do. And since the location was embedded in the handshake, I can tell you it originated from the Thames House complex—again, as it was supposed to do. So far, nothing's slapped me in the face in terms of it looking suspect. But I've got to localize it further, and that may take a while. I wanted you to at least have what I've been able to find so far. Hope it helps."

"Everything helps. I'll give you a shout soon as I can."


VAIL, KEEPING HER PISTOL trained on Buck, said, "Good news?"

DeSantos slipped the phone back in his pocket. "All depends on your perspective."

"I don't understand what you people are up to," Buck said. "You're supposed to be working *for* me, not—"

"I suggest you keep quiet," Vail said. "You'll get your chance to talk. That time is not now." She glanced out at the buildings they were passing. "How long till we're there?"

"Ten minutes, maybe. I'm taking it slow, making sure I don't run any lights."

"Playing the good citizen?"

DeSantos chuckled. "I think it's way too late for that."


THEY ARRIVED AT THE location DeSantos had previously selected as being best suited to their needs: Vincent Square in Westminster, a privately owned thirteen acre patch of parkland and sports field greenery in the heart of London.

DeSantos had assured Vail that he could disable the padlock on the black wrought iron gate that led to a small, paved parking and storage area in back of the groundsman's house.

After pulling in, out of view of the street, DeSantos shoved the gearshift lever to park.

As he twisted in his seat to face Buck, Rodman called.

"GQ, you alone?"

"No, we've got company. Why?"

"There's something you and the shrink should see."

"Now?"

"Now. I'm sending you a link."

Thirty seconds later, they were standing outside the car and a YouTube video was buffering on DeSantos's souped-up iPhone.

The BBC logo appeared on the screen, followed by a news anchor. "It's with sadness that we report the passing of beloved minister Basil Walpole. The minister was found dead late last night in his home, the apparent victim of a home invasion. Or was it? Dabir Ghassan has the story. Dabir?"

The reporter appeared on screen, microphone in hand. He appeared to be standing in front of Walpole's Edgware residence. "Truly a tragedy of tremendous proportions. We have learned that authorities now believe the murder was the result of a terrorist attack and may, in fact, be related to the recent bombing of the Turner Gallery and Embankment Underground station. The Service has released a photo of two of the people believed responsible." Ghassan's voice continued as a grainy video image of DeSantos and Vail rolled, showing them walking into the building on New Bond Street.

"This is not good," Vail said.

"...and while the identity of the woman is still unclear, sources believe that the male is Hector Cruz, a known terrorist of Panamanian descent—"

"You're Panamanian?" Vail asked, keeping her eyes on the screen.

"No. Does it matter?"

"...but what has proven particularly troubling is a photo that the BBC has obtained of Cruz attending a high level governmental meeting and socializing with Prime Minister Braxton Moore, as well as two senior members of his—"

A photo appeared of DeSantos shaking hands, and sharing a laugh with, Moore and two unidentifiable men.

"More lies?" Vail asked.

"No, that one's actually true. Sort of."

"You know the prime minister?"

DeSantos paused the video. "He was a member of parliament back then. And I met him at a conference on global terrorism, several months after 9/11. Because of my father."

"Your father? Who's your father?"

"That's a discussion for another time. But this conference, I was there presenting a case study. I thought no cameras were allowed in."

"Apparently you thought wrong."

DeSantos pondered this a moment.

"Just a guess here," Vail said, "but the suggestion that the prime minister is consorting with a terrorist could be enough to topple the government, wouldn't you think?"

"I'm no expert on UK politics, but from a perception and image standpoint, I'd say he's now got a huge PR problem."

"This was a deliberate act," Vail said. "The question is, why? Who are all the people that'd have something to gain from discrediting Moore?"

"Are we back to making long lists again?"

"No one said boots-on-the ground police work is for everyone."

"Definitely not for me. And, I might remind you, it's not for *us*—we don't have time for that shit."

"And let me remind *you* that not every situation can be resolved with guns, knives—and pliers."

DeSantos looked at her.

"I'm sorry. I didn't mean that."

Without a word, he started the video again, and the reporter continued: "Just what this means—for example, precisely what Prime Minister Moore and two senior ministers were doing socializing with a known terrorist, is unclear at this time. One intelligence source who requested anonymity stated there is evidence that Cruz and his accomplice are planning a major attack on the city. Exactly what form that would take, whether it would be another bombing or some other of type of violent act, they would not speculate. The prime minister's press secretary declined comment. Calls to the Home Office have not, as yet, been returned."

The video ended.

"As I was saying." Vail shook her head. "Just when I didn't think it could get any worse."

"Must you always look at the negative?"

"I'm sorry. Was there good news in that report?"

"Yeah. The image was so crappy they couldn't identify you."

"Yet."

"And," DeSantos said as he pocketed the phone, "at least those photos at Walpole's place were taken before I shaved my head."

"Fine. I'll give you that." She reached up and stroked DeSantos's bare scalp. "I think I'm beginning to appreciate the badass look."

"Let's get on with this." He gestured at the backseat. "Go keep him company. I need to make a call."

DESANTOS PULLED OUT Aden Buck's cell phone and dialed FBI Director Douglas Knox's private number.

"This is your man on the ground," DeSantos said. "I'll cut to the chase because I can't stay on this call very long. I need to question your friend, the one who needed me to come out here."

"What do you mean, 'question' him?"

"Interview. Very possibly without his cooperation."

"What? No. Absolutely not."

"I wouldn't ask unless I felt it was vital to what we're doing here. And because I won't have a willing subject, some…inducement will be needed."

"Have you lost your mind?"

"I believe it's necessary. And time is short."

"I can't condone that—it sets a bad precedent. You understand, don't you?"

In fact, he did. A spy agency—or law enforcement—director carried state secrets and sensitive information with him that, under duress, might be revealed. Not to mention that this violated protocol so blatantly that it could cause irreparable damage to US-UK relations. But understanding the situation did not change the facts.

"So that there is no confusion," Knox said firmly, "let me be perfectly clear. You will not cross that line. Do you hear me?"

"All due respect, I don't see an option. We don't know who can be trusted. The mole could be 'our friend.'"

"Do you have proof of that?"

"We're working on it. But part of that effort is gathering information. At the very least, we have reason to believe he's involved. In fact, he's responsible for our current situation. I'm sure you've been briefed on the news reports. If not, get the BBC video on the minister's murder. That'll tell you all you need to know."

There was a long pause and then Knox said, "Find another way."

"I would if I could. But there *is* no other way, given the circumstances. Everything's in play. *We're* in play."

"Nothing will change my mind on this."

"Sir, the only people who know what's really going on, about the imminent attack and the players behind it, are us—*wanted fugitives.* Our only hope of fixing this is by getting answers. This person has at least some of those answers."

DeSantos had already said more than was advisable over an open line. He rubbed his forehead, frustrated that Knox was not on board with the plan.

"Do I have to remind you that you're black? You shouldn't have called me. You've jeopardized my position. Your *country.* I'm telling you not to proceed. Abandon the mission. You and your partner need to find a way out. Make your way home. Godspeed."

"But—"

DeSantos stopped himself. The line was dead.

# 48

DeSantos lowered the phone. He looked at Vail through the rear window, and for the first time since she had met Hector DeSantos, she saw fear in his eyes.

She opened the door and got out. "I take it that did not go well."

He dropped Buck's phone on the pavement and smashed it under his heel. Powering down the device would've accomplished the same thing, but she knew it would not have been nearly as satisfying.

He leaned his back against the side of the car. "Anything from Uzi?"

Vail assembled her BlackBerry, checked for texts, and then shut it down and removed the battery. "No."

DeSantos bit his lip and canted his head toward the overcast night sky. Then he abruptly pushed away from the vehicle and said, "Go take a walk. Be back in ten minutes."

"What?" Vail asked, moving in front of DeSantos. "Go take a walk? What the hell does that mean?"

"Just do it. Be careful, keep your head down. Avoid people."

"But—"

"Karen, I'm going to do something that runs counter to your FBI regs. I don't want to put you in that position."

"You've gotta be kidding. I'm 'so fired' when I get back that any further breaches in procedure aren't even worth discussing."

"This may leave you with a fate worse than getting fired. Not to mention it running counter to your morals."

Vail hesitated, examined his face. In a low voice, she said, "Hector, we broke into the house of a key British politician and murdered him." *I can't believe I just said that.* She gave a nervous laugh. "What more could we possibly do now that would screw things up more than they already are?"

"You've got a point there."

"I'm in this to the end. It's the best chance I've got of helping us clear our names, to say nothing of stopping this attack before it's too late." She gestured toward their prisoner. "Go do what you need to do."

His eyes remained riveted to hers a long moment. "Keep an eye out and bang on the window if you see a problem."

DESANTOS GOT INTO the backseat of the car.

"You people are acting irrationally," Buck said. "Let me go and I'll consider not pressing charges."

DeSantos nodded slowly. "Director General, if you're innocent, then I apologize profusely for snatching you up. And I apologize even more for what I'm about to do."

"What you're about to—What are you talking about?"

"Sir, these are extraordinary times. And unfortunately they call for extraordinary measures."

"Let me out of this car. Now!"

"What happened with the search of St. Paul's? Did you actually carry it out?"

"Of course. A forensics team found slight traces of ricin in a storage room, but otherwise it was clean."

They must have moved it—if Buck was telling the truth. If *Richter* was telling the truth. DeSantos bit down hard on his bottom lip, frustrated that they could not make any definitive headway.

"Where is it now?"

Buck wrinkled his nose as if DeSantos was a daft idiot.

"Fine. We'll do it my way." He reached into his pocket and removed the syringe containing the remaining SP-117.

Buck's eyes focused on the needle. Fear enveloped his face like a sheet over a corpse. "Mr. Cruz. I strongly urge you to think about what you're about to do. I can help you get whatever it is that you want. There's nothing to be gained by killing me."

DeSantos tilted his head. "Why would you think I'm going to kill you?"

Buck looked away. "I know about Minister Walpole."

"Thanks to you, the whole goddamn world knows about Walpole!" DeSantos took a breath, fighting to restrain his anger. He leaned closer. "I want to know who you're working for."

"What in bloody hell are you talking about? I work for the British people. The government, the Home Office."

"Then why did you send me and Vail to the minister's house? Why'd you set us up?"

"Why on Earth would I do that?"

"The CLAIR. The two devices were paired, right? Yours and mine?"

"You know they are. I told you that."

"And there's no way anyone else could've sent me a message using your handset."

"Absolutely none. The first staff I vetted when our system was compromised was our tech people. It's a very small, close-knit department. And the CLAIR was in the pocket of my trousers the entire time. I sent no message telling you to go to the minister's residence."

DeSantos shook his head. He held up the syringe and removed the cap. "Give me your handset. I'll prove it."

"I don't have it."

Buck pushed his back into the seat. "Then you just have to believe me."

"I want to. But I don't. And there's only one way to find out with reasonable certainty."

"Please. Don't kill me. I did *not* set you up."

"I don't intend to kill you, sir."

Buck's brow crumpled in confusion. "Then what's in that syringe?"

"SP-117."

Buck's eyes widened. "From our Cotswolds facility?"

"Exactly."

"No, please. There are other ways of verifying that I'm telling you the truth."

"Maybe. But nothing that'll work as quickly. And in case you've forgotten—assuming you're not part of it—there's an imminent attack planned for this city. I don't have time to waste."

Buck banded his arms across his chest. "This is going to set an extremely dangerous precedent."

"Extraordinary circumstances. Extraordinary measures." DeSantos leaned his body weight into Buck's torso and plunged the needle into his neck.

# 49

U zi tapped away at his keyboard beside Rodman, who was seated in front of his own laptop. Rodman's eyes, however, were fixated on Uzi's screen.

"You following what I'm doing?"

Rodman licked his lips. "I think you lost me after you got into MI5's secured network. I was trained in cyber-warfare, so I know a bit about hacking, but you passed me by about three hours ago. You've gone deeper than I thought possible."

Rodman's baritone voice was unusually resonant, but Uzi was confident no one outside the van would be able to hear him.

"You doubted me?"

Rodman shrugged. "I've only done one op with you. Don't know your capabilities. Don't know much about you, period."

"For now, here's all you need to know: I like challenges. If you tell me something's not possible, I'll find a way to *make it* possible. I'm a persistent son of a bitch."

"Figured as much or GQ wouldn't have anything to do with you." Rodman watched Uzi's fingers play across the keyboard another minute, trying to follow the commands he was typing. "Don't you have to practice hacking to stay sharp?"

"Like anything else, yeah. Once a week I try to penetrate NSA's servers. Every few months I actually get in. But they shut me down real fast." He stopped, examined the code, then continued typing. "They're not very happy with me."

"Imagine that."

"One day they're gonna find out who's been giving them fits, and that's not gonna go so well. I may need to call in some favors to keep my ass out of Petersburg."

Rodman consulted his watch. "How much longer?"

Uzi continued tapping away. "The Brits' systems are actually pretty secure. I've had to be creative, while preventing them from figuring out who we are and where we're doing it from. Not easy to do on short notice. If I could've planted a Trojan on their system weeks ago, this would've taken half an hour."

"You didn't answer my question."

Uzi paused, read the lines of code on his screen, and then typed another command. "When I've got something to tell you, I'll let you know."

Rodman turned back to his own laptop, and, once again, checked the time.


DESANTOS GLANCED OUT the window. Vail turned to face him and they shared a look of concern. He was giving the medication time to work its magic on the brain, breaking down its conscious and unconscious barriers, loosening its internal safeguards and inhibitions.

DeSantos did not fully understand how these behavioral engineering drugs worked—particularly SP-117, which he knew next to nothing about. The last he had heard, the CIA was still attempting to obtain a viable, fresh sample to study from an FSB double agent.

That was shaky ground, given the damage the Agency suffered in the late 1970s when Project MKUltra was laid bare. It was largely believed that the idea of developing a truth drug had been put to rest. Then again, very few knew about its work on Memogen, or the research on the mind control drug China had used on Scarponi.

DeSantos had heard whispers in the intel community about a year before Scarponi was released from prison that some of the chemicals developed in the MKUltra offshoot, subproject MKAlpha, had been smuggled out of the CIA lab and kept in private university vaults for continued study. He would not be surprised to find out that the rumors were true.

Buck opened his eyes and took a long, deep breath. "Why are you still here?"

"Because I need some answers, sir. Are you working with Hussein Rudenko?"

Buck contorted his face. "Why would I have anything to do with that vermin?"

"You tell me."

"There's nothing to tell. I am not associated with that terrorist."

"Are you aware of any other member of the Security Service who's involved with Hussein Rudenko or his organization?"

"If I knew that, the Queen would've knighted me by now."

DeSantos frowned. The SP-117 did not seem to be as effective on Buck as it had been on Richter. He thought he had used the same dosage, but there was no way for him to be sure. Since he had not intended to use the drug again, he had not paid close attention to how much he had actually administered when questioning Richter. Then again, everyone metabolized drugs differently. He might simply need more time for it to take effect—or it might have no effect on him at all.

A couple of minutes later, while Buck appeared to be dozing, DeSantos resumed his questioning. "I need to know where the ricin is being held."

"So do I."

"So do you? What do you mean?"

"I need to know where the ricin is, too."

DeSantos clenched his jaw. Was the medication flat-out not working, was Buck somehow resistant to it—or was he telling the truth?

He looked at the syringe. There were a few cubic centimeters remaining in the vial. Without forethought, he emptied it into Buck's neck.

"Ow. Will you stop doing that?"

"I need answers. And this will help me get them." He waited another few minutes, then asked, "Why did you want Basil Walpole killed?"

"Basil was a dear friend. Why would I want him dead?"

"We don't have time for this," DeSantos said. He grabbed Buck's lapel and pulled him close. "You're lying. We traced the signal from your CLAIR handset to Thames House. We know you sent those secure messages."

Buck blinked. "Yes."

DeSantos tilted his head. "Yes?"

"Yes."

Buck's eyelids fluttered and his body relaxed.

DeSantos released him back against the seat and slapped him gently on the cheek. "Sir, look at me. Look at me!"

His eyes rolled back and his breathing noticeably slowed.

DeSantos grabbed his wrist and felt for a pulse. "Oh, shit."

He noticed Vail cupping her hands and looking in the driver's side window.

DeSantos opened the door. "Dial 999, emergency services."

"What? We can't call the—"

"He's having some kind of reaction to the drug. Do it now!"

# 50

Vail made the call, doing her best to disguise her voice as she provided the location and a brief, though cryptic, description of the problem.

*It's not like I can tell dispatch that we injected the MI5 director general with a truth drug and that we just may've killed him.*

She hung up and pulled open the rear door. "Help me get him out. They're on their way."

"And do what?" DeSantos asked.

"Prop him up against that maintenance shed. We can't be here when they arrive."

"Can I pound my fist into a cement wall first?"

"It went that well, huh?"

DeSantos struggled to get hold of Buck's body in the tight confines of the back seat. They finally dragged him out and leaned him against the gray stucco wall of the flat-roofed building, as Vail had suggested.

They quickly backed away and climbed into the car.

Vail started the engine. "If Buck dies—I don't even want to think where that leaves us."

"Honestly, we probably wouldn't be a whole lot worse off than we were before."

"And that accurately sums up just how fucked we were before we kidnapped Buck." She turned right onto Vincent Square and then left onto Rutherford Street. "Did you get anything worthwhile?"

"I'm not sure. I used a Russian psychoactive drug on him. A truth drug. But it didn't work as well as it did on Richter."

"You used it on Richter?"

DeSantos did not reply.

"Where the hell did you get it?"

"Reid and Carter had it at the safe house." DeSantos leaned both elbows on his knees and massaged his temples. A moment later, he said, "Buck admitted he sent the secure messages."

"Okay."

"No, not okay. I don't know what the hell that means. Did he understand which secure messages I was talking about? He sent us totally legit texts that were fine. It was the one leading us to Walpole that caused the problem." DeSantos sat back. "But his 'admission' came right before he lost consciousness. He was, I don't know...groggy, I guess. No idea what 'Yes' means. Don't know what it gets us."

Vail slowed and tried to look nonchalant as a Metro police cruiser passed.

"Hear anything from Uzi while I was with Buck?"

"If I'd heard something," Vail said, "I would've—"

"Fine. Just keep driving. Get us the hell away from here."

"Where to?"

Sirens sounded in the distance. "We'll figure it out as we drive."

UZI SAT BACK in his seat. "Whoa, got something."

Rodman slid over. "Important?"

"Yeah. Get Santa on the line."

As he confirmed what he had just discovered, the call connected. Rodman handed him the phone.

"Talk to me, Boychick. Give us something good."

"I found a signal path that leads to an office at Thames House; I believe it's the director general's office. But from what I've been able to determine, there's some kind of anomaly that could indicate it came from 2 Marsham Street."

"And what's at 2 Marsham?"

"It's the Home Office. Run by the home secretary. Buck's boss, so to speak."

"Are you sure?"

"No, that's the point. I'm not sure. It's hard to explain. Put it this way: it looks like it came from Buck's office, but I found something that strongly suggests it actually came from the Home Office. There are irregularities that don't make sense, so I've got to dig deeper. I wasn't even going to say anything until I was sure—or *more* sure. But since I don't know what stuff you're finding on your end, in case this meant something to you, I didn't want to keep it to myself."

"Okay, I'll shout at you soon."

"Look, I know this is frustrating, but I'm not entirely sure of what I'm seeing—yet. I'm gonna stay on it. But I can't guarantee I'll get any further than I've gotten. And yes. I know time's running out."

"I need help with something else," DeSantos said. "Buck had a bad reaction to a drug I used on him. Give it a bit, then find out if he's okay. We were near Vincent Square, so check the closest hospital. I don't know what their procedures are when a high ranking official goes down. But I'd have to think they're going for the closest medical facility when every second counts."

"We can check hospital databases, but do you really want us diverting our time from the problem to check on Buck?"

"Have Hot Rod give it five minutes. If he can't get anywhere, forget it. I'm sure it'll be on the news soon enough."

"Copy."

"Something else. Contact Clive Reid and Ethan Carter for us. If Buck survived and told them what we did to him—I want to make sure we're still cool with them."

"We need to find Hussein Rudenko," Vail said. "Another project for Rodman. Have him tap into the CCTV cams and see if he can locate him. Reid told me most of the cameras aren't part of the government's system, but he suggested it's possible to tap into the entire network."

"If it's possible," Uzi said, "we'll get it done."

"Buck also told me they checked St. Paul's for ricin. It was clean but a forensics unit of some kind found traces in a storage room. If true, they must've moved it. But I have no idea if he was bullshitting me. See what you can find out."

DeSantos hung up and leaned his head back against the seat.

"We need to eat. Where, I've got no idea. But we need something. Fast food, protein bars, whatever. But it's gotta be a place where we can avoid being filmed."

DeSantos closed his eyes. "Good luck with that."

# 51

Vail stopped at the Yellow House Bar and Kitchen in Surrey Quays, near where Uzi and Rodman were camped out in their mobile digital lab. DeSantos ordered several dinners to go: Scottish beef burgers with Gruyère cheese, hand-cut chips, Cokes. Once back in the car, he called Uzi and told him they would be there in five minutes.

"Good thing," Uzi said, "because I've got a few things to show you."

"You're getting my hopes up, Boychick. You'd better deliver."

"You deliver the food, I'll deliver the goods."

When they approached the cyber café, they circled the block three times, ensuring that they were not being followed—and that Uzi and DeSantos were not being watched.

They climbed into the back of the van and pulled the doors shut behind them.

"Whoa," Vail said, taking in their setup.

"Not bad for a go bag and a couple of laptop cases, eh?"

Uzi's ultrabook sat atop two stacked milk crates, with a third serving as a seat. Rodman's workstation was identical, with an extra computer sitting off to the side.

Uzi pointed to the unattended laptop's screen. "We've got three mini cameras stuck to the outside of the van, just to make sure no one suspicious comes by. Nothing outrageous, but it gives us eyes on the ground. We can play the CCTV game, too."

"You using that cyber café's wireless signal?" Vail asked.

"For now. We're doing low bandwidth stuff, so it won't raise any alarms, and I'm masking our PCs, so they can't be discovered."

"Need be," Rodman said, "we've got the ability to use an encrypted internet connection provided we have some unobstructed sky."

"Satellite?" Vail asked.

"Very good," Uzi said with a nod.

"Why is everyone so surprised when I know something?"

DeSantos chuckled. "You really want an answer to that?"

"I'm going to ignore you," she said as she reached into the brown shopping bag and pulled out the Styrofoam meal containers. "We should've brought a can of aerosol deodorant with us. It stinks in here."

Uzi sniffed the air. "Of what?"

"Hardworking men," Rodman said.

Because of Rodman's size, Vail felt it was better not to recharacterize his description. She left it at that.

"All I smell is food." Uzi popped the lid on his and sniffed the sandwich. "Oh, that's heavenly. Red meat, ketchup, and fries. Excuse me. Chips." He turned to Vail. "How'd you know?"

"Easy," DeSantos said. "*I'm* the one who ordered it."

Uzi slid over a couple of milk crates and Vail and DeSantos took seats.

A moment later, after all of them had dug into their meals, DeSantos asked, "What'd you want to show us?"

"I checked on Buck," Rodman said, his jaw working vigorously. He swallowed, then continued. "He's alive. Treated and released. Don't know what the deal was, but I figured you didn't care. He's fine."

Vail felt a sense of relief. *Guess they won't be adding Murder One to my case. Oh, wait—that would've been the* second *count. Or third?*

"Nothing yet on the St. Paul's search," Uzi said as he wiped ketchup from the corner of his mouth. "Might not be in the system yet. If they haven't filed the report, it won't be on their server. I can't find what's not there."

"Keep me posted on that. It might give us a clue as to whether or not Richter, and Buck, were telling the truth. If they lied about that, they may've lied about the other stuff, too."

"Those guys you asked us to get in touch with," Uzi said. "Reid and Carter. Spoke to Carter, but it wasn't easy. He didn't know who the hell I was, and I had to talk in circles around everything in case his phone was being monitored. I'll send you Reid's new number. When you're ready, don't use the iPhone I gave you. Since he's vulnerable to being tracked, it's not worth being voice ID'd to it and losing it altogether. Call them from a burner phone and dump it."

"We're using SIM cards," Vail said.

"Fine. Just power down the handset and remove the battery after each call. Dump the card."

*Pain in the ass.*

"At least they're still willing to talk to us, after what we did to Buck." DeSantos dug out some fries that had fallen into the bottom of his Styrofoam container. "We're gonna need more SIM cards."

"Thought you might." Rodman rooted around his backpack and pulled out a small metal box. He tossed it to Vail.

Uzi took another bite. "Got some more good news." He chewed a moment, then swallowed. "I disassembled the CLAIR and hooked up my gizmos to it. And it looks like someone else may've sent that message sending you there to kill Walpole. You were set up."

She snorted. "We already knew that. Was it Buck?"

Uzi took another bite. "Don't think so. I'm getting close to locating where the message originated from."

"How?" DeSantos asked. "It self-erases its memory."

Uzi looked over his burger, determining where he would take the next bite. "There are historic buffers available for user review, as well as internal diagnostic buffers protected by specialized hardware that self-destructs if an unauthorized person tries to access it. A number of gaming companies use this technology to protect information on systems returned for repair. The CLAIR has a specialized network chip with a circular buffer that holds a few minutes of the last communication."

Vail looked at DeSantos, who merely shrugged.

"So where'd the message come from?" she asked.

He took a bite, holding up an index finger while his jaw ground from side to side. After swallowing, he said, "That building I told Santa about, the Home Office. Because of their setup, I couldn't locate which room it came from. Or even which floor—yet. I'm still working on it. But Hot Rod found something."

All heads swung toward Rodman, who was taking a pull from his Coke. He set it down and said, "I put together a backgrounder on Walpole, to see if we could explain why someone would want him offed."

"He's a politician," Vail said. "I'm sure the list is long."

"Here's the part where you thank me profusely. Turns out that Walpole was sitting on a secret government commission that was investigating a British bank that's suspected of laundering lots of dough for Hussein Rudenko."

"Uh oh," Vail said. "Big money equals big motive."

"Walpole was the driving force to shut down the bank's operations. He apparently got a lot of pushback because the bank's a British institution and they've got a tremendous amount of influence in Parliament."

"How do you know all this?" DeSantos asked.

Rodman popped a few fries in his mouth. "Simple. I looked. They have minutes from their meetings. It may be a secret commission, but I'm guessing they think their systems are secure."

"Doesn't every government?" Uzi asked. "Until they're hacked?"

They all laughed.

The third laptop beeped and a red bar appeared along the top of the screen.

"I got it," Rodman said as he rose from his crate and took a seat in front of the other PC.

"Point is," Uzi said, "Walpole was a huge threat to Rudenko's business. I'm sure he launders money through multiple places, but if some lone wolf is pushing to shut you down, what do you do?"

Vail stopped just before taking the next bite. "If you're Hussein Rudenko, you do what you've done to everyone who's gotten in your way. You get rid of him."

DeSantos crumpled his napkin and tossed it into the empty bag. "And we were his contract hit team."

"Hey," Uzi said, "if we're lucky, when this is all over you'll get to tell Rudenko how pissed you are about it." He swiveled on his seat. "Whatcha got there, Hot Rod?"

Rodman struck several keys as he spoke. "That facial recognition software I was running on the CCTV databases. Got a match."

"For who?" DeSantos asked.

"Rudenko." He scrolled down a list of commands and hit enter. One of the photos they had of Gavin Paxton appeared. It slid left and a grainy black and white image of a man appeared on the right. Rodman struck a key and specific points where the features matched glowed yellow. "Looks good."

"Where?"

"Wait, I've got another match. I don't know how we didn't hear it before." He played the keyboard and another face appeared. "That guy you asked about—Walker."

"Yeah," DeSantos said. "Kyle Walker."

"And some other guy, George Fields. I'm pulling up some information on him."

"Where?"

"Hang on a second, I'll get you a location for both of them. Looks like the same place. They were outside a SecureStuff self-storage facility in Bermondsey, borough of Southwark. Old Jamaica Road. That mean anything to you?"

"Yeah," DeSantos said. "Near the train tracks, about a mile or so from here." He checked his watch. "Let's go now, eyeball the place, see if we can catch Rudenko or Walker coming by. What time were they there?"

Rodman struck some keys. "Give me a minute. Still figuring this software out."

"Want me to come?" Uzi asked.

"I think you two should stay here," Vail said. "No one can do what you do, and we don't want to roll in there with all hands on deck. It puts all of us in one place, and there's a greater chance we'll scare him off. Rudenko's very smart. He could have lookouts."

Uzi glanced at DeSantos, who nodded agreement. "Makes sense to me."

"Three hours ago," Rodman said. "Doubt they're gonna be sticking around. Looks like storage unit twenty-five." He kinked his neck. "Maybe thirty-five, hard to tell."

"What were they doing there?" Vail asked.

Uzi looked over Rodman's shoulder. "Don't know. If you give us some time, we might be able to tap into the feed from that camera."

"Do it," DeSantos said. "But Karen and I aren't waiting around. We're heading over there."

"And we've gotta move the van." Uzi checked his watch. "We've stayed here too long. Let's set a check-in schedule, on the half hour every hour. If you don't call within two minutes, we'll power down and try again the next half hour."

"Fine. We'll do the same."

"There's something else," DeSantos said. "Knox. He..." DeSantos shrugged. "He kind of told me to abort the mission."

"When?" Uzi asked.

"Right before I injected Buck. I called him."

"You what? You called him?" Rodman asked, his deep voice rising uncharacteristically. "GQ, what the fuck?"

"Stupid, I know. I don't know what the hell I was thinking."

"From what we know of this op—which I'm sure is less than you know," Uzi said, "we're the front line of defense in this attack. Am I right?"

Vail cleared her throat. "Unfortunately. Yeah."

"So then what the hell are we doing, sitting here and staring at each other? Get moving."

DeSantos stuck out his fist and Uzi and Rodman bumped it with theirs. Vail popped open the rear doors and they jumped out of the van.

# 52

Clive Reid sat down at a back table on the second floor of The White Lion pub in Covent Garden, where Ingram Losner had just ordered them both a pint of Nicholson's Pale Ale. He adjusted his Fedora, pulling it down a bit further on his face, nearly against the dark tinted eyeglasses he was wearing.

Losner pushed the glass across the table to his friend. "You look a bit pale, almost like the ale, I'd say." He grinned.

Reid absentmindedly examined the foam inside his glass. "I haven't been truthful with you, my friend, and I want to apologize upfront about it."

Losner laughed. "More tall stories about that buxom lass you were dating?"

Reid looked at him, his gaze stern. Penetrating.

Losner set his drink down. "This is serious, is it?"

"I've got an arrest warrant issued for me. Yeah, it's serious."

"A warrant, you say? Today's my day off, mate. What in hell have I missed?"

Reid leaned across the table. "I need your trust. What I'm about to tell you is classified, official business. Can I count on you to keep it to yourself?"

Losner swallowed. "Of course."

"I've been working undercover. For MI5." He held up a hand to deflect any questions. "'Why' is for another time. Thing is, I need your help and I've nowhere else to turn. Five's been compromised. Six too. All our agents, potentially exposed. From the inside, by the looks of it. And things are going down now that require us to think outside the box, put aside our English inhibitions and take a stand."

Losner took a long pull, then set the ale down.

Judging by the look on his face, Reid felt as if the revelation was too much to process, the favor too much to ask.

"I'm working with Director General Buck, Ethan Carter, Karen Vail, and three of her colleagues to identify who's our inside rat." He moved to within a few inches of Losner, who'd leaned his elbows onto the table to meet him halfway. "Hussein Rudenko is in London Town. He's moved a fair amount of ricin into the city. We need to find it—and him."

Losner laughed. "No one knows what he looks like. We've been looking for him for, what, thirty years?"

"Gavin Paxton, from Idris Turner's gallery. Remember him?"

"Of course."

"Now you know what Rudenko looks like."

Losner's brow lifted. "Shite."

"Shite is right. We had him, he was in the same blasted room as us." Reid shook his head. "I need eyes and ears in the Met to make sure we don't bugger this up more than we already have. Monitor what's going on, let me know if there's a problem."

"I like Vail. But how sure are you of these people? Minister Walpole, that's not exactly a thing you want on your résumé now, is it?"

Reid leaned back and took a gulp of ale. "Put it this way, mate. I've staked my career on them."

Losner let his gaze roam around the room before engaging his friend. "Okay. I guess that makes two of us, then."

# 53

Vail drove slowly along Old Jamaica Road, a residential neighborhood bounded on both sides by apartment buildings. CCTV cameras were plentiful.

Ahead on the right was the storage complex, a green- and salmon-colored low-slung brick building built beneath a broad network of train tracks. She drove by slowly and turned right on Marine Street to come around the periphery of the property.

"Pretty quiet," DeSantos said. "Lighting sucks. Go ahead and bring us around, pull into the lot. I think we can risk getting a good look around because the cameras won't be able to see much through our windows."

Vail turned the car around and headed back to the storage complex. They parked and waited twenty minutes, using the time to catalog the cameras they could see. DeSantos said he was reasonably certain they could shield their faces from the lenses.

As the minutes ticked by, Vail stirred in her seat. There had been no activity.

"Guess no one's paying their storage units a visit at this time of night."

"Let's go in," DeSantos said. "We don't have the luxury of waiting around. If the ricin's here, we need to get Reid and Carter over here with their hazardous materials unit."

"Unless they want to sit on the place, watch it in case Rudenko and his men return."

"That's up to them. But first we need to know if this is one of the three places they're storing the ricin."

"Three places. You're assuming the info Richter gave you is real."

"He was under pretty good. The drug worked on him. I think we can go with that. Let's put it this way. We've got nothing to lose. It's here or it's not."

THEY GOT OUT OF THE CAR and walked up to the building, taking care to angle their bodies and approach from a direction that prevented the closed-circuit cameras from getting a good image of their faces.

The units were numbered clearly above each green metal roll top door.

"There it is," Vail said. "Gotta be twenty-five. Thirty-five is too far down, the next block of units."

Before they neared the gate, a pair of headlights swung into the parking lot and cast a bright splash of illumination across the brick.

DeSantos pulled her back into an alcove that was draped in shadow. "Let's wait for them to leave."

Two car doors slammed, but the vehicle was out of their line of sight.

Footsteps crunched along the gravel-littered asphalt of the parking lot.

A few seconds later, a man and a woman walked into the breezeway, along which many of the storage rooms were located. Vail leaned back into DeSantos. She recognized the woman. "Nikola Hačko," she whispered into his ear. "The chemical engineer."

"And the guy's Emir Dhul Fiqar."

"We're supposed to grab them up," Vail said.

"Not so fast." He pulled her back a step. "Let's see why they're here."

As they watched, Fiqar produced a key and opened the lock. He pulled up the rolling door and they both stepped inside.

Vail reached into the small of her back and removed the SIG. She press-checked the chamber and then held the gun in both hands, pointed at the ground. Judging by the slow scrape of one mechanical part sliding on another and the accompanying movement she felt behind her, she figured that DeSantos was following suit.

Vail slowly peered around the brick wall, then drew back. "I say we take them while the door's open. We'd have both them and the ricin—with minimal risk."

"No."

Vail twisted her neck and torso to make eye contact with DeSantos. "No?"

"We've only located one of potentially three sites where the ricin's being stored. And no Rudenko. If we let them do their thing and then follow them, we may get everything."

"And if they go to a bar to throw back some shots and shoot the breeze?"

"Then after they get juiced up, we'll take them drunk. Either way, can't lose."

*I'm not so sure of that.*

They waited another five minutes before Hačko and Fiqar emerged, a heavy bag in Fiqar's hand. Hačko pulled the door down and locked it, then followed Fiqar back to their car.

"Let's go," Vail said.

DeSantos again grabbed her shirt and drew her back into the shadows. "Not yet. We've gotta do this right so they don't see us."

"And if we lose them?"

"We won't. But even if we do, we've still got the ricin."

The brake lights lit up, followed by a puff of exhaust from the tailpipe.

"Okay," DeSantos said, "let's go."

They walked back to their car, wanting to run but keeping themselves under control—just a couple returning home from a night out at their favorite neighborhood storage cubby.

DeSantos took the wheel and pulled out of the lot with his headlights off.

"Right up ahead," Vail said.

"I'm on it. Contact Reid and Carter, tell them to get over here with hazmat, or whatever they call it here."

Vail reassembled her phone and made the call, deflecting Reid's questions about the Walpole murder. "Let's just say you don't want to know, and I don't want to tell you. Short version: we were set up. We'll talk about it when this is all over and we've secured the ricin and have Rudenko in custody."

While she removed the SIM card and dumped it out the window, DeSantos remained in visual contact with Hačko and Fiqar—not an easy feat in London, even at this time of night. As they entered an industrial area, the cars thinned out, forcing them to hang further back.

"Wish I had a GPS tracker on their car," DeSantos said. "So much at stake, I don't want to lose them. Can't spook them, either."

Fiqar, the driver, made a left into a light industrial park. DeSantos pulled to the curb alongside the street and watched.

"You're not going in?"

"I'm hoping they'll choose a spot within our line of sight. Then we can go on foot. Two bodies skulking in the dark are a lot easier to hide than a moving car on the road."

Vail leaned forward in her seat and peered deep into the parking lot. The vehicle pulled into a slot in front of two warehouse-style buildings. "Looks like you're getting your wish. Let's go."

"You go ahead. I'm gonna wait till they're out of sight, then park behind them. If they get away from us, they've got no way of escaping. By car, at least."

"You're a devious sort," she said.

"Thank-you. I've been told that."

Vail got out and approached the targets, moving in the shadows. Engaging them separately, as DeSantos had suggested, had another advantage: if Hačko or Fiqar spotted one of them, the other still had a chance at intercepting them.

And since DeSantos was now, unbeknownst to them, blocking their vehicle, they should have, at the very least, increased their chances of successfully apprehending them—and hopefully the second store of ricin.

SIG in hand, Vail inched along the concrete tilt-up facing of the warehouse-style structure, taking care not to scuff a boot on the pavement or make otherwise identifiable noises that would raise their target's awareness.

Vail inched up to the edge of the building and peered around the corner—when a fist collided with her cheek and sent her sprawling backward. She looked up and saw Nikola Hačko standing over her.

Vail's SIG was a dozen feet away, where it must have landed when she hit the ground.

Hačko raised her Beretta and lined it up with Vail's face—but Vail swung her leg up, knocking the handgun from her grasp.

Hačko hesitated, as if wondering if she should go after Vail or her pistol.

Vail dove along the cement for the weapon, but they arrived at the same time.

Hačko swung an elbow and struck Vail in the chest, driving her back. As Vail tried to regain her balance, a thought flitted through her mind:

*Where the hell's Hector?*

DESANTOS QUIETLY SHUT HIS DOOR, latching and locking it to prevent Hačko and Fiqar from taking it in place of their own.

He moved quickly but deliberately, purposely approaching from the left, opposite the route Vail had taken. After stopping at the corner of the building, he listened and heard movement—but it was a distance away.

He turned the corner and kept close to the wall of the structure, remaining in a thin band of darkness and heading toward a spillage of light that was emanating from a garage-sized doorway thirty feet away. As he neared, a shadow appeared on the pavement in front of the opening.

Someone was there: Fiqar or Hačko?

DeSantos froze and pressed his body up against the cold siding. He watched as the figure stepped out of the opening and rolled a heavy drum into place by the entrance. It was a man—Fiqar.

*Where the hell is Karen?*

HAČKO SNATCHED UP the gun, but Vail punched her in the eye, knocking her head back into the concrete and stunning her for an instant.

Vail grabbed the barrel of the Beretta and twisted the tip away from her while shoving her forearm into the crook of Hačko's elbow and folding the arm against the woman's body.

But Hačko recovered quickly and head-butted Vail, driving her back.

Her face feeling like it was going to explode and her visual field charcoal-dark, Vail managed to hold onto Hačko's forearm like a rabid dog, hoping her sight would improve before the woman could get a shot off.

Hačko got to her feet, yanking and twisting, trying to dislodge Vail's grip. But Vail held on and kept the Beretta pointed away from her.

Her vision started to clear—as did her thoughts. She slammed the heel of her boot onto the top of Hačko's foot, and the woman recoiled in pain. Vail yanked the handgun away and swung it, backhanded, into Hačko's face.

The woman went down hard.

"Now," Vail said, "we're gonna have a little talk." *And if I've got a broken nose, it's not gonna be a pleasant chat.*

As she backed away to retrieve her SIG, a gunshot rang out.

DESANTOS INCHED CLOSER to the warehouse entrance, listening for people talking. At this time of night in an industrial district, there was no reason to expect company—and thus little need to keep quiet.

He heard equipment moving around, but no voices.

If his reasoning was sound, that meant Hačko was either in another area of the building, or she was somewhere else on the grounds.

*With Karen?*

Fiqar was on his list of men to eliminate, per Buck's orders. But were those orders still valid? What if Fiqar had valuable information that Buck did not want DeSantos to elicit? No—Uzi felt that the text placing them at Walpole's originated elsewhere. How sure was he? For now, until they were certain, he had to operate on the assumption that his "facts" were at best unverified.

DeSantos stood just outside the entrance, poised to enter, his back against the wall, the SIG in his hands. He waited, listened, then swung around the edge and found himself twenty feet away from Emir Dhul Fiqar.

"Don't move," DeSantos said.

But Fiqar either did not listen or did not understand English, because he did in fact move. He reached for the shiny silver pistol in his waistband.

And DeSantos shot him.

"TURN AROUND," Vail said.

Hačko did as instructed.

"Shove your hands in your back pockets and don't even think about taking them out."

Vail grabbed a handful of Hačko's hair and pushed her forward, using her as a shield as they moved in the direction of the gunshot. It sounded like it had come from up ahead. But in the darkness, she could not see DeSantos—or anyone else.

After turning the corner of a building, Vail saw light spilling out from an open warehouse door.

DeSantos appeared a second later, SIG at the ready.

"Don't shoot," Vail said, worrying that he would see Hačko and not realize that she was behind her.

"You okay?"

"Bitch broke my nose. Otherwise I'm fine."

DeSantos approached. He looked over Hačko as a drill sergeant would appraise a recruit—disdain on his face, superiority in his body language: she was trash, and he was in charge. "Tell us where the ricin is."

"We know one of the stores is here," Vail said. "That's why *you're* here, isn't it?"

"The other store," DeSantos said. "The third one. That's what we need to find."

Hačko turned away. "I don't know what you're talking about."

DeSantos got into her face. "Yes, you do. And you're going to tell me. Or I'm going to start breaking bones in your body. One by one, until you do."

Hačko faced him. Defiance in her eyes. "You wouldn't dare."

"We're not the police," DeSantos said. "We're not going to arrest you. But we are going to leave here with what we came for."

A small smile teased her lips.

DeSantos tilted his head. "You think I won't hurt you because you're a woman." He snorted. "But you're not a woman. To me, you're a terrorist dedicated to killing innocent people. All I care about is the information I need to stop the attack. And that's what you're gonna give me. *Now*."

Vail took a deep breath. She could not undermine DeSantos by showing resistance to his plan. But since she heard a gunshot, and Hector was here and Fiqar was not, it was reasonable to assume that Fiqar was dead and could not be questioned. *That's why he's leaning so hard on Hačko.*

"I can't see how it matters," Hačko said. "You don't have long. That last stock is our largest. Even if I told you where it was, it'd be too late."

DeSantos's eyes flicked over to Vail's. *Is he telling me he has no choice, and that he hopes I'll forgive him for what he's about to do?*

He punched Hačko in the abdomen, a quick, sharp thrust. She doubled over and dropped to her knees.

Vail held up a hand for him to stop. She gestured toward the warehouse with her head. Then she crouched beside Hačko, who was on all fours trying to catch her breath. "Nikola. Emir Fiqar's your lover, isn't he?"

No response—which was answer enough for Vail. She looked up at DeSantos, hoping he could read her expression, understand what she was trying to tell him.

"You've got it wrong," DeSantos said. "It's not us who's running out of time, it's you. Your boyfriend's in that warehouse with a bad gunshot wound. But it's not too late. Tell me what we want to know and we'll get him to a hospital."

Hačko lifted her head and looked toward the open doorway.

"It's not a tough decision," Vail said. "If you care about Emir, tell us what we want to know. You don't give a shit about him, fine. He dies. But either way, we're gonna get the information out of you. Might as well save his life."

After a long moment, DeSantos grabbed her by the hair and forced her to look at him. "Where's Rudenko!"

Hačko's face displayed none of the confidence and arrogance it had a moment ago. "He—He was in a flat in Camden, near the markets, above a Vietnamese restaurant. That's all I know. I was only there once, I didn't pay attention to the address."

"Where's the rest of the ricin?"

"I don't know."

"All right, forget it. Let's go," DeSantos said, grabbing her shirt collar and pulling her away from the warehouse. "Say good-bye to Emir."

"No, wait. All I know—All I know is that it's going to be an aerosolized release."

"Bullshit," Vail said. "You're the chemical engineer. You designed it, you know everything about how it's going to be deployed. And where."

"Let me see Emir. If he lives, I will tell you."

DeSantos and Vail shared a look. And that's when Vail knew that her suspicions were correct. Fiqar was dead.

"Take her to the car," DeSantos said. "I'll call an ambulance and get him taken care of."

"No!" Hačko said, yanking her arm away from Vail. "I want to see him."

"Can you handle this?"

Vail shoved her SIG into Hačko's neck. "I'm good." She led Hačko away, her prisoner twisting and looking back, checking to make sure DeSantos was doing as he had promised.

What she did not know is that it was a hollow promise, one DeSantos had no intention of keeping.

# 54

Five minutes passed before DeSantos joined them at the car. "I called Carter. Ambulance is en route, ETA two minutes."

Vail understood the code: Carter, and whatever hazardous materials crew he had assembled, would arrive in short order—which meant they had to be gone before then.

"We're taking their car," Vail said. "I think we wore out our welcome in that one."

"Good." DeSantos shoved the SIG into his waistband and turned to Hačko. "I kept up my end of the bargain. Where's the ricin going to be released?"

"I want to go to the hospital, I want to be with Emir."

"Not gonna happen. You give us the info, we'll take you there. But right now, our job is to find that toxin." He gave her a long look, but she tensed her lips.

"Fine." Vail popped open the trunk. "Climb in."

"I'm not getting—"

"Now."

She didn't move, so DeSantos picked her up and threw her inside. He removed the belt from her jeans and bound her arms securely while Vail pulled off the woman's socks and stuffed them in her mouth.

After closing the lid, Vail parked the vehicle they had been using at the far end of the complex. She joined DeSantos a moment later near the exit.

He drove Hačko's Peugot out of the lot just as the whirring lights and sirens of Carter's hazmat contingent were heading toward them, a block away.

"That'll come in handy," DeSantos said, pointing to an external GPS mounted on the dash. "Don't have to risk turning on my phone. Program in Camden."

Vail cranked the radio and set the balance to the rear to mask their conversation. Van Halen's "Panama" blasted from the speakers.

As she poked at the GPS screen, she said, "If they're releasing an aerosol, what are the options?"

"Too numerous to figure out without time, intel, and a detailed knowledge of the country."

"Is it time to bring in MI5?"

"Reid and Carter have been in contact with Buck. But there's still the problem of the mole. If they go agency-wide with this, their inside man will find out and tip them off. They'll change their deployment and Rudenko will hit the wind. We'll get nothing."

"We'd buy time. I'm not sure Reid and Carter are enough."

"They aren't, but we don't have a choice. Not until we can figure out who's working with Rudenko. So—it's time to work off assumptions and roll the dice."

Vail sighed. "Maybe we can increase our odds with some good old-fashioned reason, logic, and intelligence."

"Where we gonna find any of that?"

Vail allowed herself to smile. "If you were Rudenko and his crew, how would you pull this off? How would you release the ricin?"

DeSantos stole a look at a street sign. After a moment, he said, "I'd use a crop dusting plane.'"

"At night?"

"Absolutely. Fly under the radar—literally. Drop your load over a large swath of land, or a city, a park, the choices are endless. And no one knows what happened until they wake up sick. Or don't wake up at all."

"So an airfield. Something small."

"They're not taking off out of Heathrow or Gatwick, that's for sure." DeSantos consulted his watch. "Call Uzi, see what he can tell us."

Vail assembled her phone and put it on speaker.

"Boychick," DeSantos said, "talk to me."

"Got some more info on Buck and that secure text he sent you. Someone piggybacked on the encryption algorithm—"

"Uzi. We're in England. Speak to me in English, okay?"

"Fine. I'll dumb it down. Wait—Where the hell are you? Is that Van Halen?"

"We've got a visitor in the trunk. Music's cover. Go on."

"Right. So in simple terms, they stole the key of Buck's handset and used it to send you a message."

"Who's 'they'?"

"It came from inside the home secretary's office."

"Are you sure? The home secretary is behind all this?"

"Not necessarily. Give me a little more time. I'm tracking something down and I'm almost into their system. How about you?"

"We have reason to believe that there really are three ricin stores," Vail said. "We've secured two of them, but the third is the largest, and it's going to be aerosolized. We're guessing it's going to be spread by crop duster."

"Hot Rod'll do some research, see what he can find out."

"We don't have time for thirty minute check-in schedules," Vail said. "I'm gonna use the iPhone from now on and leave it powered up."

"Hopefully my modifications will keep them from tracking you."

DeSantos chuckled. "From your mouth to God's ears."

# 55

As DeSantos drove toward Camden, Vail dialed Reid. He answered, confused about the unknown number and struggling to hear her over the commotion at the warehouse.

"Another dead body," Reid said. "You people are getting quite the reputation."

"I think that train's already left the station," Vail said, craning her neck to get a look at the surroundings, making sure they weren't being followed. "Are you with Carter?"

"Bit of a risk, but I can't skulk around town worried about getting arrested. We've got important matters to settle."

"Is it confirmed?" Vail asked. "Ricin?"

"It's a scene here, lots of people in spacesuits. But from what they're saying, yes. Both sites check out. The preliminary mobile lab shows we've got the liquid form containing the cytotoxic proteins ricin and RCA."

"RCA? I assume you're not talking about the electronics company."

"Ricinus communis agglutinin. I think that's what he called it. Now you know why I said, 'RCA.' It's a chemical in the toxin that blows out your blood cells. I suggest you avoid exposure."

"Good thing you told me. I was thinking of snorting the powder, assuming we find it."

DeSantos turned and gave her a look.

"Got something else for you and Carter to chase down," Vail said. "Someone sent us a bogus secure text on the CLAIR. It was supposedly from Buck but it came from the home secretary, possibly his office."

"He's a she, and how did you get this information?"

"Let's just say it's not something you can use in court. So you're going to need to poke around and find whatever evidence you need to get a search warrant. When you do, you'll want the right to examine hard drives and their government server, smartphones—you get the picture."

"Who are we going after? Surely you're not telling me it's the home secretary."

"Don't know yet. We're working on it. As soon as we've got something, you'll know. Meantime, start poking around. You wanted to know about Walpole's murder. That secure text Buck sent us—He told us he'd located one of the triggers."

"Ah," Reid said, understanding. "But it wasn't one of the triggers, it was Walpole."

"Right. Uzi—the guy you spoke with earlier—he did whatever geeks do and traced the message we got from Buck. It was bogus. It was sent from inside the home secretary's office—by her, or her assistant, or someone else. Find whoever sent that bogus message and chances are good you'll have the guy who betrayed all your colleagues."

"Bloody good."

"Is Buck back on the job?"

"You could say that. Chap's got a screaming headache and I believe he would like to shove his boot up both your arses. But yeah, he's in the office."

"One other thing you should know: Walpole was sitting on a secret commission that's investigating a bank that's been laundering money for Rudenko."

"He was also the major architect of legislation for the UK to have a unified fiscal and foreign policy," DeSantos said. "That put him in the crosshairs of a number of interested parties."

Vail glanced out the window, taking in her surroundings. "Not sure how all that fits in with the Home Office, but what doesn't make sense to us may make sense to you. Like, what does the Home Office do?"

"It's run by the home secretary, whose official position is Secretary of State for the Home Department. She's got an executive who works alongside her, the Permanent Secretary, which is a senior civil service position. The Home Office oversees immigration, security, and law and order—meaning MI5, police, border control, passports and ID cards, and counterterrorism."

"So it looks like we're hiking in the right forest."

"Let's hope so. I'll get to work on this. Ring me up if you hear anything else."

As soon as she hung up, her phone rang.

It was Uzi. She put him on speaker. "What've you got?"

"How about malware," Uzi said, "on the home secretary's PC. A Trojan."

"You mean, like a virus?"

"A virus infects other files and self-replicates. A Trojan looks like a legitimate program or service, but it hides malicious code. The one I found on the home secretary's PC was designed to record her keystrokes and transmit them back to its origin."

"How can that be, Uzi? I mean, we're talking about a secure facility. Wouldn't it be like our Department of Homeland Security? I'd think they'd take security seriously."

Uzi laughed.

Vail looked at her phone. "That wasn't funny."

"More funny than you know. Things are not as locked down as you think. Here's how it's sometimes done: the home secretary has meetings every day, right? So one day she gets back to her office, and she's just had lunch with Joe. She gets an email from Joe—only it's not really Joe. It's someone who either knows that she's recently had a meeting with Joe, saw her in a restaurant with Joe—or at least knows that she knows a Joe."

"An insider," DeSantos said.

"Doesn't have to be, but it increases his chance of success. So fake Joe sends an email to Elizabeth with the subject line, 'As we discussed.' She opens the email, thinking it's from her colleague, and there's a note that says, 'Elizabeth, thought you'd be interested in this article, which goes to what we were discussing.' She clicks on the link in the email, which takes her to a webpage that's spoofed to look just like the BBC. When the page loads, it doesn't really pertain to anything she and Joe discussed. Still, it's an interesting article on immigration legislation. Elizabeth closes the webpage and moves on to a call she needs to make.

"What she doesn't know is that by clicking that link and going to that fake BBC webpage, she's downloaded an executable file onto her PC. It starts logging all her keystrokes. Passwords, emails, documents, anything she types gets transmitted to the fake Joe, who also now has a backdoor that gives him total access to her PC."

"And she's clueless."

"Clueless. It's happened to more Fortune 500 companies than you'd believe. And high-ranking government leaders. You can have great security protocols, but people are always going to be the weakest link."

Vail sat forward in her seat and did another scan in all directions for tails. "I've got Reid and Carter working with us on this. Is there any way to tell where that malware is sending the data?"

"Sending the keystroke data would likely be when the PC is in an environment where a firewall would not prevent the transmission," Uzi said. "The keystrokes would likely be packaged up and sent to an anonymous IP address on the Internet, like StuxNet does. Let me see what I can find out, but it takes time. And time's not on our side. Santa, you listening?"

"I'm here."

"We need to discuss our exit strategy."

"Exit strategy?" DeSantos stole a glance at Vail. "We don't have all the ricin yet. And Rudenko's still at large. This is our best ch—"

"Look," Uzi said. "There's only so much we can do here. Working against the clock, against law enforcement, against the Security Service— if we can't secure the toxin soon—and I mean, soon—we need to get our asses out of Dodge. We'll turn over all our intel to Buck on the way out of the country."

"But—"

"You know I'm right, Santa. It's gotten too messy, and if we stick around, we may not get any further than we've gotten. We've been lucky—and we've been good. But the longer we hang around, the more likely our luck's gonna turn bad. And if we're arrested, you and Karen are toast. As it is, I don't see a way out of this for you guys without some serious diplomatic maneuvers. And we both know that just doesn't happen when you're black. Especially when there's a body count that can't be easily explained away."

DeSantos again looked at Vail. She tried not to let her face betray her feelings, but she agreed with Uzi. Jonathan was on her mind—and she had already expressed her feelings over getting duped into this mission.

DeSantos sighed. "Since when did you become the parent in this relationship?"

"Are you with me on this?"

"Yeah" DeSantos said. "Fine. You're right."

Vail sat back, relieved—yet still hoping they would get to finish what they had started.

"Of course I'm right," Uzi said. "That's why I've already worked out a solution."

"Why am I not surprised?"

"'Cause I'm freakin' awesome. You think I'd come over here without a plan to get us out? Hot Rod and I worked it out on the flight over and cleared it with Knox. We're gonna head over to Mildenhall."

"The Royal Air Force Base?"

"In Suffolk, yeah. The US has a big air force base there that happens to be well stocked with a fleet of Ospreys."

"There aren't any Ospreys there."

"Apparently, my man, there are now. They're retiring all the CH-46 birds and replacing them with Ospreys. And Hot Rod and I are going to borrow one and pick you up."

"You're going to steal an Osprey?"

"Borrow, Santa. Borrow."

"And go where?"

"First things first. We're heading out to Suffolk. Hot Rod's going to drive, and I'm gonna keep working the keyboard. I'll let you know where it leads."

# 56

"What the hell's an Osprey?" Vail asked. "I assume you're not talking about the bird."

"It *is* a bird, just not one that flaps its wings."

"Helicopter?"

"Not really that, either. It's a plane and a helicopter all in one. A tilt rotor aircraft, vertical takeoff and land. First of its kind. It flies twice as fast and twice as far as a chopper."

Vail snapped her fingers. "Yeah, I saw one of those at an air show a couple of years ago. Very cool demonstration. But didn't they have a lot of problems with them?"

"Define problems."

"Crashes."

"That'd be a yes," DeSantos said. "Don't worry about it. The criticism was overblown."

Vail looked at him, hoping to see a broad grin. But he was not smiling. And that's when she felt a serious knot tighten in her stomach.

FIVE MINUTES LATER, Vail's phone rang.

"Got something," Rodman said. "Put me on speaker." After Vail complied, he continued: "I've located Rudenko, outside a flat in Camden."

DeSantos accelerated. "That's where we're headed. When was he there?"

"He's there now. I tapped into the Met's CCTV network and set the system up to set off an alarm if it got a facial recognition hit. I had to pull off the road, but I'm now on a live feed. Rudenko came out of a building and headed northwest. I'm trying to follow him, pick him up on different cameras. If you're anywhere close, I suggest you get your asses there fast, because I don't know how long he'll keep walking where we've got eyes. He's in a black overcoat and a top hat. And he's got a handlebar moustache. Doesn't look like he's as good as you when it comes to disguises. Attracts attention to himself, if you asked me."

"Goes with the personality of successful, wealthy businessmen," Vail said. "They think they're impervious. Some lose the filter for being careful. They become overconfident. They're accustomed to doing what they want and winning, like a gambler who keeps getting positive reinforcement. He loses the inhibition to be careful; he forgets he could still lose everything."

"Don't know if that applies to Rudenko," DeSantos said, squealing the tires as he pushed the Peugeot too hard on a turn. "He's survived decades in weapons dealing because he's extremely smart. I can't imagine he's suddenly lost his edge. You sure it's him, Hot Rod?"

"Hundred percent match. I pulled up a good image from his gallery cameras. Wait, he's passing the Costa Coffee Shop on Chalk Farm Road right now. Across from the Stables Market."

Vail pulled out her iPhone and dialed Reid, who answered on the first ring. "Can you get CO19 to Camden, Chalk Farm Road? Sighting on Rudenko, real time. By the Costa café, across from the Stables Market."

"Will do," Reid said, and clicked off.

DeSantos hung a hard left. "Just turned onto Camden High off Jamestown."

Residential apartments sat atop storefront businesses, restaurants, and coffee shops on both sides of the street.

"Looks like Camden High becomes Chalk Farm," Vail said, reading the GPS and glancing up at her surroundings. "I think we're close."

"A few blocks," Rodman said. "But—Oh shit."

*"Oh shit" is not what I want to hear right now.*

"I can't—"

Vail heard Rodman tapping his keyboard.

"Damnit. Lost him."

*You've gotta be kidding me.* "Find him! We may not get another chance."

"I can't see him if there aren't any cameras," Rodman said, his voice tense, yet controlled. "I can try tapping into private cams, but he'll be long gone by then. Keep driving along Chalk Farm. Maybe you'll be able to get a visual."

DeSantos slowed the car to a crawl. "Passing Stables Market."

"He was on the north side of the street," Rodman said. "If that helps."

"See anything?" DeSantos asked.

"There," Vail said, pointing at a man walking in a black overcoat a block away. "We've got a possible. Vail out." She pocketed the phone and drew her SIG. "Pull ahead and let me out. He won't recognize me until he's on me. By then you'll be there, behind him."

*It'd be a whole lot better if Brits drove on the right side of the road.*

DeSantos accelerated gently and passed the man.

"That's him," she said, looking in the side view mirror.

DeSantos pulled the Peugeot to the left curb and Vail got out, hiding her handgun and avoiding eye contact with Rudenko as she crossed the street.

Apparently Rudenko had seen this maneuver before, because he turned and ran in the opposite direction. He ditched the overcoat, hopped the adjacent construction enclosure, and landed in a vacant lot alongside a backhoe.

Vail followed but lost sight of him as he scaled the far fence thirty feet away, and then disappeared up the side street.

She heard footsteps on the asphalt behind her, which she sure hoped belonged to DeSantos—but she was not about to take her eyes off the area where Rudenko had disappeared.

Vail climbed the chain-link and landed squarely on the sidewalk. Ahead of her was a dimly lit residential area featuring modest two-story attached homes fronted by brick walls.

She moved up the street slowly, SIG at the ready, eyes scanning the block, looking for any form of movement.

"Karen!"

She heard DeSantos's voice an instant before the gunshots.

# 57

Ethan Carter accelerated as he rounded the curve, forcing Reid's left shoulder into the car door.

"You think we'll get there before CO19?" Carter asked.

"Depends on where they were when the call came through from dispatch. But their average response time is something like four minutes."

As they turned onto Chalk Farm Road, they saw the ARV, or Armed Response Vehicle, ahead of them, two blocks away. The BMW was moving quickly, its light bar whirling in a dizzying rhythm.

"There's my answer," Carter said. He accelerated and came up behind the white, yellow, and orange vehicle.

"What do we do if Vail and DeSantos are still around?"

"Once we grab up Rudenko, we'll help them make their exit. But they knew the score when they summoned CO19."

Reid clenched his molars. "They asked for CO19 because it was the right thing to do. They shouldn't be punished for putting aside their own interests and making the right call."

He did not want to see Vail and DeSantos go through the penal system for risking their lives on behalf of the United Kingdom. Still, there was little he could do to help them. His first priority was to secure Rudenko. The rest would have to take care of itself.

DESANTOS APPROACHED with his SIG down by his knees, oriented toward the ground, as he shuffled toward the houses. When he had gotten out of the Peugeot, he angled away from Vail, taking a different approach while heading down Hartland Road.

Because of his route, he had seen what Vail could not: Hussein Rudenko perched behind the brick wall, his handgun aimed at her, the barrel poking over the top.

"You okay?" he asked.

"I'm fine. For someone who nearly had her head blown off. Thanks."

"I told you I'd never let anything happen to you."

"I'm starting to believe you."

DeSantos looked at her. "Starting?"

Ahead of them was Rudenko's inert form, his gun lying impotently on the pavement a few feet from his hands.

Just then in the windows of the adjacent house, Vail saw the flicker of a police light bar. "Shit. They're here."

"Hang on," DeSantos said as he started toward Rudenko's body.

Vail grabbed his sleeve. "They're down the block, we've gotta go."

"Just wanted to be sure he's dead."

She pulled him down Hartland, away from Chalk Farm. "Can't go back for the car, we'll never make it."

"What about Hačko?"

They crossed to the other side of the street and ran down the sidewalk, using the parked cars as cover, headed toward what looked like a train trestle.

As the Armed Response Vehicle passed Hartland—they were headed to Rudenko's last known location, the Costa café—Vail saw a car on the side street off to her right: Hawley Road. The vehicle flashed its headlights and Vail and DeSantos ran toward it.

As soon as they pulled the backdoors closed, Carter hung a right on Hartland.

"Did you find Rudenko?" Reid asked.

"We more than found him," DeSantos said. "I shot him. No choice. He's probably dead."

"No choice?" Carter asked, not doing an effective job of concealing his anger.

"No choice," Vail said. "He was about to kill me."

"He was a high value asset. I still think there was a choice."

"I won't take that personally," Vail said.

"Turn left up ahead," Reid said. "Let's try to get some distance from CO19." He turned around to face DeSantos. "So there were gunshots?"

"Two."

Reid and Carter shared a look.

"Gunfire's rare in London," Reid said. "More units are gonna respond. Go down Adelaide, see if we can circle around, get us away from the crime scene." He rooted out his phone. "I'm going to see if I can point them where they need to be. It may take them off their search grid."

"And out of our hair," Vail said.

"Exactly. Where's the body?"

"Near the vacant lot," DeSantos said, "on Hartland, in front of the first or second house, by the brick wall."

"Have them search our car," Vail added. "An idling Peugeot on Chalk Farm by Hartland. They'll find Nikola Hačko in the trunk."

He initiated the call. "This is DCI Carter. I've got some intel from an informant on the location of the victim and possible suspect that CO19's responding to in Camden." He gave them the directions and shoved the phone back in his jacket pocket.

"Get anywhere with the Home Office?" Vail asked.

"Working on it. I've enlisted a prosecutor's assistance, someone we can trust. He nearly laughed me out of his office. No evidence—at least none he can present to a judge. I mean, we're going after the Home Secretary. That's not something you want to be wrong about."

"We're not sure it's her," Vail said. "Uzi's still working on it, but you may need to set a trap, plant some information and see who takes the bait."

"Now *that* I may be able to pull off." He pointed at the approaching intersection. "Left on Finchley, it turns into Park."

Reid wiped the fogging window with his jacket sleeve, then scanned the streets. "We've got Rudenko and two of the three batches of ricin. And we've got some direction on who might be our mole. No offense, Karen, but I think we can take it from here."

"So we've been told. Uzi reached the same conclusion."

"You need a way out, then."

"Uzi's going to pick us up in an Osprey. I assume he's gonna fly us out of the country."

Carter took his eyes off the road to glance at Vail. "An Osprey, did you say?" He shook his head. "Don't think I want to know how he's going to get one of those—or get you through British air space without the air force shooting you down."

"Thanks for the vote of confidence. Got any better ideas?"

"Not one," Carter said.

Reid leaned forward and peered out the windshield. "Where's the rendezvous point?"

"Don't know," DeSantos said. "We're going to choose one and hope it works. We're running out of time."

Vail swiveled in her seat and looked out the rear window. "We'll need to get to a place where cameras aren't likely to be monitoring us. Any suggestions?

"The Thames," Carter said. "Get there, take a boat, and you'll be off the grid as much as possible in this city. The Met's got a Marine Support Unit, but the river's still your best bet. Uzi should be able to pick you up somewhere along the shoreline."

DeSantos nodded. "Works for me. Get us to the Thames. We're not that far from it."

"No," Vail said, swiveling around in her seat. "Angles and distance, right?" She got a surprised look from DeSantos. "If we take a straight line to the Thames, we'll lead them right to our only way out of this mess. We need to escape and evade."

"She's right," DeSantos said. "What's the most direct roundabout way that'll get us there?"

"The mail railway," Carter said.

"Yes!" Reid said. "Brilliant, mate. Paddington, then?"

"What's the mail railway?" Vail asked.

"Hold that thought," Carter said. "We've got company."

Vail twisted in her seat and saw a Metropolitan Police cruiser swinging onto Finchley behind them, light bar flashing.

# 58

"Let us off!" Vail said.

Carter glanced up at his mirror. "I'm gonna slow without touching my brakes. If they don't see the lights come on, they may not be close enough to realize that I've stopped. Get ready."

"I'm going with them," Reid said as he turned off the interior dome light. "I'll get 'em to the railway. Can't stay here, anyway. They'll arrest me and make your life hell for harboring a fugitive."

"Very well, then." Carter downshifted to first and they lurched forward as the engine groaned. He pulled up on the handbrake, and when the vehicle had slowed enough, they popped open their doors and got out in front of a stone gazebo.

An adjacent sign told them there were standing just outside Regent's Park. Reid led them around the far side of the structure, out of the approaching cruiser's field of view. The police car pulled up behind Carter and flashed its lights. Carter, who had continued on after dropping off his passengers, brought the vehicle to a stop half a block away.

Vail, DeSantos, and Reid moved to the far side of the small building and waited. She heard Carter identify himself and imagined him pulling out his credentials. They would comb the sedan's interior with their flashlights, and then send him on his way. In this neighborhood, at midnight, there were few cars on the road. Carter's vehicle was an easy target for search, in case their shooter had escaped via automobile.

Vail watched the light bar's reflection off the area's buildings diminish in intensity. As she shifted position, she saw that the cruiser was headed down Park, Carter just ahead of them.

She poked her head further around the edge of the gazebo and signaled the others that it was clear.

"Looks like Carty left us a gift," Reid said, heading for a couple of short, rod-shaped objects in the street where Carter had parked. He picked them up and handed them to DeSantos. "Flares?"

DeSantos grinned. "So Uzi can see us from the air."

We carry 'em around in our cars for emergencies. Carter must've dropped them out the bottom of his door before pulling away."

"Now what?" Vail asked.

"Baker Street Underground station." Reid stole a look at his watch. "We'd better hurry. It's a half mile up the street and the last train leaves soon."

# 59

U zi tapped away on his keyboard as Rodman consulted the GPS and exited the motorway. "Time to pack up, Uzi. They're gonna be here in ten minutes."

"I'm close. It's—Wait, there it is. Got it. Get Santa on the phone."

A few seconds later, Rodman put the call on speaker.

"Talk to me," DeSantos said.

Uzi started shutting down the third laptop while he spoke. "Only got a few minutes. We're just outside the base perimeter. But I've got some answers and I don't know when I'm going to be able to contact you after we're airborne. And we need to set an RVP."

"Carter suggested we set the Rendezvous Point for the Thames. No CCTVs. Harder to track us. Makes sense, so pick us up there."

"Uh, last time I checked, Santa, that's a long freakin' river—like a couple hundred miles."

"Somewhere near city center. I've got flares. Look sharp."

"No problem. I'll make it work."

"You said you've got something for us?"

"I do." Uzi shoved the laptop into his backpack and then shifted the phone from his shoulder back into his left hand. "That CLAIR message. It was definitely spoofed to make us think it came from the Home Secretary,

ALAN JACOBSON                                                    353

or at least the Home Office. But some of the information in the packets
didn't match up. The location and date/time packets appeared to be pasted
in, like they mixed in identity tokens from another Home Office message."

"That makes you sound like a freaking genius," DeSantos said,
"because I've got no idea what you just said."

Uzi climbed back atop the milk crate seat in front of his laptop and
opened an email. "Bottom line. I was able to locate the true origination
point of the message. I've got an address for you, but you're not going to
like it."

"I already don't like it."

"Then you're *really* not gonna like it. It's the Shadow Home Secretary's
*house*. His personal computer."

# 60

Vail leaned closer to the phone.

"What did you call it—the *Shadow* Home Secretary?"

"I'm sending the address to Reid right now," Uzi said. "And yeah, that's how the cabinet directory listed the address. Monty Gallagher, Shadow Home Secretary."

"What the hell's a Shadow Home Secretary?" DeSantos turned to Reid.

"Part of the shadow cabinet. Basically, the shadow cabinet's senior members of the main opposition party scrutinize their corresponding ministers in the government. They create alternative policies and hold their counterparts accountable for their actions."

"So the Shadow Home Secretary keeps the Home Secretary on her toes?" DeSantos asked.

"More or less. He looks over her shoulder on policing, national security, immigration—everything she's responsible for. And if the opposition party's elected to government, the Shadow Home Secretary often becomes the new Home Secretary."

"Wait," Uzi said. "Did I hear Reid right? If the opposition party takes over, the Shadow Home Secretary can become the new Home Secretary?"

"That's what he said."

"That's our motive right there," Uzi said.

Vail stopped walking and brought them together in a huddle. "This might be a power grab. The Shadow Home Secretary sends us off to kill Walpole, a minister who's clamping down on policies that the more extreme parts of government don't want to see passed. He eliminates the threat and then frames the prime minister and a couple senior members of the government by giving the media a photo of us—the people who murdered Walpole—and labels us international terrorists. The prime minister is guilty by association, and he resigns. His government falls and the opposition takes over."

Reid shook his head. "Not exactly. You're right—by discrediting the prime minister, they'd discredit the governing party. But the only way that the government can 'fall' is if the matter were so serious—and this obviously qualifies—that the opposition parties bring a motion of no confidence. Basically, when it passes, the government falls. Assuming the opposition party does well in the new election, it takes over. But they're not aligned with the extreme parties of the government."

"That you know of. Tell Carter to pick up the Shadow Home Secretary—"

Reid's brow rose. "On what?"

"Find something," Vail said. "An unpaid parking ticket. Start sweating him and show him the proof that Uzi just emailed you."

"The docs he got by *hacking* secure government servers?"

"C'mon, Reid," DeSantos said. "You're a spook. You know how to do this. Bluff him."

Reid nodded. "I'll tell Ethan to pick him up." He pulled out his handset and started dialing.

"If you've got someone you can trust," Vail said, "have him start going through the Shadow Home Secretary's phone records, emails—you're going to find at least one accomplice, maybe more."

"How do you figure?"

"I doubt he has the technical expertise to reroute and piggyback secured signals. Or whatever Uzi called it."

Reid brought the handset to his ear. "Good point."

"Let's get moving," DeSantos said. They started forward, headed for the station.

Uzi's voice crackled from the speaker. "I had the same thought, Karen. I've got a tracer program running, but we've gotta shut it down in a minute. Buck can hire an independent hacker he trusts to finish what I've started but I—" A beeping sound interrupted him. "Hang on a second. I think we've got a hit."

"Hot Rod," DeSantos said. "While Uzi dicks around with that, where do we stand on the crop duster?"

"I got Mac over at Geospatial to give us some satellite time. He's looking at a live feed, but it's gonna take some time. A crop duster only needs a tiny airstrip of compacted dirt. That could be almost any rural area."

"And that's the problem," Uzi said. "Trying to find these bastards means scouring huge swaths of the country for active infrared signatures moving around a single-engine biplane agricultural aircraft. Not as easy as it sounds."

"Obviously not," Vail said. *Who said that sounded easy?*

"My buddy's got a friend with the Royal Air Force," Rodman said, "pretty high up. I'm gonna give him a call, alert him we've got intel on a small craft ready to deploy a chemical weapon. They can notify whoever should be notified. I'm sure they've got more eyes on their skies than we do."

"Definitely have something here," Uzi cut in.

"Would you like to share?" Vail said. "We're getting close to the tube, and once we go down, we'll lose you."

"And *we've* got a meet," Rodman added, "any minute."

"Fine, fine," Uzi said. "I had a program looking for unusual activity going to or coming from Monty Gallagher's PC or phone—emails, calls, texts, anything—to see who it'd lead us to. One person stands out, a spike in texts and phone calls over the past week or so. That's not a smoking gun by any stretch, so I looked into this guy's background while running a different program to search his PC to see if anything interesting came up."

"Boychick," DeSantos said. "Get to the point."

"It found about a dozen encrypted files, all using the same encryption scheme that's on Gallagher's computer. We don't have time to decrypt them, so I picked the smallest one to see what we'd get."

"And?"

"And I found the smoking gun."

# 61

"It's a database of names," Uzi said. "What do you want to bet that it's your stolen list of intelligence agents."

Reid lifted his brow. "Read me a few of them."

They heard the click-clack of a keyboard.

"Pearson, Marsdon, Hanley, Spicer, Rigo—"

"Bloody hell, that's it. We've got to secure that hard drive, see who he's sent that list to—"

Rodman's voice boomed through the speaker. "Uzi, we've gotta go."

"Okay, okay. Just need another minute." More keyboard work.

DeSantos leaned closer to the phone. "Hot Rod, did you get through to that air force contact?"

"I left a voice mail on his cell for him to call me back. But he doesn't know who the hell I am, and I couldn't reach my friend to give him a shout."

"Uzi," Reid said, "Who's this guy, the one who had this list?"

"Name's Richard Price. And he's a—"

"Holy shit. He's a junior minister, very bright guy."

"With an interesting background," Uzi said. "Double major from Cambridge, computer programming, political science. That probably says all you need to know."

"The hacker who got elected to the government," Vail said, "combining his talents to influence policy."

"I've zipped and encrypted everything," Uzi said. "It's on its way to you, Reid."

"This is it," Reid said, stopping in front of The Globe restaurant, which Vail remembered reading had been around for two centuries and had served Arthur Conan Doyle and Charles Dickens. "That's one of the main entrances." He nodded across the street, where there was a blue Baker Street station sign mounted above the doorway. "We'll avoid that because of all the cameras, and go down here." He placed his hand on the long wrought iron fence that bordered a staircase bearing a sign that read, "Pedestrian Subway."

Another series of beeps blared from the speaker.

"Uzi," Rodman said, "ignore it. Our ride's here, and he can't wait."

"Okay, okay. Reid, listen to me. The program just got another hit. Wes Collingsworth. I've run out of time, so the rest you're gonna have to—"

"Wes Collingsworth, you sure?"

There was a click and the noise of shuffling feet. "I just shut everything down, but yeah, that was the name."

"Wes is a friend of Carty's—of Carter's—from JTAC. I know him, too. Bloody hell."

Vail shared a glance with DeSantos. They both knew that JTAC stood for the Joint Terrorism Analysis Centre. *This just keeps getting better.*

"Good luck with that," Uzi said. "Sounds like you're gonna need it. Signing off. Karen, Santa, see you two over the Thames."

# 62

As they walked into the station, looking down to avoid the entry cameras, Reid's phone rang. He answered it as they swiped their Oyster cards.

He listened a second, then said, "You sure?" He swiveled around, his eyes searching the area.

"What's up?" Vail asked.

He rotated the handset away from his mouth and quickened his pace. "It's Ingram. The Met's CCTVs picked us up, they've got a fix on us. They're a block away. We've gotta move, get on a train. At this point, doesn't matter which direction. We have to change our location."

They wound their way into the bowels of the station, passing through its myriad tunnels, passageways, and levels. Built in 1863, Baker Street was a mix of modern retrofit and antique fixtures, with nods to its Sherlock Holmes literary celebrity. Cameras were everywhere—cameras readily accessible to Scotland Yard. If they knew Vail and DeSantos were nearby, they'd be doing a search of all video feeds coming in from the station's cams.

They neared the platform that Reid led them to: they wanted the Bakerloo line, he told them, exiting at Paddington. He said it was a short, four minute ride.

A moment later, a train was rumbling toward them. Once inside, Vail sat down heavily. "Hopefully no one'll be waiting for us when we get off."

"Ingram said the Met's got an alert out to all officers and CO19 units. They've got checkpoints set up around town. We should avoid cars, taxis, buses, and trains."

"So naturally we're on a train," Vail said.

"Perhaps you wanted to walk?"

"It's a short leg," DeSantos said. "Not like we had a lot of choices." He took a seat beside Vail, facing Reid, who'd sat down across the way. "What's this mail railway you mentioned?"

"A 'secret' underground rail system designed to move mail across London. A six or seven mile trip from its east end to its west end. The trains only go about thirty-five, forty miles per hour, but the best part— the most important thing for you—is that it's underground, and there's no CCTV. Well, there are cameras, but they closed the railway in 2003, so they're not being used."

Vail looked at the overhead graphic showing the station map. The last thing she wanted was to miss their stop.

"You sure it'll still run?" she asked.

Reid shrugged. "Wish I could tell you for sure, but yeah, they supposedly only mothballed it. I'm told the controllers go down there periodically, fire things up and run the trains. It's a good emergency system."

"And how are we supposed to 'fire things up'?"

"I was down there a few years ago and watched a demonstration they did. Hopefully it'll come back to me."

*Hopefully?*

The tube's public address system announced that they were approaching Paddington Station.

"This is us," Reid said. "Let's see if we can throw them off. Cover part of your face. An eye, your nose. Looks a bit suspicious, but it supposedly prevents the facial recognition from, well, recognizing you."

The train stopped. The "Please mind the gap" announcement began as the doors parted.

"Stay close," Reid said. "I'm going to try to lead you out of here without too much drama."

*Yeah. I'm not holding my breath.*

# 63

Uzi and Rodman stuffed all their equipment into a black backpack and left the van, which Rodman had meticulously scrubbed before heading off toward Suffolk.

A US Air Force troop carrier was idling parallel to their vehicle, lights off. Uzi peeled back the canvas cape covering the rear of the truck and they climbed inside. A uniformed man sat there, gear off to the side. He extended a hand and Rodman took it.

"Trip, good to see you."

"Another time, Hot Rod, I'd say the same thing. But you're putting me in a real bad way. The risk—"

"Has been huge. For *us*. In the next few days, when things start coming out, you'll be telling me how much you appreciate what we've done here."

Trip frowned, then pulled out a duffel bag from beneath the seat.

"But we're grateful for your help," Uzi said. "Getting out of here would've been a whole lot harder, if not impossible."

Trip grunted. "Don't thank me yet. You're a long way from being out of this. There are a million things that can go wrong—starting the minute you stepped into the back of this truck. Trust me, you don't want to know all the ways you can fuck this up." He unzipped the canvas bag and removed a couple articles of clothing. "Assuming you're not shot down and I'm not court martialed, you owe me a beer stateside someday."

"Deal," Uzi said.

"Flight suits," Trip said as he tossed them onto their laps. "You've got two minutes to get 'em on before we hit the base perimeter."

Uzi and Rodman complied, slipping them on over their clothes.

"Assuming we get through the base's security checkpoint, the flightline has tighter controls. There are other access points with video and electronic surveillance that require electronic passes. If we make it through all of those, the runways themselves are very isolated. But the Air Force is notorious for its overbearing patrols of the flightline. Wearing those," he said, gesturing at the flight suits, "and acting like you know what you're doing, we should be okay."

As Uzi adjusted the fit atop his shoulders, he said, "So how's this going to work? Can't imagine we're just gonna walk up to an Osprey and fly it away."

"Short answer is yes, that's basically what you're going to do. Long answer's more complicated. Aircraft stored out on the flightline are mostly ready to fly. At the end of regular flight ops, sometimes there are inserts—basically, big red plugs—that go in the intakes, pins for the landing gear, and various 'remove before flight' flags on certain gear. The planes are chained down and their wheels are chocked. That's the bad news. The good news is that they'll probably be fully fueled and ready to go."

"Doesn't sound 'ready to go' to me."

"Removing the 'red gear' and chains only takes a few minutes," Rodman said. "It's not as bad as Trip's making it out to be."

"Look," Trip said. "These are very expensive, very unique planes. The Air Force doesn't want anything happening to them, right? That includes theft. Don't forget that no one knows you here—you may be wearing the right uniform, but everyone here pretty much knows everyone else. You'll be exposed while you're unhooking the chains, removing the red gear, and boarding. Those a very dangerous 'few minutes.'" He gave Rodman a stern look.

"Just how many bullets are we going to be dodging?" Uzi asked.

Trip stole a quick look out a small grommet hole in the canvas covering. "The late night hours are usually pretty quiet for flying. Since you're doing this after regular flight hours, the tower's closed. Obviously that's a big deal. So as long as you fly low and don't turn on your transponder, no one'll be able to track you once you're airborne.

"So that brings us to your biggest problem. This is the busiest time for the maintainers. They're in and out of the aircraft on the line throughout the night doing maintenance. So even if you're able to remove the gear and get into the plane, it's gonna be tough to start it up without drawing attention."

"How quick can we lift off once we start the engines?"

"Not quick enough. But here's the thing: when certain kinds of maintenance are done on the engines, they need to be turned on and run up to various power settings before they're certified to fly again. Not many maintainers are certified to start these planes, especially for high power checks. But I'm the maintenance officer, and I'm certified. So I volunteered. I'm flying an important joint exercise tomorrow. No one questioned it."

"So," Rodman said, "you'll be making a lot of noise on a plane nearby."

"Right. When you start your engines, no one should notice."

"How long will it take to get airborne?"

"If we do it right," Rodman said, "ten, fifteen minutes."

"And if we do it wrong?"

"Not an option. I can do this."

"How many times have you flown one of these?"

Rodman's face hardened, his eyes locking on Uzi's. "Half a dozen."

Uzi was sure he was unsuccessful in hiding his surprise. "I don't know a whole lot about the Osprey, but I do know it's a complex machine that's had a number of crashes, mostly from pilot error. And you've only flown this thing six times?"

"You have a better idea," Rodman said, "now would be the time."

"Look sharp," Trip said, peering through the canvas hole. "We're here."

# 64

Vail, DeSantos, and Reid successfully navigated the surface streets without "drama," as Reid had put it.

Now, with the lift unavailable until they turned on the power, Reid led them down the steps into the Royal Mail railway station. The pungent smell of long-undisturbed darkness irritated Vail's nose as she descended the staircase.

They used their smartphones as flashlights until they reached the metal fire door, which they pushed through onto the platform. Reid told them to wait while he located the control room. A minute later, he lifted a large lever into position. It slammed home with a metallic clunk.

The lights flickered, lit up, and then switched off. Reid made some noise, clicking and clattering as he reset the circuits. The fixtures came on once again—and this time they burned brightly.

The station wasn't in as much disrepair as Vail had feared. As she looked around at the rounded, gray-white metal walls, her concerns over being trapped underground, seventy feet below the surface, where no one traveled for perhaps months at a time, started to dissipate.

"Not many people know this place," Reid said as he ducked back into the control room. "It's been called 'the secret railway,' because unless you were one of the staff who worked down here moving mail, or a controller working the trains, the public rarely, if ever, heard about it. They just got their letters and parcels on time. I think it's the only mail railway in the world."

Large steel bins on wheels stood off to the side along the station's wall. To her left, a train sat on the tracks, its red locomotive covered in a thick layer of dust. "Royal Mail" was lettered in yellow script across the bottom of the row of cars.

Reid threw a switch and the ventilation system started up with a roar. Air blew down onto Vail from a square duct above.

Vail walked into the control room and looked at the row of computers. The brand name "Vaughan" was molded into the side of the plastic housing. "Monochrome cathode ray tube monitors? These PCs are museum pieces." She chuckled. "In fact, I think I *have* seen stuff like this in a museum somewhere."

"Karen," DeSantos said, "you're not instilling a sense of confidence."

"That's okay. I'm not feeling it either."

Reid hit "enter" and examined the lines of code. "System's booting up. We should be ready to go in a few minutes."

"And how sure are you," Vail said, "that the computer's gonna work?"

Reid lifted his hand off the keyboard. "I'm not sure at all."

*Lovely.*

"If I remember right," Reid said, "each station has its own computer that's connected to the relay system. The computer controls the progress of each train on the system automatically, but the line controller can take control of any part of the system, and reroute the trains if needed."

"And you'll stay at the controls till we get out?" Vail asked.

"I'll be here. But I won't know when you're out because we don't have cell service down here. A text might go through. Give it a shot."

"If not," DeSantos said, "six miles, forty miles an hour. Give us half an hour, then figure we're out. You can leave. If we're not out, we'll be close enough."

Reid examined the archaic monitors. "We're booted up and functional."

Vail looked over Reid's shoulder at the text on the screen. "Do you actually know what all this means?"

Reid nodded. "Not a clue."

Vail gave DeSantos a look.

"We'll be fine." He took her by the elbow and led her toward the tracks. "C'mon, the faster we get to the river, the faster we'll be on our way out of England."

She placed both hands on her hips as she surveyed the train. "Where do we sit?"

"The railway didn't carry passengers," Reid said. "It carried letters and small parcels. You two are somewhat…larger parcels. I guess we'll call it steerage class." He chuckled.

Vail looked over the mail cars. "You expect me to get in that tiny bin?"

"This is no time for a claustrophobic fit," DeSantos said.

"Oh." Vail slapped her forehead. "Silly me. What the hell was I thinking?" She realized he did not get it. "It's not a conscious decision. I see a tight space and the anxiety builds in my chest."

DeSantos placed his hands on her shoulders. "You're gonna have to do this. This is our best chance to get to the rendezvous point. I'll be right behind you."

The two stepped into their respective compartments and Reid started to pull the top over Vail's car. She raised her arm to stop him. "I'll pass."

"I don't know the condition of the tunnels," Reid said. "You don't want something falling from the ceiling and hitting you in the head, now, do you?"

"If it means not being trapped in some kind of tiny metal coffin, yeah. At least I'll get some air movement over my face."

"Suit yourself."

He attempted to pull back the covering, but it was connected to a metal plank that bridged the gap on the side of the train where it met the platform. "Can't do it, Karen. The train won't move with the ramp open. You're gonna have to deal with it."

DeSantos pulled out his knife and sliced through the canvas. There were still bars above her, but it was an improvement.

"Thanks," she said. "I think I can handle that."

After DeSantos settled into his car, Reid secured the cover over him.

Cramped in the compartment, knees against her chest, Vail felt her chest tighten. She slowed her breathing by thinking of Robby. Of making love, going to dinner, listening to music at a local Washington blues club.

"All right, then," Reid said as he walked over to a switch that hung by a thick wire suspended from the ceiling beside the tracks. "Talk to you on the other side."

Vail was able to block her anxiety until Reid pressed the button-operated control and started the train.

They lurched forward and began a bumpy, swaying journey into darkness.

# 65

U zi and Rodman leaned back in their seats, doing their best to appear calm—and bored: this was just another night reporting in for their shift. A moment passed as the driver spoke with the man on duty at the security checkpoint.

"He might come back here to inspect," Trip said. "Just be cool, talk about sports stuff."

"Nationals have a kickass team this year," Uzi said.

"*British* sports, dumbshit. You're stationed in England, remember?"

"So, soccer?"

Trip rolled his eyes. "The Brits call it football. *We* call it soccer."

The rear canvas was peeled back and a flashlight combed the interior.

Uzi casually glanced at the roving beam. "So who do you like?"

"Man United," Trip said. "Evra's my guy."

"True dat. He's my guy, too."

After two passes, including one underneath the metal bench seats, the cover closed.

"'He's my guy, too?'" Trip repeated. "That was pretty weak."

"Hey, we made it through, didn't we?"

After successfully passing challenges at the other access points, the transport pulled up along the flightline. Trip tapped Uzi's knee, and they jumped down onto the tarmac.

A dense mist hovered over the light stanchions, a steady drizzle falling as they set off toward the Osprey that Trip had identified as the one they would procure.

Rodman went to work removing the chains tethering the wheels to the pavement. Uzi pulled out the red gear while keeping an eye on the maintainers, who moved freely about the flightline. The area was the antithesis of the rest of the base, which, other than security patrols, was quiet. Here, it was like a busy city in midday.

Moments later, they boarded the plane and climbed into the pilot and copilot seats. Ahead of them, below a rectangular split windshield, lay an array of screens, digital displays, levers, and switches.

They slipped on their flight helmets and seated them firmly.

"ICS check," Uzi said.

"Roger. Loud and clear."

Uzi patted down his pockets. "Crap. You get the key from maintenance to start her up?"

Rodman looked at him. "That's not funny."

"Just trying to lighten things up."

"Okay, you want funny?" Rodman asked as his eyes roamed over the control panel. "I've never really flown one of these."

Uzi swung his gaze over to Rodman. "But you said you—"

"Sorry, bro, it was all simulator work with the 8th Special Operations Squadron. You've just gotta trust me on this."

"And how is that funny?"

"Here's a quick and dirty flight lesson," Rodman said. "The hover's a lot of fly-by-wire. You've been there, done that, so no biggie. The catch comes in the transition to and from vertical flight. Only way to learn it is by doing it. It's not too overwhelming. That small thumbwheel there," Rodman said, pointing at the device, "slowly turn it to rotate the nacelles. Eight degrees a second. You just need a little finesse, is all—the right touch.

"Biggest difference from a helicopter is that the controls are kind of reversed. This thing's designed to be flown like a plane, not a helicopter. In a helicopter, you pull up, or back, on the collective to increase lift. Right?"

"Right."

"In the Osprey, you push the throttle *forward*, or away from you, to increase lift. For a jet guy this makes sense, but some of the early accidents in the Osprey were caused by helicopter pilots instinctively pulling *back* to increase power in a hover during a moment of distress."

"Definitely want to avoid that."

"Good," Rodman said, with a wink. "Then we're on the same page." He turned his attention back to the panel, found what he was looking for, and threw a switch. "Rotor brake."

Uzi examined the dashboard, a large rectangular control panel that contained two color screens in front of each seat, and a plethora of gauges and buttons. "Rotor brake. Off."

"Nacelles. They should be at ninety degrees."

"Nacelles? Sounds like I'm in some kind of starship." He searched a second, but Rodman pointed and Uzi said, "Got it. Ninety."

"Intakes?"

"Clear."

"Okay, we're in business. Ready to fire her up. Now we just need Trip to make some noise."

As Rodman finished his sentence, they heard the low-pitched whine and roar of nearby engines turning over.

Uzi grinned. "Good to go."

"Okay then. Number one ECL."

Uzi's hand hovered a bit, and then he pressed the button. "Start."

The left engine came to life, the massive thirty-eight-foot propeller-like blades rotating slowly and increasing in speed as the seconds passed.

Rodman glanced out the window to his left. "Looking good. Number two EC—oh wait. Shit."

"Shit?"

"I forgot something." Rodman's gaze roamed the panel. "Right, Ng, Np, Nr." He pointed and Uzi followed his finger. "We want it stabilized."

"Yeah, stabilized."

"All right, let's fire up the other engine. Number two ECL."

"Start."

"APU."

"Holy crap—" Uzi leaned forward in his seat and peered out the side window. "The nacelle's spewing white smoke!"

"That's normal."

"May be normal, but it's gotta be visible for at least half a mile."

"Forgot to mention that. Nothing we can do about it."

Uzi peered into the side view mirror mounted just above the control panel. There might not be anything they could do about it, but it was disturbing, nonetheless.

The second engine spun up and the rotors gained speed as the first one had, reaching maximum power within twenty seconds.

As they continued with preflight checks and the minutes ticked by, Uzi grew increasingly anxious. He glanced in the mirror and then out the windows, craning his neck to get a view of as much of the tarmac as possible.

"Uzi," Rodman said. "C'mon, man. It is what it is. We're committed now. Ready to advance power for takeoff."

"I'm good, let's go."

"Flaps."

"Auto."

"ECLs."

"Fly."

"Here we go. Increasing TCL and applying slight aft cyclic pressure, lifting the nosewheel off the ground."

As the craft rose, Uzi thought the sensation felt like a normal helicopter takeoff.

"Landing gear," Rodman said.

"Up. Lights out."

"Interim power."

"Um...okay. Selected."

As the aircraft climbed, Rodman used the cyclic to maintain position and the directional pedals to preserve his heading.

"Keep her low," Uzi said.

"Copy."

"Shit—we've got company!" Uzi leaned toward the convex mirror mounted to the right of his windshield, then twisted in his seat, trying to get a better view of the tarmac beneath the massive nacelles. "Two or three chase vehicles, coming up fast. Get us out of here."

"Rotating nacelles," Rodman said, trying to keep his voice—and the craft—steady as he rotated the dial slowly. "We need twelve seconds."

"How about five?"

"This is our most vulnerable time. We screw this up, this close to the ground, we crash and burn."

As the vehicles neared, Uzi felt a distinctive shove against his torso and he was pressed into the seatback as the plane shot forward.

"Transponder's off," Rodman said. "Sure hope they don't scramble anything. EAPS?"

"Closed," Uzi said. "Showing above eighty knots."

"Nacelles."

Uzi leaned forward to check. "Clean and dry." He threw a switch. "Extinguishing exterior running lights. You know, if they do scramble something, Trip would be the one they send because his engines are hot."

"Not sure that's good or bad. Puts him in a tough spot. Status."

Uzi studied the screens. "So far so good."

"Keep her steady," Rodman said as he pulled out his cell phone.

"Seriously? Who the hell are you calling?"

"You can handle this. Once we're airborne and in forward flight, it's no different from anything else. Same with a stabilized hover. It's the transitions that can get you." Rodman pressed a button on his handset. "I'm calling the RAF guy again to see if I can catch him. Now that we're airborne, we can give them an extra set of eyes."

"I'd leave out the part about stealing an Osprey from the US Air Force."

"Really? Dude, you've gotta give me more credit than that."

Uzi's face cracked a smile as he looked out over the English countryside.

# 66

Reid stood over the computer, watching the train's progress as it moved along the rudimentary blue and white electronic map. He hoped the tracks were switched properly to take Vail and DeSantos to the easternmost station, which, if he remembered correctly, was the Whitechapel mail facility.

As he studied one of the monitors, he heard a noise coming from the lift area.

But there wasn't anyone else down here.

He made his way out of the control room and was met by a dozen armed men from CO19's SFO unit—Specialist Firearms Officers. Decked out in Kevlar body armor and black PRO-TEC assault helmets, they approached with Glock-17s in hand, their frame-mounted red lasers trained on his torso.

"Get down!" the lead officer said. "Down on the ground."

"What in bloody hell's going on?"

"Do you have any weapons?" he asked, his tone stern and forceful.

"Do you know who I am?"

"DCI Reid. Yes sir, we know who you are. Now get down on the ground and interlock your fingers behind your head. You know the deal. Don't make me shoot you."

"Bollocks," Reid said as he dropped to his knees. Bluff and bluster was not going to work with these men.

Two officers shoved him prone and then applied handcuffs, while another walked into the control room.

"Name's Billingsley. And I don't have to tell you that I need to know where they are."

Reid lifted his head. "Who?"

"Look," Billingsley said, pulling off his goggles, "don't insult me. We've got Cruz and Vail on CCTV entering the Mail Railway with you twelve minutes ago."

The officer poked her head from the control room. "Clear."

Billingsley turned to Reid. "Are they on the train?"

Reid nodded.

"Cut the power to the tracks and tunnels," he said to the officer.

A moment later, they heard a loud click. "Track control relays and circuit breakers for the track blocks are down," she said.

Billingsley nodded. "You're already in a heap of trouble, Reid. Tell me where they went."

"Mount Pleasant. That's all I know."

"Why?"

"Can't be tracked down here."

Billingsley activated his radio. "Mount Pleasant. Send an ARV. Over."

Dispatch acknowledged his call.

"All right, get him up," Billingsley said. When his men lifted Reid to eye level, Billingsley got in his face and said, "I have no idea what motivated you to aid and abet terrorists, Inspector. But it's something you'll regret, that much I promise you."

Reid could not help but laugh. He had experienced a lot of feelings regarding Vail and DeSantos during the past several days, but regret was not one of them.

# 67

T he train swayed as it rattled through the tunnel. Vail guessed they had another six miles to go, but as her car passed under the occasional overhead light, she wished she knew their intervals, in distance. She could then count them and figure out how close they were to reaching the end—and forget she was holed away in a metal coffin hurtling through darkness.

After coming around a gentle curve, there was a lurch and the train ground to an abrupt halt.

Vail struggled to push herself up onto her knees, to get a look around. "What the hell was that?"

There was a ruffling sound as DeSantos pushed aside the top covering his car.

"It's totally dark. Power go down?"

"Looks like it," he said. "C'mon. I don't like this."

Vail climbed out and onto the rough, graveled ground beside the tracks. She activated the flashlight on her phone and moved it in an arc to get a bearing on their location. "Middle of goddamn nowhere."

"Yeah. Let's continue in the direction we were headed. No idea how far we got, but there's gotta be some kind of emergency hatch."

"Nice thought," Vail said as they set off along the track. "But this thing only carried mail. Why would they need an emergency hatch?"

"Then a maintenance panel. Anything that'll get us out of here."

"I'm all for that."

They walked through the tunnel, its cement and steel-skeleton walls varying in texture, but largely featuring a honeycomb pattern. Cabling and conduit, black from a thick mixture of soot, dirt, and grease, ran along the sides of the tunnel and continued into the distance as far as their weak flashlights could reach.

DeSantos's light passed over Vail's face and he stopped her. "You okay? You're sweating, and it's cold in here."

"I'm fine. It's just the tunnel." *And the claustrophobia. And the anxiety.* "Let's keep going. I—we—have to get out of here."

They continued for another few minutes when Vail focused her light on what appeared to be an access pane in the ceiling, directly above the tracks. "Got something."

DeSantos came up alongside her and reached up to get a look. There was an iron handle protruding from the bottom. He pulled, then pushed, but it did not budge.

"Give it a twist," she said.

He rotated his wrist and the panel moved with the kind of scratchy, metal-on-metal scraping squeal when two iron parts that have not been lubricated in years are forced to pass over one another. After a dozen full turns, it came loose and nearly smacked him in the head. "Heavier than I thought." Rust flecks floated down across his face. He shooed them away.

Vail shined her light up into the abyss and saw, in the dim illumination, a narrow tunnel with protruding rungs, a space not much greater than the width of DeSantos's shoulders.

"Uh, that's not gonna work."

"You go first," he said, ignoring her. "I'll give you a boost."

"Hector, I can't—"

He took his face in her hands. "You can and you will. I know this is tough. Think of it as a way to desensitize yourself."

"Thinking's not the problem. I can't *think* this stupid phobia away."

"Fair enough. But you're going up into that shaft." He interlaced his fingers and created a step for her.

"The tunnel's bad enough, but this tube is—It's like my worst fear. It—It reminds me of when I was held prisoner behind that closet. I—"

"Karen, I'm here with you. We're going to do this together. But we have to *do* it. We don't have a choice."

"But—"

"I don't know why the electricity went down, do you?"

She shrugged. "I just assumed it was a power failure. The system's old; it's not being used."

"Or CO19 knows we're here and they shut it off. Now if that's the case, they could be on us in minutes. We can't stay here."

*Damnit, he's right.*

DeSantos gestured toward his cupped hands.

Vail hesitated a second, took a deep breath to calm herself, then lifted her right foot into his artificial step. He lifted her swiftly and efficiently, right into the mouth of the shaft.

She grabbed onto metal rungs that jutted out from the side of the tube. And she ascended into the dark void.

# 68

"I see something," Uzi said.

Rodman disconnected his call before anyone could answer. He leaned forward to examine the dark skies. Pinpoints of light were clearly visible in the distance. "You think that's our guy?"

"At 2:30 in the morning, there's no other small, low-flying aircraft around for dozens of miles. I think there's a good chance."

"What do you want to do? Head for the Thames or divert?"

Rodman clenched his fingers around the control stick. "GQ and Vail are waiting for us."

"Does this thing have a weapons system?" Uzi asked.

"Used to have only a .50-cal machine gun mount on the rear ramp. But they're retrofitting the fleet with remote-controlled 7.62 millimeter miniguns. It's called something like an interim defensive system—defensive *weapon* system, that's it. The IDWS. I think I saw the targeting eye on the belly when I was dropping the chains."

"Try your RAF contact. If he doesn't answer, we're going for it. If that's the crop duster, we've gotta take it down before it can deploy the ricin."

Rodman pulled his phone. "I've only got one bar." He dialed, waited while it rang, and shook his head.

"Okay," Uzi said, "let's do this."

"Roger. Give me a heading."

Before Uzi could respond, a light turned yellow on the control panel and began flashing.

"No way," Rodman said.

"We're low on fuel?"

Rodman slammed his fist on the armrest. "Goddamn it. It was on the flightline for maintenance, they probably hadn't gassed it up yet."

"But Trip said—"

"He was wrong. What do you want me to say? That we're in the shit? Because we are."

"How long you think we've got?"

"Don't know. But that warning light's like the one in your car: when it goes on, we're near the bottom of the tank. What do you want to do? We're not even sure it's a crop duster."

"If we divert to take out this plane—assuming we're right and it's our aerosolized ricin—we may not have enough gas to pick up Santa and Karen and make our rendezvous."

"We may not have enough as it is," Rodman said. "Veering off course could seal the deal. Every drop counts. Literally."

Uzi stared off into the distance at the small craft's taillights. If they did not shoot down that crop duster...how many would die? He was not sure, but he knew it would be significant. Ten thousand? Twenty? Did the number matter?

On the other hand, if they shot down the plane, the extra fuel they used might force them to land before they made it out of the UK. They would be arrested, and they might never see freedom again.

"It's your call, Uzi. But every second we delay—"

"Shoot the bastard down. We'll take our chances with the fuel."

Rodman shook his head. "Hope you're right. Heading?"

Uzi provided it, Rodman made the adjustments, and the plane banked right and increased airspeed. At 230 knots, they would be at an intercept point in two minutes.

Uzi unbuckled his belt. "I'll go get ready."

"The weapons system looks like an Xbox controller with a color monitor. Think you can figure it out?"

Uzi moved out of the cockpit and into the rear compartment. "Did you really ask me that?"

"Sorry. Lost my head for a minute."

Uzi settled himself in the seat and examined the system. "Forward-looking infrared and 28x zoom. Sweet."

"Let me know when we're good to go, I'm going to take us in as close as possible to get a look at that plane."

"If it's a crop duster," Uzi said as he took the controller in his hands, "it's going down, agreed? No other good reason for one of these to be up this time of night."

"Roger that."

Behind him, the million dollar weapon pod deployed below the fuselage, unfolding and running through a self-diagnostic. "Just about ready to engage. We're over open fields, no houses in sight. Now would be a good time."

Rodman brought them behind the craft and cut back on his forward thrust. "Definitely a crop duster. An Air Tractor 802, if I'm not mistaken. She's a beauty, pity we have to destroy it."

Uzi focused on the monitor, tracking the plane on the targeting sensor. "Bring us up and alongside. Looks like I need a thirty degree shooting angle to clear the rotors."

"Copy."

The Osprey rose and Uzi moved his left thumb on the controller, remotely adjusting the minigun's barrel. The screen displayed the green hue of the crop duster's aft as they came up alongside it. "Firing on your mark."

"And...mark."

Uzi depressed the trigger mechanism and a trail of bright red light exploded forth into the darkness. A second later, the rounds struck the AT-802, pumping holes into its skin. He couldn't see the impact, but the crop duster veered sharply to the right and rapidly lost altitude.

"Piece of cake. Just like Call of Duty," Uzi said, referring to the Xbox game.

"Really?" Rodman asked.

"No. Much more satisfying." Uzi unbuckled and returned to the copilot's seat, where he watched the small craft disappear from the sky. He threw a switch on the panel and leaned back in his chair. "Get us back on course."

# 69

Vail kept moving hand over hand, pulling herself higher, trying to focus on the task. Somewhere seventy feet above her, in the pitch darkness, was the end of the shaft. She did not know what they would find when they got there—nor did she want to consider the possibilities. God forbid there was a sealed or locked lid. Would they be staring at a CO19 team of armed officers?

*Stop it. Keep going up.*

Behind her, a voice in the darkness: DeSantos, chatting her up, trying to take her mind off the tight quarters.

She blinked away the beads of perspiration rolling down her forehead and into her eyes. Whatever it was—the physical exertion of the climb, the stress of being trapped in a narrow cylinder, or the temperature of the tube itself—her entire body was coated in sweat.

"Is it hot in here, or is it me?"

"Definitely you. I'm pretty sure I've told you that before."

"Huh?" She paused with her hand in midair, the comment finally registering. "How can you joke at a time like this?"

He waited for her to lift her foot before grabbing for the same step. "I wasn't joking. But this is exactly the time to have a laugh, don't you think? Reduces stress, keeps you sharp."

Vail reached up for the next rung—and her hand hit something hard: some kind of metal plate. "I think we're there." She felt around to get a sense of the size of the obstruction barring her escape from this claustrophobic's nightmare. "It's big—kind of feels like a square manhole cover. Can you reach your light?"

DeSantos slowly removed his phone. Taking care not to let it slip from his slick hand, he shone the beam as best he could toward the top. "Looks heavy, like a hunk of iron." He shut the handset and shoved it in his pocket. "Think you can push it up?"

"Doubt it."

"Give it a good shove, see if you can get some movement. Let's just make sure it's not locked down. I'll hold your legs in place. Use two hands."

Vail pushed overhead, grunted, then gave it another shove. The cover shifted slightly. "This thing weighs a ton. I got it to move a bit, but there's no way I'm going to lift it off. You're gonna have to do it."

"Karen, there's barely enough room for you to get through. How can both of us fit? And we can't trade places unless we go all the way back down and start over."

"Not gonna happen," Vail said. "You have to get up here."

After a moment's hesitation, DeSantos said, "Fine, I'm coming up. Hold on and make sure your feet are stable."

DeSantos flinched as he lifted himself, scraping his back along the concrete wall of the shaft. If his foot or hand slipped off the rungs, he would likely not survive the seventy foot fall as he plummeted down the narrow tube, smashing his head on not only the iron bars but the rough cement.

He pushed himself up, his face resting against Vail's thigh as he repositioned his body. "Okay, I'm ready. I'm gonna have to come up in front of you, and reach behind you for the rungs. Don't move."

*Where the hell am I going to go?*

DeSantos grunted and reached between her legs, got a firm hold on the handle, and then shifted his weight and brought his foot up to the next tier. He moved his hand and—

"Hector, that's my crotch."

"Don't move. The sweat's pouring down my face, getting in my eyes, and I don't want to lose my grip."

"Fine. Wipe your face on my pants."

DeSantos was pinned and had a difficult time moving his hands. He turned his face left and right, Vail's damp cotton pants absorbing most of the perspiration and clearing his field of vision.

"Another time," he said, "I might've found that enjoyable."

"Shut up and finish."

"That's what my wife says."

He pushed himself up and came face-to-face with Vail. Their cheeks were touching, his beard stubble rubbing against her smooth, sweaty skin. The wall behind him kept his head pinned where it was.

"I'm gonna bring my arms up to see if I can get that cover off. When I remove my hands and start pushing on that lid, I'm probably going to lose my balance. I need you to put your arms around me, hold me in place. Can you do that?"

"I can do that." Vail removed one hand and slid it behind his waist, followed, slowly, by the other.

"Okay. Here I go. Don't let me fall."

"I got your back, don't worry."

"Is that a joke?" he asked as he carefully shifted his hands above his head.

"Just sayin'. You've got mine, I've got yours."

DeSantos pushed up on the metal lid. "Finally." *Grunt*—"Glad to see—" *grunt*—"you've—" *grunt*—"come around."

"Shut up and focus."

He yelled, then shoved the side of the cover as hard as he could. It moved a couple of inches. He slid the fingers of his right hand through the slim opening and further angled the edge up onto the surface above. "I can see some light. Not a whole lot, but—"

"It's dark out."

"Right."

He twisted his torso as much as he could, his chest rotating into Vail's breasts and compressing her ribcage, making it difficult for her to breathe.

She heard the scrape of metal on the hard substrate above her, and she knew that they were seconds away from climbing out—to freedom, unencumbered space, and fresh air.

DeSantos gave the lid a final shove and it moved enough to create a sufficient opening. "Go ahead. Hands first. Move them back onto the rungs, and I'll give your rump a boost out."

"I think I've had enough of your body parts touching enough of *my* body parts for one night. I can climb out of here without your help. I've got plenty of motivation."

Two minutes later, with the lid back in place and abrasions crisscrossing their arms, they were standing in the middle of a street. "I think I know where we are," he said. "Not far from Covent Garden. We need a cab."

"Cameras?"

"Across the street. Keep your back to them, and walk this way." He took her hand and led her down the block, and then pulled her into a dark alcove. "We'll wait here. Hopefully a taxi will come by soon."

"We're supposed to avoid cabs."

"If I'm right, it's a five minute ride. And I hate to keep saying this, but we've got no choice."

A couple of minutes later, Vail saw the familiar shape of a black cab approaching. She stuck her arm out and flagged it down. "You sure about this?"

"We've got to get to the river, and we don't stand a chance on the streets." The car pulled up in front of them and they met it at the curb. "Get in, I've got an idea." He pulled the door open.

As DeSantos settled into the seat, he directed the driver to the Embankment tube station.

Vail wanted to add, "And step on it," but she didn't want them getting pulled over for a traffic violation. Besides, on such a short trip, speeding might, at best, gain them mere seconds.

"So what's your idea?" she asked.

DeSantos grabbed the back of her neck and pulled her close, then brought his lips against hers.

She pushed against his chest. "What the hell are—"

"Shut up and kiss me," he said by her ear. "No one can see our faces if we're kissing, not even the CCTV's facial recognition software. And it looks perfectly normal."

"Robby's going to kill you for this."

"You know, that's very medieval," he said as he kissed her lips. "That a man has to fight for his woman. Still, I don't think he'll be upset."

"Really."

"Yeah. He'll thank me for keeping you alive." He pulled back a bit, then kissed her on the lips again.

It was a quick ride, as DeSantos had said.

When the driver pulled up to the Embankment Underground, he said, "Station's still closed, that bombing—"

"No worries. We're good here." He gestured at the Costa café. "Guess we'll have some coffee and dessert first."

The driver craned his neck to get a look at the coffee shop. "It closed hours ago."

DeSantos laughed. "So it did."

Vail paid the man with the last of her pounds and they got out, shielding their faces with a hand, as Reid had suggested.

"We've gotta get across the bridge, and then we can get hold of a boat."

They climbed the Hungerford Bridge's wide staircase and headed out onto the walkway.

"I feel very vulnerable. There's no one else around. We kind of stand out like a red elephant."

"I've got no idea where the cameras are, so we're blind. Assume they're everywhere. Cup your hands in front of your mouth and nose, like you're blowing on them."

Vail pulled her coat a bit tighter around her chest. "I was going to do that anyway. It's goddamn cold out here." As she said that, a light rain began to fall.

*Terrific. On the water, in the winter. And in the rain. Sounds like fun.*

"I'm going to hang back," DeSantos said, "so it doesn't look like we're together. They're looking for a couple."

As they crossed the apex of the bridge, a constable passed, headed in the opposite direction. Vail nodded at him and he lingered on her face a bit, but gave her a wink and continued on.

It got her heart going at a gallop, but—

"Hey!"

*Oh shit.*

Vail turned to see the cop aiming a Taser at her.

DeSantos grabbed him from behind and yanked back, the darts deploying into dead air. He hooked the inside of his elbow against the man's neck, applying intense pressure and holding it. The officer tried to resist, but DeSantos was prepared for whatever countermeasures the constable could manage. Seconds later, the man sank to the ground, unconscious.

DeSantos tossed the Taser aside and found flexcuffs on the copper's utility belt. He pulled them around his wrists and sat him up against the wall of the bridge.

"Let's get out of here. I have no idea if they patrol in pairs."

A minute later, they were across the Thames and headed down the staircase toward the Riverside Walk promenade and pier. Ahead of them, the futuristic London Eye Ferris wheel rose into the night sky.

"Now we go shopping for a boat," Vail said. "Any ideas?"

DeSantos peered into the darkness. "Kind of like what I was looking for when I bought my 'vette. A convertible. Fast and sporty."

# 70

U zi tapped out a message to Clive Reid, telling him that they had taken care of the crop duster. He provided the exact coordinates and recommended that a hazmat team respond to the crash scene in case the ricin had aerosolized on impact.

After returning the handset to his pocket, he peered out the Osprey's front windshield. "How long till we reach the Thames?"

"About ten minutes. Meantime, see if you can locate the flight manual. Check under the seat. Maybe it can give us an idea how much fuel we've got left. We may need to abort."

Uzi fished around but felt nothing. As he was withdrawing his hand, it hit something. "Got it." A moment later he slammed the book shut. "This is a stupid problem to have. To come all this way and run out of gas?"

"What'd it say?"

"We've got a range of about nine hundred miles, but I don't know this thing's burn rate. If we had inboard wing and auxiliary tanks—which we don't—we'd have an extra thousand gallons. It's got a refueling probe, which doesn't help us unless there's a C-130 flying around somewhere."

"Anything else?"

"Flying like a plane uses less fuel than hovering like a chopper. But I couldn't find anything on how much is left when the warning light comes on." Uzi's gaze fixated on the blinking yellow fuel light. "Thing is, we don't need a manual to tell us we'd better find Karen and Santa real fast."

# 71

DeSantos pointed at a boat moored along the pier beneath the majestic London Eye. "A RIB. Perfect."

From where they were standing, it looked to be a gray powerboat with three rows of pod seats and a tall console that was protected by a severely curved windscreen.

"What'd you call it? A rib?"

"A Rigid Inflatable Boat."

*Looks like the Zodiac I took to Alcatraz.*

"Hopefully we'll make it to the dock without getting picked up on the cameras. I've gotta believe they're deployed all around the Eye."

"Do we need keys?"

"Normally, yes." He winked at her. "I'll go first, get her ready. Give me thirty seconds, then follow." He vaulted the metal gate beneath the large white Ferris wheel and jogged down the pier that extended dozens of feet into the river.

Vail stood in the shadows, watching while DeSantos hopped on board and removed some kind of square panel beneath the steering wheel. She could not make out exactly what he was doing, but she supposed he was hotwiring the electronics. After counting off the seconds, she made her way to the boat.

DeSantos had moved aft and was starting up the twin Yamaha outboard motors. Vail removed the ties from the cleats, then climbed into the RIB. Seconds later, with Vail at the wheel, they swung out into the center of the Thames, spewing white foam behind them.

"Heading?" she shouted over the din of the engines.

"Straight down the center of the river. We'll keep going until we hear from Uzi. Hopefully we'll be able to put some distance between us and the heart of London."

They passed beneath the Hungerford Bridge, its dramatically angled white spires rising into the rainy, ink-black sky.

A moment later, Vail banked right along one of the Thames's sharpest curves, nearly a ninety degree turn, as they zipped under the Waterloo Bridge. She took a seat behind the wheel to get the windscreen's benefit of keeping the oncoming rain out of her eyes. "Got the flares?"

"Oh shit!"

She swung her head to the left. In the low light, she could barely make out the white teeth of DeSantos's smile. "You suck, you know that?"

He pulled the two flares from his pocket and shielded them from the rain. "Ready to deploy. But you know you're not supposed to use road flares on boats, right?"

"When did we start doing things by the book?"

"Good point." DeSantos looked down and patted his pocket, then rooted out his phone. "Text from Uzi. Five minutes out."

After passing by the massive legs of the Tower Bridge, Vail caught sight of a yellow and blue police boat along the left river bank. *Crap. Did they see us?*

She glanced over her shoulder and got her answer: the copper was arcing around, preparing to come up behind them. "We've got a problem!"

DeSantos swung his gaze around the river just as the marine unit's forward overhead spotlight lit up, illuminating them like a diamond in a black velvet display case.

"Hang on!" Vail reached for the throttle on the console and pushed the black handle up. The craft accelerated abruptly, forcing their bodies into the pod's seatbacks.

Vail tightened her grip on the wheel. The last thing she wanted to do was lose control of the RIB at high speed. She turned her torso toward DeSantos and yelled, above the engine's roar, "Light the flares!"

But DeSantos had already turned his back to the wind, popped off the caps, and struck the ends against the rough deck pad. The phosphorous ignited instantly and burned a deep, bright red. He averted his eyes so as not to burn out his rods, and then lifted the flares up, away from his torso—and the boat's rubber skin. He slowly turned around, trying to keep sparks from falling inside the RIB.

In less than a minute, they had opened up a considerable distance between them and the patrol boat. But considering what was to come, was it enough?

# 72

U zi sat forward in his seat. "There, I see them."

"Got 'em," Rodman said, looking from the nightscape through the windshield to the nav screen in front of him. "Altering course to intercept. Looks like they're in a boat. And it's moving."

"Nothing like a little challenge. You up to this?"

Rodman ground his jaw. "We'll find out soon enough."

Uzi studied his monitor. "There's somebody behind them, maybe a few hundred yards. Police?"

"Probably. Fuel status?"

Uzi tapped the digital gauge, even though he knew it was a futile gesture. Part habit, part wishful thinking. "Not good. We'll need an hour's worth of gas once we pick them up. If we hover too long here we probably won't have enough range to make our rendezvous."

"Then we'll have to get this right."

Uzi pressed the release switch for the rear loading ramp, and then unbuckled and moved out of the cockpit into the Osprey's cabin. As the aft of the plane lowered, Uzi saw the pitch darkness of the horizon and the choppy waters of the Thames below. Cold, damp air settled around his neck, sending a chill through his body.

In the dim light, he examined the empennage structure above the cargo ramp door to familiarize himself with the rescue hoist assembly. He figured that an electrically driven winch like this had a weight capacity of at least five hundred pounds, if not a bit more—certainly enough to lift both Vail and DeSantos to safety.

Still, between the downwash—which was intense given the two thirty-eight-foot rotors—the pursuing craft, and the fact that both the Osprey and Vail's boat would be in motion, getting a rescue line onto their vessel would be more than merely difficult.

"Fifteen seconds," Rodman said in Uzi's headset. "Stand ready."

# 73

V ail saw the Osprey first. She nudged DeSantos with her shoulder. His head was turned, checking on the Met police boat behind them.

She hoped that they had not called ahead for reinforcements to flank them from the other end of the river. Or—if they had, that the distance from them was too great to matter. It was a very long river.

DeSantos had explained a few moments ago that the flares were burning at nearly 1,500 degrees, so he could not drop them on the boat's floor; they would set it ablaze.

"No," Vail said. "That's exactly what we want."

"Torch the boat?"

"We do it just as we're ready to leave. It'll confuse the cops, slow them down. They won't be able to get close to us. We'll need that time."

"I like the way you think. Okay, that's the plan."

"That's *our* plan. What's Uzi's?"

"I assume they're gonna drop us a line."

"But we can't stop or the patrol boat'll be on us in seconds."

"Uzi and Hot Rod know that."

After a beat, Vail turned to face DeSantos. The bright red phosphor lit his face and allowed her to see his expression—and him hers. "You mean they're going to try to pluck us off a moving boat, while they're in a moving plane?"

DeSantos did not reply. His silence was answer enough: this would be a difficult extraction.

He looked out at the cluster of well lighted, modern office buildings just ahead. "If we're where I think we are, we're about to enter a straight portion of the river. After that jug handle turn up ahead, we'll pass Canary Wharf. We'll have about three-quarters of a mile before the next turn. We'll jam the steering wheel in place. That's our best chance."

"Not much of a margin for error."

"That just about describes the entire mission, doesn't it?"

DeSantos crossed his arms overhead, then brought them apart, waving the flares like a signaler on a tarmac. If he figured correctly, Rodman was piloting the Osprey and Uzi was prepping whatever type of winch they had onboard. He hoped Rodman understood his silent message.

RODMAN'S VOICE STARTLED Uzi, booming in his ears. "GQ's signaling us. Looks like they're about to enter a straightaway. I think this is it."

"Copy that."

"Slowing to thirty knots and transitioning the nacelles."

Uzi activated the hoist assembly and the weighted, open-throat stainless steel hook began its descent. He wished he could see below the fuselage, but he had to trust that the winch was deploying directly beneath them.

Uzi felt the drag of the engines and vibration of the craft as the nacelles began rotating. He moved to the cabin's side window and watched as the rotors assumed a vertical position. "We're gonna have to match their speed to make this work."

"Already on it," Rodman said.

VAIL JAMMED A SEAT PAD into the space between the steering wheel's spokes. She gave it a good shove and felt confident it would maintain their course.

"Here she comes," DeSantos said.

As the Osprey descended, the rotor downwash began intensifying.

"Cut back on the throttle a bit. Let's not make this harder than it needs to be. The fire should buy us the time we're gonna lose by slowing down."

Vail pulled on the handle and the RIB decelerated, but still maintained a decent rate of speed.

"Incoming!" DeSantos yelled.

Vail looked up to see a large, shiny silver hook swinging toward her face. She reached for it, but DeSantos yanked her down, then twisted around as the hunk of metal passed over them, just missing the windscreen. He dropped the flares on the floor and steadied himself as the hoist reversed course and started back toward them.

"Let it hit the boat first," DeSantos yelled. "The static electricity from the rotors'll shock you."

They stayed down as the hook swung back like a pendulum, slamming into the control panel and dissipating its charge. DeSantos caught it sloppily as it rebounded, the momentum nearly pulling him out of the boat. Vail tried to steady him as he wrestled with it, the cable swaying and yanking both of them to and fro.

"Get it around you!"

Vail tried, but the constant pull in multiple directions made it impossible for her to wrap it about her torso.

Just then, the fire flared, burning faster—and more intensely—than she had anticipated.

DeSantos swung his head around toward the flames. "The gas tanks!"

*Oh my God. Didn't think of that.*

"We've gotta get off this thing now. Before it blows."

"FIRE," RODMAN SAID into his mic.

"What?" Uzi struggled to see out the window, but he had the wrong angle. He moved forward, attempting to get a glimpse out the front windshield—but the action was *below* them.

"Must be the flares. Pull 'em up, Uzi. Now."

"Are they secured?"

"Now, before that thing explodes!"

Uzi ran aft to activate the rescue hoist assembly. As soon as it began reeling them in, Rodman's voice filled his ears: "Police boat closing."

*Shit.* "I can't see!"

"There's a hatch by the machine gun console."

Uzi scrambled back toward the cockpit, beside the control panel, and found the switch to open the door.

"Let me know as soon as you've got 'em on board," Rodman said. "Need to go to forward flight ASAP. The fuel."

"Copy that." The hatch was opening slowly—and he did not want to leave the hoist mechanism unattended for too long. He slammed his hand against the bulkhead, willing it to move faster, then stepped across the cabin to look out the window. But between the huge spinning rotors and the fuel tanks below him, the view was limited. He turned around to check on the door's progress, and found the opening large enough to fit his helmet through. He leaned out into the cold darkness and searched the murky waters below.

But what he saw in that instant made him wish he had never looked.

"YOU OKAY?" DeSantos yelled over the roar of the rotors as the braided metal line swung them violently to the side. The winch cable was between them, their arms wrapped around it as the momentum carried them back toward the flaming boat.

Afraid to move—to lose her hold—Vail merely nodded in response.

He reached out and put his arm around her, pulling her closer against him. "Hang on!"

*No worries—I'm not planning on letting go.*

Just then, a booming blast exploded skyward, pieces of flaming shards blowing in all directions. Either the shrapnel struck DeSantos, or the large, open-mouth hook did.

Whatever it was, he was no longer on the rescue hoist.

# 74

"Man down! All stop—"
The scream, with uncharacteristic panic permeating Rodman's voice, blasted through Uzi's earpiece. He had seen what Rodman had seen, yet he was helpless to do anything.

Vail was on her way up—that much was clear. But DeSantos was nowhere in his field of vision. He had fallen from the cable, but where he ended up—and if he was conscious or not—was impossible to determine. At this point, the best Uzi could do was get Vail onboard and take the cable down to see if he could locate DeSantos.

"Found the spotlight," Rodman said. "Looking for GQ. You see anything?"

"Negative."

*C'mon, Santa, stay on the surface till I can get down there.*

VAIL WHIPPED AROUND to get a look below her, trying to locate DeSantos. Meanwhile, the cable continued to pull her up toward the Osprey.

*Hector!*

She spun dizzyingly as the hoist rose. Finally, she found him—what she thought was him—floating on the water...and—

*Holy shit, he's going under.*

Vail did the only thing she could: this was not a moment to think. It was a moment to *act*. She let go of the cable and plunged into the cold water of the River Thames.

# 75

C old did not begin to describe what Vail felt when she penetrated the surface. It was numbing, paralyzing, and breath-taking; she literally could not breathe.

*Find Hector, Karen. Focus.*

Vail opened her eyes, now completely submerged, and looked around. Nothing. *Where the hell is he?* The Osprey's spotlight provided some illumination, but it was moving, searching, which did not help. And the fire from the boat, while intense, was not nearly luminous enough to pierce the dense water.

She was suddenly bathed in darkness.

Vail forced herself up and broke through the surface. She kicked her feet in all directions, hoping to—*Wait, I hit something.*

She turned toward the object and reached out with her hands, and felt something hard, floating—a body. *Hector.* She pulled him up, doing her best to keep his face out of the water. Whether he was conscious or not—alive or not—she could not tell.

Vail craned her neck up toward the sky, hoping to catch the spotlight so that Rodman or Uzi would see her.

She could no longer feel her feet, her legs, her arms. She fought to maintain a grip around DeSantos's torso, counting the seconds, willing the light to hit her in the face.

A moment later, it did just that.

And then it was gone, as the Osprey rotated away from her.

*Wait—where the hell are you going?*

After completing a 180 degree revolution, the hoist swung toward her again. Uzi was hanging from the rear opening of the plane, steadying the cable, attempting to prevent it from swinging. Steering it toward her.

Vail caught the hook with her right hand, the electric shock and smack of cold metal against her skin numbingly painful. She secured it around DeSantos's torso and signaled Uzi to raise them up. It took a moment for him to climb back into the cabin, but seconds later, the hoist lifted them from the water.

The chill became worse as they rose toward the plane, and the downwash was blowing so forcefully that they found it difficult to breathe. Halfway up, the plane started moving forward, away from the burning wreckage below. Vail fought to hold onto the cable—and DeSantos—but they were now only about fifteen feet from the open mouth of the cabin.

As they approached, Vail looked up—and saw Uzi on all fours, ready to receive them. When his hands gripped them and guided them aboard, she felt a sense of relief envelop her. More likely, it was sheer exhaustion.

# 76

"They're aboard," Uzi said into his mic as he struggled to unwind the cable and hook from DeSantos's body.

"Copy that," Rodman said. "Heading out to sea. Let's hope our tank doesn't run dry—and we're not intercepted by a very pissed off air force."

Uzi reached over to the cabin wall and pulled the lever to close the ramp loading deck.

"How's GQ?" Rodman asked in his ear.

"Working on it," he said as he tossed the hoist assembly aside. He took DeSantos's pulse and checked his airway. "Nice work, Karen. Are you all right?"

"Frozen to the bone," she said with a shiver. "Nothing a hot chocolate and a change of clothes won't cure."

"Let's get him on his side."

Uzi delivered a few blows between the shoulder blades and DeSantos coughed up some water. He slowly opened his eyes and tracked from Vail to Uzi, and back. He coughed again and tried to sit up. They helped him onto one of the padded seats along the side of the cabin.

"Welcome back," Vail said.

DeSantos rested his head against the bulkhead, but an intense shiver racked his body, sending him forward. "My skull feels like it's gonna explode. And talking over the engine noise definitely doesn't help. Makes it pound."

Vail wrapped her arms over her chest. "Can we shut that window?" she asked, gesturing at the hatch Uzi had opened earlier.

He closed it, then gave DeSantos a cursory exam. In addition to a large welt and laceration on the back of his head, there were several gashes, none requiring immediate attention. "Looks like the hook may've swung around and clocked you good."

Uzi checked the cabin and found a pair of communication headsets, which they slipped over their ears, and a couple of thick military-grade needle-punch wool blankets.

He handed DeSantos a gray hand towel that was protruding from a metal task bin along the cabin wall. "Hold this over your scalp wound. You could use a few stitches, but the pressure will slow the bleeding. And no jumping out of planes for a while. Best guess, you've got a concussion." He changed the frequency on his helmet and spoke to Rodman. "Hot Rod, I'm gonna need your flight suit."

Uzi unzipped his overalls and handed them to Vail. "Take off your wet clothes and change into this." He unfolded one of the blankets and held it up as a curtain. A moment later she emerged, still shivering. Uzi wrapped the blanket around her and then retrieved Rodman's flight suit from the cockpit. He helped DeSantos change, then likewise swathed him in the other wool shroud and propped the towel between his head and the cabin wall.

"How you doing?" he asked.

DeSantos reseated his headphones. "Starting to feel a little more human. Head's not as fuzzy. We got any water?"

"We don't have much of anything. We'll get you looked at as soon as we get there."

"Get where?" Vail asked. "What's our end game? Can this thing make it all the way back to the States?"

Uzi took a seat beside her. "We're rendezvousing in the Atlantic with an amphibious transport dock. The USS *New York*. It's going through ship handling drills."

"And they happened to be in the neighborhood?" Vail asked.

"Not exactly. They were a couple hundred miles away. They've been underway for nine hours. They should be closing in on the RVP."

"I can't believe they diverted here for us," DeSantos said.

"Make you feel important?"

"Kind of," DeSantos said, touching the back of his head—and wincing.

"We're talking Knox and McNamara." Uzi chuckled. "I'm not surprised."

"That's gonna be a tricky landing, especially at night. Can Hot Rod set an Osprey down on one of those ships? Landing pad's not that big."

"Of course. Piece of cake." *More like: we have no choice.*

"Can't be any worse than what we just went through," Vail said. "Can it?"

Uzi and DeSantos looked at each other.

"I'd better get up there," Uzi said, "and help fly this thing."

"HE DIDN'T ANSWER ME," Vail said.

"Just a guess, but you probably don't want to know," DeSantos said as he warded off a shiver.

"Still cold?"

"May take me weeks to warm up."

Vail moved closer and wrapped her blanket around the both of them. DeSantos shivered again.

"You know, you don't make it easy, Hector. Trust is important to me."

"This again?"

"This again. Trust is everything."

"In a marriage, I totally agree with you. But this isn't a marriage. It's black ops. Sometimes your life depends on what you *don't* tell people. It protects you—and it protects them."

"I get it," she said. "I just don't like it."

"You want to tell me what happened back there?"

"You're changing the subject."

"I really want to know what happened. We were on the RIB, we saw the Osprey approaching...and then I woke up in here."

Vail pursed her lips. "We were on the cable, about halfway up, when the boat exploded. The flares ignited the fuel tank. And something slammed you in the back of the head. Next thing I knew, you were in the drink."

"Considering how wet I am, that much I figured out."

"So I jumped in after you."

DeSantos tilted his head and twisted his torso to get a good look at her face. "No shit?"

"No shit."

"I don't know what to say. Thanks."

"You look surprised. Don't you know I wouldn't let anything happen to you?"

DeSantos grinned. "I thought that was my line."

# 77

U zi settled into the copilot's seat and took another look at the fuel gauge.

"Yes," Rodman said.

Uzi faced him. "Yes, what?"

"Yes, I'm worried. I don't think we've got enough in the tank."

"This thing can fly on one engine. What if we shut one down to save—"

"No. Don't even go there."

"I know it's normally prohibited, and definitely risky."

Rodman laughed. "I was thinking more like 'insane.' Seriously, if you were my pilot and you said something like that, I'd push you out the back of the plane."

"I still think we should consider it."

"Uzi, shutting down an engine is a drastic measure, even to save fuel. We'd be dooming ourselves to some kind of crash landing if we couldn't get the engine relit. And don't forget—we're landing on a ship, which is tough enough."

Uzi knew Rodman was right—but he could not take his eyes off the fuel gauge. Either they would run out of gas and plunge into the Atlantic Ocean, or they would be unable to restart the engine and crash onto the flight deck. Tough choice.

"What if we flew a bingo profile?" Rodman asked.

"I flew helicopters, Hot Rod. And I tend to stay out of churches. Don't know what this bingo thing is."

"We climb high and fast to max altitude, then pull the power back to an idle and basically coast the rest of the way in. It's the best way to conserve fuel in a fixed wing craft."

"Sounds like we'd be turning this baby into a flying Prius."

Rodman looked at him. "You didn't just say 'Prius,' did you?"

"You ever done it? This bingo profile?"

"Once. Almost ran out of gas in a U-28 over Iraq. Bailing out was not an option. It worked and the Air Force was thankful I didn't ditch a seventeen million dollar plane."

"Can't see where we have much choice," Uzi said, "or much to lose. If we're gonna take a swim in the ocean, we may as well do it knowing we tried everything."

"I agree. So grab that flight manual again and look in the back for bingo profile numbers."

Uzi reached beneath the seat, pulled out the book, and located the section. "Whoa. You've gotta be kidding."

"Ignore all those confusing charts. We just have to crunch some numbers, calculate the climb airspeed and distance to begin a descent. Here, let me see it."

Uzi handed it over, then switched channels on the comms. "Karen, Santa, you there?"

"Here," Vail said.

"We're going to change our flight plan. I need you two to strap in. We're gonna make a high power climb. It's kind of abrupt."

"A max-range profile?" DeSantos asked.

"Hot Rod called it a bingo, but it sounds like the same thing."

"If you're looking at a max-range profile, then that means we're seriously low on fuel."

"Need to know, Santa."

"Boychick, that makes no sense."

Uzi cleared his throat. "After what you'd been through, I didn't think you needed to know."

DeSantos groaned. "Fine. We're ready."

"Wait," Vail said. "We are?"

VAIL NUDGED DESANTOS. "Now you know how it feels when you're not told everything."

DeSantos gave her a look.

"Just sayin'." As she latched her belt, she asked, "So what the hell is this 'max-range bingo' thing?"

"A way of conserving fuel. You climb toward your maximum altitude and then turn your plane into a huge glider."

"That doesn't sound reassuring."

"I wasn't trying to reassure you, Karen. I was giving it to you straight. Don't ever say I never tell you the truth."

Vail pulled the seat restraint tight. "This is one of those times when lying to me might've been the better way to go."

DeSantos shook his head. "You've spent this entire mission lambasting me for not telling you the truth, and when I finally do, you say you would've preferred a lie. I don't think I'll ever understand the female psyche."

*You wouldn't be the first.* "Will this max-range idea work?"

DeSantos turned to Vail, his eyes searching her face.

"What?"

"I'm trying to figure out if you want an honest answer or not."

"Yes—give it to me straight."

"If Uzi and Rodman are doing it, they feel it's the best course of action. But I've never actually done it. A buddy of mine has, and he told me it works. Of course, he's a habitual liar." DeSantos laughed, a release of nervous energy. "Sorry, couldn't resist."

Vail closed her eyes. *I'm in a flying metal coffin rocketing toward the sun. How did I get myself into this?*

UZI SWITCHED OVER comms and nodded at Rodman. "They're ready."

"We've got another problem." Rodman set the pocket checklist down. "The cabin's not pressurized, so we'll have to use our oxygen masks, but—"

"Karen and Santa don't have any."

"Right. So they're gonna pass out once we climb past eighteen thousand feet."

"Do we have to go that high?"

"We'll actually be going to twenty. But I'm not sure how the Osprey uses gas, and the checklist doesn't cover it. But one thing's for sure: the lower we go, the less fuel we save. And the more we sit here and dick around about it, the more we waste."

Uzi swung his head around and looked into the rear cabin. He keyed his mic. "Uh, one more thing, guys." He explained the situation.

"Hypoxia," Vail said. "You're joking, right? Are we really gonna wake up?"

Rodman broke in. "Somewhere between ten- and thirteen-thousand feet, you'll feel a bit lightheaded. When we get closer to eighteen, you'll drift off to sleep. After we drop down below that, you'll be fine. There's a risk of altitude sickness, but we won't be above eighteen thousand very long."

"Understood," DeSantos said.

"Karen?" Uzi asked.

"I was held prisoner in a closet and came down with claustrophobia. Now you're trying to give me acrophobia. Sure, let's go for it. I don't mind being a mental wreck by the time I hit forty."

Uzi switched channels as he swung his head back to the front of the plane. "Let's take her up."

"Just so you know, the bingo is charted in the checklist for a max altitude of thirteen thousand feet. For twenty, I've had to extrapolate."

"You mean *guess*."

Rodman shrugged. "Basically, yeah."

They donned their oxygen masks and made the necessary flight adjustments. A moment later, the Osprey began a rapid ascent of three thousand feet per minute, pinning them into their seatbacks.

As they climbed, Uzi's eyes found the fuel gauge. The numbers were dropping precipitously, like an elevator in free-fall. "Uh—Jesus Christ. Our fuel is—It's—"

"Don't watch the levels, Uzi. It's going to freak you out."

"Going to?"

"It's only gonna get worse. Those numbers aren't going to reverse. But soon as we reach max altitude, the fuel burn will drop and we'll be sipping gas the rest of the way down—when we 'go Prius,' as you put it."

"I'd feel a little better if we'd done the calculations so that we know for sure we've got enough fuel to pull this off."

"If it makes you feel any better, I didn't really guess."

Uzi tilted his head. "You didn't?"

"No sir. No point in guessing. We didn't have a choice, remember?"

"Doesn't make me feel any better."

A minute later, Rodman said, "We're at our ceiling, twenty thousand feet. Cutting back." The drop in velocity, as well as the change in pitch of the plane, was immediate.

Uzi stole a look into the rear compartment and saw Vail and DeSantos slumped against each other. When he turned back to the cockpit, he did what Rodman told him not to do: he snuck another look at the fuel gauge. And immediately wished he hadn't.

# 78

V ail licked her lips, blinked her eyes, and then pushed herself off DeSantos's shoulder. He was still unconscious, so she shook him awake.

He took a deep breath, wiped away the saliva dripping down his chin, and stretched his arms above his head. "Guess we're on our descent."

"We've been on our descent since the moment we landed at Heathrow."

"Jesus, Karen. Don't be such a downer. We got Hussein Rudenko. We really haven't had time to process that. He's escaped law enforcement for decades. He's, what, number nine on your FBI Most Wanted?"

"Number four," she said as she unbuckled her restraint. "So what? You think we should pat ourselves on the back?"

"Don't you?"

Vail went silent for a moment. "I don't know. I guess so. If we hadn't—If Walpole—"

"Look, once in a while you get an op that runs into some kind of FUBAR scenario. Walpole's death definitely qualifies. But I've learned to take my wins where I get them. A guy like Rudenko, who traveled the world wreaking havoc, feeding the war machine in a dozen countries…I mean, eliminating him is a huge victory. To say nothing of preventing the ricin attack. How many lives did we save?"

Vail sat there a moment, lost in thought. Then she bolted upright, threw the blanket aside, and began pacing.

"Uh oh. I don't like that look. What's wrong? Something I said?"

"Yeah. Something you said." She looked toward the cockpit. "Uzi, can you hear me?"

"I was just going to come wake you," he said through her headset. "Welcome back to consciousness." He twisted his body to face her. "Everything okay?"

"No," she said. "I mean, I don't know. Hector and I were talking about things, and I may have—I'm not sure, I may've screwed up. Can you reach Clive Reid or Ethan Carter?"

"It's, like, four in the morning."

"Between getting warrants and rounding up junior ministers, they've been plenty busy. They're not sleeping."

"I'll see what I can do."

DeSantos pushed himself up and then sat back down. "Between the blow to the head and that little hypoxic episode, I'm not quite ready to stand yet. What's going on?"

Vail rubbed her temples, still pacing. After a minute, she said, "I hope I'm wrong. But something Idris Turner told me. I didn't think anything of it at the time, but I just thought we were dealing with a terrorist bombing of an art gallery to destroy a rare manuscript." She stopped and faced him. "You see? You should've told me everything from the start—"

"Karen. Get to the point."

"He told me that—"

"Karen," Uzi said, "Reid didn't answer. But I've got Ethan Carter."

Vail ran to the cockpit and took Uzi's phone, slipped it under her right earpiece. "Carter, can you hear me?"

DeSantos grabbed onto an overhead pipe and pulled himself erect, slowly making his way toward Vail.

"Hear you?" Carter asked. "Barely. Where the hell are you?"

"Uzi," Vail said, "can you put this call through so we can all listen in?"

He took a patch cord from the comms and plugged it into the earphone jack on his handset. "Go for it."

"Carter," Vail said. "Listen to me. I think I fucked up. Where's Reid?"

"Arrested. Not looking too bloody good. Why?"

"We need to talk to Idris Turner. You know where he is?"

"We're ready to release the gallery back to him, but he's not answering his cell. The Met doesn't want to just pull the constables and abandon the place because it can't be adequately locked and there's still a lot of valuable stuff there. How important is it that you talk to him?"

"Very. I need to know about the Turner Gallery, its history."

DeSantos, who had made it to the cockpit, was holding onto Rodman's seatback. He shared a concerned look with Uzi.

"I was briefed on it," Carter said. "What's the problem?"

"Just tell me what you know."

Carter sighed. "When the director general was setting up the op, he gave us a backgrounder. The gallery's been around about a hundred years. Been in the family, passed down over the generations. Started in Manchester. About twenty-five years ago, after the father died, Idris took it over and moved it down to London."

"Was the elder Turner married?"

"Widowed, from what I recall," Carter said.

"Children?"

"One son. Idris."

"You're sure Idris is the son?"

"I only know what I was told," Carter said. "Why?"

Vail took a deep breath. "Because I think you're gonna find that Idris Turner is not a descendant of the Turner family. I think you're going to find that Idris Turner is an alias."

"An alias? For who?"

Vail closed her eyes and cursed herself. "Hussein Rudenko."

# 79

"What?" DeSantos said.

"Reid told me you killed Rudenko," Carter said.

Vail massaged the bridge of her nose. "We killed the man we *thought* was Rudenko: Gavin Paxton. But we got the wrong guy."

"Are you sure?" DeSantos and Carter asked simultaneously.

"Get something from Turner's house. Hair, saliva—whatever—and do a DNA profile. You'll find a match for the Rudenko sibling's exemplar that we've got on file."

"We already got a match," Carter said. "For Paxton."

Vail shook her head. "We got a match against the exemplar, and the exemplar was his sibling. Paxton could've been another sibling."

"Back up," DeSantos said.

Vail thought a moment, reasoning it out. "Stay with me on this. Carter, you're gonna find that the Idris we know and the one from Manchester are two different people. That's why when 'Idris' took over the family business, he moved it to London. The local clientele in Manchester would know what the real Idris looked like, and they'd know an imposter right off. So Rudenko moved the well-known business to London and assumed Idris's identity."

"And what about the real Idris?" Carter asked.

DeSantos snorted. "Pretty obvious. Dead. Like his father. Rudenko needed a front for his business, a place where he could launder large sums of money. An art gallery, a rare manuscript broker, dealing in high-end merchandise, fit the bill."

"Londoners wouldn't know that Hussein Rudenko appropriated the identity of the real Idris," Vail said. "Check around, find some family photos. You'll see."

"I'm on it," Carter said.

"And you'll also want to look into old man Turner's death. You'll find it was murder, made to look like natural causes. Heart attack or some kind of 'unfortunate accident.'"

"Heart attack," Carter said.

"If they've still got the tissues," DeSantos said, "check them for high levels of insulin. There are other drugs, but that's a good place to start."

"Hang on," Uzi said. "What makes you so sure Gavin Paxton wasn't Rudenko?"

Vail let her head fall back against the bulkhead. "Turner told me, and I was too dense to see it. He said he travels the world collecting art and making buys. Paxton stays behind and manages the shop. Turner's been making buys, all right—weapons."

"Wait," Uzi said, "I'm not following you."

"A guy like Rudenko has to travel to do his illicit business," DeSantos said with a slow nod. "And who was often out of town? Not Paxton, the guy we thought was Rudenko, but Idris Turner."

Carter groaned, then said, "Fak me."

*Not exactly how I'd phrase it, but I agree.* "Get with Buck and lock down all air traffic, trains, boats—anything and everything out of England. Find him."

Vail handed Uzi back his phone. They were silent a moment before Vail sank down to the cabin floor and cradled her head in cold, rough hands. "We had the bastard. I had coffee with him. He played us!" She kicked the bulkhead.

After thinking a moment, DeSantos said, "Paxton's gotta be Rudenko's brother. That would explain the DNA similarity. But he's also a conspirator, Karen. And we got him."

"Small consolation."

Uzi swiveled in his seat. "That gallery—because of its history in Manchester—Rudenko gained instant credibility in the business community. In the art community. It's an institution." He shook his head. "It's hard when criminals are smart."

"I like to think we're smarter than most of them," Vail said.

"We are," Uzi said. "But it's also why a guy like Rudenko is unique, why he's escaped law enforcement for so long."

"Here we go," Rodman said as he tuned up the USS *New York*'s navigation frequency, channel 78Y on the military's Tactical Air Navigation system, or TACAN. "I've got a good lock on the ship. Three-one-zero at about thirty miles. Right where we want to be."

Vail pulled herself up from the floor. "Sorry for letting you down. I totally missed it."

"Missing Rudenko...it sucks," Rodman said. "But shit happens. Can't beat yourself up over it. On the other hand, I just realized I should've dialed in the TACAN when we were climbing to twenty thousand. If the *New York* wasn't exactly where we expected her to be, I could've adjusted course. If they got delayed or weren't in the right spot, we probably wouldn't have had the fuel to change course. They'd have been fishing our bodies off the floor of the Atlantic. *That's* a fatal error, Karen."

"Exactly." DeSantos steadied himself as Rodman reduced their speed. "Like I said, we take our wins where we can get 'em. We stopped the terror attacks. We eliminated several of Rudenko's accomplices, secured the ricin, and closed down his base of operations. We did our best. We're not perfect. *You're* not perfect."

"Okay, you two," Uzi said as he squared himself in his chair and pressed a button on the panel. "This is gonna be a rough landing. Take your seats and belt yourselves in."

"I thought Hot Rod could handle it," DeSantos said.

Uzi glanced at Rodman, who busied himself with the controls. "Well, Hot Rod's never actually flown an Osprey before. And since we're almost out of fuel, we're only gonna get one shot at this."

Vail closed her eyes. *Terrific.*

# 80

DeSantos sat beside Vail in the cabin and fished around for his seat restraint. He clicked it home and then glanced at Vail. She looked like she wanted to rip her headset off and smash it against the bulkhead.

"Worried about the landing?"

"No. Yes. And I'm pissed at myself."

"He can do this," DeSantos said. "Hot Rod's a good pilot."

"You trying to convince me, or yourself?"

DeSantos knew that touching down on a ship required skill and practice. A pilot who was unfamiliar with shipboard landings could get disoriented very quickly and end up crashing into the water—or against the side of the ship.

While he didn't doubt Rodman's skill, DeSantos knew that even if he had done this before, it had been at least several years. And he had never done it in an Osprey.

"How's your head?" she asked.

"Bleeding's stopped. I'll live."

Vail snorted. "Assuming we don't crash and burn."

UZI TOLD RODMAN he was letting him take the plane in—a hollow gesture since Rodman was the only one who had any experience piloting an Osprey—even if it was in a simulator.

Judging by how tightly he was gripping the thrust control lever, there were other places Rodman would rather be right now.

They had "glided" in on low power, and when they reached five hundred feet, they increased engine thrust.

The flashing yellow fuel light turned red, and an adjacent warning light came on. Uzi ignored them; there was nothing he could do about it. They had done everything reasonable to conserve fuel, so now they could only hope there was enough in the tank to safely touch down on the flight deck.

Uzi consulted the TACAN, which showed that they were about twenty-five miles out. The plan was to come in astern at a slight angle, along the port side of the ship.

When Knox had set up the rendezvous point and provided them with the TACAN code, he instructed them to use the USS *New York*'s alias, "Liberty." To maintain anonymity in open, international waters, ships preferred not to use their real names over the radio. Uzi depressed the communication switch on the stick.

"Liberty, this is Shadowrider, approaching in a CV-22 squawking 1200, on emergency fuel. We've got sweet lock, request permission to land on arrival. I say again, we are on emergency fuel."

"Roger, Shadowrider, this is Liberty control. Liberty is setting emergency flight quarters now. Expect a BRC of 275."

"BRC," Uzi said to Rodman. "Rings a bell, but—"

"Base Recovery Course. It gives us the bearing that the ship's traveling. The flight deck's not a stationary landing field, so there's no runway heading. The BRC points us toward the ship."

"Emergency fuel acknowledged," Liberty control said. "Please squawk 0421."

"Copy that." Uzi twisted the identification, friend or foe code into the Osprey's transponder, allowing their aircraft to be identified on the controller's radar scope and telling the *New York* that they were who they said they were. Otherwise, the ship would lock them up with its self-defense weapons and shoot them down as an unapproved, approaching plane.

"Liberty control has you sweet-sweet on the 060 radial at sixteen nautical miles. Continue your descent to cherubs five. Report a 'see me.'"

Even at this distance, Uzi thought he could make out the flight deck lights. The sizable landing pad he had expected to see looked more like a postage stamp. "We really going to set down on that thing?"

"Let's hope so."

"See you at fifteen," Uzi said into his mic, informing the *New York* that they had a visual on the ship and that they were fifteen miles out.

"Roger, Shadowrider," the controller said. "Check in with the air boss on 231.5."

Uzi dialed in the UHF transmitter to frequency 231.5 and keyed his radio. "Liberty Tower, this is Shadowrider checking in."

"You are cleared to spot four. Relative winds are 003 at twenty knots."

Uzi glanced at Rodman, who shrugged. He reached out and pressed the "radio call" button. "Uh, Liberty Tower, where exactly is spot four?"

"Are you not familiar with shipboard ops, son?"

"Well—" Uzi cleared his throat. "We've never done this before."

"Say again? You've never done *what*? Landed an Osprey on a ship at night? Or landed an Osprey on a ship?"

"I guess we can start with we've never *flown* an Osprey before, and then the rest is kind of self-explanatory."

"You gotta be shitting me." The air boss was silent a long moment. Then: "Best you stay the hell away from my deck. Land that thing on a nice, long, Air Force runway—where you belong."

Rodman's face hardened. "Liberty Tower, we don't have enough fuel to land anywhere but on your deck."

"So either clear us to land," Uzi said, "or you'd better launch the SAR helo to pick up the survivors from our crash off your port side. Assuming we survive."

"Boss," Rodman said, "bring your captain online. But make it fast, because we don't have enough time or gas left to debate this. We're on approach."

A moment later, another voice: "Shadowrider, this is Captain John Dunbar."

"Captain," Uzi said, "I don't understand the problem. You were expecting us."

"I was ordered to divert to these coordinates to pick up a package. Nothing was said about some greenie trying to land a goddamn Osprey on my deck—at night."

Rodman set his jaw. "Don't take this the wrong way, sir, but we *are* coming in. If you deny us access, you're going to have to explain our deaths to Secretary McNamara. Because that's who I report to—directly."

"Captain," the air boss said, "I don't care who he reports to. I can't clear these guys to land. They're not qualified."

After a long pause, Dunbar said, "My ship, my decision. Get that Huey off the flight deck and into the hangar. And get the Cobra airborne. Everyone but the LSE off the flight deck when that Osprey comes in."

The air boss started to object, but Dunbar cut him off. "Those are my orders. Have the Officer of the Deck set General Quarters."

Uzi knew that Dunbar was maximizing readiness for the crash he was anticipating. Uzi did not appreciate the lack of confidence, but what he and Rodman were attempting carried low odds of success.

"Shadowrider," Dunbar said, "I'm clearing as much real estate as I can, but we're full up. We're putting one in the air to give you spot four, port side, just aft of the hangar bay. Look for the yellow shirt waving his wands."

"Can you turn up the lights," Uzi said, "help us out a bit?"

"Copy that, but we're set up on night vision. We'll need time to change it out from NVG-compatible deck lighting."

Uzi consulted his watch. "You've got five minutes. Sir."

They heard the captain say something over the open channel. It was muffled but sounded like "All lights to full bright." The mic cut out, then came back on. "—don't care, you've got two minutes to make it fucking daylight out there!"

Rodman winked at Uzi, as if to say, "That's more like it."

Uzi figured they would be mobilizing a crash crew to be prepared to douse the deck with A-Triple F, a chemical that smothered fire. Unfortunately, Uzi was familiar with the stuff.

As the Osprey neared the *New York*, the dim postage stamp in the dark ocean lit up like Times Square, and the two squat masts and smooth, flat sides of the massive vessel came into full view.

Uzi had seen pictures of the ship when it was commissioned; a big deal was made of the fact that its bow had been constructed of several tons of steel from the Twin Towers in the aftermath of 9/11. If there could be a fitting use of the ruins of a terror network's destructive act, it was as part of a United States warship. In a sense, it was the military raising its middle finger to al-Qaeda and anyone else who would mount an attack on US soil.

Uzi felt a sense of pride as they approached the *New York*. He pushed it aside and concentrated, ready to lend a hand as the landing pad grew larger through the windshield.

"Holy shit," Rodman said. "He wasn't kidding about the deck being full."

"You can do this."

"Find out soon enough. I'm bringing us in closer than I should before switching over to a hover. Hover uses—"

"More fuel. I remember."

Waiting till the last possible moment, Rodman cut back on the thrust and, using the thumbwheel, began transitioning the nacelles to a vertical orientation.

The pace of the blinking red fuel light immediately quickened. An alarm sounded. Moving to hover mode was like sucking the last drops of water from a cup with a straw.

"Call out airspeed and altitude," Rodman said.

Uzi tore his eyes from the flight deck. "Twenty knots, 475 feet. Eight knots, 410. Bring us in lower—drop, drop, drop!"

Rodman corrected—and then overcompensated. They fell toward the water, like an elevator in free fall.

"Holy Christ, too low!"

The plane rose abruptly, like an amusement park ride, rocking side to side.

"Wave off," the air boss yelled over the radio. "Wave off!"

"Negative," Rodman said. "No gas."

Rodman brought them along the port side, as if to parallel park. There were two slots open; spot four was exactly where Dunbar said it would be, on the edge, behind the hangar and in front of another chopper.

A sizable CH-53 Super Stallion helicopter sat to their right.

They were swaying wildly as Rodman attempted to line up the Osprey with the margin of the flight deck.

He was overcontrolling the aircraft. Uzi knew it, Rodman knew it—but this was where actual in-flight scenarios came into play. Simulators could only take you so far.

A crewman in a yellow jacket and helmet began moving his arms, using hand signals to guide them in.

Rodman inched over the port side and hovered there a long second, the wings continuing to rock from side to side, the rotors coming dangerously close to striking the helicopter on his right.

A moment later, he stabilized the plane and lowered it slowly—but unevenly. The crewman held his arms straight out at his sides, then dropped them rapidly to his hips, signaling Rodman to bring it home.

But at that instant, the fuel pressure indicator dropped to nearly zero.

Every buzzer sounded. Every light on the forward display lit up.

And the Osprey dropped like a rock toward the flight deck.

# 81

The right side of the plane dipped hard and the rotors skimmed the nearby CH-53. By design, the Osprey's blade shredded into hundreds of spaghetti-like strands.

"Cut power!" Rodman said.

"Cutting power. Roger."

As Uzi reached for the engine control switch, the fuel pressure zeroed out and the craft settled onto the tarmac like a sixteen-ton weight.

It hit hard and nearly bounced off the edge.

Upon impact—by design—the pilot seats "stroked," or collapsed to the floor. Uzi and Rodman yanked off their restraints and pulled themselves up to reach the buttons on the dashboard.

"Brakes," Rodman said. "Brakes!"

"Brakes. Roger." Uzi drew the lever back and stopped the plane just short of rolling off the flight deck and into the ocean.

"Shutting down systems," Rodman said as he jabbed his index finger at multiple buttons on the control panel.

Outside, the crash crew rushed the plane, securing it with chains and dousing it with A-Triple F.

Emergency lights whirred and the tarmac was a mass of activity.

ALAN JACOBSON

423

Uzi and Rodman collapsed back into their seats and started laughing. Uzi reached over and slapped his pilot in the chest. "You did it, man. Congrats."

"Welcome to the *New York*," Dunbar said over the radio. "Ugliest goddamn landing I've ever seen."

"Hey," Vail said, coming up behind them. "Don't listen to him. You got us home safely and we lived to tell about it. I thought it was *beautiful*."

# 82

*USS New York*
*Hospital Ward*
*North Atlantic Ocean/Celtic Sea*
*49.65° Longitude, -8.25° Latitude*

Hector DeSantos and Karen Vail were lying on Hill-Rom electric hospital beds, IV lines hooked up to their arms, despite their protestations. The suite was generous, with exposed ductwork and dozens of rows of neatly bundled cables snaking along the bulkheads and ceiling, as was common in most naval vessels.

At the far end of the room, above a freestanding Sanyo Biomedical freezer, was a flat screen television, images rolling by without sound.

The *New York* was a new ship with state-of-the-art equipment; what's more, everywhere they had walked upon deplaning was obsessively clean and maintained with pride.

While Rodman went to the crew's lounge, Uzi accompanied his friends to the hospital.

"The sleeping quarters are a bit tight," he said as he took a seat on the edge of Vail's bed. "You going to be able to handle that?"

Vail, who had used the remote to raise herself into a seated position once the corpsman had left the room, waved her free hand. "After climbing seventy feet in a tunnel about three feet wide, I think I'll be able to manage it. I'm so exhausted, I'll be asleep before I have a chance to think about it."

"I'm tired just thinking about going to sleep," DeSantos said.

"So." Vail folded her arms in her lap. "We've done a good job avoiding the red elephant in the room."

DeSantos laughed. "Again with the red elephant? If I didn't know you any better, I'd think you've got an elephant fetish."

Uzi looked around. "Red elephant?"

Vail play-slapped him. "What do you think they're going to do with us? We only broke about nine million UK laws, killed an innocent man—an up-and-coming, well-liked politician, no less."

"We haven't been shackled and flogged yet," Uzi said. "I take that as a good sign."

"As well you should."

The voice came from the doorway, where a suited FBI Director Douglas Knox stood, hands in his pockets, hair immaculately combed.

They all turned simultaneously.

Uzi rose and shook Knox's hand. "Sir."

Knox pursed his lips and made eye contact with each of them. "Let me be the first to commend you on an extremely difficult operation. Hector, Secretary McNamara's been briefed." He consulted his watch. "Right about now, he's on the phone with the home secretary."

Vail wanted to ask what this meant for all of them, but Knox anticipated the question.

"In the end, I think everything will settle down and this will all blow over."

"Blow over," Vail said. She looked at DeSantos and then Uzi, but neither was forthcoming with a comment. "Sir, I don't think you know everything that's happened, what we...everything we did."

"I've been fully briefed by my counterpart. Director General Buck told me the bad as well as the good. And let me say this. Hector, if you ever stick a goddamn needle in me, no matter what the circumstances, so help me God—"

"Understood, sir."

Knox let a smile flit across his lips. But it was as fleeting as it was noticeable. "I'm well aware that everything about this case was foreign to you, Agent Vail—and no doubt incredibly difficult. Covert ops work is...well, it takes a certain type to carry out these missions. And that's why this was black. To allow you to do things that, well, ordinarily aren't done by law-abiding law enforcement officers. As it turned out, the United Kingdom, and the United States, benefited from the actions the four of you took during this mission. And for that, I am personally and eternally grateful." He cleared his throat. "That said, you will need to lie low for a while, until we can get all this sorted out."

Vail sat up straight. "What about my ASAC?"

"I've already spoken with Thomas Gifford."

"You have? He knows?"

"He knew you were working a case for me. That's *all* he knows. That's all he *can* know. Understood?"

"Yes sir."

"Hector, you'll explain the parameters to her? What she can and cannot disclose—and with whom?"

"I'll take care of it."

Knox nodded.

"So how is this being handled?" Vail asked. "Does the president talk to the prime minister? How do things get...excused—or explained?"

Knox chuckled sardonically. "The president and prime minister do not know the full story—nor will they. If we involve them, it could degenerate into a three ring circus. Congress and Parliament would get involved, years-long inquiries with task forces would be set up, the media would give it a good ride, and nothing would get resolved—certainly not the way we want it to be.

"This is the kind of thing that, without full disclosure and proper perspective, could irreparably damage US-UK relations. No, this is best handled quietly. The press will be fed a story. They may not like it and they won't believe some of it. They won't be able to verify a lot of it."

"But the involved parties have a vested interest in keeping their traps shut," Vail said.

"That's the idea."

"And," DeSantos said, "if anyone does talk, there'll be no proof to back it up."

Knox looked around the room. "You have to realize what was at stake, Agent Vail. The entire UK intelligence apparatus was paralyzed. The country was in grave danger because they had to recall all their agents here and abroad. They were essentially blind to everything Rudenko's crew was planning. You four stepped in and not only thwarted the attack but you identified the source of their leak, made it possible to restore a good number of their agents—and dealt a serious blow to one of the most notorious weapons traders and money launderers the world has known."

"About that," Vail said. She glanced at DeSantos, then said, "I believe I scr—"

"Hussein Rudenko is still at large," DeSantos said. "He posed as an innocent party and we mistook his accomplice for him."

"Mr. Buck just informed me," Knox said.

Vail explained her theory regarding Rudenko and the Turner Gallery. Knox absorbed it and rocked back on his heels as he considered it. Finally he said, "I'm sure MI5 will put it all together. We'll leave it to them to dot the I's and cross the T's. I think we've done our part."

"But Rudenko's in the wind," Vail said.

"That he is, Agent Vail. But all's not lost. We now know what he looks like. We've got photos and video footage of him. As we speak, those files are being distributed to Interpol and every other major metropolitan police force in the world. And we'll soon have a complete DNA profile. It's only a matter of time before we get him."

"I'd sure like a piece of him." *Did I say that out loud?*

Knox stepped between their two beds and extended a hand to Vail. "Thank-you."

"Agent Vail did extremely well," DeSantos said. "We couldn't have pulled it off without her. In fact, she saved my life."

Knox lifted a brow and looked at DeSantos, who nodded. Knox turned back to Vail and tilted his chin back. Unless Vail was imagining it, his eyes seemed to convey newfound trust and respect. Having heard Uzi's account of when he had "earned" that same look from Knox—which no doubt led to his being given this UK assignment—she was not sure this was a welcome development.

A Secret Service agent entered the room and whispered something in Knox's ear.

"Fine," Knox said, "Tell him I'll be right there."

As the agent left the room, Knox turned back to DeSantos.

"Hector." He held DeSantos's gaze a long moment, but no words were exchanged. He finally reached out and squeezed his shoulder. "Agent Uziel," Knox said as he turned for the door. "With me. Now. For your debriefing."

Uzi reached out and bumped fists with DeSantos, then gave Vail a wink. "Catch you in the morning—or, at this rate, the afternoon. I think we all need some shut-eye."

They walked out, leaving Vail and DeSantos alone.

"How do you deal with things like this, Hector?" She knew that DeSantos would understand she was talking about Basil Walpole.

DeSantos sighed. "Honest answer or bullshit?"

Vail smirked.

"Right. I wouldn't disrespect you with a bullshit answer." He took a deep breath and looked down at his lap. "Despite what you think, Karen, I'm not a psychopath. It's tearing me up inside. But what can I do? When I get home, one day when my guard's down, it'll hit me across the back of the head and I'll self-medicate with booze and Xanax." They both fell quiet a moment before he turned to her. "How are you going to handle it?"

"I'll probably take a more traditional approach."

"Counseling?"

"No, I think I'll bottle it up, have nightmares, compensate, sublimate, and try to find meaning in the 'greater good' of what I did."

"What *I* did, Karen. You didn't kill him."

Across the room on the television, a BBC early morning news report rolled footage of hazmat investigators sifting through the wreckage of a downed aircraft in a remote field.

DeSantos shook his head. "Wonder how the talking heads are going to explain a crashed crop duster that's riddled with machine-gun rounds and a belly full of ricin powder."

"Really." Vail laughed. "I mean, how could something like that possibly happen?"

DeSantos pursed his lips. "Ever hear of don't ask, don't tell?"

"Of course," Vail said. "That's got nothing to do with this."

"It's my version. Don't ask me, because if I tell you, I'd have to—"

"Kill me?"

DeSantos furrowed his brow but did not answer.

"You would, wouldn't you?"

"Karen Vail, you've got a very active imagination. What makes you think I do shit like that?"

## Acknowledgments

The research for *No Way Out* presented a challenge on many levels, not the least of which was its setting. Errors of fact are my own, though a few details were modified for specific reasons. I owe sincere thanks to all the experts and professionals who helped me bring *No Way Out* to life:

**John Hudson**, graduate of the Shakespeare Institute at the University of Birmingham, and founder of the New York Shakespeare ensemble, the Dark Lady Players (www.darkladyplayers.com), for sharing his comprehensive analysis of Amelia Bassano Lanier, the Shakespearean plays, and authorship issues with me. John's review of *No Way Out*'s "Shakespeare chapters" ensured that I didn't muff his groundbreaking research.

**Ingram Losner** and **Jane Willoughby**, for being my key UK consultants; their comprehensive background on England, its society, political pressures, phraseology, and English culture were invaluable, as was Ingram's thorough review of the manuscript.

**Mark Safarik**, supervisory special agent and senior FBI profiler with the FBI's Behavioral Analysis Unit (ret.), for information regarding threat assessment as well as his contacts within New Scotland Yard, the Madrid police department, British law enforcement, and Interpol. Thanks, as usual, for his review of the manuscript.

**Jason Rubin**, captain, United States Marine Corps. I cherish experts who are outside-the-box thinkers. Jason is that, and more. What started as a casual conversation at a fraternity convention about the Marines and their various jets and helicopters turned into an in-depth primer on the Osprey, which is a cool plane, not to mention an amazingly complex aerospace machine. Jason is now an instructor pilot, and when I told him how I wanted the scene to unfold, what it needed to accomplish—and that it had to be accurate—he kind of laughed. His expression said, "Is that all?" Over a period of months, our brainstorming discussions led to the awesome scene in *No Way Out*. Any questions, look it up in the Osprey flight manual!

**Steve Garrett**, US Navy hospital corpsman senior chief (Diver/Free Fall Parachutist/Fleet Marine Force)—or in military parlance: HMCS (DV/FPJ/FMF) (ret.), for his thorough review of the manuscript and for correcting my Special Operations Forces terminology and procedures, secure communications, and the like.

**Kevin Kelm**, resident agent in charge, Bureau of Alcohol, Tobacco, Firearms, and Explosives and supervisory special agent, Arson and Bombing Investigative Services Subunit at the FBI's Behavioral Analysis Unit (ret.). Kevin is a walking encyclopedia on bomb-related information and bomber profiling. I also valued his London stories of working with Scotland Yard. Thanks as well to **Ron Tunkel**, supervisory Special Agent, Bureau of Alcohol, Tobacco, Firearms, and Explosives, at the FBI's Behavioral Analysis Unit.

The unnamed **New Scotland Yard detective chief superintendents** and **detective chief inspectors** who spent a great deal of face time with me. They gave me invaluable background information on crime in London, general police procedure, gun laws, and political issues facing the UK, as well as tours of their facilities. Since UK policing is so different from that in the US, their candor, insight, and stories gave me an important window into how it's done across the pond. They preferred to remain anonymous.

**Mary Ellen O'Toole**, supervisory special agent and senior FBI profiler with the FBI's Behavioral Analysis Unit (ret.), for her assistance with, and information on, threat assessment.

**Bill Urban**, commander, United States Navy, Naval Surface Force Atlantic, for reviewing the pertinent USS *New York* chapters for accuracy— and his invaluable input and suggested changes. **Callie Ferrari**, lieutenant, United States Navy Office of Information East, for her assistance (and persistence!) in obtaining clearance for me through the Navy's chief of information.

**Tomás Palmer**, cryptographer, for his time, expertise, and patience in helping me understand the CLAIR technology and the paths Uzi needed to take to find the answers. Tomás, you may recall, helped me with similar aspects relative to technogeekery in *Crush*. As Tomás said, "What would Karen Vail do without me?" Indeed!

**James Alvarez, PhD**, international hostage negotiator and police psychologist for Scotland Yard and the NYPD, for his counsel regarding the cultural personality differences between American and British societies. It was a "lightbulb moment" for me.

**Peter Clarke**, former deputy commissioner at Scotland Yard; and both **Tom Neer**, supervisory special agent and senior FBI profiler, Behavioral

Analysis Unit–Counterterrorism (ret.) and **Stephen White**, chief constable Northern Ireland, for connecting me with Peter.

**Colin Bexley**, a senior executive in the UK National Health Service, for deftly answering my sensitive questions regarding the service's databases and how information is maintained.

**Steve McEvoy**, US Air Force first sergeant (E-7, retired), for vetting my Mildenhall scenes for accuracy. **Paul Ortega**, AT&T Senior Emerging Technology Manager, for reviewing my terminology regarding wireless technology. **Steve Evans**, tour guide extraordinaire. I told him what I was looking for, and he turned me onto the secret MI5 disused Underground facility and the Royal Mail Railway.

**Ann Hamilton** and **Miriam Rose**, for their background on "must-visit" non-touristy places relative to my story outline and for answering miscellaneous England-related questions before I ventured across the pond.

**Davina Fankhauser**, president and co-founder, Fertility Within Reach (www.fertilitywithinreach.org), for assisting me with obtaining information regarding DNA familial probabilities; **Selwyn Oskowitz, MD**, reproductive endocrinologist, for connecting me with **Marcus Hughes,** MD, Ph.D., professor of genetics, pathology and medicine, Genesis Genetics Institute. **Maury Gloster**, MD, for assistance with the medical scenario involving Vail's and DeSantos's hypoxic episode.

My London family, **Geoff** and **Val Bard**; **Caroline Rabin** and **Steven Green**; Geoff and Val threw my life upside down when they said, "Get to London before the end of October because the weather turns awful and it's dark by 4:30, which'll really shorten your research days." Within three weeks, we built a trip, scheduled hotels, booked flights, and landed at Heathrow. Steven and Caroline gave us a car tour of London, including the American Embassy, which helped me gain a feel for the city.

**Corey Jacobson** for his review of portions of the manuscript for the accuracy of Madrid geography, London landmarks, British language nuances, and British politics. **Ilanit Sisso** for the Spanish translations in the Madrid chapters; **Lauren Dellar** for arranging for the Arabic translations. **Matthew Jacobson** for his naval primer and research relative to carrier and amphibious landing vessels. **Jeff Jacobson**, for his input and review of the manuscript.

**Kevin Smith**, my editor. The beauty of having collaborated on six books is that we work so well together that we're like—pick your simile—a well-oiled machine? A symphony? Well, it may not be that graceful, but Kevin knows how to coax those final ounces of polish out of the tube.

**Chrisona Schmidt**, my copyeditor, for her vitally important role in ensuring the quality of the final finished product. **C. J. Snow**, proofreader extraordinaire, for his usual fine job as my last line of editorial defense.

The terrific, hardworking crew at Premier Digital Publishing: **Thomas Ellsworth, Hutch Morton, Julie Morales**, and **Ryan Shaw**. You are my army in battle, and it's fun going to war with you.

My hardcover publishers, **Virginia Lenneville** and **John Hutchinson**, at Norwood Press. They're not just the best publishers an author could ever hope to write for, but they're special people, too.

My agents, **Joel Gotler** and **Frank Curtis**. Joel works tirelessly behind the scenes to make sure my works are well-represented around the world, as well as in Hollywood. Frank is one of the finest entertainment law attorneys I've ever worked with, and his guidance and advice have proven essential to how I write my novels.

**Roger Cooper**, former publisher of Vanguard Press, Perseus Books Group. Several years ago, Roger had the sagacity to convince me to turn Karen Vail into a series character. That was never my intent. Without Roger, the adventures I've had so much fun writing—and you've had so much fun reading—might never have occurred.

**My fans and readers**. Receiving an email, tweet, or a Facebook post telling me how much you've enjoyed my novels brightens my day. Without you, my efforts would feel hollow because there wouldn't be anyone to share my stories and characters with. I'd also like to give a special shout-out to the two administrators of the Fans of Alan Jacobson Facebook fan group (www.FansOfAlanJacobson.com), **Terri Landreth** and **Sandy Soreano**. You two do an awesome job! I love your enthusiasm.

Last, though it really should be first: my wife, **Jill**, is my front line editor, finding those things that somehow escape my eyes and sensibilities. Much more than that, however, all authors know that it takes a significant other with a strong constitution to keep the ship on course. For the past twenty-five years, Jill has helped me navigate the choppy waters with aplomb, keeping the bow pointed in the right direction. Unlike the Osprey, our tank will never run dry.

## The Works of Alan Jacobson

*Alan Jacobson has established a reputation as one of the most insightful suspense and thriller writers of our time. His exhaustive research and years of unprecedented access to law enforcement agencies bring realism and unique characters to his pages. Following are his current releases.*

## NOVELS

### False Accusations

Dr. Phillip Madison has everything: wealth, power, and an impeccable reputation. But in the pre-dawn hours of a quiet suburb, the revered orthopedic surgeon is charged with double homicide—a cold-blooded hit-and-run that leaves an innocent young couple dead. Blood evidence has brought the police to his door. An eyewitness has placed him at the crime scene...and Madison has no alibi. With his family torn apart, his career forever damaged, no way to prove his innocence and facing life in prison, Madison hires an investigator to find the person who has engineered the case against him. *False Accusations* is a psychological thriller that instantly became a national bestseller and launched Alan Jacobson's career, a novel that spurred CNN to call him, "One of the brightest stars in the publishing industry."

### The Hunted

How well do you know the one you love? Lauren Chambers's husband Michael disappears on a ski trip. As she searches for him, she discovers Michael's hidden past involving the FBI, international assassins—and government secrets that some will go to great lengths to keep hidden. As *The Hunted* hurtles toward a conclusion mined with turn-on-a-dime twists, no one is who he appears to be and nothing is as it seems. *The Hunted* introduces the dynamic Department of Defense covert operative Hector DeSantos and FBI Director Douglas Knox, characters who return in *Velocity, Hard Target,* and future Alan Jacobson novels.

### The 7th Victim (Karen Vail #1)

Literary giants Nelson DeMille and James Patterson describe Karen Vail, the first female FBI profiler, as "tough, smart, funny, very believable," and "compelling." In *The 7th Victim*, Vail—with a dry sense of humor and a closet full of skeletons—heads up a task force to find the Dead Eyes Killer, who is murdering young women in Virginia...the backyard of the famed FBI Behavioral Analysis Unit. The twists and turns that Karen Vail endures in this tense psychological suspense thriller build to a powerful ending no reader will see coming. Named one of the Top 5 Best Books of the Year (*Library Journal*).

### *Crush* (Karen Vail #2)

FBI Profiler Karen Vail is in the Napa Valley for a vacation—but the Crush Killer has other plans. Vail partners with Inspector Roxxann Dixon to track down the architect of death who crushes his victims' windpipes and leaves their bodies in wine caves and vineyards. But the killer is unlike anything the profiling unit has ever encountered, and Vail's miscalculations have dire consequences for those she holds dear. *Crush* is not only a twisting and compelling read, but it brings the wine country to life in a story that *Publishers Weekly* describes as "addicting" and *New York Times* bestselling author Steve Martini calls a thriller that's "Crisply written and meticulously researched," and "rocks from the opening page to the jarring conclusion." (Note: the *Crush* storyline continues in *Velocity*.)

### *Velocity* (Karen Vail #3)

A missing detective. A bold serial killer. And evidence that makes FBI Profiler Karen Vail question the loyalty of those she has entrusted her life to. Squaring off against foes more dangerous than any she has yet encountered, shocking personal and professional truths emerge—truths that may be more than Vail can handle. *Velocity* was named to *Strand Magazine*'s Top 10 Best Books for 2010, *Suspense Magazine*'s Top 4 Best Thrillers of 2010, *Library Journal*'s Top 5 Best Books of the Year, and the *Los Angeles Times*' top picks of the year. Michael Connelly said *Velocity* is "As relentless as a bullet. Karen Vail is my kind of hero and Alan Jacobson is my kind of writer!"

### *Inmate 1577* (Karen Vail #4)

When an elderly woman is found raped and murdered, Karen Vail heads west to team up with Inspector Lance Burden and Detective Roxxann Dixon. As they follow the killer's trail in and around San Francisco, the offender leaves behind clues that ultimately lead them to the most unlikely of places, a mysterious island ripped from city lore whose long-buried, decades-old secrets hold the key to their case: Alcatraz. The Rock. It's a case that has more twists and turns than the famed Lombard Street. The legendary Clive Cussler calls *Inmate 1577* "a powerful thriller, brilliantly conceived and written." Named one of *Strand Magazine*'s Top 10 Best Books of the Year.

## Hard Target

An explosion pulverizes the president-elect's helicopter on Election Night. The group behind the assassination possesses far greater reach than anything the FBI has yet encountered—and a plot so deeply interwoven in the country's fabric that it threatens to upend America's political system. But as covert operative Hector DeSantos and FBI Agent Aaron "Uzi" Uziel sort out who is behind the bombings, Uzi's personal demons not only jeopardize the investigation but may sit at the heart of a tangle of lies that threaten to trigger an international terrorist attack. Political thriller master Vince Flynn calls *Hard Target* "A smart, complex novel that explodes from the page." *Note: FBI Profiler Karen Vail plays a key role in the story.*

## No Way Out (Karen Vail #5)

When an exclusive London art gallery is bombed, esteemed FBI Profiler Karen Vail is dispatched to England to assist with the investigation. But what she finds there—a plot to destroy a controversial, recently unearthed 440-year-old manuscript—turns into something much larger, and a whole lot more dangerous, for the UK, the US—and herself.

## SHORT STORIES

## Fatal Twist (featuring Karen Vail)

The Park Rapist has murdered his first victim—and FBI profiler Karen Vail is on the case. As Vail races through the streets of Washington DC to chase down a promising lead that may help her catch the killer, a military-trained sniper takes aim at his target, a wealthy businessman's son. But what brings these two unrelated offenders together is something the nation's capital has never before experienced. If you want a taste of Karen Vail, *Fatal Twist* will whet your appetite.

## Double Take

NYPD Detective Ben Dyer awakens from cancer surgery to find his life turned upside down. His fiancée has disappeared and Dyer, determined to find her, embarks on a journey mined with potholes and startling revelations—revelations that have the potential to forever change his life.

For news and a free personal safety booklet coauthored by FBI Profiler Mark Safarik, please visit Alan's website, www.AlanJacobson.com.

## About the Author

Alan Jacobson is the National Bestselling Author of eight critically

acclaimed thrillers. His two decades of research and training with the FBI's Behavioral Analysis Unit, the Drug Enforcement Administration, the US Marshals Service, Scotland Yard, SWAT, and the military have helped shape the stories he tells and the characters that populate his novels. His books have made numerous Top 10 Best Books of the Year lists and five have been optioned by Hollywood.

You can reach Alan through his official website, www.AlanJacobson.com, or follow his social musings on Facebook (www.Facebook.com/AlanJacobsonFans) and Twitter: @JacobsonAlan.

## *Acronyms used in* No Way Out

| | |
|---|---|
| ASAC | Assistant Special Agent In Charge (FBI) |
| BHP | British Heritage Party (UK) |
| BRC | Base recovery course |
| CARD | Covert Arms Research Division (US) |
| CCTV | Closed-circuit television |
| CIA | Central Intelligence Agency (US) |
| CLAIR | Device that enables secure communications; unstated acronym |
| COFEE | Computer online forensic evidence extractor |
| DCI | Detective chief inspector |
| DOD | Department of Defense (US); also used as DoD |
| DOJ | Department of Justice (US) |
| FLEOA | Federal Law Enforcement Officers Association |
| FSB | Federal Security Service (Russia) |
| FUBAR | Fucked up beyond all recognition (military acronym) |
| ICS | International Counter Terrorism branch (UK) |
| IDWS | interim defensive weapon system |
| IFF | Identification, friend or foe |
| JTAC | Joint Terrorism Analysis Centre (UK) |
| LED | Light emitting diode |
| Legat | Legal Attaché (top FBI position in a foreign country) |
| LSE | The London School of Economics |
| MO | Modus operandi (or method of operation) |
| MI5 | Military intelligence, Section 5; also Security Service (UK) |
| MI6 | Military intelligence, Section 6; Secret Intelligence Service (UK) |
| MP | Military Police |
| OPSIG | Operational Support Intelligence Group |
| RAF | Royal Air Force (UK) |
| RIB | Rigid inflatable boat |
| SEAL | Sea, air, land team (US Navy's special operations force) |
| SecDef | Secretary of Defense (US) |
| SitRep | Situation report (military) |

| | |
|---|---|
| SCO19/CO19 | Specialist Crime and Operations Specialist Firearms Command (UK) |
| SO15 | Special Operations (Counter Terrorism Command) (UK) |
| SERE | Pentagon's Survival, Evasion, Resistance, Escape program |
| SIM | Subscriber identity module (for cell phones) |
| SFO | Specialist firearms officer (UK) |
| SP-117 | Drug used by Russian security forces for mind control |
| TACAN | Tactical air navigation system |
| WMD | Weapons of mass destruction |